A FORENSIC MYSTERY THRILLER

BLUFF CITY BUTCHER

STEVE BRADSHAW

Barringer Publishing, Naples, Florida
www.barringerpublishing.com
Cover, graphics, layout design by Lisa Camp
Editing by Carole Greene

ISBN: 978-0-9851184-8-8

Library of Congress Cataloging-in-Publication Data
Bluff City Butcher / Steve Bradshaw

Printed in U.S.A.

ACKNOWLEDGMENTS

I owe special thanks to:

Dara Bradshaw, Barbara Albiniak, Jason Talavs, Larry Kluge and friends for their critical reviews of first drafts and their personal investments in the creation process,

Carole Greene, my gifted editor, for showing me the ways to grow in the art of storytelling,

Jeff Schlesinger, my valued publisher, for seeing and believing,

My family, from ages four to sixty-four, for their relentless and enthusiastic encouragement,

And to my wife, Suzanne, for her unwavering support…as always.

PROLOGUE

October 1983—a child is taken off the deck of a Memphis restaurant during a Sunday brunch. A patron sees on the bluff a tall man with a ponytail. The next night, four men sitting at the infamous table at sunset are drawn into the deep grass. One returns in shock, covered with blood. Later that night, Memphis police chase a stranger wielding a butcher knife onto the Harahan Bridge; he jumps into the dark, turbulent waters of the Mississippi River, his body never recovered. But the missing three men are found: decapitated, dismembered and selected organs harvested. *The Memphis Tribune* names the killer…the BLUFF CITY BUTCHER. Most believe he survived the river, and the Midsouth is his killing ground. Officially, the MPD rejects his existence and denies any connection to the rise in missing persons and unsolved deaths (by knife) in the region.

The Memphis urban legend is born….

PART ONE
THE SUPERIOR FORCE

CHAPTER ONE

[Mon-ster]…a legendary creature, combining features of an animal or human, grotesquely deviating from the normal shape, behavior, or character. An unnatural person who excites horror by wickedness and cruelty…

Twenty-five years later

Steel blue eyes cut through the smoke and bodies to study the hooded shadow in the darkest corner of the crowded pub. Half on a stool, nose in a mug, the shadow twitched like a cockroach under a loose brick. The faded camouflage parka was tight on its belly and black Serpentine mud was high on the left boot, size fourteen. Elliott found another one…a real monster.

It was midnight in London when the three mini-skirts paid their bill. They were followed out of the Victoria; only an empty mug sat in the darkest corner. Oblivious, the three sloshing beers-on-heels walked wet sidewalks on Strathearne Place and split-up at Stanhope Terrace. The one taking Brook Street to Hyde Park was chosen, her hotel a kilometer walk through one of the famous Royal Parks of London. Thick trees, now sparse pedestrians, and long shadows presented ample opportunity.

They never linked the deaths publicly. Parts of the first body were found in 2004, in Serpentine Lake. Two more bodies were found that year, in Kensington Gardens and Greenwich Park, young women brutally raped, necks crushed. The Yard found three each year, always in one of the Royal Parks—no DNA, no physical evidence except boot prints, size fourteen, in the black mud of Serpentine Lake. Five years and fifteen bodies later, Scotland Yard turned to the forensic specialist out of Texas: Dr. Elliott Sumner. He named their serial killer…he had the *Serpentine Strangler* in his sights in eleven days.

He preferred to take them at the moment of attack; they would be focused on their prey and vulnerable. There were other possible approaches, but they introduced more risk that could end badly…losing a predator and more innocent victims; and without solid forensics, losing them in the legal system was always a concern. Elliott hunted the worst of the worst, the most demented, psychopathic, double digit killers in the world…the *real monsters.* He made sure his never got back on the playground.

August 2nd, Detective Chief Superintendent of Scotland Yard deployed a task force into Hyde Park. Like most law enforcement professionals, he paid close attention to the hunches of the world-renowned serial killer hunter. Elliott's unparalleled success over the decade was beyond extraordinary: forty-nine serial killers hunted, forty on death row and nine rotting in the ground.

The task force was in position before sunset. When Elliott stepped out of The Victoria Pub at midnight he took lead of the operation and followed the Serpentine on foot. Once in the park, Elliott would transmit position; a dozen sets of eyes and high-powered rifles with night vision would make pinpoint adjustments and close the circle. But, as with all plans, there were unknown variables. Elliott lost both after the curve on Brook. The path of park entry was unknown; the labyrinth of dark trails proved impossible to cover.

Elliott stepped to the edge of the grass with six options; picking the wrong one could mean death to the girl and the Serpentine Strangler's escape. He took the darkest path under the thickest canopy, the farthest from sidewalks and trails. He moved fast, listening and scanning the dense surroundings for anything atypical. His brisk pace turned into a loping gait as he covered ground in a desperate attempt to reconnect…his cell phone vibrated. *Maybe someone spotted the Serpentine. But they would use the two-way.* "WILCOX" appeared on his screen. The call was from the States—Memphis Homicide.

"Tony…I'm busy at the moment. Can I get back to you?" whispered Elliott.

Without hesitation, Tony replied, "He is back!"

"Hold on, Tee…" Elliott caught a break, an opening in the foliage, some moonlight and perfect timing. He saw the girl in the distance; she was on West Carriage Road. Elliott moved to the nearest tree to minimize damage. There was a chance his cover was still good. The girl was alone, and he detected no other movement in her vicinity. The Serpentine may cling to modus operandi—setting his trap near the Lake where five other bodies were found. *Maybe he has gone ahead…has seen nothing,* Elliott hoped.

Wilcox crackled back to life on his cell. "We need you in Memphis. Wade and Bates have extended a formal invitation."

They must be scared. "Tony…I can't deal with this now. My hands are full at the moment." He moved along the darkest shadows of towering shrubs while eyeing the girl.

"Where are you, Elliott?"

"London. Wait a sec…" He pressed his inline mic. "I have a visual on our girl, West Carriage moving east toward Averard Hotel and lake…no visual on Serpentine…I repeat…no visual on Serpentine. Hold positions or we lose him for sure. I'm closing. Someone tell me you have our girl in your sights, over."

"…ORCA here, I have her, Sir," the voice was unwavering but youthful.

ORCA…? *Hope you are as bad as your handle.* "Here's how this will work; I'm going for Serpentine before he reaches our girl: six-two, two-hundred fifty pounds, a belly and wearing an army green, camouflage, hooded pull-over and jeans tucked into boots. If I am unable to neutralize our man, do not let him touch a single hair on our girl's head. Gentlemen, keep your eyes on a twenty-foot circle around our girl. You move if you see Serpentine enter that space. ORCA, not one hair, son…"

"Not a problem, Sir…"

Elliott moved in parallel to her. She was slow enough for him to scan the dark surroundings.

Wilcox crackled alive again. "The bastard cut the heart out of a young Beale Street musician and—something new, Elliott. He put this one on public display."

The last piece of information was the last thing Elliott wanted to hear, but at the same time he spotted a dark figure in the bushes straight ahead, at the edge of the sidewalk, and his girl was approaching. The shadow was a man…it moved…stood up and leaned forward.

"Tony, hold on."

I'm too far out. He accelerated, pressing the cell tight to his ear—he needed to get there first. "Tony, we have a real problem if your victim is the work of the BCB. You do know that…right?"

"Yes. We need you here…now, Elliott. This is going to get crazy fast."

"Tell Dr. Bates to delay the autopsy a day if they want me in this; set it up for Monday morning. I will meet you at the *Peabody* tomorrow night…GOT TO GO!"

He slid his cell into a pocket with his eyes on the girl nearing the Serpentine. *What are you holding…is that a club…a metal pipe? Shit…that's new. Forensics shows you beat your girls after the rape. She might not survive one hit.* Elliott accelerated.

He was blindsided. It came out of nowhere. He was hit hard and went down in a daze. When he opened his eyes he was on his back, pinned and in a devastating chokehold. The grip was perfectly positioned and the pressure perfectly applied; Elliott's carotid arterial blood flow to his brain was essentially cut off. As a doctor, he knew he had fourteen seconds before the dominos would start to drop: blackout, unconscious suffocation, and then death were minutes away.

He looked above the fat, slimy hands clamped down on his neck—the powerful vice grip of the laid-off ironworker—and followed camouflage arms to the hooded face. Just as he had imagined as a kid: a sick smile and fiendish, empty eyes were dancing with a primitive rage and hideous joy that was not from this world. Elliott looked into the desolate eyes of a *real monster* and again saw a stark wickedness that took over a man from a place inside.

ORCA was the shadow in the bushes and his rifle was the metal bar, the club. Elliott allowed himself to lose focus; his mind was on his nemesis, the beast that resurfaced in Memphis, Tennessee with new needs. He let the London operation spin out of control at the very end…he took his eyes off the lion in front of him. Now, he would pay the price. The day he feared all his life had arrived; he would be dragged away and die a horrible death.

The Memphis Tribune

Beale St. Entertainer Dead;
Memphis Police Bring In Specialist

August 4, 2008

The Memphis police responded to a call at Tom Lee Park around 5:30 a.m. Saturday morning. They found a man on a park bench dead with knife wounds. The twenty-six-year-old, black male was later identified as Panther McGee, a visiting musician on Beale Street. McGee was found by a jogger. "He didn't look well. I got closer to see if I could help. He was unconscious. I called 911," said Jesse Fordham.

Memphis Police Homicide Detective Tony Wilcox said McGee was the victim of a knifing that occurred at another location. They believe he was left at Tom Lee Park moments before being discovered. "Aspects of this homicide are concerning and must be carefully assessed. We will bring in another forensic specialist to assist," said Wilcox.

In an unusual move, Shelby County Medical Examiner, Dr. Henderson Bates, delayed the McGee inquest to Monday morning. "This homicide case has unusual characteristics. We believe bringing in another specialist will enhance our efforts to reach a successful conclusion," said Bates. "This is not the first time I have used consultants and it probably will not be the last." When asked to explain, the M.E. had no further comments on the active investigation.

Sources close to the Panther McGee investigation say the Memphis PD hired Dr. Elliott Sumner, the noted Forensic Pathologist and a serial killer specialist. Once a medical examiner in Texas, he formed the Sumner Forensic Institute (SFI) and provides special services to law enforcement and government agencies, the private sector and others around the world.

Scotland Yard credits Elliott Sumner for the August 3 apprehension of the *Serpentine Strangler* alleged to have raped and killed fifteen women over a five-year period in the *Royal Parks of London*. The recent accomplishment achieves an unparalleled milestone for the sleuth of international acclaim as this is the fiftieth serial killer Sumner has brought to justice.

FBI Behavior Sciences Unit estimates there are as many as 400 serial killers in the world and 80% in the United States. Sumner's stated mission is to remove these dangerous criminals from society by employing advanced forensic technology and investigation techniques with sustained pursuit.

Dr. Sumner was recognized in March by the *International Forensic Science Society and World Law Enforcement Academy* for his special contributions in the field and academics. Sumner is traveling, unavailable for comment.

Anyone with information about Mr. McGee is asked to call the Memphis police crime line: 888-CAN HELP. Your call is confidential.

■ ■ ■

"People only see what they are prepared to see."
Ralph Waldo Emerson

4 August 2008

4,375 miles and twenty-three hours later Elliott was sitting in the *Peabody Hotel* with an Irish coffee, unopened *Memphis Tribune* and a badly bruised neck. On the fourteenth second, the butt of ORCA's rifle met the back of Serpentine's skull; the crushing grip went limp and he flopped over like a cheap lawn chair. A few slaps later, Elliott saw the smiling face that went with the now familiar voice, "Welcome back, Sir," said ORCA. Scotland Yard was on the Serpentine Strangler before he could open his beady eyes.

He tossed his bags on the bed. He would change clothes after meeting with Wilcox. Elliott was comfortable in his khakis and blue blazer after he lost the tie and unbuttoned the collar, and he always had on his Merrell Kaolins, no socks; it was his official uniform when he was not in jeans or workout gear.

The headlines caught his eye; *Usain Bolt sets 100-meter record 9.69 seconds at Beijing Summer Olympics.* Although fast and interesting, it was not the story he wanted. He flipped the paper. It was under the fold. He scanned…*in the early morning hours a young, black male is found dead in Tom Lee Park…multiple knife wounds. Identified as Panther McGee…visiting musician on Beale…knifing occurred at another (unknown) location. McGee is left moments before discovery by jogger.* If that was the whole story, Elliott would still be in London tying up loose ends and getting drunk with ORCA.

Over the brim of his coffee, he watched Wilcox navigate the buzzing crowd and fluttering applause; local celeb status comes with the territory, too many TV cameras in the face at too many homicides. His rangy stature, wispy, brown hair and shaggy brow hid the rock-hard persona chiseled over twenty years as a Midsouth cop, homicide detective the last ten.

"Great you could make it," said Tony, his words sincere.

"Wouldn't miss it…." They embraced and held a firm grip. Elliott's penetrating eyes level with intensity few understood; Tony did. Both stood at six-foot-four and projected a natural deterrent. The *Peabody* minions slowed, heads turned and curious eyes hovered. The usual clamor and bustle of the five-star hotel dropped off the cliff, replaced with sizzling whispers and the cascading fountain at the hotel's epicenter. A fortuitous audience gaped, putting it together. They had read the *Tribune* or caught the news—there was another one dead by knife. They saw that Wilcox was meeting with that Sumner guy, the International Forensic Pathologist and serial killer specialist, but why? What are they not telling us? Is the Panther McGee homicide the work of the Bluff City Butcher? What did the M.E, mean…*some aspects concerning and unusual characteristics?*

They expected to see an older man, doctor type, one that spent a life in a cold, dark morgue with dead bodies and microscopes and thick glasses and filthy saws and scalpels and suction devises, a doctor that goes outside only at night to poke around blood and guts and murders. He would have corpse-like features: pale, maybe thinning, translucent hair, blue lips, pearly eyes and maybe powdery skin…and definitely atrophied muscles from sitting and thinking and solving sick, hideous death puzzles that would make normal people puke. But that man was not sitting across from their favorite homicide detective.

He was thirty-nine with a tan, athletic build and thick, coffee-brown hair combed back with a single pass of a few fingers. His chiseled brow, high forehead, cut jaw line and square chin better fit an *NFL* quarterback than a death doctor. Memphians expected to see another Dr. Henderson Bates type, their Shelby County Medical Examiner, the model of a forensic pathologist…but they didn't get one.

Few knew Sumner was a rarity, a genius with a perfect, photographic memory. By twenty-one he'd graduated *Southwestern Medical School;* by twenty-six he'd completed residency programs in Clinical and Anatomical Pathology and a dozen medical/legal specialties: Forensic Pathology, Criminal Psychology, Serial Homicide Behavioral Sciences and Modern Crime Scene Investigation. Most read about the youngest medical examiner in Texas history and his perfect record solving hundreds of the most complex, unexplained, violent deaths. It was the big story that got national attention and launched Sumner's career as an international serial-killer hunter.

They called him the *Western Sherlock.* At last, the national news media had found a perfect, modern-day hero: a young, handsome and humble doctor deep in the heart of Texas solving horrific homicides every day. This forensic pathologist was different. He did not stay in his scrubs and latex gloves all day, slicing organs and looking in microscopes. He spent most of his time in the field with law enforcement hunting the bad guys. His gifts, education and hands-on approach gave him a remarkable edge. He honed his superior skills of observation. At a death scene he identified, collected and processed more information in one hour than a CSI Team could in one day. From the crime scene to the autopsy table and into the forensic laboratory he applied advanced, analytical and deductive reasoning skills, produced remarkable results and achieved unparalleled success catching killers. Everything he did was as captivating as a scary movie and just as newsworthy. Requests for his services poured in from law enforcement all across the country and governments from around the world. In 1996, Elliott Sumner opened a private practice to direct his special talents on the worst of the worst, the *real monsters* in the world…and his life would never be the same.

A lot was kept from the public; Panther McGee's heart was cut out of his chest and his body tied to the park bench. When an organ was taken from a victim, it got the increased attention of law enforcement and jurisdictional medical examiner's office. When pristine incisions, intricate sutures and multiple cases with cool-down periods were found, it got the attention of specialists. Memphians were not aware of the extent or nature of the terrible trauma Mr. McGee endured, and in accordance with standard operating procedure the Memphis PD had every intention of keeping it that way...until they caught the perpetrator.

"Congrats on number fifty...unbelievable accomplishment. Never imagined there were so many damn serial killers in the world..."

"Thanks, although I'm not sure I know what it all means. From where I sit it's just a drop in the bucket." Elliott sipped his coffee, his thoughts drifting somewhere dark.

"You look good, except for the handprint on your neck...a parting gift from the Serpentine?"

"Let's just call it a limited edition imprint." They both smiled. "Talk to me about Memphis, Tony."

"I started liking the quiet around here..." He slid back and sunk into the sofa. His legs poked six inches above the seat and his gun pushed his coat up. "...him being gone and all, I assumed he was someone else's problem. Well, I am sure...now he's back."

"We will see," said Elliott. "I don't jump to conclusions." He would need to take a close look at Panther McGee, even though Tony was one he never doubted.

"He came home for a reason, Elliott. I want you here at the beginning. We have got to stop him this time. He's working up to something." The attractive waitress leaned over in all her bountiful beauty. Tony ordered. "Coffee...black and give him another Irish...thanks."

"What is the early thinking?" asked Elliott.

"You know the drill. Some see stitching on a corpse and think surgery and that means the killer is intelligent and the kill had to be thought out.

Reasons for the murder must be highbrow, esoteric…stuff like that."

"You mean they don't see that they are dealing with a genius psychopath with an obsessive-compulsive personality disorder that likes to sew?" They smiled again.

In twenty-four hours, Elliott would know more about Panther McGee than anyone on the planet: life, death, forensics and evidence. Tony learned long ago no one was better at finding and assembling the pieces of the puzzle that led to a killer, but they both knew the beast they were after this time was very different.

Tony recalled how their paths first crossed in 1998. Elliott was in Memphis meeting with the police officer that worked the 1983 triple-homicide on the bluff. Officer R.L. Thornton was the only one that got to spend time with the fleeing suspect that night in October, although the visit was brief. The suspect jumped into the Mississippi River and a body was never recovered. The night before, a five-year-old girl was taken off the deck of a popular Memphis restaurant on the bluff. Thornton was there the next night when three young men were found dead, unmercifully butchered like cattle in a slaughterhouse. Back in 1998, Elliott was working a string of homicides in north Texas similar to the Memphis carve-fest. He had a hunch: the Memphis killer survived the Mississippi River and took his skill-sets on the road.

Wilcox was new in Homicide. He sat in the Sumner-Thornton meetings and was drawn into the nightmare. His off-the-clock research of unsolved Memphis homicides uncovered more cases with obvious linkage, but his "serial killer" theory was rejected by top brass and he was directed to keep his unproven speculations to himself and focus on his new job.

Over the years, more unsolved homicides with linkage found their way into the growing cold-case files. The departmental denial of a Memphis area serial killer became entrenched. Tony's urgings were dismissed but tolerated to an extent because he was the most productive homicide detective in the city.

They developed a long-distance friendship, sharing findings. Elliott and Tony believed they were on the trail of the most dangerous serial killer in American history. If they were right, the Bluff City Butcher had killed over a hundred people and was young enough to double the number. So far, the BCB was unstoppable.

"As I shared the other day, your formal invitation is from the top," said Tony. The Memphis PD Director, Collin Wade, and Shelby County Medical Examiner, Dr. Henderson Bates, were the self-appointed protectors of turf. Some said their decision process put jurisdictional concerns above catching the bad guys. Tony's opening comment was code; the political environment in Memphis was neutralized.

"How is your FBI weighing in on this one?"

"Dexter Voss is still the regional director and he opposes outside interference. At one time his position aligned with the turf-gods, but times have changed. He can't stop anything. Director Wade has the final word, for now anyway."

Elliott talked into his coffee mug as if he'd found a bug. "Apparently Voss failed to make the progress Wade had hoped for." They panned the lounge with discerning eyes, always looking for the unusual and suspicious. "Politics gums up the works for most things in life." He had no appetite for the ramblings on the sidelines. Elliott was already moving into the hunting mode. After tonight, the political topic would be dead.

"To finish the point, Director Wade is hanging on by a thread."

"He has fallen from grace?" asked Elliott.

"The mayor gave him enough time to solve the mystery in Memphis. That short, rotund career cop-politician may be losing his hair and nerve, but I don't think he has any intention of losing his job."

"Although he strayed from the mission and principles that attracted him to law enforcement in the first place, and took him to the top, it appears Director Wade is waking to the reality of it all," said Elliott.

"I agree with that."

"Is he clinging to standard protocol?" asked Elliott.

"Yes. Still keeps things tighter than a frog's ass."

"If we're right, that's about to change on its own."

"Memphians know nothing, Elliott."

"Look around. They know a lot more than you think."

"I mean the lion is loose in the neighborhood and the people are still lacing-up their running shoes. They should be told it ain't safe to jog at night."

"The low profile treatment of serial-killer investigations has been judged to be one of the most expeditious routes to catching them. But the world is changing. Today, serial killers are smarter, better educated, have access to more information, are disciplined and even organized."

"Counting Panther McGee, I have linked five more kills over the last few years to the Butcher," said Tony.

"The real number is ten times that in the Midsouth. He is a master at hiding his work: missing persons, suicides, accidents and even natural deaths."

"We are seeing victims exposed to a five-step process; stunned, abducted, tortured, exsanguinated and harvested. Conventional explanations are falling apart. Director Wade and M.E. Bates are forced to deal with a set of crumbling premises."

"Their positions require they approach the ominous with caution."

"Ten years is a lot of caution, Elliott."

"True. Maybe they fear it is apocalyptic. Few are prepared to see or acknowledge what is really out there. I have been hunting the Bluff City Butcher for a decade. I met the *real monster* in 1995. Before that day, I was blind. What's the status on the Memphis urban legend?"

"In '83, the Bluff City Butcher came into the world…jumped into the river…the body never found and so on…"

"BCB took Sabina Weatherford and killed Cory Fortis, Roger Kent and Teddy Morgan," said Elliott, remembering every fact and detail.

"The triple homicide and kidnapping found its way into the cold-case files after two years of dead ends. In '92, the unsatisfied families of the slain boys held a press conference and told the world everything: the decapitations, amputations, heart removals and exsanguination. Those revelations lit another fire of fear that continues to be stoked by the mysterious disappearances of Midsoutherners, and the continuous knifings in the region that just don't get solved."

"Facts mix with fantasy, superstition, mistrust and ignorance," said Elliott.

"The Butcher is the *Big Foot* of the Metro Area. A lot of our most educated people around here believe he survived the river in '83, and has been killing ever since. People believe he is responsible for all unsolved homicides and many of the missing persons in the region." Tony looked at his vibrating cell. "Today, growing segments of the community are convinced the Bluff City Butcher lives in the fog of this urban legend. They are convinced he has superior physical and intellectual assets that allow him to kill at will and to avoid capture, maybe the worst in America ever, Elliott."

"It appears he put Mr. McGee on display."

"And that would be a first. What do you think it means?"

"I have not seen McGee, so I cannot confirm it is the work of the BCB. However, if it is, something is changing in his world. Living in the shadows of legend may no longer meet his needs. If he came home and did this to McGee to send some message, I think that message is…he wants more attention."

"The sick bastard needs more attention? Shit! What's he willing to do now?"

"For twenty-five years he went to great lengths to hide his work in six states that I know about. If I'm right about this, you cannot begin to fathom what is coming our way. This is the most prolific, elusive serial killer I have ever encountered in the world. The Bluff City Butcher is the most dangerous serial killer in the country. He sits at the very top of the food chain. He is smarter and physically more gifted then his prey and law enforcement."

"I was afraid you would say that." Tony's phone vibrated again, another text. "What are your plans tonight?" he asked while reading the message.

"Walk Beale, prepare for the eight o'clock inquest." *I need to climb into the head of the Butcher…his most recent movements and thought process.*

"Ever been to Beale?"

"No, but I know enough to…"

"Since the '20s, it's been known for its carnival atmosphere, smoked pork and great black entertainment. It is also known for the shadows around the perpetual party: the place for gambling, prostitution, bootlegging, voodoo, petty crime and murder. Almost ninety years later, little has changed; the party got bigger and the shadows got deeper."

"Ok, thanks for the history lesson."

"The fringe of the neon is where things get dicey sometimes."

"Really…I understand. Meet me here at ten for shooters. I will have some questions after Beale and before the autopsy. Good?"

"Good. Enjoy your stroll in my fine city." Tony's cell vibrated a third time. "Shit, that domestic dispute just got uglier—got to run."

Wilcox took off. The *Peabody* crowd parted for their local hero as Elliott went in the opposite direction and stepped onto the elevator to go change. The Memphis sun dipped below the horizon. Soon Elliott would be in the head of the Bluff City Butcher back on the night he took Panther McGee from Beale.

■ ■ ■

Along the two-story buildings that frame Beale, his old jeans, shabby t-shirt and faded Texas baseball cap moved with the throbbing chaos of the loud beer drinkers and dawdling tourists oblivious to their surroundings.

The Butcher started here, the corner of Second and Beale. He was dining out, a buffet. The perfectionist would begin at the beginning—had to see everything before a selection. I smell the smells, hear the sounds and feel the crowd…the exposure and the risk. He moved in inches, processing pieces of information often missed and seemingly meaningless that could be important. Elliott was in a constant and deliberate search for an unexpected advantage.

Did you stay in the shadows on the sticky sidewalk, surrounded by these eyes and the smell of meat slow cooking over hickory and funnel cakes frying in old canola? Or were you drawn to the alleys and abandoned property, the parallel world with its own distinct aromas; the bitter stench of spilled booze and vomit and urine soaked garbage? In both worlds, the Blues flowed from BB Kings and mixed with light Jazz and hot Rock 'n Roll that poured from the bars crammed into three blocks of blazing neon and wandering hordes. *Which way did you go?* He thought. *When did you choose Panther McGee and why? Was his heart special for you…or someone else?*

When the Bluff City Butcher stepped onto the hot asphalt Saturday night, the herd was thicker, the flow slower. The prey was more distracted than tonight but undercover cops were more abundant. The Butcher would be cautious and not deterred. He would take the one he wanted and use the crowd, darkness and technique to position for the ultimate kill. No one would see all of him at any time. He would blend into the night.

After an hour, Elliott approached the entrance to Handy Park. He felt a familiar chill down his spine; something was not right. *The Butcher stood here for only a moment. He wouldn't stay. He would look for another way inside the walls, fewer eyes.* Handy Park was the last place McGee was known to be alive.

"That nice black, singin' man is dead, yah know."

He heard the thin puff of a voice; his eyes adjusted to the darker shadows. He saw the pile of dirty rags and the matted hair. The red bandana caught his eye first.

"Hello," he replied, still not in focus.

"Not so bad a singer, yah know. I heard worse."

"So you have, have yah?"

"Seems they all start here like that...on the grass...in front of that cement stage. They don't ever let new ones use that stage, not til they got them a crowd or got them a bigger name or somethin'."

"Is that right?"

"Yup, it tiz."

She was in her late sixties, homeless a while, teeth in bad shape and would probably kill her eventually if nothing else did—roaring gum infection, but the alcohol helped. Her left eye was closed and crusted over. Her arms were crossed tight over her chest, and the neck of a pint stuck out her armpit, no cap. The smell of bourbon was strong.

"So, I guess you saw Panther McGee Saturday night?" Elliott asked. She took her time, confused or stubborn, he wasn't sure which.

"Watched him the whole ten minutes—got no respect. Sometimes peoples aren't good to the new ones."

"Really?" Elliott moved from the entrance and sat on a portable bench to get closer. She seemed to like the attention from the tall, handsome man.

"Yup, world's different now...peoples don't care much about others no more."

"Were there very many watching him sing the other night?"

"Plenty here but few watchin'." She looked to her left and right, pulled *Jack Daniels* from her armpit and took a swallow. She showed her three teeth to Elliot and put the pint back where it was safe. "Keeps me alert...don't need it, yah know."

"I see that. Do you come here oft…?"

"I count thirty-two peoples here last night. I like countin'; twenty-seven of um drinkin' and smokin' and talkin' while that poor man was singin'…"

"Thirty-two?" Elliott nodded.

"…pourin' his guts out right there in that grass; it was pit-tee-full."

"And why was it pitiful?"

"He had five watchin', counted them too; teenager couple sittin' over there and a fat, black lady in white tights standin' over there, and a real big man in a long black coat squattin' by the tree over there…and me, sittin' right here out of the ways of everybody."

Did she actually see the Butcher? Only two people alive have seen him, Marcus Pleasant and R.L. Thornton, and that was twenty-five years ago. Maybe she saw something that can help.

"My name is Elliott." She jerked back from his hand and tightened her arms around her chest, protecting her dinner. She looked up with her good eye and then relaxed.

"I'm Joey. I liked the name and took it last year." She stuck out her little hand. She was missing the tips of three fingers, probably amputated after frostbite or diabetes; at least she had seen some medical care along the way. He held her little hand between his two. He would let go when she was ready. She started talking even more.

"You're a nice man, Elliott. I bet you have a bunch of girlfriends."

"Thank you for that but I really don't, Joey. Can you tell me more about the big man you saw, the one by the tree?"

"Why, you think he killed that McGee feller?"

"Oh, I wouldn't know about that. I'm just curious. I heard this park was the last place anyone saw Mr. McGee; the man you mentioned seems suspicious to me. Why, did you see him with Mr. McGee…did he hurt him?"

"I think he hurt that black man."

"I see. Why, Joey?"

She showed him her three teeth again and leaned closer. "I put my good eye on that big man when he looked in the park. He didn't come in the front like everybody else. He looked in the front and he came in the back. I saw him jump that gate back there under the light. He went high and hit the light under that roof."

"That light?" Elliott pointed to the one twelve feet off the ground.

"Yup, he hit it and it aimed on the spot where he comes down. I never saw a man jump high like that, not even them basketball peoples on the TV. He was like one of those Olympians."

"What did he do next, Joey?"

"That man stayed low to the ground and followed those hedges along that wall. He never got out of the dark all the way to the tree where it's always dark. I saw how big he was when he stood up to look for the singin' man over here." She pointed. "He was big, like you, but could make himself look less big."

"Crouching down in his coat?"

"Yes, Sir. He kept watchin' the singin' man. I kept my good eye on him."

"That seems suspicious to me, too," said Elliott, still holding her hand.

"After he finished singin' he passed a hat. It came back and he got mad, cussin' and all. Nobody was lookin' at him 'cept me and the big one."

"What happened next?"

"The McGee fella drops his money on the ground and leaves in a huff."

"Did he leave out the front gate?" asked Elliott.

"I picked up that seven dollars, each rolled into a little, dirty ball; I didn't care, I got 'em all and I saw the singin' man climb out the back gate. Never saw him again."

"And what did the big man do, Joey?"

She pulled her hand from Elliott's and took a couple more swallows of bourbon. "Not for sure…I'm thinkin' he climbed the wall behind the tree."

26

"He was gone?"

"I'm thinkin' that singin' man is gonna get hurt and there wasn't nothin' I could do 'bout it. I see stuff and it scares me, been tryin' to stay out of the way most all my life." Joey sunk in her dirty laundry and leaned back against the wall, her head down and hands balled in her lap. "He hurt that singin' man."

Elliott reached for her shoulder. Joey looked up with her good eye. It was wet. "Miss Joey, I want to give you a couple things. Will that be ok with you?"

"I don't know. What I gotta do?"

"Only what you want to do."

"Ok...then," she said. Elliott gave her five ten-dollar bills and watched her eye go wide and sparkle. She folded two and put them in one sock and folded two more for the other sock. She put the last ten-dollar bill under her rags into a little purse on a knotted string around her neck, probably her dinner stash.

"Can you read, Joey?"

"Some. But I'm real good with numbers."

"That's ok because this card has mostly numbers. It's my phone number. Joey, when you are ready, I want you to call and tell me what I can do to help you."

"But I don't need no help. I'm real good with my tens."

"I know, Joey, but I'm a doctor and a little worried about you getting sick out here. I know your teeth hurt and your eye is infected, Joey. If you let me give you some medicine, I promise you'll feel a lot better when you're sitting out here."

"Ok. You can be my doctor." She stuck his card in her sock; that meant later. Their three eyes met a last time. Elliott left the Park the back way.

The gate was seven feet, the light twelve. The side street along the wall was one of those dark edges of Beale's neon and crowds that Tony was talking about. The whole block was a "no parking" zone but there was a cluster of fresh oil drops…just one spot. Elliott knelt to look closer and to take in everything that happened there. It felt right. The oil was gritty, dirty, thick…*an old car, no doubt.* In the gutter two feet away was a guitar pick, the only shiny thing on the dirty cement. *Panther McGee was taken here.* With tweezers he dropped it into a small, plastic baggy…*maybe a print?*

The lame battery desperately struggled. From haunches, he looked at the sound, the single, red taillight that dimmed with each feeble effort. It was a dirty white van at the end of the next block. The mud smeared plate was not a surprise. Elliott started toward the coughing heap; the engine growled to life and the loose pile of metal rocked and creaked around the corner. It lumbered into the night, leaving a cloud with the crickets. Rubbing the drop of dirty oil between his fingers, Elliott smiled. It was a good day. He got close to the Butcher on day one. That would anger the demented killer. *Joey saw you Saturday night…and I found you Sunday night. Every inch from here matters even more.*

Standing on the edge of Beale's perpetual party after his encounter with the Bluff City Butcher, Elliott felt something new. Was it another gift…one he did not yet understand? Was something inside speaking to him? *It is going to end in Memphis. Something is changing in the life of this serial killer. Who is the hunter and who is the hunted?*

CHAPTER TWO

"I never sleep, because sleep is the cousin of death."
Nasir Jones

5 August 2008

The walk-in refrigerator at the Shelby County morgue could easily bed twenty on gurneys with wheels and twice that in crash bags. On August 4th, twelve were spending the night, including Panther McGee.

Elliott arrived early and befriended the night shift with *Starbucks*. Within ten minutes the field agent in charge took him on a predawn tour of the facilities. Dr. Bates would arrive precisely at seven o'clock and the rest would dribble in for the McGee inquest scheduled for eight o'clock. Elliott would have everything he needed well before the circus came to town. He worked best alone because he was much more efficient at capturing and processing enormous quantities of relevant forensic information, and he could see the pieces to the puzzle that are often difficult to explain.

The pneumatic door gushed open, a crystalline cloud rolled into the barren hall and Elliott followed Roger Knox inside. The door released like a train leaving the station. Flood lights at the corners flickered long enough to trigger doubt. They popped back on at the last moment and provided ample illumination for the frigid bowels of another county morgue; he'd been in too many over the last decade.

There were two lines of ten gurneys. Six on each side holding the bodies, heads at the walls and bare feet in the narrow aisle. Elliott scanned the twelve bumps from the door. Each was tucked under a disposable white paper sheet splashed with a cocktail of stains created by the last trauma they endured. Roger Knox moved slow, a young *Dom DeLuise* before the weight gain and hair loss, in his mid-twenties, a fourth-year med-student thinking about forensic pathology. Knox eased into the narrow aisle, the feet sticking out from under drapes; he read the toe tags aloud, the fog shooting from his mouth with each syllable uttered.

"John…Sanford, Beatrice…Blair, Henry…Potter…where did we put Panther McGee?" He straightened up and nudged his glasses back on his nose. "Dr. Sumner, we have five naturals, three accidentals, two suicides and two homicides on board. Been relatively quiet around here for the last year, but I think things are going to start picking up again." Knox moved to the next pair of feet and groped around for the toe tag.

"Quiet?" asked Elliott.

"Well, I say quiet. What I mean is…bizarre cases are picking up."

"Bizarre?"

"Well, I say bizarre. What I mean is…yup, bizarre is what I mean." He stood up again. "Yah know…a guy could go nuts knowing the stuff that goes on around here. I have seen a whole lot, and I have more questions today than the day I arrived."

"I understand that feeling. This world is life unedited. Sometimes we need to talk it out just to keep our sanity." *That should loosen you up. Tell me what's on your mind.*

"I've been interning with the medical examiner's office for eighteen months now. There have been dead people pass through here that were ruled suicide, or accidental, or death by natural causes that, well…I just didn't see it that way."

"You believe they were homicides?"

"Yes. I thought they were."

This could be interesting. "It is normal to have doubts. Take the Memphis Metro Area; the population is 1.2 million people. That makes it the third largest city in the southeastern United States. This medical examiner's office reported 686 autopsies last year and you are on track to do 815 this year. I will estimate 1,200 bodies come through these doors, maybe 400 inspections and the rest autopsies. Some disagreement on the cause and manner of death among staff is bound to come up."

Did he just say all that? Stats…? Shit, the man is a genius, like it says in the textbooks…probably knows more about this place then me, thought Knox. He stopped looking at toe tags and turned to Elliott. It was time to take a chance. "It's more than that, Sir. Suicides, unwitnessed accidental deaths and some natural deaths, fine…but they shouldn't be missing body parts when they are found."

Did you say missing body parts? "Body parts missing?"

"Yes, body parts missing: hearts, livers, stomachs and other things. We are told it is not that unusual. We are told body parts can be taken by family members or friends for a multitude of reasons: religious, superstition, money and even keepsakes," said Knox, as he bent over the next toe tag.

"Is it possible you are missing something, maybe another step in the investigative process? Are these cases—with missing parts—handled differently from other suicides, accidents and natural deaths?"

"Well, I guess so. Dr. Bates takes them off-line. The field agents are pretty much cut out of the circle. There is no oversight, if you know what I mean."

"How are they carried in the system…the computer…paperwork?"

"Manner of death is ruled 'undetermined,' the bodies are released and the case files disappear. They are not in the Shelby County Medical

Examiner data base and do not appear in reports or in any statistical analysis that I've seen. Out of curiosity, I tracked a few of these cases. It was almost like they never happened."

"I'm sure there is some explanation. You should ask Dr. Bates."

"I have. He said the confidential cases are complex and could require several years of investigation. Therefore, they must be handled in a more protected process…off line…with the FBI."

Dr. Bates, MPD Director Wade and FBI Director Voss know more than they are sharing…even with Wilcox, their top homicide detective. But why? Do they know they are dealing with the Bluff City Butcher? Is there something else going on here? Why go to such great lengths to bury possible BCB kills…and organ harvesting…and for how long?

"I guess I am over thinking, as usual," said Knox. He started to shiver as the cold sank into his clothes. "Let's see, we have Margaret Grover…and…"

The dark, damp prison of a fungal-laden world and endless poundings created the boney, gnarled stubs covered with dried, cracked skin, bunions, blisters and calluses. The toenails were too long or too short, overgrown or ingrown, discolored or missing. After a lifetime of faithfully transporting the body, the poor feet seem to be the most battered and unattractive appendages of the human anatomy. Elliott's swift survey of the twenty-four quickly located Panther McGee on gurney #12, the youngest African American feet in the group. He would let Knox make the discovery.

"Here we go, Mr. Panther McGee. I knew he was here somewhere."

"The only things removed from the body at check-in were shoes and socks, correct?" asked Elliott.

"Yes, Sir," said Knox.

And they were carefully bagged, I'm sure. "I will want to see them later." *And the rest of the clothing and possessions that will come off at the inquest…to be photographed, inspected and processed according to the standard operating procedures and this medical examiner's suspicions that could be shallow if he continued to avoid looking for the Butcher.* Elliott's needs were different. He knew better than anyone how this monster killed and processed his victims.

Elliott came early to validate whether Panther McGee was a BCB kill or the end result of a copycat. If it was the Butcher's work, Elliott would begin the process of differentiating the kill from his others; what changed and what did it mean? And every step of the way he would continue his search for the next unexpected advantage that he knew he would need.

They pulled on disposable gloves. Knox flipped the paper sheet off the body and made room between the gurneys. "I don't want to interfere but can you educate me…tell me along the way some of what you see and think as an expert?"

"Sure. First, I try not to over think." *Something I have yet to master.* "Don't miss the big things." *Is this Panther McGee…is always a good place to start?* "Don't begin with a set of expectations or pre-formed conclusions. I represent the deceased. It is his or her turn to speak. I must pay close attention and let them tell me their story."

"That's incredible. I never thought of it that way," said Knox.

Elliott visually inspected the bagged hands and forearms. "I see no defense wounds. He was not surprised." *Panther was subdued rapidly…no time to react.* "I see at least one broken fingernail." *He pulled at the Butcher's iron-arm that lifted him like a child off the sidewalk and into the death van.* "Dr. Bates may find trace blood and tissue from the killer…a possibility of DNA." *Probably not.*

The shirt was open, revealing a seven-inch sutured incision under the left breast. "There are fifty tight stitches, each with a packer's knot—*the Butcher's favorite*—and the edges of the incision are neatly trimmed. The wound has been scrubbed and rinsed and a portion of the ribcage has been removed with the heart."

I have seen the characteristic cave-in so often that palpation is not necessary. The Butcher is consistent with his surgical procedures.

"What have we learned in the first minute?"

"The killer is a doctor?"

"Not necessarily…possible, but I'm going for indisputable findings. Listen and learn. The killer has surgical skill and enjoys his work—he took his time to savor the experience. He has a steady hand and a plan." *I see the Knots of Isis at both ends of the incision…and the missing ring finger from the left hand. I will not share those observations.*

He felt the top of Panther's skull with his index fingers, his hands cradling the head, ears in his palms. Elliott focused on Panther's glassy eyes, drawing Knox into the moment; he would not share the discovery of the cranial puncture wound he located in the usual spot. He laid down the head, stepped back and, they returned the paper drape over the cold, rigid body. Standing at the refrigerator door, they looked back at the empty shells.

"A certain reverence comes with the privilege of being with them at the end. The good ones never lose touch with that, Dr. Knox."

"I understand, Sir."

The pneumatic door sucked open. Dr. Bates stood outside in the growing cloud as the two worlds met. His hands were on his waist and head cocked forward like a parent looking for kids at dinner time. His body said he was pissed-off…his domain had been violated.

"Well, the famous Dr. Elliott Sumner. You are early. I didn't plan on finding you in my refrigerator," said Bates, attempting intimidation. Elliott stepped from the arctic cloud into the barren hall, towering above Bates. His presence crushed all attempts of Bates to distract him from what was important. Knox thoroughly enjoyed the moment. Bates stepped back and began to unscrew his face. *You are different…so big and your eyes…intense, penetrating. Why do I feel like you see all of me? Is it true?*

Maybe you are the most revered serial killer hunter in the world for reasons I have not considered.

"Excuse me one moment, doctor," said Elliott politely as he returned attentions to Knox with an extended hand. "Thank you for your time and brief but prideful tour of the operations. I always value the field agent's perspective...the eyes of the medical examiners everywhere. I am sure Dr. Bates values your internship and I certainly hope you choose to pursue a career in Forensic Pathology. If you do, maybe one day we will work together."

"Yes, Sir, and thank you, Sir. I am honored to meet you. It's great to talk with someone who is actually in some of my forensic textbooks. Your contributions have been phenomenal...incredible stories. And I am sure Dr. Bates will show you far more than I could." They shook hands and Knox left them alone.

"I don't believe we have formally met." Elliott smiled. He had everything he needed. The rest of the morning would be a plus. Bates was still back on his heels.

"Yes. Dr. Sumner. It is my profound pleasure to meet you, Sir."

■ ■ ■

"Loneliness is about the scariest thing there is..."
Unknown

6 August 2008

The Bell estate was in east Memphis on Walnut Grove Road, fifty acres of prime real estate behind a twelve-foot brick wall covered with ivy and moss. Tall iron gates and a stone guardhouse marked the only way on and off the property. The wall around the estate was steel-beam reinforced with embedded day/night vision cameras, motion detectors, sound sensors and flood lights every twenty-five feet.

At the gates a brawny, uniformed man stepped onto the driveway as two limos pulled up. Another guard of equal proportion and attitude stood halfway in the doorway of the guardhouse, with busy eyes leveled and a hand on his unsnapped, holstered gun; the Bell estate welcome mat was out with intent to discourage foolishness.

After a few quiet words, a look at selected documents and an accusing eye into the backseat, the guard waved the limos on, Elliott Sumner in one and Max Gregory the other; they were expected.

The iron gates parted and the limos moved onto the hallowed grounds, accelerating through the gradual climb across a field of rolling wheat. Inside the brick wall were walking rifles and German Shepherds. Max was impressed with the security but curious, because he felt it was more elaborate than he expected. His visits were always at night. *What is Albert trying to keep out?* He wondered.

At the southern edge of the amber fields, the driveway began its gradual descent toward the sprawling Bell mansion surrounded by pristine lawns, manicured hedges, flowering gardens and glass ponds framed by a hundred weeping willows and giant oaks. Twenty feet from the house proper the limos pulled up to the famous stone arch supporting the Bell family crest and the imposing spear atop the gothic spire, one of the most photographed entries in the country, where many a visiting dignitary had passed. William stood under the famous arch; he would escort Max and Elliott to the study. Tony was already with Albert Bell.

"In the fall of '83, I received a hand-written note mailed at a roadside postal unit, downtown Memphis. I thought it peculiar at the time and held onto it."

Albert Bell, Jr., a young seventy-six and a billionaire international cotton merchant, turned from the second-floor window and view of his expansive estate. A tall, willowy framed man with a bronze complexion, his wavy, silver hair wild on the forehead gave him an eccentric, elder statesman appeal. He returned to his desk and the discolored file folder at its center. With one finger he opened it and pinched a corner of the plastic baggy containing a single sheet of tattered stationery. He held it up like a dirty diaper.

"Gentlemen…I would like you to examine this first." He walked it around to Dr. Sumner sitting in one of the three high-backed, hunter green leather chairs that surrounded and were dwarfed by the hand-carved mahogany monstrosity at the center of the cavernous study. Albert's desk was the primary site for everything including the lighting for the most strategic room in the mansion. The walls were filled with priceless oil paintings, bookcases with first-edition classics, urns with exotic plants from around the world and two fireplaces cloaked in an abiding shadow on the edge of creepy. Tony Wilcox sat in the next chair and Max Gregory in the third.

"Mr. Bell, I am honored with the invitation this evening and pleased to look at whatever you have, but handwriting analysis is a talent I do not possess," said Elliott as he accepted the protected document from Albert as he would grasp the original copy of the *Declaration of Independence.*

"Please, Elliott, call me Albert." This was the first time they'd actually met, although both knew of the other's status and accomplishments

"Albert," he confirmed.

"I assure you such an expectation, I do not have. However, a man of your unique talents and considerable experience may have some worthwhile comments.

"I see. Sure, that's fine," said Elliott.

Albert returned to his chair and scotch. Elliott studied the note for several minutes as the room watched. He then passed the document to Tony who gave it to Max. The room was quiet, all eyes on Elliott. His hand made the crystal goblet of scotch look like a shot glass and his other hand propped his chin, a finger moving back-and-forth on his lower lip. Max cleared his throat like a smoker paying the price.

"Albert, as you said at the onset, you have information to share that is relevant to unexplained events in the Midsouth—the Panther McGee homicide was mentioned. Is it your contention this twenty-five-year-old note has some bearing?" asked Max.

"I have the same question," said Tony. "A man of your wealth and notoriety must receive *love letters* like this all the time. What possibly could make this one special?"

"I am confident you both will agree this note is special once you have the opportunity to see all the information."

They nodded.

Max Gregory had met Albert Bell by accident in Tel Aviv, 1982; they were barefoot on the beach of the Mediterranean. Business suit pants were rolled to the knees and socks hanging from the pockets. It had been a day of meetings for both…they needed an out. Albert was puffing on an expensive cigar when he bumped into Max; he had an unlit Chesterfield hanging from a frown. The strike of a match launched a friendship that endured the next twenty-five years. They met each year at the same bar in Tel Aviv to complain, solve world problems and drink; Albert scotch, Max vodka. After Max retired from CIA Secret Ops, he started Spyglass, LLC, a private investigation agency.

"You have everything and I have nothing…now. I will kill you slowly," said Elliott while looking at the ceiling. "My first impression…the message says little that should alarm a billionaire or anyone of wealth and privilege. Seven of thirteen words have errors; one misspelled, three missing a letter and three words with backward letters.

"The fifty-four percent error rate suggests the author desperately crafted this message for you, Albert. That makes it more personal and more important; it makes it relevant. Let's consider the following; *'I have nothing…now,'* implies that a condition that is bad will be changed for the better. *'I will kill you slowly,'* implies that you are responsible for the bad condition and the author will make it better at your expense."

"I felt the note was different," said Albert

"A legitimate threat, but as Max pointed out, a twenty-five-year-old threat."

"I would have agreed but there is another letter. This time it was delivered to the mansion, wedged in the gates the morning of August 3, 2008."

"The day Mr. McGee was found in Tom Lee Park?" said Elliott.

Tony sat up, displaying the first sign of life since his arrival.

Albert went back to the window and looked to the far reaches of the estate. "This requires some setup. I'll be brief.

"I was in El Paso, Texas in December 1967, attending our annual Texas Cotton Banquet. Mr. Philippé Ramirez was the independent meeting planner handling the event. He was a wonderful individual, hard worker. He had a severe degenerative disease of the hip; I wanted to help. We brought Philippé to Memphis for surgery; it was a success. He decided to stay in Memphis and joined the Bell family business as our exclusive meeting planner. Sixteen years later Philippé disappeared without a trace."

"Albert, if I may," Max interrupted.

"Gentlemen, Albert asked me to look for Mr. Ramirez. Our agency specializes in locating missing people. We are pretty good at it, with a ninety-nine percent recovery rate. Unfortunately Philippé fell into the dreaded one percent.

"His apartment was on the bluff downtown. He was last seen by his neighbors on October 14, 1983. Spyglass got involved five days later. There were five newspapers on the doorstep, dirty dishes in the sink, the TV was on and a two-inch ash was clinging to a cigarette in the ashtray next to his chair.

"No signs of foul play, no forced entry, nothing taken and no disturbance noted by neighbors. Ramirez was a quiet, friendly man of petite stature whose last moments in that apartment were in front of the TV after dinner, smoking a cigarette. Whatever happened was sudden and unexpected. We dusted the place for prints, none unknown. Ten years later we ran DNA on the cigarette filter and other known specimens collected at his place at that time, confirmation: all Ramirez."

"Albert, what does this all have to do with the August 3rd letter?" Tony's patience was wearing thin; he had a serial killer to catch and every minute was important.

"The August 3rd letter is on the same stationery as the letter of 1983, the same handwriting and errors." Albert pulled out the second plastic bag and read; *"I have been busy but all are stupid and do not see. I want YOU to know. I was shocked to see these similarities twenty-five years apart."* Albert passed it around the room and purposely did not comment on the human finger in the baggy with the letter.

"My God, what is this dried up finger?" asked Tony.

"Actually, *mummified*…prolonged refrigeration." Elliott tilted the shade of Albert's desk lamp and held the specimen to the bulb. "Did you get a look at the ring?" He enjoyed how Albert let them discover the finger without a prelude.

"Yes, we gave it to Philippé on his ten-year anniversary."

"And the string…does it mean anything to you?" Elliott asked. *The string is tied at the proximal end, possibly intended to stop drainage long ago.*

"No," said Albert.

"Unusual knot." Max peered over Elliott's shoulder.

"The *Knot of Isis*," he passed the bag back to Tony.

"And what is a *Knot of Isis?*"

"Isis is an Egyptian goddess—protector of the dead. Tony, we need DNA testing to confirm the finger belongs to Ramirez."

"We'll get it started tonight. I'm sure they have Max's '93 profile in the system."

"Albert, it's safe to assume your pen pal killed Philippé Ramirez—for reasons unknown—and he seeks your attention."

Why is the Bluff City Butcher reaching out to Albert Bell? Why twenty-five years ago and why did he kill Philippé Ramirez? But…most important, Albert Bell, why does a demented, psychopathic serial killer have a relationship with you? And how much do you really know about it?

"Gentlemen, this brings me to why I asked you here tonight."

"There's more?" asked Tony.

Albert removed a third note from the file. It was neatly encased in another plastic baggy. He read from his chair. *"I am keeping the one I got on Beale for now, left ring finger…that is."* The signature was…ADAM.

Max jumped out of his seat. "Tony…can you tell us? Was Panther McGee missing a finger? It stays in this room, Sir."

"Only those in a very tight circle around the McGee investigation know a finger was taken…and the heart. Yes—since we are sharing—the killer took the same finger from McGee that was taken from Ramirez."

"May I see the third note?" asked Elliott.

"Yes, of course." He started to get up but Elliott was on his way. Max started with the predictable barrage of questions; Elliott understood that old CIA guys couldn't stand surprises or being the last in the room to find out anything. Max would scramble to connect the dots but would never have enough. The three-way gave Elliott the diversion he needed.

Elliott's mind pursued the implications; the third message identified the author but, more importantly, the stationery opened a door into the Butcher's world. There was an imperfection, a blemish or smudge, unworthy of attention. It was in the same place on all three, the lower right corner. The faint oval discoloration was the size of a grain of rice and contained a single word on the edge of microscopic, but for Elliott…visible. The word was *Gilgamesh*.

His photographic memory reached back to his junior year at the University of Texas, English literature. *Gilgamesh* was the king of Uruk— modern day Iraq—in 2500 BCE. He was a demigod of superhuman strength that reigned 126 years. Gilgamesh was also the grandson of the King of Babylon, who, out of fear, had him thrown from the highest tower; the oracles said Gilgamesh would kill the king. But an eagle broke his fall and the infant was raised by a gardener and eventually became king. Elliott remembered the entire text of the *Epic of Gilgamesh,* the first story on the pursuit of immortality. *How does this relate to the Bluff City Butcher?*

■ ■ ■

9 August 2008

It was scheduled for Saturday night, *Grisanti's Italian Restaurant* in Midtown. Elliott had nothing planned. He accepted Albert Bell's dinner invitation; something about new biotechnology, a risky investment and input from a non-biased medical professional. And Albert said he wanted to know the international forensic sleuth better. That suited Elliott because he wanted one-on-one time with the billionaire patriarch. Revelations at the first meeting opened new areas to explore; why the twenty-five-year relationship with a serial killer, the Bluff City Butcher? What was the basis of the enduring interest on both sides? Was there more to the three cryptic notes? The elaborate security measures at the mansion were telling. Albert knew more. And *Gilgamesh,* what was it and how did it fit?

Elliott was met at the front doors of the Italian restaurant by a plump smile and red cheeks in a white apron with sleeves rolled up. She took him the opposite way from the dining room, through the bustling kitchen and down the dark, damp hall of piped music to a stream of soft light pouring from an open door. She left him there.

Albert Bell was at the far end of the long, empty table that was draped in crisp white linen and had two elaborate place settings. Little light came from the ornate, cut glass chandelier in the center of blood-red walls and dark molding. Most light fell from the dozen small lamps above the small paintings surrounding the table. A man was leaning toward Albert, sunken eyes beneath a black knit cap pulled over his ears, a wisp of grey poking out the back. The black shirt and black trousers clung to his lean body. He was in his early seventies, hundred-and-fifty pounds, six-two, *Rolex* with a black face, no wedding band—Elliott saw everything in seconds. The man was very close to Albert, a trusted relationship, the way they looked into each other's eyes and spoke, one reaching for total understanding and the other guiding with patience and confident expectations. They had done this many times before. Albert whispered. The man wrote in his small leather binder. Elliott would need to meet the man in the knit cap…somewhere along the way.

"Good evening, Dr. Sumner." Albert was the first to see him step into the dim light. His words were for the benefit of his associate. The binder snapped closed and he disappeared into a dark corner, a door to somewhere. Elliott thought it all quite odd but he had not run with many billionaires so it could be perfectly normal.

"Hello again, Sir," said Elliott. Albert extended his hand; they gripped…equal in size and surprisingly equal in strength.

Elliott returned the smile and saw his place setting was in a subordinated position, Albert at the head and he the side. A fresh scotch on the rocks was waiting. It was new, the glass and napkin still dry next to a sweating glass of ice water. Albert's controlling nature was not hidden.

"I hope you don't mind, I took the liberty of assuming you are a scotch man."

And, how did you know I am a scotch on the rocks man? "An excellent assumption and liberty well taken." They clicked glasses with intense, steel blue eyes locked. *What have we here?* Elliott wondered. *I need to know more about you, and already I sense the task may be one of my more challenging.*

New gifts suddenly presented. Elliott learned to pay attention. The wash of anticipation, a vague premonition of danger or the foreboding cloud that he met at Grisanti's front door was a warning. He was unlike any other man that sat across from the patriarch and had not yet considered the possibility the same was true for Albert Bell.

After the customary courtesies, dinner was served and the evening progressed. Elliott admired Albert's worldly ways, humble demeanor and razor-sharp intelligence honed by the wisdom of years and a lifetime of opulence and absolute excess. He was impressed with the effortless projection of a durable confidence, tranquility and measured patience few in the world would ever know. Elliott yielded to Albert's command of the evening's conversation because his skills of observation and deduction delivered results without a requirement of predetermined path or controlled examination. Elliott extracted slivers of relevance and assembled multiple puzzles concurrently. Although the content of discussion was important, the words used and avoided, inflexions, the flicker of an eye, misplaced reactions, transitions and knowledge denied were all captured, assimilated and assessed.

"As you would surmise, the Bell family is presented with investment opportunity and participates in numerous ventures around the world."

"I would imagine it is a full time job keeping billions working…or out of harm's way, depending on point of view." Elliott held little interest in financial matters unless they were relevant to a diabolical puzzle. Serial killers were rarely in it for the money. Navigation of a P&L and balance sheet was easy enough. The perfect selection of a certified public accountant was more his style.

"In March 2005, I invested in a startup—the *Life2 Corporation*—conveniently headquartered in Memphis."

"How obliging." They laughed as plates were taken.

"*Life2* is a biotechnology company focusing on genetic engineered solutions for medical conditions. Their first target…osteoarthritis."

"They certainly know how to pick them. That is the number one degenerative condition today," said Elliott.

"They said exactly that."

"When I was in medical school my rotation through orthopedics exposed me to an impressive array of medical devices and wonder drugs to help these people. Today, the advances in restoring pain-free mobility are miraculous."

"*Life2* has one product they will talk about. *Ossi2* is for regeneration of cartilage. Their research has steadily progressed since 2004, laboratory testing and animal studies completed. Controlled human clinical studies are underway in Europe. So far, the results appear to be favorable, but I'm no scientist. I just know what they tell me." Albert downed the rest of his scotch. A wisp of a waiter eased in and out of the light. A fresh scotch on the rocks replaced the empty without a word spoken. By Elliott's count, number four in an hour.

"So, they claim they are regenerating cartilage?"

"Exactly. Their studies showed new cartilage cells populating boney surfaces where old cartilage was obliterated."

"Do you know the people heading up this company?"

"Jack Bellow is the President/CEO and a friend of the family. I have invested in two of his companies. He is a revered biotech entrepreneur. *Life2* is his fourth company."

"And the top technical guy?"

"Dr. Enrique Medino, a Vanderbilt geneticist. I never heard of him before, but he checked out during the 2005 due diligence process;

University of Texas El Paso, Southwestern Medical School and Vanderbilt…M.D. and PhD."

"Molecular biology and geneticist?"

"Yes…director of the genetics outfit that worked on the human genome project. Medino studied organic chemistry, cell biology and molecular biology. He got his medical degree and was an OB/GYN doctor a few years."

"Did he practice medicine?" asked Elliott.

"According to the private placement memorandum, he had a clinic for a few years in Pecos, Texas."

"Pecos, Texas…I wonder what got him out there?"

"1968 to 1970," said Albert without thinking—*why did I just do that? Now he has date, location and name. If he is as good as they say, he will eventually make the connections, but maybe not before the time is right. Gloss over the whole thing.* "The company was formed December 2004, a fifty-fifty proposition between the two founders. Bellow put in $10 million seed capital and leased the Old Exchange Building to *Life2* for a dollar a year, global headquarters. Dr. Medino brought the intellectual property, knowhow and breakthroughs to the company, and leased his private research facility to *Life2* as well, a farm in east Nashville. The Series A Preferred Stock offering raised $50 million in April, 2005, and the Series B offering brought in another $150 million, as I recall. I'm in for $35 million."

"I'm sure you didn't bring me here for the financials," said Elliott as he leaned back and absorbed every ounce of data he could extract from the Bell patriarch.

"I am curious to know what you think about the biotechnology and the company." Albert produced a half-inch bound document and set it next to Elliott with an encouraging nod. Elliott turned it with one finger and read the cover; *Life 2 Corporation, Private Placement Memorandum,*

Series B Preferred Stock offering. Their eyes met as he picked it up; he knew what Albert wanted to see. For him, it was not that great but for the rest of the world it was somewhere between dazzling and mind-blowing. The PPM was 275 pages: twenty pages for investor notices, five index, twenty-five exhibits, thirty forward-looking statements and routine legal disclaimers. That left 195 pages of substance: business plans, technology, risk factors, and use of proceeds, management and capitalization. He fanned the pages, allowing a view of each. He was done before Albert set his glass back on the linen. Elliott slid it back with one finger.

"Impressive," said Albert.

"Not really. Speed reading is something people do now," said Elliott.

*But few remember every single word...*smiled Albert, knowing his homework would pay off.

"The *Life2* biotechnology...I have some observations, questions and recommendations...is that good for you?"

"Exactly what I was hoping for this evening."

"Good. Observations, the PPM is not telling the whole story. It is a veiled attempt to sell stock without selling out the technology. The technical section is written by one person, an MD/scientist, which is odd. I assume the author is Dr. Enrique Medino."

"Why odd?" asked Albert.

"New ventures raising capital fold sections of their business plan into the private placement documents. Corporate attorneys and SEC specialists pore over the draft docs and clean them up: make sure claims are sufficiently vague but tempting, informative, legal. Then they fix grammar and punctuation and position ideas properly. That means each discussion stream in this document has a beginning, middle and end. Dr. Medino's words are unedited throughout the entire document. That is suspicious. I see beginnings, vague middles and incomplete endings."

"Why is that significant?"

"Not knowing the man, I can only guess he is shielding something. He is writing to other scientific types and is extremely careful to protect knowhow and any underlying intellectual property."

"Wouldn't that be expected from a scientist-inventor?"

"To some degree…yes."

"But what?"

"He is hiding something more than he is protecting something. If I were you, I would try to find out what he is hiding, because it may have a bearing on your investment. It may be a problem."

"Hiding?"

"Development of *Ossi2* was an enormously complex project probably taking several decades of research and development. Dr. Medino presents the *Ossi2* biogenic mechanism as limited to the repair and regeneration of chondroblasts, only one human cell type. If you read between the lines he is avoiding discussion of broader applications. That is illogical. Why avoid that discussion? I would assume future possibilities of the technology have value to an investor and would be an appropriate forward-looking statement."

"Universal, meaning it works with other types of cells?"

"Yes. The genetic on-off button for the chondrocytes is very likely the same for other cells."

"Why would he hide that, I wonder?"

"The most obvious answer is protecting confidential information and staging the business for technology roll outs."

"And the less obvious?"

"Could be anything from the product is going to fail, to the development of the product is suspect—a broad application means there was extensive testing and that means there were enormous requirements for a wide variety of fresh, human tissue over time."

"Why is tissue an issue?" asked Albert.

"Human tissue is regulated and tracked. It is not readily available and not as fresh as it must be for delicate biogenic testing. It is extremely expensive, and some tissues are next to impossible to get: heart, brain, liver…for example."

"I see." *So…Enrique Medino didn't abandon his work on life-extension as he said to me in 2005. He has been working on it since 1965. The Ossi2 is a ploy, a way to get the international network in place for the ultimate product,* Albert thought.

"I suspect *Life2* has a much broader application of their biotechnology under wraps: treatments for other medical conditions like cerebral-vascular disease, diabetes, atherosclerosis and maybe some cancers. They could be sitting on a goldmine and be pacing themselves. I would, however, have to spend time with Dr. Medino and Jack Bellow to get a better insight into that."

The man in the black knit cap stepped into the private dining room from the shadows, this time without the cap. "Excuse me, Sir, someone to see you."

"Can it wait?"

"He said you would want to know. It should take but a minute, Sir."

"Will you excuse me, Elliott? I will be right back."

After Albert left the room the table was cleared and reset for coffee and dessert. He got up and meandered around the room, examining each oil painting: originals, unknown artists, dark, gothic, Italy landscapes. He neared Albert's chair and could see through the cracked door a short, plump man with a handlebar mustache talking to Albert. Next to the chair was an opened briefcase with files, one tab was visible…*Carol Mason.*

Albert reentered the room, his eyes following Elliott's as he reached for his drink, number seven. Albert picked up where he had left off. "Is the *Life2* technology real, Elliott?"

"Based on my limited view, I can say the technology looks promising but this whole area of science is new. Breakthroughs can be fleeting, simply fail at some unexpected moment, develop unacceptable side effects, or even worse they can produce outcomes more damaging than the condition they attempt to treat."

"Do you suspect the *Ossi2* biogenic technology has broader applications?"

"Yes, I do. If it can wake up the chondroblasts and reverse the natural degenerative process in joints then you are really dealing with a 'life extension' breakthrough. I am sure other biotech experts know Medino may have something big."

"What are your questions?" asked Albert.

"I have many, but you will not have the answers. I would want to know more about the animal testing and human clinicals. I would want Dr. Medino to tell me about the genetic manipulations that allowed aged cells to revitalize and encourage repopulation. I would ask Jack Bellow to share his vision, where they are relative to his goals. Albert, there is more going on at this company than is in the documents. I cannot determine from the PPM if it is a good thing or bad."

"The *Life2 Corporation* has an investor meeting in the fourth quarter. Jack said one more round of financing. I can arrange for you to get an invitation."

"An invite would be good. I will be in Memphis most of the month working with the MPD." *I have no interest in the investment opportunity, but I need time with Dr. Medino to learn more about how he fills his enormous research needs for fresh human tissue, and what about Jack Bellow's involvements, depths of understanding? Why does the business plan drop off a cliff in five years? Something big is going to happen after the last funding event. Their research expense going forward is easily addressed with revenues. The capital infusion can only be aimed at international distribution, and that is far more robust than would be needed for any one-of-a-kind orthopedic solution.*

"Albert, I promised you a recommendation. Why don't I save that until after the investor meeting?"

"Certainly."

The dessert cart wheeled in, shifting attentions. *You are as sharp as I thought you would be…before the end of the year you will tell me all I need to know about Enrique Medino and the veiled biotechnology,* thought Albert.

CHAPTER THREE

"Revenge is a confession of pain."
Latin Proverb

11 August 2008

The rusted and faded NO BOAT LAUNCH sign leaned toward the river at the north end of Mud Island across from the only bend in Island Drive, three miles from downtown Memphis; a shotgun blast had taken out the "NO" a long time ago. Few people traveled that way anymore; fewer knew about the hidden trail behind the crippled sign.

The narrow opening in the thick brush turned into a trail that dropped into a ravine and snaked through a hundred years of river debris and wild growth. After a while, it opened onto a small, isolated clearing on the east bank of the Mississippi River. That's where Elliott saw the little girl on display.

It was after two in the morning. The milky, moonlit surroundings moaned as the river winds pushed anything that could move. From the trail, he was sure she was dead. She had been taken twenty-five years ago...off the back deck of a restaurant on the bluff. *Why present her to me here, this way...and why now?*

He approached the mound of sand where she was lying on her side in a contracted, fetal position; she wore the same dress and single red shoe, as described in the 1983 police report...Sabina Weatherford was five then. The smell of natron was thick, but it was the sight of a mummified child that made his eyes water. Kneeling over her in a wary silence, Elliott took in every infinite detail, including the victim's pain; one day that would kill him.

Leaning over the little girl, Elliott thought back to the phone call just hours before. It was late. He was preparing to return to Dallas to handle loose ends with other cases. He would return to Memphis at the end of the week and pick up where he left off. But then Elliott was startled by his cell phone vibrating on the nightstand. Only four had his number: William and Martha Sumner, Tony and the Bluff City Butcher.

"Hello, Dr. Sumner, miss me?"

Elliott knew the voice well: deep, confident, edgy. It had been two years since they last spoke. Now, Elliott was anxious for something new: a clue, an error, another thread of insight.

"Always," he replied sharply.

"Does my heart good, you know."

"I'm glad for that."

"How are the Brits?"

"Wet."

"Cute. I'm pleased to see you made the Royal Parks of London safe again, my good doctor."

"I'm pleased you're pleased."

"Another obnoxious, disgusting animal taken out of service by the world renowned serial killer hunter," said the Bluff City Butcher tauntingly.

"I'm sure you didn't call to sing my praises. It's late." Elliott ignored the taunt and pushed just enough to have a chance at substance. The Butcher couldn't help himself, needed to be in control. It was the only predictable behavior after ten years of scrutiny by the best.

"Welcome to the City on the Bluff...home of the King."

"Thanks. I came as soon as I could get away, once I heard you were in town."

"So, you did miss me?" BCB let a puff of sick joy hit the phone. Elliott was quiet; something was different.

"It is time for our relationship to evolve, Elliott Sumner."

Everything you say has meaning, each word a purpose. The only time you speak without thinking is when you are angry...you struggle with the consuming rage that controls you. Where are you going with me tonight? What do you want to accomplish? Time to go fishing...I need something that gets me closer. I cannot and I will not let you get away again. This stops in Memphis.

"I believe in evolution, too. What do you have in mind?"

"My time...I will call back tonight with instructions. Goodbye, Dr. Sumner."

"Goodbye...ADAM," he replied like ordering a burger. The BCB stayed on the phone; that answered one question. The next words would answer even more.

"I don't like YOU using that name," he said with churning rage.

"Then why did you put it out there for me...ADAM?" he pushed harder.

"Maybe a test...that someone failed."

"That someone is Albert Bell. How could Mr. Bell fail you...can you tell me that? Really, did you think he would keep it a secret? Do you think you have that kind of power over a billionaire?" *Confirmed your name is Adam and have known Albert Bell for twenty-five years. But why search out and kill Philippé Ramirez? Why...Panther McGee? What do YOU think Albert Bell owes YOU? And, for that matter, what does Albert Bell know...about you? Elaborate security at the mansion, the saved messages over the years, a private detective on payroll, and the impromptu meeting with Memphis Homicide...and me...what does it mean?*

He'd hunted him since '96 across six states and twenty-two kills, at least the ones he knew about. When Elliott met R.L. Thornton in '98 he got the name of the monster he had been hunting; the Bluff City Butcher was on his way to classification as the most prolific serial killer in American history. So far he was unstoppable.

"Just maybe you made a mistake," said Elliott.

"I expect more from you, Sumner. You are slipping. Keep it up and I will lose interest. I DON'T MAKE MISTAKES. Who got everyone here? Who is in control? And you still have nothing?" he said hypnotically.

Elliott would keep him off balance, not give him the satisfaction of winning a debate or completing a thought. "Saw you on Beale this week. You need a new battery for your van. Seems to me you would have better wheels, a man of your talents."

"I have plans. If you want a chance at me, be ready for my call tonight."

"Maybe I'll pick up." The phone went dead. *Can the Butcher diagnose his own mental deterioration?* Elliott wondered as he looked out the ninth-floor window of the *Peabody Hotel*. *Can a genius, psychopathic anthrophobe with agateophobic tendencies know when he has begun to unravel even more? If the Bluff City Butcher can diagnose himself, he will be even more desperate to complete whatever mission he has in mind, and that cannot be good for me or the Midsouth…less time than I hoped for….*

He refocused on the little girl before him. She was thirty-nine inches and forty-one pounds when she was taken in 1983. Now, she was a leathery, desiccated carcass twenty-eight inches and weighing ten pounds, if that. The mummification process was implemented perfectly: the original incision scar was barely visible, thin on the lateral aspect of the abdomen, the port of entry for removal of internal organs and packing the thoracic and abdominal cavities with sawdust, natron and other embalming salts. With his pen light, he confirmed brain removal was through the nose—another practice thousands of years old. There was evidence of oils and resins on her amber skin and signs that she was wrapped tightly during the dehydration phase following death.

The child's face was gone, replaced with an old man's face. Her skin was stretched across edgy, protruding facial bones, and her eyes were wide and fused to surrounding plastic-like tissue. Her small, dried lips were still taut from an agony endured, and her throat scars showed she was cut ear-to-ear. The clean edges twenty-five years later told of a single pass of a sharp blade deep enough to sever the carotids and jugular—complete exsanguination.

Elliott carefully inspected her skull; the sparse, straw hair was brittle, broken and in places fused to her dried skin. He located the Butcher's signature puncture wound. It was in the usual location, the medial aspect of the coronal suture. The small entry hole in the center and top of the skull was consistent with twenty-two other homicides in the area. *The Bluff City Butcher had showed no mercy.* The ice pick was used on the child just like on the adult victims. The kill process never changed.

Elliott put off his Dallas trip. The Bluff City Butcher was in the mood to share.

■ ■ ■

A crisp wave of river wind ran across Mud Island, spraying the loose sand and lifting his hair. Elliott's thoughts shifted from the child back to the Butcher and the immediate dangers around him. He felt the presence, probably a sense shared by prey when their predator was near. Between courage and conviction, he feared death like all men; his decision to accept the invitation was tantamount to opening the lion's cage at dinner time, but he had no choice. Time was more important than ever before. Elliott's demons were gaining strength and the Bluff City Butcher was evolving into something the world had never seen. Elliott's mission was set, but could he live long enough and was he smart enough to find the unexpected advantage that would end the sick legend?

Shadows moved and dark waters lapped the banks. The river breeze mixed odors of the wild, combing the brush, and bending the saplings with an eerie rhythm. He could smell a faint, foul odor laced in a single stream of air from the southwest, a wisp of an acrid stench and then sounds of movement. He reached for his cell and aimed his light at the sound. He pressed "record" and set his cell on the sand next to the child. If Elliott died this night, Tony would find the phone and move another step closer to stopping the monster.

Brush moved as he slid his hand to his ankle holster and discovered his gun was gone, the strap unsnapped...*when?* The holster empty...*it could be anywhere; the car, the parking lot, the trail...anywhere.* His heart was in his throat. He was never very good at keeping track of a gun because he rarely used them. Again, like with the Serpentine Strangler, he faced one of his childhood fears—monsters. The Bluff City Butcher was the one that would kill him. The gun was not that important anyway. It would only hold the Butcher for a minute or a second...to talk. It would not stop him: too smart and way too fast. *Stick to the plan,* he said to himself. *The Bluff City Butcher is not going to kill me tonight. It would make no sense. This encounter is my chance for information unless I get lucky.*

It happened fast: splashing water, thrashing weeds and flying sand. Before he could turn, the Butcher lunged from the black river's edge with a hideous, gurgling squeal like a wounded animal; he crossed ten yards in a second. Elliott could taste the sweet stench of bloody kills clinging to the dark, steaming hulk that was pressed against him. Elliott had ruled out an attack from the river: illogical, impractical and impossible to surprise. But that was how the Butcher operated, always the unexpected. Elliott turned to see the ONE that had killed so many and escaped him for a decade. Elliott wanted to see the face of the demented, twisted creature that tortured and killed so easily. Tonight Elliott would get him to talk. Something could be said that made all the difference...an unexpected advantage.

He fought his fears to stand up straight, defiantly holding his head inches from the snorting, slimy thrusts of hot, rancid breath that shot from the raspy lungs of a beast. The immensity of the Butcher was crippling. *Is this more animal than man?* As it was for a wild animal, killing was a part of life. However, the nourishment the Butcher took from his victims was different.

He blocked the morning sky and looked down onto his next kill. Elliott looked up at the Butcher; the moon was centered in each glassy black eye, and the muscular brow was slanted with demonic passion. Maybe Elliott was wrong. Maybe the Butcher was done with him. Without thinking, Elliott reached to deflect the ten-inch knife he knew was in the Butcher's left hand. The knife was moving toward Elliott's belly. Time stopped. He never had a chance. Everything went black and then the muffled sounds of life.

Is this death...?

■ ■ ■

14 August 2008

He pulled up to the gates in a black *Lincoln*. It was six o'clock, another steamy August evening after a short, miserable sprinkle in Memphis. The Director of the MPD was known as a man with every minute of every day planned. There was no other way to lead the city's 2,300 strong, law enforcement team or manage the $200 million budget. The unplanned visit was odd and alarming. Albert asked security to take Director Collin Wade into the study while he excused himself from an international conference call. This would be Albert's second meeting with the director over the man's five-year tenure. Albert did not like the first meeting.

"Thank you for seeing me." Police Director Wade approached, hand extended and eyes everywhere but on Albert. The greeting was predictably awkward.

"Good to see you again, Director Wade." *Something awful must have happened,* Albert thought. *Why else would he drop by without even a phone call?*

"I don't know any other way but to just get started. It's time to think outside the box."

"Outside the box?" Albert leaned back in his chair and leveled his eyes.

"In 2005, there were 154 homicides in Memphis; in 2006 we had 160, and last year 164. We do a pretty damn good job solving ninety-six percent of these atrocities, but over that three-year period we had nineteen killed that remained a mystery. Sure, we may reduce that number some over time, but most become cold cases—inactive, unsolved homicides. And yes, our Cold Case Team makes some progress; however, the majority of these cases sit for years with no resolution; they get colder and more come each year."

"And am I correct to conclude this 'cold case process' is…your BOX?"

"Yes. Mr. Bell, I propose a collaborative effort between the Memphis Police Department, representing all Metro Area law enforcement, and the *Memphis Tribune.* I want a new look at a decade of cold cases, 1995 through 2005. The high-profile collaboration would raise community awareness that could generate new leads that could help solve more of these lost homicides. We could take more bad guys off the streets and give the Midsouth families of victims some closure. What do you think?"

"Director, you are the subject matter expert. I'm sure you have given this a lot of thought. As you know, *The Memphis Tribune* has been in the Bell family a long time. We have done all we can to support the community and that will not change."

"And we all appreciate that help, Mr. Bell."

"Well then, I will call Ed Cole this evening. I suggest your people meet with him Monday morning so he can get your information in the paper."

"I'm sorry. I guess I have been unclear on the role of the *Tribune* in this collaboration. I propose the decade of cold cases be reviewed by your best investigative reporter without police impediments…I mean to say…involvement."

"I don't know if that is something we could or should do, Director Wade."

"Mr. Bell, an independent review is the key. A nonbiased, unencumbered, outside review of these cases is the giant step outside the BOX we need."

"I see…and how many cold cases are we talking about?"

"Looking at the Metro Area, eight counties in three states, I estimate fifty to sixty unsolved homicides over the ten-year period."

What are you really looking for? Albert pondered. *Police departments don't turn their case files over to city newspapers every day. How bizarre is this?*

"What is the role of the Memphis Police Department in this collaboration?"

"We will manage the proprietary information flow from Metro Area law enforcement agencies to the *Tribune*. I will assure unfettered access to case files and evidence chains so your designated specialist can focus on the research and associated investigations."

"And what about confidentiality and liabilities?"

"Shared confidentiality with your specialist; what we know they will know. Our only requirement is that you agree to present all findings, conclusions and make recommendations to the MPD prior to the release of any information to the public."

"And liabilities?"

"After presentation to the MPD the *Tribune* is free to disclose at your own risk, releasing the MPD from culpability. We may ask you to not release certain information, but the final decision will be yours to make in all cases. I would hope that we could work through those few situations in an amicable manner but understand your needs."

"How big is the access window for case files and evidence streams?"

"I think two years is reasonable with one-year extensions by mutual agreement."

"We are talking to a *Pulitzer Prize* winner currently. If my editor-in-chief is good with the fine print we can accelerate."

"Excellent," said Wade, deriving some comfort from the tentative agreement.

"Assuming Ed Cole is on board, I have two requests," said Albert. "First, the city and county mayors must sign-off on this program in advance and second, the Memphis PD must hold a press conference. I want you and Ed to launch the program and to introduce the designated *Tribune* specialist to the community. This person must be supported by everyone from the start."

"Agreed."

He watched Wade's black *Lincoln* climb to the crest of the driveway and then dip into the valley that led to the gates on Walnut Grove. "Janet, get G.E. Taft on the phone."

"Right away, Sir."

Albert pulled a file from the bottom drawer, *Carol Mason* on the tab. He thumbed through the letters, clippings of newspaper and magazine articles, a half dozen photographs from her childhood to present day, college transcripts, a resumé, PI report and a handful of recommendations. Albert had been watching Carol a very long time, a talent brought to his attention by Rudolph Kohl, an old friend of the family. Albert interviewed her ten years ago and watched her progress as a freelance reporter. He wanted her on staff one day. Now, the time was right for more reasons than one.

Janet poked her head in, "Mr. Bell, Sheriff Taft is on your phone."

"Thank you, Janet…Hello, G.E."

"Albert, how in the hell are you?"

"I'm good. Thanks for asking. It's been a while. Are you up to tasting some old scotch and smoking a few cigars?"

"You talked to Wade, did yah?"

"Yes."

"I'll see you in an hour, my friend." G.E. had met with Wade three days earlier. He didn't like the program; it was a desperate reach and Albert Bell would see right through it, which he did.

Albert hung up and looked back at the stack of papers he had pulled from Mason's file. Under an old picture of Elliott Sumner was a three-page report on faded stationery. This time the watermark was centered and large with a tagline; *Gilgamesh*…confidential vessel preparation….

■ ■ ■

"Justice delayed…is no justice."
Unknown

"The most important news stories are found in the dark alleys of life. I have rarely found them under the bright lights of Main Street," said Carol.

"Probably the most dangerous too, Miss Mason," said Albert.

"I suppose that would be a true statement, Sir."

Carol had climbed to the top of her profession as a nationally syndicated, free-lance investigative reporter known for taking on the tough stories: unsolved murders, drug smuggling, kidnapping, banking scams and government fraud. She had her Pulitzer and most other awards ten years out of the Ole' Miss Journalism program; the position at the *Tribune* was created for her: director of investigative reporting. It was set up parallel to the editor-in-chief position and also reported directly to Albert Bell. From the start the MPD/Tribune Cold Case Collaboration was a high profile project. She got on the first plane from Los Angeles after Albert's call. They met for the second time in ten years at the Bell mansion.

Albert lit a small cigar with a steady hand. After a few puffs, he turned to her, cigar in one hand and burning match in the other.

"Miss Mason, my family is primarily in the cotton business, and then there is a parade of less interesting ventures around the world. We are most proud of The *Memphis Tribune*. Did you know we have been in the newspaper business for a century?"

"Yes, I believe your Grandfather, Alberto Antonio Bella, purchased the *Memphis Daily News* in 1905." Her due diligence was fresh on her mind.

"Yes, that he did, Miss Mason."

"In 1915 your father was twenty. He was given full responsibility for fixing the faltering city newspaper. The first thing he did was change the name to test Alberto's pledge to let go completely. Your grandfather never said a word."

"Very good, Miss Mason, and it is well known that grandfather did let go. What you might not know is he never gave father the satisfaction of using the name in a sentence until the day he died. In his final moments he pulled father close and said. *Never let The Memphis Tribune go, son...you have made it our family's single greatest asset.*' Thank you for bringing up Father. I miss him to this day." Albert tossed the match into the fireplace.

"There is more going on here than you are sharing, Sir. If I am going to sign up, I need to know." Carol sat in the chair next to the fire with her long legs crossed and her green eyes following Albert's every move. She was stunning.

"You are quite right; more is going on than a collaborative exercise. Miss Mason, I am one who tends to protect by nature, but you must know my motives with you are quite different. You see, I am sure of one thing. I must bring you in my way if we are going to benefit from your fresh eyes and investigative prowess. I fear anything less will be disastrous."

"Where are the police on this?"

"They are holding their cards close. Either they know something and are worried or they have little and are desperate. The collaboration was their idea. I believe Director Wade was forced into the proposition."

"Such a collaborative arrangement is bizarre…suspicious."

"Exactly my words, Miss Mason; my methods never vary. I find the best people in the world for a particular task, give them all I have and then get out of their way. I am not a hands-on person. My information transfer process will allow your instincts and skills to drive the investigation wherever it may lead, and you can be assured you always have my unwavering support. I have your back, young lady…no matter what."

"I know. And that is why I am here. I am comfortable with your approach, Mr. Bell. However, my nature is to push and prod."

"What is your view on cold cases, Miss Mason?"

"The first homicide investigator on a case has the greatest prospect of catching the killer. Each hour that passes is another wave reaching across the beach of justice, taking another truth away, sometimes forever. When we talk about unsolved cases ten years old, the prospect of figuring it out and catching the killer is not great."

"Sounds defeating."

"Each year about ten percent of all deaths in our country are trauma induced: homicide, suicide and accident. Homicide is about one percent of all deaths; roughly seventeen to eighteen thousand people are murdered each year. The bad guys try to hide their work in all the other categories, including natural deaths and missing persons."

"I assumed today the medical examiner system, modern forensics, and advanced crime scene investigation caught most of those," said Albert.

"They often do…when those resources are available. Unfortunately, that expert level of scrutiny is typically unavailable in the rural areas of the country. The best forensic investigators are in the major cities. This Midsouth Metro Area is a cluster of a dozen counties primarily rural. Most handle their own death cases alone. Although investigation skills have greatly improved across the country, many have limited experience with death and killing, and the bad guys are getting smarter."

"Homicides are made to look like accidents and suicide?"

"Yes. To do this right I will need to review all traumatic, unwitnessed accidental and suicidal deaths in the Metro Area that we know the medical examiner and a trained forensic team did not see. We should also take a look at deaths ruled undetermined, and I would like to review the missing person files for the same period."

"Why missing person?"

"Memphis reports around 4,000 people missing each year. Two thirds can be eliminated as typical runaways. I suspect we will find homicides in the remaining third. All together—unsolved homicides, questionable accidents and suicides, undetermined rulings and missing persons from 1995 to 2005—I would plan for 150 case-file reviews. I can get started right away."

On September 1, 2008, Carol stepped off the elevator onto plush, hunter green carpet, the executive floor of *The Memphis Tribune*, and walked through the renovated suite of offices designated for the director of investigative reporting and staff. At the window on the third floor, she felt the tremor of the presses rolling two floors down and smelled the fresh newsprint. She craved the business: electricity in the newsroom, chasing stories, the sources and the pressure of deadlines. But now, surrounded by boxes of cold case files from around the region, she knew there was more going on in the Bluff City than anyone was willing to talk about at the moment. No police agency shared confidential files with a newspaper. No billionaire patriarchs were protected more than the President of the United States, and the white van on the other side of Union Avenue had been following her ever since the taxi from Memphis International Airport to the *Peabody Hotel* two days earlier. She smiled. The world famous serial killer hunter, Elliott Sumner, was here in August. She had a pretty good idea there was a serial killer in Memphis.

CHAPTER FOUR

"Not the power to remember, but the power to forget,
is a necessary condition for our existence."
Sholem Asch

18 August 2008

"**W**e need to know everything." Dr. Sidney Gilmore, Chief of Neurosurgery at Parkland Memorial Hospital took lead; the Chiefs of Cardiology and Internal Medicine, Dodson and Bennett, sat at his flanks with the intensity of soldiers disarming a bomb ready to blow.

"You know him better than anyone and were there when it happened. He is dying in my ICU and I don't know why." With that declaration, Gilmore sucked the rest of the oxygen out of the room; Tony Wilcox was already crippled with the unexplainable events of the last twenty-four hours. None of it made sense.

"DYING?"

"Yes, DYING."

"That's not possible." *You're the strongest guy I know…come on now. You can pull yourself out of this…somehow,* he thought, his heart beating in his ears.

"This is a medical dilemma we have never seen."

Never seen? What the hell does that mean? You are the chiefs, the top dogs, the best at this shit, Tony thought, although he knew nothing about medicine and doctors. *The man is thirty-nine, for God's sake. You guys are supposed to be able to do anything, surrounded by all these fucking diplomas and this big hospital complex.*

"What are you going to do?" asked Tony as he loosened his tie.

"We are going to listen to you. Our hope is that you say something that points us in the right direction, tells us what to do, and, just as important, what not to do," said Dr. Gilmore. He leaned over the small conference table crammed in the tight alcove with three walls of bookcases packed to the ceiling: medical books, dog-eared journals, stacks of patient files, x-rays and a dozen slide-carrousels. Gilmore's short, gray-haired assistant emerged from the mess, carrying four coffees on a silver tray. She set it down and vanished.

Although you're a small man you speak with the conviction of a giant killer. But I can see desperation in your eyes. That's what I do, read people for a living. You are the chief of neurosurgery for one of the most prestigious hospitals in the fucking country and you're LOST. "What do you want from me?" asked Tony. *Two weeks after Panther McGee had his heart cut out in Memphis, Elliott Sumner collapsed. Now he was lying unconscious in an Intensive Care Unit in Dallas, on life support.*

"Your friend has been in a coma for twenty-four hours and is at risk of another cardiac arrest triggered by unknown factors; the next one could be fatal," said Gilmore. "Just start talking. Tell us about you and then everything you know about Elliott Sumner: his life story, career, interests, habits, physical constitution, gifts, problems and idiosyncrasies… everything."

"That makes no sense. I could meander all day long and get absolutely nowhere. How could that possibly help Elliott? Your plan is pitiful. Is this all you've got?" Tony's anger started to surface. He did not like the direction things were going but had no idea how to change it. He hated being dependent on others. From his perspective, the doctors in Dallas had him by the balls.

Chief of Cardiology, Dr. Dodson, held up his hand to get Gilmore's attention; he wanted a shot at handling Tony's mounting frustration. Dodson was Santa Claus with red cheeks and a twinkle in his eye but without a beard and wearing a white lab coat with crisp, green scrubs and white *Crocs*.

"We understand your confusion and get your discomfort, but please work with us; do as we say and we will guide you, based on medical relevance and the critical path treatment options. We will keep you from wandering too far from the path, Mr. Wilcox. We are on a slippery slope with Elliott Sumner…we are losing him. We are not sure what is keeping him alive. Textbook treatment regimen seems to be taking him down faster. We need to work outside our comfort zone if we are going to have any chance at saving this man. The decisions we make from here forward are risky, and selection of one route can eliminate others that could be the lifesaving ones." Dodson looked at Gilmore. He was done.

"Elliott Sumner is on a high-wire. An error on our part could be that gust of wind that pushes him into the abyss. We could lose him," said Gilmore.

Dr. Bennett, Chief of Internal Medicine, was sitting next to Dodson, an attractive, hardy woman in her fifties with expressive, deep-green eyes that revealed the greatest angst of the three staring at Tony. Her soft facial features framed in a gentle flow of blond curls projected a sense of calm and confidence, and probably helped move her along to the top of her profession.

"Mr. Wilcox, all his life systems are functioning perfectly, yet he requires life support to keep breathing. If I were only to look at his numbers, he would not be in a hospital; it is mind-boggling. Right now we have a handful of colored wires and one chance to cut the one wire that disarms this ticking bomb, the bomb that will end Elliott Sumner's life. Your job is to point us to the correct wire."

At that precise moment Tony got it. Dr. Bennett smiled. They all saw he was ready.

"Please, go ahead, Mr. Wilcox," said Dr. Gilmore.

"I'm a twenty-year Memphis cop, the last ten a detective in the homicide division. The first week of August the Memphis PD engaged Dr. Sumner as an expert consultant to work on a homicide case. He flew in from London the day after we spoke."

"Flew in from London?" asked Gilmore.

"Yes. Elliott's agency is based in Dallas. The Sumner Forensic Institute, SFI for short. He provides very specialized forensic investigation service to law enforcement, governments and private interests around the world. Elliott was in London working with Scotland Yard. He tracked down a serial killer—the Serpentine Strangler."

"I see, please continue."

The three leaned closer. Tony was not surprised. Homicides and serial killers fascinated everyone. Like human nature itself, such aberrations were hypnotic, like a house fire or a train wreck.

"I called Elliott on a Saturday evening, after midnight London time. He was in pursuit of the Serpentine at the time but took my call. We met at the *Peabody Hotel* in Memphis twenty-four hours later."

"He booked a flight sometime well after midnight London time—after chasing a serial killer—and was sitting in Memphis with you the next evening?"

"Right. Elliott has a private jet. His pilots took off the next morning, a nine-hour flight London to Memphis and he picked up seven hours jumping time zones. For Elliott, he was two hours away and got seven hours sleep on the plane. He does it all the time."

"Ok, please go on."

"Elliott worked on the Memphis homicide case over the last two weeks and traveled back to Dallas a day here and there to handle other SFI commitments."

"And, you came to Dallas to confer on something that could not wait?" asked Dr. Dodson.

"Yes, exactly."

"And what brought you to Parkland Hospital?"

"Elliott was scheduled to interview a witness and asked me along." *You look more like a Sidney than a chief of neurosurgery. I probably beat up a few Sidney-types along the way. I'm glad one of you survived...I think...we'll see.*

"That morning we met for breakfast at the Hyatt at eight o'clock. He had scrambled eggs, bacon, toast, orange juice and coffee. We left for Parkland at 8:45."

"And the events leading up to the collapse please," asked Gilmore.

"We were walking down the corridor on the third floor, a normal pace. I remember Elliott talking at the time. He was in mid-sentence when he stopped and clutched his chest like he had been shot or something. I got to him right away and held him up against the wall. I got in his face and asked what was wrong. His face was blood red, eyes bulging. He gripped my arm with a God-awful iron claw and forced four words through his clenched teeth, *'cardiac arrest get help.'* Fortunately, God damn doctors were everywhere. I yelled and they got to him on the spot."

"Did he say anything else?"

"No, when the doctors stepped in his lights went out. Those guys started ripping off clothes and hitting his chest, pinching his nose and blowing in his mouth as others wheeled up all sorts of shit. They zapped his chest with those electric paddles, he jumped a few times and then everything got real crazy: needles, syringes, IV bags, rubber tubing, white tape, sheets, towels, tanks of oxygen, monitors and gurneys were coming from all directions.

70

Someone took me by the arm and led me out to the lobby and I haven't seen him since." Tony slumped back in his chair as a drop of sweat rolled down his sideburn. He relived it. He was scared for Elliott.

"Ok, and he is still unconscious in ICU. It's best that we keep going. Was he acting like?"

Tony cut Gilmore off. "No, God-damn-it. I told you that he was the same as always." The helplessness was hitting Tony hard. Elliott was dying. Dying! Tony grabbed the steaming coffee in front of him and drank it in three giant gulps, slammed it down on the table and pushed the empty mug at Gilmore. It slid five feet and stopped an inch from Gilmore's clasped hands; he didn't move. Tony noticed. And Gilmore saw Tony's eyes: no more questions. *My friend is dying.*

Dr. Dodson tried to sidestep the Wilcox wood-chipper. "Was he under any pressure? Did he have any significant stress in his life?"

"That's it. Who are you people? What doctors play these games? Do you have any idea who is lying in your ICU? How long are you going to waste time with this ridiculous go-nowhere process while my friend waits for you to do your jobs?'

"We know very little. We now know Elliott Sumner is a successful forensic pathologist today. We remember he was a medical examiner in Texas, 1994 to 1998. Until you told us, we were unaware of SFI and his international interests," said Dr. Gilmore. Dodson and Gilbert sat quietly, nodding in affirmation.

"That's it? That's all you know about Elliott Sumner? Do you ever leave this damn building? Do you ever watch television, listen to a radio or read a newspaper? Really, do you have any exposure to the world around you, the things that change lives every day, the things that can take everything away?"

The three moved in their chairs and each hoped the other would speak to Detective Wilcox's extreme frustration and growing anger.

Dr. Gilmore cleared his throat, got up and moved to the chair next to Tony. "I know it will be hard for you to accept, but most of our time is spent in an operating room, with patients or teaching at the medical school. Like your profession, ours too is all consuming, Detective. Our exposure to the outside world is extremely limited. I am sorry we do not know what you think we should know."

"I'm not buying any of it. There are no excuses. You should know the man you have in your ICU is the world renowned forensic pathologist and premier serial killer hunter. You asked me if he had pressure or stress in his life—HELL, YES! Pressure and stress IS his life. Over the last decade he personally hunted and captured fifty of the world's most dangerous serial killers—the FBI estimates there are 400 to 500 active today. Each one hunted tried to kill him first. His nemesis, the only one that got away, is in Memphis now…the most dangerous…the one that has killed over a hundred people and is just getting started. Hell, yes, Elliott is under pressure. That genius psychopathic killing machine in Memphis is smarter than law enforcement in six states and the FBI and has been killing for twenty-five years. Elliott Sumner is the only one with a shot at taking this monster off the streets. Does he carry stress? SHIT! HE HAS AN UNSTOPPABLE KILLER ON HIS MIND AND ON HIS ASS."

Tony started to get up to leave. Gilmore grabbed his wrist with a firm grip, much more powerful than Tony expected from such a little man.

Gilmore stood with eyes locked on Tony's. "Son…he is at death's door. Elliott Sumner is thirty-nine in the body of a twenty-year-old…and you know it. Put your anger away and tell me the secrets you carry for your friend, your burden… the true source of your anger today. If you hold back I can promise you that the next opportunity you have to help your friend will be to carry his casket."

The old pendulum clock behind Gilmore's desk took over the room as a cloud killed the sun and the air blower in the tight doctor's office shut off on cue—the only thing missing was the cricket. Seconds were an eternity as Tony eyed Gilmore and the other two watched.

I never knew what any of it meant, thought Tony. *Elliott just started telling me things…the brother he never had. We are loners. We see the world the same way: good guys, bad guys and monsters, and we want to fix things the same way.*

Shit…at first the stuff he told me was interesting. I couldn't believe it. But then it got scary. I got worried, especially when I realized he was frightened about some of the stuff he could do. He didn't know what it was all about, what it meant or where it would take him. He always said he had a tiger by the tail and no idea how to let go. He showed me each gift once and then we wouldn't talk about it again unless it came up during a case or was needed to solve a problem. I even tried to tease him about it, to make light of it all, but behind the smiles we worried about the unknown…what was going to happen someday…unexpected shit. I knew deep down this day was coming. I knew the good would be offset by the bad. Gilmore was right; I'm pissed-off at me. I knew all this shit a long time ago but have never done anything to help Elliott…my brother.

■ ■ ■

"Everything stays in this room."

"Of course."

"How do I know?"

"The doctor-patient relationship, confidentiality, it is protected. And I give you my word anything you tell us will only be used to save Elliott's life." Gilmore did not flinch. Tony leaned back, closed his eyes and got to a good place.

"November 5, 1968, Martha and William Sumner found a baby on their front porch at their ranch in Abilene, two weeks old. The note said, *'This is Elliott. Please give him a good life.'* That was it. Since that day all efforts to find his natural parents were unsuccessful and continue to this day. Ok, where do I begin?"

"Tell his story…like that…it will happen."

"He could read at age four. Soon, he could read a book as fast as he could turn the pages—age seven. He read all the books in the Abilene Public Library by the time he was twelve."

"Was he tested…a genius IQ?" asked Gilmore.

"Oh, yes. The Sumners were educated people; they knew exactly what to do. William was a retired prosecutor and Martha a retired family physician. They owned a small cattle ranch, a thousand acres. They knew how to help Elliott from the start. They had him privately tested. His IQ was measured at the 175 level, a gifted genus, top one-tenth of one percent of the tested population. Elliott was home-schooled, by a parade of tutors and specialists. Every decision the Sumners made about Elliott's development was preceded by protection of his privacy—he would not be someone's sideshow."

"An exceptional IQ is rare but not lethal," Dr. Dodson noted.

"Elliott also has what they call a perfect, photographic memory."

"Total, instantaneous recall?"

"Yes. He remembers everything and can retrieve it rapidly and perfectly. The Sumners hired specialists to teach him to manage that gift, how to suppress the automatic flow of data and images. He learned to access only the information he wanted.

"Please continue." The doctors looked at each other and nodded.

"Memory is just one of his assets. His mental processes pertaining to observation and perception, analysis, deductive reasoning and judgment are all advanced.

"Have these been measured?" asked Bennett.

"I will say yes but with a caveat. M.I.T., Harvard and Stanford tried to measure them, but Elliott was already functioning well beyond their tools, and he was still a teen. All testing was conducted under the strictest confidentiality agreements. I believe Elliott even helped those schools upgrade their tools. They never knew his real name."

"And what about physical assets and liabilities?" asked Dodson.

"He avoids talking about physical gifts. I never pushed. I think because they are tangible things. He is always aware of them and has always tried to minimize them."

"That makes sense. We do know he is aging slowly. What do you know about that?" asked Gilmore.

"Nothing really. I didn't notice. He looks thirty-nine to me. But I do recall an eye examination. About two years ago we were at a forensic medical conference in San Diego. His dinner date lost a diamond stud. Elliott walked across a ballroom and picked it up; I saw him. Later he pretended to find it under our table. I asked him about it on the return flight."

"Did he see the diamond across the room?"

"Yes. He did: fifty feet, floral carpet and poor lighting."

"Interesting," said Dodson.

"He told me he had his eyes examined. Actually, he said 'analyzed.' Elliott told me he has five times the retinal light receptors as the average human eye."

"And how does that manifest?"

"He said his retinal construct is closest to that of an eagle. The human eye discerns three colors while an eagle's can distinguish five."

"Don't know much about eagle eyes. Did he say anything else?"

"An eagle can see a rabbit in a field a mile away; Elliott said he can see the proverbial needle in the haystack, easily. Those visual assets are huge in forensics. He can process a crime scene and examine a body unlike anyone else. He sees things some never see…clues never found."

"Are his other senses enhanced?" asked Gilmore.

"I don't know about that, but I suspect they are."

"Does he offer any explanation for these gifts?" asked Bennett.

"Just his natural parents, who he does not know," said Tony.

Gilmore leaned over and whispered to Dodson, who then leaned over and whispered to Bennett.

"This might be important. He recently captured serial killer number fifty," said Tony.

"However, one has escaped him for years and is now threatening," said Gilmore.

"Correct."

"Did Dr. Sumner have any contact with that serial killer recently?"

"Yes, August 11, on his cell, and I think they met face-to-face."

"Why would you think that?"

"Well, I have him watched in Memphis—protection. He ditched my guys around midnight one night and didn't get back until the morning. I had lunch with him that day."

"How was he?" asked Gilmore.

"He was behaving oddly: quiet, lethargic, distracted and puzzled."

Dr. Gilmore made a notation. "Ok…helpful."

"I guess serial killers take a lot of lives," said Dodson.

"Yup, by definition, they kill at least three with cooling-off periods between."

"How many lives did Elliott's fifty take?" asked Bennett.

"Six- to seven-hundred victims, we estimate."

"According to your definition, I was thinking a hundred and fifty."

"Elliott had criteria; he focused on the worst of the worst, those with ten or more victims, many linked to thirty or more victims and a few over sixty."

Dr. Gilmore held up his hand to stop questions from his colleagues. "Detective Wilcox, we will need time to ponder and confer. I think we have enough and thank you for your disclosures. If you agree, my assistant will take you to see Dr. Sumner and then we can meet again this afternoon."

Tony entered ICU. Elliott was tied to the bed on a thick foam pad with green sheets tight over his torso and arms outstretched with fists clenched. Tubes were running in-and-out of his body everywhere and mechanical pumps jerked his chest up and down accompanied by robotic noises. The incessant beeps and busy monitors with jagged lines said he was alive. But Elliott's taped eyes and his bloated and bruised face said he was a fish out of water…dying.

Gilmore had sent Tony to say goodbye to his friend.

■ ■ ■

"A ship is safe in harbor, but that's not what ships are for."
William Shedd

"Rita, hold my calls."

"Certainly, Doctor." Rita deposited Tony in the alcove. She smiled and vanished; it was something she seemed to do well. The three doctors sat with perfect posture in their white coats and blank faces; they were experienced purveyors of bad news.

"I won't keep you waiting," said Gilmore. Tony looked. Bennett and Dodson gave nothing away.

"He's going to die; I know. I'm not blind. I just saw him," bellowed Tony.

"What? No. We don't think he is going to die…this time anyway."

"You don't? Shit…he looks terrible. Hell, he looks dead already."

"No," said Gilmore. "Let's back up. We now understand what is going on with Elliott Sumner."

"You do?"

"Yes. The best way I can explain it to you is to say that Elliott is rebooting."

"Rebooting?"

"Yes, rebooting…like a computer that crashed. Fortunately, we believe this time the crash was not fatal."

"Ok, I think," said Tony looking at the other doctors. They pushed out half smiles.

"We are certain that Elliott had a neurological overload that induced the coma—a natural protective function in his case—intended to minimize damage and focus limited physical resources to repair. The cardiac arrest was secondary and he quite possibly could have survived it on his own…the first time around."

"Then why does he need all that damn equipment to stay alive?"

"When we got him we didn't know what we were dealing with and…well, we just about killed the man." Bennett and Dodson looked at their hands.

"I see."

"Let's just say we each have our secrets now; that should provide you with some added assurance of containment," said Gilmore, attempting to be light.

"Yes…of course." They smiled uncomfortably.

"What's going on with Elliott? What does this all mean?"

"Ok, allow me to speak in simple terms; otherwise this can get quite complicated quickly for all of us."

"By all means."

"This is about the human brain handling information and how that information can stimulate physical response. As you can imagine, our brain processes an enormous amount of data continuously, data coming to us through all our senses: sight, sound, smell and touch, for example. This information is carried in the form of memory. Most stored information is inconsequential to the function of the human body, but some information can trigger significant, biophysiological events."

"Biophysio…what?" asked Tony.

"An illustration might be best. A memory of a burning car at the city dump is insignificant information that would have little or no physical impact on someone. However, a memory of a burning car with your mother trapped inside is very different. It holds onto emotionally charged information that triggers physical responses beyond your control: changes in heart rate, increased blood pressure, changes in circulation and body temperature and breathing pattern, mental confusion and more.

"We all essentially store emotionally charged information in subconscious places. Otherwise, we would live on a biophysiological rollercoaster. Unfortunately, some people do live that way. They need therapy and medication. They can die young, commit suicide or go insane. It is very difficult to cure if your traumatic emotional memories stay in the forefront of your mind…vividly and constantly."

"Are you saying Elliott's emotional experiences did this to him?"

"Yes, and those experiences are vast, detailed and remembered perfectly."

"My God."

"We believe a significant portion of Elliott's emotional experiences moved from his subconscious to his conscious world abruptly. Further, we believe he exceeded some neurological capacity. The dam broke and he was deluged with raw pain and terror."

Dr. Bennett interrupted. "When you walked down the third floor corridor Elliott Sumner thought about something that put him over the top."

"He was overwhelmed. A lifetime of 'mothers trapped in burning cars' poured into his conscious world."

Gilmore nodded. "That overload triggered an autonomic nervous system response, the body's natural mechanism to cope. This peril is tantamount to being eaten alive. Elliott's ANS started shutting down systems and moving him into survival mode."

"His own body started to kill him?" asked Tony.

"Not exactly…something went wrong. The ANS process somehow interfered with Elliott's heart. I am convinced it was a flaw in his makeup…an error…a short circuit," said Dodson. "But that doesn't change things for Dr. Sumner."

"I understand. You think the error will happen again," said Tony.

"Yes. The medical term is idiopathic cardiomyopathy," said Dodson.

"And that means?"

"The heart stops for unknown reasons."

"Is Elliott going to die from this idio-whatever?"

"Not this time. We have him on the right program now, recovery in a week."

"But Elliott is neurologically at capacity," said Gilmore.

"What does that mean?"

"He must avoid traumatic, painful, terror-laden events from this day forward. One more will likely kill him immediately," said Gilmore. "Sumner must abandon his career—step away—if he wants a chance to live."

"And that may not be enough," said Dodson. "But that's because I'm a cardiologist. I worry about hearts."

"He is not going to like it. His work is his life. Is there anything he can do to rechannel dangerous, emotional information or to strengthen or expand his subconscious memory capacity?" asked Tony.

"Those are exceptionally good questions, but I'm afraid the answers would be well beyond the current body of knowledge," said Bennett.

Gilmore closed the notebook in front of him where he had been jotting down some thoughts and observations during the discussions. As he pocketed his *Mont Blanc* he looked over the tops of his glasses at Tony. "How do you suggest we handle this with Dr. Sumner?"

Without hesitation he said, "You tell him everything. Remember, he is a genius. Before he leaves this hospital he will know more about his condition and his options than you and have a set of potential solutions…if they exist."

"Tell him everything?" asked Dodson.

"Yes, he is practical and realistic by nature. Elliott will want to know what happened from the moment he checked out until now. He will understand the medical issues and implications. I bet he knew he was bumping up to some limits before he crashed."

Gilmore stuck out his hand for a firm shake. "Tony Wilcox, you are a good friend. Without your help, Elliott Sumner would not walk out of this hospital. Take a moment for yourself. After all, you did find a way to help your friend live with his gifts."

"Thanks for that. But there is one thing only Elliott can decide," said Tony.

"And what's that?" asked Gilmore.

"William Shedd, an American theologian, said something that really hit me. It carries me through the tough times in my life as a cop. He said, *'a ship is safe in harbor, but that's not what ships are for.'*"

Dr. Gilmore personally walked Detective Wilcox through the maze of offices to a long and empty corridor that led to a set of double-doors. The sun pierced the two small windows shooting two lines of light from the end of the otherwise dark tunnel. They both looked and felt the relief that Elliott would live and they felt a new friendship, one born from surviving a great test in life…together…dependent upon each other.

"I'm curious. Do you remember what Dr. Sumner was talking about that morning when he grabbed his chest?" asked Gilmore.

"Yes. He was talking about his nemesis."

"Ah yes, his nemesis." Dr. Gilmore rocked on his heels and waited for more.

"The ONE still out there…the unstoppable…the Bluff City Butcher."

"I see."

They shook hands and then embraced. "Thanks, Doc…and I mean it."

Gilmore smiled.

Tony walked down the dark tunnel and out into the bright light of day. The double doors opened and let some of the world in as Tony disappeared.

Gilmore returned to the quiet confines of his empty office. He would sit for a moment before checking on Dr. Sumner. His eyes adjusted to the lights being off. He sat at his old desk with memories of the day he arrived twenty years ago: the same smell, the same sounds and mostly the same furniture. For the first time, it dawned on him that he was the only thing in the room that had changed.

From his desk he lingered over his college and medical degrees, recognitions and awards neatly organized on a wall of accomplishments. But this time he would home in on his medical degree; *The University of Tennessee College of Medicine, Memphis, Tennessee…graduated 1983.* He could never forget what happened on the bluff in Memphis the year he graduated from medical school. The atrocities behind Captain Bilbo's Restaurant, the place he drank many beers on many a night, the little girl that was kidnapped and the three young men that were butchered. Sidney Gilmore was one of the believers in the Memphis urban legend. He thought then that the Bluff City Butcher survived the jump into the Mississippi River. *That monster is still out there,* he thought.

Gilmore looked up to the ceiling, in the direction of ICU, where Elliott Sumner was now recovering. He closed his eyes. We need to find a way back for you. *We need you to leave the harbor again, Elliott Sumner.*

■ ■ ■

It was as if he was abducted by aliens. August 27, Dr. Elliott Sumner walked out of *Parkland Memorial Hospital* and vanished. Blackwell, Stone & Associates closed the doors and the books of SFI seven days later. All consulting contracts were cancelled, confidential files returned and monies refunded. The twenty-four SFI employees were terminated; each valued member of the team was offered a $1,000,000 severance package and letter of recommendation from the renowned forensic sleuth…provided no questions were asked, no interviews were given and the terms were undisclosed—the arrangement was 100 percent acceptable.

His medical condition was known only to Gilmore, Dodson, Bennett and Wilcox. Bennett took the lead as the attending physician and released to the media that Dr. Sumner suffered a severe allergic reaction that triggered anaphylaxis and a grand mal seizure. Fortunately, the medical emergency received immediate attention and serious complications were averted. The famous Texas medical examiner was treated and released. The Dallas *Morning News* reported Bennett would have no further information to share concerning Dr. Sumner's private medical care.

Sumner's disappearance could only mean the forensic icon was recovering at an undisclosed location—surely the revered serial killer hunter of the decade would return soon. But, just days later, the world headquarters of SFI closed its doors in Dallas. The press didn't know where to turn. Absolutely no one was talking and before they could react, everything on the forty-seventh floor of the *Renaissance Tower* in Dallas was gone, even the letters on the frosted glass doors. Speculation ran from relocation to resizing to the restructuring of the international forensic enterprise. Some were convinced their beloved Western Sherlock was going solo…going underground. And rumors circulated that Sumner was moving operations to Memphis, Tennessee. Following the capture of the *Serpentine Strangler* and after reaching the extraordinary milestone—fifty serial killers in ten years—moving the world headquarters to a centralized base made perfect sense.

■ ■ ■

On September 24, Elliott decided to kill himself. On September 27, he settled on the method and means.

The nose of the cold, steel barrel was pressed to the roof of his mouth, a .357 magnum *Smith & Wesson, Model 686 double action revolver.* He used it to kill monsters; now he would use it to blow off the back of his head. On the bed and the walls of the cheap hotel room would be his blood, brain matter and the invisible remnants of fifty demons that lived in his head. Elliott considered every option and concluded he had no other viable choice. He would finish the job and kill the monsters for the last time.

The hollow-point was an expanding bullet designed to disrupt tissue and transfer kinetic energy to the target. Only one was needed; neither Elliott nor the monsters on board would survive. With the gun pressed deep inside his mouth and his finger on the trigger, and his demons daring him to do it, he realized the monster that mattered most was still out there…a decade later. The Bluff City Butcher would avoid death. He realized, in the end, the sickest, most twisted predator would win.

The BCB was the last one with him, and then Elliott collapsed. Did he know how to push Elliott over the edge? He had years of experience manipulating the forensic sleuth. The Mud Island encounter was bizarre, more than an opportunity to taunt or play a game. The Butcher wasn't ready to kill Elliott; he said their relationship was going to evolve. A swift pass of the butcher knife would have dropped the world renowned forensic pathologist, but the opportunity was not taken. Did the Butcher have more elaborate plans for Elliott Sumner's ultimate demise…and that of others?

Is the Butcher doing this to me…is he in control now? I don't remember anything after that hot breath in my face and the blocked morning sky…those eyes…the anger. But…what happened after that? I reached for the knife…and then I was on that park bench next to the river…it was morning. What did the Butcher do to me? Did he say something to me? Did he drug me? Why didn't he kill me? No. This is all part of it, my unique medical condition…exhaustion…confusion and the booze is not helping me. I'm doing this….to myself.

Fifty monsters and 600 victims sat with Elliott on the edge of the bed. The rain tapped like a snare drum on the old window unit spitting wet air into the dank motel room. Elliott's hands trembled and the four-inch barrel clicked on his teeth. He pushed the monsters back one more time and squeezed out a tear that found the hand and suicide note in his lap. Elliott opened one eye—a paper thin slit—and saw the odd man on the other side of the room. *Who the hell are you? How in the hell did you get in here? Are you a roommate…or another drunk looking for a place to stay? Did I agree to this and forget about you? How long have you been watching?*

Elliott's cell phone buzzed, causing the loose change and rental keys on the nightstand next to his leg to bounce. Keeping the gun in his mouth and watching the man watching him, Elliott instinctively reached for the vibrating phone. The note slid off his lap and made a perfect arc under the bed. *Damn. The keystone cops will never look down there*, he thought. *But Tony would come. He would check the room close. He would think the BCB paid me a visit. Tony would find my letter.* Elliott stopped worrying and focused on the cell phone screen…UNKNOWN NUMBER.

With the gun in his mouth, there was an eternity between each cell phone vibration. Elliott raced through scenarios as usual, rethinking his suicide and the state of affairs leading to the moment. *Have I missed something…anything? Is this the best way? Have I been duped into doing what the Bluff City Butcher wants me to do? I don't see any other way out.*

My life no longer has purpose, my existence is unbearable and there is no treatment for my GIFTED condition.

Like a terminal disease—a cancer—the serial killers that lived in Elliott's head methodically devoured everything good: innocence, wonder, beauty, the capacity to love, life…and his humanity. Although the flow of emotion triggered more physical pain, the loss of his reason to live was what brought the ultimate, crushing blow. Elliott experienced something on Mud Island he would never fully comprehend. The Bluff City Butcher did something. The unstoppable killing machine, the genius psychopath, found a way to give Elliott Sumner more than he could handle, and it would prove to be as effective as a butcher knife in the gut or across the throat…a death blow from a genius.

With his finger on the trigger, he recognized the man on the other side of the room. The cell phone was quiet. Everything stopped.

CHAPTER FIVE

"If you can find a path with no obstacles, it probably doesn't lead anywhere."
Frank A. Clark

27 September 2008

"**I** am no longer active in forensic pathology and homicide investigation," said Elliott with as much edge as he could muster. He ignored the phone calls and half a dozen text messages over the last two days, but Mason persisted.

"Dr. Sumner, do you know who I am?"

"Yes. Someone calling me incessantly that doesn't take a hint…"

She ignored his sarcasm. "I am Carol Mason, Director of Investigative Reporting at *The Memphis Tribune*."

"Congratulations to you. And that is important to me why?"

"The Memphis PD and *Tribune* have launched a collaborative program to review the unsolved homicides in the Metro Area for the ten-year period of 1995 to 2005. I joined the *Tribune* September 1st to lead the project, working for Mr. Albert Bell."

"Ok…good…congratulations and good luck with that. But, as I said, I am not in the business anymore. I suggest you contact Memphis Homicide Detective Wilcox."

"Buford Forrester is dead in Blytheville, Arkansas," she said.

"How was he murdered?" asked Elliott.

"I never said he was murdered."

"Miss Mason, you said you were investigating unsolved homicides. You then said a man was dead…my question is very logical." *Nice try on her part; quick recovery on mine.*

That was so stupid. Now he will be on guard. Be direct. "Does October 17 mean anything to you, Dr. Sumner?"

"Is this a courtroom? No, not a thing." *Yes, it means things to me but I'm not telling you.*

"I find it odd that October 17 is your birthday and the same day that Buford Forrester was killed."

"So Forrester was murdered?"

"I have a prediction," said Carol.

"You can see into the future, too?"

"A man with your capabilities and passion for justice must be in the hunt. I do not know why you stepped away, but I have important information that can help you with your ten-year quest. But I need some help from you."

"Miss Mason, I have no idea what you are talking about, and I can assure you that I have no interest in your information—I will say goodbye, now."

"Buford Forrester's death was investigated by an insurance adjuster, the elected coroner. He botched up the whole investigation; he confused, ignored or destroyed every piece of physical evidence the killer left behind. He did such a great job on his first case that he saved money by not sending the body to the Shelby County Medical Examiner's Office for an autopsy. He ruled the death an accident."

"And that troubles you why?"

"Buford did not fall out of his fishing boat and drown; both carotid arteries were severed, his feet were tied at the ankles with the anchor line…a packer's knot."

"It is difficult to tie your ankles accidentally. Did you consider a tangle?" *I heard 'packer's knot,' but maybe that means nothing to you so I will let it be.*

"A packer's knot by mistake would be a miracle. And I have already found three other people with similar injuries and circumstances. I think there is one guy killing people...a serial killer. When I am done with my review, there could be twenty or thirty homicides hidden in accidents, suicides and missing persons."

"I think you have an overactive imagination, Miss Mason."

"I really don't know much about you, Dr. Sumner, and I am quite certain you know nothing about me, but if you are trying to mislead me or play games then I am not helping the real victims here. I need little but will pass if you don't want to help at all."

"Miss Mason, I still really do not know what you want from me. And, I will choose to ignore that last inflammatory comment concerning my behavior." *Does she know how Forrester fits?* "Ok. I will listen...not promising anything." Elliott tossed his shirt over the screaming bottle of *Dewar's*, set the full glass of scotch in the bathroom out of sight and put the pillow over the gun...for the time being. "Tell me what you know about Forrester."

"Retired from the restaurant business and left Memphis to live in Blytheville, Arkansas, the spring of 1990...a loner. He never married...lived the simple life: cooked every day, bowled Tuesdays, played checkers, and fished once a week."

"I assume that's where they found him...his fishing spot."

"Yes...Mallard Lake, rain or shine...his special spot on a corner of the lake."

"Go ahead."

"October 17, 1995, he didn't show up for the Mississippi County Regional Bowling Championship; he and his team had prepared for weeks. The next morning, they pulled him out of the lake. He was at the bottom, tangled in his anchor beneath his capsized boat. Buford had a gash across his neck. The coroner believes Buford bled to death.

"They reconstructed as best they could and decided that Buford fell out of his boat, tried to climb back in and his arm slipped. He came down on an unprotected edge of the aluminum boat and sliced his neck open. They surmise he panicked, capsized the boat, got tangled in his anchor, passed out from loss of blood and died."

"No autopsy?" asked Elliott. *That's why Wilcox missed it…probably happens a lot. The people in the surrounding counties don't talk.*

"No autopsy and no experience taking a look at dead bodies and potential crime scenes."

"The coroner concluded no foul play?" asked Elliott.

"Correct. The report describes Forrester as a quiet old man…no enemies. When they pulled him out of the lake he still had his wallet, money, Rolex and diamond rings."

"Nothing taken from his automobile?"

"No. The keys were in his truck with expensive fishing gear; nothing was touched. The coroner was confident the neck injury was from the boat. He explained the other trauma to the body as turtle induced."

"What did the turtles do to Forrester?" asked Elliott.

Carol flipped through the open file on her lap as she sat in the middle of her suite at the *Peabody Hotel;* her new home…it came with the employment package. "Here it is…let me read you the relevant paragraph. *'Forrester body found 0900 at bottom of lake 3.65 meters beneath capsized aluminum fishing boat with ankles entangled in anchor line. The body was recovered from 16.67 Celsius water. Skin was mottled and wrinkled with slight petechiae. The straight-line neck wound, 7.63 cm length, 2.21 cm depth matched with exposed, sharp edge of the fishing boat (see photographs). Marine life (fish and turtles) fed on body for twelve-hour period. When recovered, body was missing eyeballs, lips, nose, both ears and all fingers and thumbs. A small, inconsequential puncture wound was noted at the top-center portion of head, likely caused by head hitting the underside of boat during resurface attempts.'*

"That's a lot more detail than I was expecting. Any more on the head wound?"

"No. I looked; it is familiar," replied Carol.

"Familiar…you have seen it before?" asked Elliott.

"Yes."

"When and where?"

Carol had his attention. "I've seen it enough to know it means something. Just like the October 17 date that you are dodging."

"I think you may be chasing ghosts if this is all you have."

"I have more."

"Ok."

"You know R.L. Thornton?"

"Yes."

"How do you know him?" asked Carol.

"We met in '95, homicide cases of mutual interest." *I remember everything about him: smart, committed, empathetic, detail-oriented, believed there was good in everyone, cared about the inner city kids—reason he stayed in the field. He gave me good info; only one alive that looked in the eyes of the Butcher…and then watched him jump into the river.*

Carol felt Elliott's relationship with R.L. Thornton would be important to her research. "In 1995, the national media was all over you, Dr. Sumner, the youngest medical examiner in Texas history that solved 500 unexplained deaths…100 percent success…a perfect record."

"That was all hype. I was given credit for a lot of other people's work. You know how the news media operates—I was a story that sold newspapers and moved TV dials. I was the walking train wreck in those days."

"Is that right? Well, I'm not buying any of it, Doctor. Help me understand why the hottest forensic pathologist in the country makes time for a Memphis street cop."

"First, at that time I was just getting SFI started; I traveled a lot. Memphis is a hub, a central point with the most convenient international connections. Being from Dallas, I passed through Memphis International Airport several times a week. A short visit with a colleague was not only feasible, it was as convenient as picking up a barbecue sandwich."

"Ok, I'll buy that for now, but why meet with Officer Thornton?"

"He worked a triple homicide in 1983 that had some similarities to cases I was investigating at the time in Texas. It was a long shot…I wanted to know more."

"How many meetings did you have with R.L. Thornton?" asked Mason.

"I think I met with him three times that week. That was it."

"Did you ever see or speak to him again after that week in 1995?"

"Did you know Officer Thornton took early retirement after your meetings…well, actually, the spring of 1996, several months after?"

"I did not know he retired, but I am glad to hear that he did." *Maybe I am letting myself get worked up for no reason at all. I thought she was going to say something bad happened. Thank God, he retired.*

"He and his wife moved to Millington. He disappeared October 17, 1996."

■ ■ ■

"He disappeared? What happened?"

"I am sorry you don't know what I am about to tell you, Dr. Sumner. I know he was your friend."

"Please…go ahead."

"Officer Thornton was taken from a golf course, a late afternoon; he was walking the back nine alone. The Millington PD found his golf clubs thrown behind the eighteenth tee box, into the bushes…some clubs broken and bloody. He clearly put up a fight. The blood trail went into the woods where he was killed, a gruesome site. DNA confirmed it was Thornton. CSI came up from Memphis, estimated twelve pints of blood at the scene, total exsanguination, and they recovered a variety of tissue types: skin, muscle, bone and cartilage—he was butchered, Dr. Sumner."

"And was his body found?" Elliott was more sober than he had been in the last month. At last, he recognized the man on the other side of his hotel room; it was his reflection in an unframed mirror stuck on floral wallpaper. *How could I be so stupid?*

Carol emptied her wine glass in three gulps. Elliott was quiet. "In 2002…boys were fishing the Wolf River north of Mud Island and saw a skull; the water level was way down. Later, Memphis CSI recovered the adult male skeleton; it was Officer Thornton, all bones accounted for except the spinal column."

"Did it just float away?" Elliott knew the answer, but was hoping for another.

"The M.E. determined the spine was removed at time of death…in 1996."

He sat on the edge of the bed, phone pressed to his ear, staring at his bare feet pressed into the carpet. Elliott was beginning to lose control, as the Parkland doctors said he would. If the door from hell opened a crack he would unravel; first the body tremors and rapid breathing, then the increased heart rate and blood pressure ramp, and then the hallucinations that would push him…arrhythmia and unconsciousness. No one would be there for CPR…he would die. Which might work for him now, but he would stall.

"I guess an ex-cop has enemies," he said. "Did they find who killed him?" *Maybe that would throw her off some.* Although he'd just met Carol, he had a strange desire to risk something to help her, but he fought it. The consequences would be too great.

"No. The killer is still out there; it will be twelve years next month."

"Twelve years is a long time. Tough case to solve," said Elliott.

"He had a puncture wound on the top of his skull," said Carol.

"Like the Forrester case?"

"Yes, exactly the same location. I *Googled* 'brain' the other day and learned some interesting medical facts. The cranial puncture wounds on Forrester and Thornton were directly above parts of the brain that control major motor skills…the ability to move. A person with similar brain damage could survive but would experience paralysis of the arms and legs and loss of speech. They would retain their sense of awareness and would feel pain. But you probably knew all that, being a medical doctor."

"I have politely listened. I see your strong desire to find answers to these horrible crimes. But the October 17th date for two deaths is not that bizarre. Thousands of people died that day in the country; hundreds murdered, committed suicide or died in suspicious accidents, and thousands were reported missing…all on October 17. You cannot build a serial killer case on a date.

"Yes, the puncture wound to the head is peculiar. But there are literally a dozen ways for that type of trauma to occur. The top of the head is exposed more often than not…a typical and likely location—blunt and penetration trauma.

"I am sure you are a very good investigative reporter, Ms. Mason, and I am sorry you think I can help you, but I cannot. I have stepped away for personal reasons."

"Teddy Morgan was killed in Hernando, Mississippi. He was found with two five-inch butcher knives stuck in each eye. They ruled it a suicide, Dr. Sumner. I guess they thought the circular puncture wound on the top of his head was due to one of the dozen other ways…Oh…Mr. Morgan killed himself on October 17, 1997…along with the other unrelated thousands."

"Teddy Morgan is dead too?" asked Elliott in a fading voice.

Carol fanned through the stack for Morgan's cold case file. She had already interviewed the mother; Mrs. Morgan convinced her that Teddy did not commit suicide. The signature on the note was a duplicate of her husband's…he had been dead five years. Carol found the police report and scanned it while Elliott sat quietly…too quietly.

C O N F I D E N T I A L

Hernando Police Department

Case: 3554   Date: October 21, 1997
Name: Teddy Morgan   Officer: T.O. Bradford
COD: Exsanguination   MOD: Suicide
DOB: October 7, 1965   DOD: October 17, 1997
Coroner: J.L. Benson

Summary Report

Teddy Morgan (32/W/M) was found dead in his apartment with seven-inch steak knives in each eye, lacerations to both wrists and laceration to the throat. At the scene, Morgan appeared to die from loss of blood.

Morgan was a Hernando, Mississippi resident at 2345 Beachwood Cover, Apartment 12. He was self-employed providing a residential tree trimming service to north Mississippi. Morgan was in an automobile accident on October 7, 1997, leaving a bar where he was celebrating his birthday. Morgan received a DUI citation and was arrested. Friends of Morgan said he was depressed. He was getting married in the spring, but he found his fiancé with another man and cancelled the wedding. The day he was found, parents of Morgan were unable to reach him by phone for several days. They contacted the apartment manager and requested a check on their son.

Morgan was discovered in the bedroom October 21, 1997 at 1135. The death scene was the bloodiest in this officer's twenty-year experience. Coroner J.L. Benson visited the scene with HPD and estimated time of death to be in the a.m. hours of October 17, 1997.

Morgan's wrists were cut superficially. The throat was cut and severed the jugular vein. There was incidental trauma to the top of the head, a circular puncture wound. Morgan apparently walked around the room for some time before collapsing on the bed and thrusting two seven-inch steak knives in his eyes. Morgan's hands were gripping the knives when he was found. Morgan had a history of depression and recent traumatic events to explain his rash behavior. There was a suicide note left to his family. Manner of death was ruled a suicide. The cause of death was exsanguination. There was no autopsy ordered.

SPECIAL NOTE: The Morgan family disagreed with the ruling. They were adamant he was not capable of killing himself. They said the suicide note was not her son, it was rushed. The mother of the deceased claims the son's signature was purposely made to look like his father's signature, not his own. She is positive her son was sending a message…he was killed and it was made to look like a suicide.

When she looked up it dawned on her that Elliott Sumner was no longer fighting her…he was non-responsive…he was struggling, somehow limited. She had said too much, pushed too hard…something was wrong.

"I am sorry. I am being unfair. I forced myself on you, dumped shocking pieces of information and expected you to get involved without any regard for your personal matters. You have saved many lives by capturing or destroying serial killers…fifty of the worst human beings that ever lived. Here I am, I have never even seen a serial killer and I am pushing you around, and I really don't know you except I know of your extraordinary accomplishments and that it takes a very special man with a depth of character, something far more than a high IQ or photographic memory. There I go again, rambling when you deserve your privacy.

"Thank you for listening to me…most of the time, anyway. And please, forgive my selfish behavior; I'm really a nicer person than that. I will not bother you again."

"Miss Mason?" It was good if she had gone. He could not take much more. She would blame herself for what he was about to do…kill himself.

"Thank you for taking my call. Goodnight, Elliott." Carol disconnected and looked at her phone. She had feelings for a man she had never met. What was that?

"Miss Mason?" The demons were held off when he was talking to her; there were moments, but fleeting…when she spoke they passed. Why? he wondered.

Elliott lifted the pillow and tossed it across the room. He picked up his gun. He would leave the suicide note under the bed. The demons would be back soon; he just couldn't bear any of it anymore.

Carol pulled out the 1983 clipping she had found in the archives at *The Memphis Tribune*. Elliott didn't intend to, but he confirmed everything. The Bluff City Butcher survived the river and was very active and unstoppable.

The Memphis Tribune

Three Found Dead on the Bluff; Suspected Killer Jumps off Harahan

October 18, 1983

Staff Reporter

Memphis, TN—Three killed last night behind a popular restaurant on the bluff. Memphis Police were called to the 200 block of Wagner Place, Captain Bilbo's Bar/Grill, at 6:10 p.m. Monday night by owner/manager, Buford T. Forrester. According to Memphis Homicide, three men in their early twenties were fatally attacked on the bluff by an unidentified man on foot wielding a knife.

According to Teddy Morgan, a Captain Bilbo's employee and eyewitness, victims were dining on the hospitality deck in rear of the restaurant when they heard something in the nearby brush. Three went to investigate. At sunset the fourth member of the party went to find his friends and returned covered in blood. The Memphis police were called.

The three killed were found several hours later by police in a remote area of the bluff. "Identities are being held until notification of family," said Officer R.L. Thornton, the first responder with the Memphis PD. "Details on the homicide scene and victims are proprietary."

Sources close to the investigation said the one who survived the attack told police he came upon a large man with long black hair in a ponytail wearing a dark coat. The man matched the description of the suspect seen the day before when Sabina Weatherford was taken from the same restaurant and is still missing.

Any information regarding an active police investigation is appreciated and should be brought to the attention of the Homicide Department – Detective Anthony Wilcox

Later that night Memphis police received a call that a large man fitting the description was seen in the vicinity of the Memphis-Arkansas Bridge. The suspect was carrying a sack and moving at a rapid pace along the river. R.L. Thornton said, "I can confirm that at 9:45 p.m. witnesses saw a man fitting the description of the primary suspect that fled the scene of a triple homicide behind Captain Bilbo Restaurant. The man attempted to cross the Harahan Bridge."

According to Memphis police, the assailant jumped off the Harahan Bridge and has not been found. Efforts to locate the assailant continue. Sources say it is unlikely the man survived the 100 foot fall or the turbulent waters of the river. Experts say the impact would likely kill or injure a man, knocking him unconscious and breaking several bones. The injured man would be swept under water by stiff currents and undertows.

"The most likely outcome is death upon impact. Anyone that survived the fall would drown in the swirling waters of the Mississippi River," said Thornton. The Memphis police plan to continue their search. "His body could be in the Gulf of Mexico in a week," said one observer.

16 October 2008

"Where in the fuck have you been, Sumner?" Tony walked into his office. Elliott was looking out the blinds, one slat up.

"Well, good morning to you too, Detective Wilcox." He kept looking out the window.

"Seriously, Elliott, what is going on with you? You check yourself out of Parkland, shutdown SFI and vanish…no cell…no cards or letters. Are you into something you can't talk about, or are you in trouble with your…you know…the shit that happened in Dallas that put you in ICU?"

"What do you think?" Elliott asked as he dropped the slat and turned.

"Well, I think I should whip your ass. That's what I think." They embraced and Tony poured coffee from the big thermos on the edge of his desk. "It's cold but good. I got a call about you from Carol Mason at *The Tribune*."

"She called about me?"

"Yes, she called me on a weekend—September 27—she said she talked to you and was worried."

"She was worried about me?"

"Yes, God damn it, she was worried about you, Elliott. She said you seemed to be in a bad place. She was concerned…you needed a friend."

She said that…about me?

"Anyway, you never answered your fucking cell phone. I called you a good twenty times. GPS had you in South Carolina until you took the battery out of your phone or flushed it down the commode or crushed the damn thing. Why?"

"It's not important now, Tony. I am going to try to fix things."

"What does that mean? I mean, I'm sure it is important, but I thought the Bluff City Butcher got his stinking claws on you, or you did something stupid like killed yourself."

"Listen to me, Tony. It's not important now. Just leave it alone. I needed some time. There are more important things going on."

"Ok, but you owe me something. Can you at least tell me; are you learning to manage your emotional trauma like Dodson said?"

"I will say a few things about that and then no more. Agreed?"

"Agreed."

"Ok…I was losing it completely. I could not escape the torment of the demons in my head…much less take on new ones. Tony, I could see all of them, their evil and sick, twisted ways. And the hundreds of victims, I lived their pain over and over again. I tried hypnosis, serious drugs and a lot of alcohol to block it…to numb me, but nothing worked. It was like an exposed nerve that felt the slightest wind and delivered unbearable pain constantly. Nothing worked.

"Tony, I was going to kill myself."

"God damn it, Elliott…no…no…please don't do that…don't give up, Brother, ever…don't." Tony dropped in his chair.

"I'm sorry, but I am struggling with unbearable pain at times and…"

"So there are times when you are ok?"

"Yes."

"And you are ok now?"

"Yes, at the moment."

"Do you know why?" Tony moved around his desk and sat next to Elliott. As usual, he was looking into his coffee mug. It helped him focus.

"I know exactly when, but I do not know why," said Elliot.

"And?"

"The last half of my phone conversation with Carol Mason…she was talking about the Bluff City Butcher. I think she knows but is not yet certain. That's when the demons stopped. For some reason, they went away."

"Have they been back?"

"No…but a few times I felt them at the door." Elliott got up, went to the window and opened the slat. "I realized then it was possible to have a life again. Tony, my path to that life goes directly through the heart of the Bluff City Butcher."

"I don't know what that means, Elliott, but I will do anything I can to see that you get through this. If the Butcher is the key, I am with you every step of the way."

"Tony, come here." He joined Elliott at the window, the fourth floor, the Memphis police headquarters downtown. "You see the white van?"

"The old one with the motor running?" The smoke trailed from the tailpipe, front wheels aimed away from the curb for a quick departure.

"You will not get there fast enough, so just listen. He knows we are looking at him right now. He sees your eyes and my eyes. That will be enough." The van jerked alive and crawled away. They dropped the slat. "That was the Bluff City Butcher. He knows I am in town and he is ready. He has very big plans."

"You can't handle another emotional crisis. Dodson said it would trigger that unique medical crap that makes your heart stop…and next time is the last time."

"Somehow, the Butcher knew before it happened. Tony, I met the Butcher on Mud Island a few days before Dallas and my collapse."

"That night you disappeared. My man said you walked into the *Peabody* the next morning like you had been out on a stroll. I was waiting for you to tell me what in the hell you were up to all night, but you never said a damn word so I figured I'd let you work it out."

"For now, you need to know the Butcher wanted to meet me at Mud Island. I saw the Weatherford child; she was mummified. I think he needed her for a reason we do not yet understand. I think he took her for someone else. The Sabina child just doesn't fit him at all."

"Whoa. I don't have a clue what that would be all about or how that could help us catch the sick bastard," said Tony as he lifted a slat for a second look out the window.

"The Butcher sprang on me from the river. I was ten feet away. He closed the gap in a second. Next thing I knew, I was on McGee's bench in Tom Lee Park."

"Shit, Elliott…he could have killed you that night; wonder why he didn't."

"He is more complex. He wants to kill me a certain way at a certain time. But he must have done something to me on Mud Island that night.

"What could he have done?"

"Maybe a combination of drugs and hypnotic suggestion; somehow he put me on a path with no way out—a manipulated, neurological overload. Remember, he is a genius and now he knows I survived his test and sees I am back. I think that will launch whatever he has in store for us…the city…and maybe even the country. I am nowhere close to figuring him out."

"What next?"

"I am here for a reason, Tony."

"And what is that?"

"It is October 16th. The Bluff City Butcher will kill again…after midnight. He always kills on October 17th. I need to be in this now."

■ ■ ■

Raymond and Martha Munson had lived on Jefferson Avenue for the last eighteen years in a modest three-bedroom ranch. It was the house with all the trees and an aluminum bass boat on a trailer stuffed under pin oaks next to the carport. Even though it broke every code, it had been there so long it was part of the landscape.

He was born and raised in Dallas, studied at SMU and found his way to Memphis as an assistant English professor at Memphis State University. He and Martha Waverly were married in 1968, and they moved to Texas where Raymond taught English for eight years at the new Carrollton Junior High School and then six years at North Texas State University in Denton. His dream position finally materialized and they returned to Memphis, where he became professor of English Literature at the University.

Munson retired on his sixty-fifth birthday in June of 2001, because of declining health. Seven years later, his plan to write a novel was still just a plan, but he did figure out how to get the bass boat out from under the pin oak. He found a fishing hole far enough away to feel like a get-away and he discovered how to get the boat in and out of the water with his bum hip.

It was like any other autumn day in Memphis, a bit chilly but sunny and low humidity. Raymond was all set to take the boat out that afternoon. Martha was going to visit her sisters in Germantown so he had no pressure to be home at any certain time; she would shop all day, have dinner with her sisters and that would turn into a sleepover, which was fine by him.

At three in the afternoon, Martha was long gone and Raymond was just backing his boat out of the driveway. He would be at his fishing hole in thirty minutes and wet a hook in another ten, tops. One hour should get him two or three fish and then home to fry them up. His hip was not acting up, so he would enjoy himself more than usual.

After a half dozen attempts he got the boat onto Jefferson with his car pointing in the right direction, toward Cooper Road. Murray Fitzberg sat on his front porch, watching, when Raymond clipped his mailbox. No major damage, but it would need some attention later. He waved, but Fitzberg was pissed, standing on the porch in his baggy pants and plaid flannel shirt, waving his middle fingers with both hands. Raymond got a kick out of watching Fitzberg almost fall off his porch.

Distracted, he almost ran into the big black van at the end of the street. *Shit. Who would park this big damn thing here?* He pulled the wheel sharply just in time to avoid clipping the bumper and slowed as he passed. *Dodge Sprinter…what the hell…I didn't know Dodge made a van this big. What's it doing? Oh yeah, probably looking at the Morgan house…damn thing has been on the market for a year now.*

He pulled around the *Sprinter*, stopped at Cooper and looked in his mirror. The van looked empty, but the windows were dark so he couldn't tell much. *Damn tinted windows should be illegal…damn mysterious. Hope they don't buy the Morgan place or I might hit the damn thing sooner or later,* he thought as he turned onto Cooper and his boat followed.

The *Dodge Sprinter* started up and pulled onto Cooper, too. Soon it was close enough to follow Raymond but far enough not to be noticed.

CHAPTER SIX

"Vengeance is in my heart, death in my hand,
Blood and revenge are hammering in my head."
Shakespeare

17 October 2008

Tony Wilcox got the call at 5:37 a.m. In ten minutes he was pulling up to 3030 Poplar Avenue. All entrances to the Memphis Central Public Library were blocked by squad cars, blue lights spinning. He was waved through.

The scene was live. Memphis PD shut down a quarter mile of Poplar Avenue to the south and Walnut Grove to the north. The four-story glass building was surrounded. Tony hopped the curb and drove down the sidewalk to the SWAT Mobile Unit that was smoking at the east entrance. A perimeter was set; media and gathering crowds were kept back a hundred yards and all eyes were on the fourth floor.

He slid to a stop, stepped out and was met by the first responder holding a pen and clipboard with an inch of dog-ears. "Morning, Sir. We've got us a situation here," said the officer. Without a word, Tony closed his door, looked at the brass name plate and up; he liked to see a little grey on the temples—increased chances the physical evidence wasn't screwed up.

"Got some info on the way; tell me what you have, Officer…Holt." Wilcox stood a head above most everyone at the crime scene and projected an aura of dogged confidence fitting the most productive homicide detective on the force. Only his brow revealed he was already pissed-off at the bastard that could stir-up so much attention so early in the morning.

Officer Kent Holt was the lucky patrolman in the area; he took the call. Equally unshaken by the growing dimensions of the crime scene, he responded unemotionally. "10-31 came in at 05:22…Memphis Central Library, Poplar 3000 block. An elderly white male was found by Lamont Otis, the night watchman, on 05:00 rounds." Holt looked up from his notes. "The poor guy is messed up bad…never seen anything like it…butchered and hung like a scarecrow." Tony kept looking up at the fourth floor; he showed nothing. Holt flipped the page and continued. "Otis found the deceased when he stepped onto the fourth floor, in a chair about twenty feet from the east staircase. At that moment he heard the whine of a squeaky wheel moving in the book stacks. The rest of the floor was dark. Otis said he ran down four flights and out of the building while calling it into MPD. I just got confirmation as you drove up; SWAT said all possible exits are locked. Otis kept a watch on the front doors. SWAT thinks the guy that did this is still in there somewhere."

"And did you get a good look at the body?" asked Tony.

"Maybe a minute…it was enough."

"Is he dead? Did anyone check his pulse?" Tony lowered his head and locked his eyes on Officer Holt.

"No…impossible to check for a pulse…"

"Why?"

"The guy's hands were cut off at the wrists. The stubs were stitched up like he had an operation or something."

"What else, Holt?" Tony backed away from the building to look up, get a glimpse of the body, to see what everyone else was seeing, especially the growing crowds behind the lines.

"Same thing was done to his feet, Sir. Cut off at the ankles and sewn up." Holt stared blankly at his clipboard. "The victim was drained of his blood, but there was no blood anywhere. I just ran tape around the death scene for forensics and came down."

"Thanks, Holt." Tony put his hand on the officer's shoulder. "Good job…tough circumstances. How many have seen the victim?"

"Five: me, Otis, a couple of SWAT and one EMT. We kept everyone off four. Told them the medical examiner and forensic team would need a pristine scene to work, especially on this one."

"Good. Do me a favor and focus on containment, Holt. Get to those other four guys and remind them…nothing gets out."

"Yes, Sir," said Holt.

Fuck…Elliott was right. The bastard struck October 17…like clockwork.

Tony headed to the front entrance. The undulating crowd of Memphis police, fire and support opened as he approached without a word. Tony passed through as if he owned the place, which he did; it was his crime scene. His eyes were straight ahead. The last person he passed was the tactical squad leader.

"Wilcox, where do you think you're going?" said Delaney.

"In. Bye." He didn't even look over.

"Whoa…you do that and I will think you are compromising my scene. I'd have to shoot you in the ass."

"You couldn't find an ass during a lap dance, much less get anywhere near it." Tony kept walking.

"You're tempting me to practice on your skinny ass, boy."

Tony stopped at the glass doors and turned his head. "Franco, can you focus? I need you to keep everyone off four until I hook up with a contingency of your finest on three—then we can all go up together holding hands."

"You got it, Tee…and watch out; I think the sick prick that did this is hiding up there somewhere."

"Will do…I just hope I find him…please God. Oh, Dr. Sumner should be pulling up any minute. He is the only one you let in. I give you permission to shoot everyone else."

"And who said Anthony Wilcox was not a thoughtful man?" *It's been a long time since we got caught in that crossfire…Tee almost took one for the city that day. I saw the guy behind the stack of pallets. I had no choice but to tackle Tony and get a shot off…my lucky day…got the homicidal freak between the eyes. I didn't even feel the hit in the leg. Got an artery…all the damn blood and I blacked out. Tee put a belt on my thigh and got me to The Med…no time for calling anyone. They said no one survives a femoral artery sliced by a bullet…but I did. That day we found a way to save each other's ass. Guess that's what it's all about…fighting the good fight and all. I'd do it again.*

Delaney pulled down his head-set mic. "T 3030, hold your positions, D…Wilcox is in the building. I need a hookup on L3. Wait for signal from D…Franco out."

Tony eased through the propped open glass door and moved through the foyer to the south side of the elevators where a team was hunkered down waiting in the shadows. He came up from behind on his newest partner, the only one that didn't see him. Tony gripped Harris's shoulder; "Hey, you young guys ever sleep?"

"Shit…Sir!" Harris jumped short of throwing his glasses off his head. The four SWAT guys on the flanks with rifles smiled and got serious again in two seconds, all business. Harris pushed his glasses back on his nose with one pudgy finger, still gathering himself. "Shit…Sir."

"You said that, Harris." Tony looked around. "Let's go." They pulled out their .38s and Tony signaled SWAT. They were going up.

The front reception area of the library was open air all the way to the top of the building. Two sets of suspended stair cases began at the second floor and ended at the fourth. The place was lit up like a Christmas tree, as ordered by MPD; their people were everywhere but floor four. The stairway and glass walls made the climb risky but still the best option. They climbed without incident to three; Tony led. He held up four fingers and pointed up. Four SWAT wearing black jump-suits, flak jackets and helmets took their positions.

The climb to four was text book; it took longer than the first three. Anything could have happened from an impossible number of directions if the killer wanted to make a statement. Tony was the only one that knew the climb would be uneventful; this killer had much grander plans. The director's orders kept him from saying anything.

Heads emerged on four, eyes at the floor level. The victim was on chilling display. One SWAT lifted his helmet visor and puked. He spit and closed his visor, waiting for the signal from Wilcox. "We good?" he asked. All nodded.

SWAT scanned the area as Wilcox studied the victim from the stairs, the next chapter of a sick story by a twisted mind. The ashen face was stitched-up like a stuffed doll and arms outstretched, suspended from the ceiling, creating a welcoming illusion. The old man had been meticulously transformed into a hideous ghoul, a Halloween character. The creation was an abomination.

Tony gave the signal; the SWAT leader in their group relayed on his helmet mic. They rushed the floor, fanning out according to protocol, and a dozen more poured onto the floor from every portal.

Tony moved to the victim and knelt, looking around, with Harris close behind. *Why kill this old guy?* He wondered.

They were facing opposite directions with guns out. Tony whispered, "Keep your eyes open until SWAT gets done with their sweep. It's going to take a while, so get comfortable and pay attention. Did anyone think to call the medical examiner?"

"Yes. They will send him up when the place is secure."

He's learning. Not bad for three months trying to keep up with me. Third generation cops sometimes don't fit, but Alex has it. He got the highest scores on the detective test and the kid memorized the police manual…and he has good police sense. But I need to shake him up some.

"Why do you think this guy was…you know…and put on display like this, Sir?" Alex leaned closer to the body and touched the arm with one finger. "He is cold. I guess he has been dead a long time."

"We'll let the medical examiner handle time of death, Harris. But I'd say we are dealing with someone who likes his knife and hated this old guy."

"Do you think this was done by a serial killer?"

"Most murders are crimes of passion, fits of rage. Few murders are planned. This kill is personal and elaborate. The killer was mad at this guy. When we identify the victim we will have paths to investigate." *I wish I could get you off the serial killer angle, but when Elliott gets here you will put things together anyway.*

"This had to be planned to get this guy up to the fourth floor of a public library. He was cut up somewhere else and brought here. And I think the killer has done this before."

"Harris, why do you want to push the serial killer angle first?"

"Sir, I may be new, but this is nothing like any of the shootings or stabbings in the books I studied. This is very weird and elaborate. If this is a serial killer, we could get FBI resources behind us to catch the guy." Harris wiped the sweat from his face, but it was back before his wet handkerchief found his pocket.

Tony watched SWAT comb the building like a swarm of army ants. "Harris, you better hope we don't have a serial killer. No one knows how to catch those sick bastards…no one."

■ ■ ■

"It's a new, damn world; killers are smarter, meaner and crazier than ever before, and serial killers are worse. They hide among us, operating quite well in our communities, in multiple cities and states and even countries. The freaks are more efficient because of the movies and the *Internet* They are more unpredictable because their targets may be defined but their selection is random. The obscure movements of a serial killer are difficult to find and follow and next to impossible to predict. FBI and law enforcement agencies across the country and around the world have done a pitiful job of catching serial killers." Tony looked at his watch; *I wish these boys would hurry it up and where the hell is Elliott?*

"I thought the FBI was successful catching serial killers; Ted Bundy, the Zodiac Killer, BTK and others. It's been in the news."

"You disappoint me. I assumed you were well read. Ted Bundy killed two dozen college girls over a seventeen-year period. BTK killed at least ten that we know about over twenty years and Zodiac killed thirty over his most active ten years."

"That is my point, Sir. The FBI caught those serial killers…right?"

"Let's see, Bundy and BTK were caught by chance, making stupid mistakes. The Zodiac was never caught," said Tony. "You tell me. Seventy-five people killed over three decades by three serial killers, one of which is still loose. Does that say the system is working?"

"No, but today we have profilers and forensics that helps."

"Ok, I will give you that, Harris. But, open your damn eyes, son. When a boat is sinking, a bucket helps, but the boat is still going down."

"I guess I never thought of it that way."

"Have you ever heard of Carl Eugene Watts?" asked Tony.

"No, Sir."

"Watts was one of the most prolific serial killers in American history." *Probably the one with more kills is the Bluff City Butcher and that psycho is just getting started,* he thought. "More people know about Ted Bundy. Watts killed four times as many women. The guy started killing when he was fifteen. He just did not like girls."

"Did an FBI profile or modern forensics catch him?" asked Harris.

"He was of African-American descent; that didn't fit any of the profiles," said Elliott from the stairs, only his head at floor level. Tony didn't move. Harris jumped into action, pointing his gun at Elliott. "Tony, tell your partner not to shoot. I'm one of the good guys." Tony smiled and whispered to his partner. Harris lowered his gun and Elliott scooted over to them, his eyes on the victim all the way.

"Sorry for the gun, Dr. Sumner," said Harris.

"Not a problem, young man. Tony, Frank gave me the lay of the land. And I could hear you two bickering on the second floor." He winked at Tony. "This place is an echo chamber."

"We were having a discussion," said Tony.

"To be fair, Harris should win the debate. Watts was caught by DNA testing. Thus, forensic advances did come into play." Elliott studied the body as the others stood up and started to follow him, Harris stayed close and Tony kept an eye on the surroundings; he hated surprises.

"True, but if the idiot had not attacked two girls in an apartment complex, the neighbors would not have complained about a loud party and the patrolman would not have arrested Watts for a domestic disturbance," said Tony.

"Correct, but they did run his DNA, fed it into the National Missing Person DNA Database and got a match to an unsolved homicide in another town," said Elliott

"True, but the idiot started to talk to the police. He told them everything he could remember: who, how and where to find the bodies." Tony walked with his gun ready at his side. SWAT darted in and out of book stacks as far as he could see.

Why have you gone overboard on this one? What are you saying? This kill is a labor of love you want to share with the world, but the Memphis Police Department is not about to let this get out…you should know that…or maybe you don't. Elliott examined the dismemberments, trimmings, cleansings and stitch work that were always intricate, tight and in numbers that related to seventeen. Packer knots were always most prevalent and the *Knots of Isis* were only on the face: both ears and the corners of the mouth.

"You know he died in prison last year…prostate cancer," said Elliott as he studied the back of the victim.

"How did you find out?" asked Tony, looking around.

"Checked every year; I wanted to be sure he didn't get out."

The SWAT commander approached Tony, "We're secure…no one is in the building. Hello, Dr. Sumner. Good to see you here, Sir. We can send up the M.E. when you're ready."

Tony holstered his gun. "We're ready. Remind your men to forget what they saw up here."

"Nothing seen, Sir." He turned and disappeared with a dozen guns trailing. Two stayed—they would be the last out.

The library would open late. Tony watched the crowds on the ground thin out. The sun peeked over the city, burning off the morning mist, and traffic started to flow on Poplar and Walnut Grove. Tony had worked hundreds of cases, only five were pure evil. This one made six. But something bothered him; his instincts were the best. Before CSI and the M.E. made it up to the death scene Tony used the quiet time to focus. Harris stayed busy over the victim with his magnifying glass and notepad, following Elliott around.

Tony stepped back twenty feet and walked a slow circle around the body. *I feel you and I smell you. You are here, aren't you?* Once again he looked up and down aisles between the stacks as shuffling shoes on the stairs got louder. He stepped out of the way.

The CSI photographer's camera popped across the death scene like a thousand lightning strikes with the whirring buzz of the recycling strobe. The forensic entourage fanned out, each knowing exactly what to do, and the medical examiner emerged wearing his official white lab coat.

"Morning, Detective Wilcox," said the M.E. with eyes already on the body and Dr. Sumner. "Is that man going to be at all my homicides?"

"Yes…get used to it. He is the fucking best in the world, Dr. Bates," said Tony.

"Did we wake up on the wrong side of the bed?" Bates continued to the death scene. He couldn't argue the point.

A few hours later Tony and Elliott stood at the stairs, looking at the sun cut through the morning and shoot light across the fourth floor. They were unsettled, uneasy. Something was not right…but what?

"This is worse than I thought, Tony."

"You were right on the date—October 17—but did you expect him to do this much…he was pretty pissed-off at this guy."

"No…this is not anger, Tony. This is vengeance. He took the heart, the hands and the senses…sight, sound, smell, taste, touch. And, he took all of the blood. What bothers me most is, once again, he put a victim on display. The first victim was tied to a park bench in the middle of a public park. Now, he tied up this one in the Public Library."

"He wants the world to know. He is GOING PUBLIC."

"Vengeance is in my heart, death in my hand, Blood and revenge are hammering in my head…Shakespeare," quoted Elliott. "And he is still here, Tony."

"I feel it too, but they have looked everywhere."

"Not everywhere, because I feel him. He is here," said Elliott.

They walked around the library for another hour. The body was removed, the Memphis police were pulling out and the cleaning crews were coming in to erase another death scene from the world. It was time for them to leave, too.

There were thousands, but only one ceiling tile within earshot moved…and softly reseated.

Steve Bradshaw

PART TWO
THE SECRET TO KEEP
2004

CHAPTER SEVEN

"The first person to live to be 1,000 years old is certainly alive today...
whether they realize it or not."
Aubrey de Grey
Geneticist, Cambridge University

28 June 2004

The streets were steaming in Las Vegas after a brief morning shower. Sparse lines of suits and high heels trickled through the Venetian hotel lobby and casino, noses in BlackBerrys and each carrying a box almost too big for one to manage. Like bees to the honey pot, the dutiful sales reps descended upon the exhibit hall to set up their company booth. *The 12th Congress of Anti-aging Biomedical Therapeutics* was anticipating 25,000 attendees. The doors officially opened in three hours.

Jack Bellow preferred running through exhibits alone, during pre-convention hours on the first day. Although such practices were strictly prohibited and security measures were in place, Jack was never one to follow rules. It was more important he scope-out technology space and competitive landscape with the fewest hassles, exhibits free of annoying personnel and literature free for the taking.

New, leading-edge technology would be missing from the meeting; why educate competition? These meetings were for repositioning marketed technology and deals. Although Jack was a master of surveillance, this trip would be different. The pre-convention visit would supplement prior due diligence. Jack was in Vegas to meet Dr. Enrique Medino, a quiet pioneer in the Anti-aging Medicine segment. Medino had a breakthrough to discuss with one of the most sought after biotech entrepreneurs in the country. Medino was about to die.

The *American Association of Anti-aging Medicine* was formed in 1992 and became a driving force in the promotion of science and research to prolong the healthy lifespan of humans. Jack knew of the organization but had little time to give it until the summer of 2004, after his fourth company was acquired by a market leader, making him even wealthier—with time to kill.

Although membership steadily grew, attracting respected healthcare practitioners and top scientists from all parts of the world, the Anti-aging proponents were discredited by the *status quo*. The pioneers were accused of taking advantage of the aging population, making promises of impossible human life spans and treating aging as a grotesque human condition that should be eradicated—like measles.

The Anti-aging advocacy organizations, physicians and scientists were driven by a simple premise: aging may not be inevitable. The new mindset created an opportunity for new possibilities. Pioneers viewed aging differently, as a collection of degenerative medical conditions. Osteoarthritis, cancer, heart disease, type II diabetes and Alzheimers at one time were thought to be results of the natural aging process. Today, every one of them was known to be a treatable disease process.

The Anti-aging field was ready to produce a game changer. Jack knew how to read the signs. He understood steady, documented scientific progress: stem cell study, genetic engineering, regenerative medicine, nanotechnology and therapeutic cloning. He had already read a third of the 3,000 peer-reviewed articles on Anti-aging in the *National Library of Medicine*. Jack saw the future in the making when a new specialty struggled to survive, unrecognized by *American Medical Association, American Board of Medical Specialties* and other established groups.

He was a successful independent businessman who believed in a free market economy. All companies had the same objectives: find customers and keep them—best model on earth for determination of relevance and value. When it came to trailblazing and innovation, Jack held little interest in the views of the *AMA, ABMS* or the *FDA*…the gatekeepers, the protectors of the standard-of-care. The innovators must be strong enough to take the beating as they hauled the gatekeepers kicking and screaming into the future.

The Anti-aging Medicine specialty was a *mega-trend* so far ahead that the *status-quo* was in pre-denial. The new, developing consumer base had already created a $96 billion global industry without permission from the gatekeepers. Jack was certain the field was fertile ground for an earth-shaking game changer, or he wouldn't be in Vegas. He was ready for the ultimate challenge. After successfully climbing mountains, Jack was looking for the Pike's Peak of breakthroughs. His due diligence suggested Dr. Enrique Medino might be the one.

■ ■ ■

"At the moment, we're stuck with this awful fatalism that we're going to get old and sick and die painful deaths. There are 100,000 people dying each day from age-related diseases. We can stop this carnage. It's simply a matter of deciding that's what we should be doing…."
Aubrey de Grey
Geneticist, Cambridge University

The elderly, large-bellied Latino-American gentleman walked down Las Vegas Boulevard toward the Venetian Resort Hotel and Casino. He stopped several times along the way; it was hotter than he had expected for a late afternoon and he was feeling weak. Wearing a floral Hawaiian shirt, white Bermuda shorts to his knees, sandals with socks, a Panama hat and an orange backpack, he looked like any other retired tourist out for a stroll in Sin City. But Enrique Medino was more than a wandering tourist. He was a brilliant geneticist with a very big secret, and today he was working. This trip was about Enrique, his wife of forty-five years and his discovery—a quantum leap for mankind. It would change everything, and Enrique had decided it was his turn to be a millionaire.

The last round of chemotherapy was the worst. He had lost the rest of his hair, including eyebrows and eyelashes. He was dizzy and his eyesight was changing daily. He could live with the poor eyesight, night sweats and the burning diarrhea for a while but not the dizziness. Fortunately, a few days before he was booked to leave for Vegas the dizziness went away. He saw that as a sign…and he could keep his food down too.

His wife wanted him to have fun this time. She would never say it out loud, but she feared this would be his last medical convention; the cancer was worse. But none of that mattered to Enrique; his mind was on his discovery—it was too big for anyone to comprehend, and those that could would kill him and steal it. Since his first option had failed to materialize, his meeting with Jack Bellow was the best plan.

Enrique methodically gathered the tools to serve his genius mind in his lifelong quest to unlock the deepest secrets of the double helix—DNA. Through high school and college he was immersed in cellular biology and organic chemistry. He graduated medical school and opened an obstetrics and gynecology clinic in Pecos, Texas a few years before going over to Dallas to pursue a master's degree in molecular biology and Tennessee for his doctorate in genetics at Vanderbilt.

Since their inceptions, Enrique had attended the *American Academy of Anti-aging Medicine, American Society of Longevity Medicine,* and the *Academy of Successful Aging and the Board of Anti-aging and Regenerative Medicine.* He served on committees, participated in studies, shared research and supported educational programs. Enrique did everything asked of him; over the years, he'd been overused and under-recognized. The loss for the emerging specialty was their failure to recognize true genius among them. Enrique's introverted nature was enough to keep the world from knowing.

He never purposely withheld his knowledge; his peers either failed to ask the right questions that would have revealed his genius or they didn't listen. Enrique was so far ahead that he was unable to put his private research into words. He began to invent a new scientific language to deal with his new world of genetic breakthroughs in 1995. Enrique reconfigured the tools of interpretation to make his journey possible.

Over twenty years as the Director of Molecular Biology and Genetic Research at Vanderbilt University Medical School, Dr. Enrique Medino met the terms of his contract consistently. University research projects were completed on schedule and on budget, research awards were bestowed, and budding scientists flourished under his tutelage. Each chancellor that served over his twenty-year tenure was honored to have the demure Dr. Medino on staff and each put forth great effort to accommodate his withdrawn nature by providing a low-profile work environment with no demands in the spotlight.

At the time, it seemed harmless and no other changes to the agreement were proposed. The provision stipulated that the research facilities of the school would be available to Dr. Medino for his personal and private use after normal operating hours. The privilege would be provided without any obligation of sharing intellectual property rights associated with private research. The university would be given recognition regarding the site where research was conducted. The contract provision was agreed to by the university twenty years ago. It would prove to be a costly accommodation.

Enrique never wanted an audience, encouragement or recognition. His world was a mystery for most. Few people could grasp basic genetics, and molecular biology was a foreign language. In the early days, his research at Vanderbilt interested his friends and family. They understood enough to know he was working on the human genome project. Interest waned: long test cycles, small successes and continuous failures. People failed to see the value of each piece to the puzzle. Enrique lost the rest of his audience—students, faculty and peers—when diagnosed with pancreatic cancer. The irony of a terminal patient searching for the genetic secrets of life dampened the allure, and Enrique did not have the personality, the inkling or the time to explain. The genius was on a mission that only he could comprehend.

■ ■ ■

On the steps to the Venetian, he was starting to think it was a bad idea to walk. The desert air should be good for him, but he felt as if a sock was stuck in his throat. As he climbed the God-awful steps one at a time, sweat poured from every pore. Even with all his discomfort, he had a point to make, and arriving in his present state to meet with Jack Bellow for the first time was pivotal. But still, Enrique couldn't help but think how ironic it would be for him to croak in front of a casino with the knowledge he carried. Alone.

By the time he got to the lobby he was officially late. After mopping his face and arms and catching his breath, he made his way to the TAO Lounge. Enrique stepped in the door and all heads turned to see the walking dead man. There was a tall gentleman in his late thirties standing near the windows, the only one with a smile. Jack Bellow.

Enrique walked slowly toward Jack, carefully navigating the tables and eyes and whispers. *Unbelievable, the likeness is amazing except for length and color of the hair;* he thought, realizing *Gilgamesh* had been thirty years ago. Jack was a child then. He would remember nothing, and Enrique would leave it that way…for now.

Show me you can do this—you must be ready.

CHAPTER EIGHT

"I just don't think immortality is possible."
Sherwin Nuland
Professor of Surgery, Yale

"I am working on immortality."
M. Rose
Prof. of Evolutionary Biology, UCI

The gorgeous waitress stood behind Enrique in all her splendor. After Jack and Enrique shook hands and exchanged pleasantries, she tapped his shoulder and he stepped aside. They immediately appreciated her Venetian apparel that left little for the imagination. Following the drink order and flirtatious banter, they enjoyed her magnificent exit. Enrique looked back at Jack and winked. Jack nodded in agreement. The ice was broken.

Jack Bellow had presence. He projected confidence and adventure. Enrique Medino was a very sick man. He looked as if he could die at any moment. The TAO Lounge was ideal for the private discussion in wide-open spaces. They were isolated in one of several intimate conversational niches, each furnished with a teakwood coffee table, a short, red satin sofa with gold piping, and two black and gold striped armchairs. A glass tube, protruding from the ceiling from twenty feet above, delivered soft light that added to the overall sense of privacy.

Jack stood long enough to allow Enrique first choice of comfort. Enrique struggled to get out of his backpack; one complete rotation and he was free. He plopped it onto the coffee table and sat on the edge of the sofa with his knees spread like a kid sitting on a bucket at a fishing hole. Jack returned to his armchair and picked up the remains of the drink he had been nursing. Enrique fumbled through papers, pamphlets and spiral notebooks that he had squirreled away in his backpack. Jack watched patiently. They smiled politely. For that brief remaining moment, they would both gather their first impressions that would prove to be most important later.

"I hope it was not too difficult for you to get here, Dr. Medino," said Jack. He knew he'd have to work to hide how stunned he was by Medino's deteriorating health—a walking skeleton. The cancer had taken him over, the battle in year-two of a three-year prognosis; pancreatic cancer was one of the worst.

Enrique, perched on the edge of the sofa, was pulling papers from his backpack as if each was a wonderful surprise. His shiny white head was sparsely populated with long strands of unruly black and gray hair that he was determined to keep until they were taken from him by the disease. His head was halfway inside the backpack when he spoke.

"Please, let's go by first names." He popped out with a smile and a crumpled piece of paper. "All this doctor stuff and etiquette really means very little to me anymore. I have wasted time on the wrong things; titles, recognitions, being polite to people I don't like, wearing a tie…you know what I mean?"

"My sentiments exactly," Jack said with a smile. They shared a short laugh. The drinks arrived; Scotch for Jack, a fruit drink with a strawberry and little umbrella for Enrique. In silence they clicked their glasses and with polite appreciation watched their Venetian beauty depart once again—making no secret of how she loved putting on a show.

Enrique began. "Jack, please allow me to start with an obvious update. Since we last spoke on the phone, my wealthy oncologist has advised that I have one year or so left to crawl around on this planet, assuming I have some success with the treatment regimen provided for my kind of cancer."

"Enrique, I'm really sorry to hear that." *He goes right to the tough stuff and tells the truth, no sugar coating,* Jack thought.

"Yes, so was I." Enrique stirred his drink with the ridiculously tiny straw as he watched Jack's reaction to his news. "I hope your investigation of me was as enjoyable as I found yours. I was impressed with your many successes as an entrepreneur in the biotech field."

"It was, and I try…thank you for noticing, Enrique."

"Yes. You are surprisingly successful at the ripe age of thirty-five. I still have lab coats older than you."

"I have been fortunate…good genes, I guess," Jack said with a cordial smile.

"As a geneticist and physician, I would agree. Saying you have 'good genes' is possibly a more accurate observation than you realize at the moment." Enrique sipped his drink through the silly straw, his nose in his glass.

He pulled another wad of crumpled papers from the backpack and un-balled them with a confident smile. "Your resumé is quite impressive too. Thank you for sending it to me." He flipped to the last page of the stapled mess. Jack got a kick out of the coffee stains on his expensive stationery, *lab geeks are all alike…you got to love them.* Jack noticed scribbled notes on the back, a molecular structure with labeling at the intersections, chemical bonds, a three-dimensional octagon with a double helix spiral through the center and protruding at both ends of the octagon, difficult to read the label in bold print. The reddish-brown stain could have been old ketchup or new pizza.

"I see here you did your undergraduate work at Yale, got your MBA at Harvard School of Business and then went for your Ph.D. at Stanford in operations, information and technology. Was that last one helpful in running your companies?" asked Enrique.

"I probably could have stopped with the MBA but the opportunity presented when I was bringing up a company on the west coast. At the time, I was encountering operational challenges in the emerging markets: Brazil, Russia, India and China. The time was right to gather a few more weapons for future battles. I guess the short answer is yes and no." They both smiled.

"Your ventures have taken you into several biotech areas: orthopedics, cardiovascular, neurological, plastic surgery, transfusion medicine and some oncology. I like the versatility." Enrique's eyes were sharp even though his body was not.

Jack was uncomfortable talking about himself. He preferred to focus on less personal things like business opportunity. However, he was sensitive to the importance of letting others get comfortable their way. At the moment he was interviewing for a technology opportunity probably more than Enrique was interviewing for a business partner.

"Thank you, Enrique. I've been moving fast most of my life, always able to learn quickly. The sciences grabbed me at ten and I stayed with it for the next twenty-six years. Along the way, the business bug bit me. I merged my interests. I see *biology* as a perfect science and *technology* as an imperfect effort—and probably the place where I could make a difference."

"I see you had success with four companies you formed over the last fifteen years."

"Yes. Those successes were possible because of good people and good ideas." Jack waved to their waitress, who was bending over a nearby table, revealing her most bountiful breasts. Jack smiled with the appropriate appreciation then held up two fingers. She returned a playful kiss with a mischievous smile and swung her hips toward the bar with a suggestive thrust. Jack winked, *nicely done.* He looked back at Enrique, who was staring at him with a benevolent smile.

"Are you involved with these companies today, Jack?"

"I've sold two and consult as a contract courtesy. It's unlikely they will seek my guidance since I am now a potential competitor. I gave my third company to the management team and serve on their board; a good group of people. My fourth company went public against my wishes, a hostile takeover by investors. After the IPO, I exercised my options and exited."

"Number four sounds a little messy."

"Let's say I learned some new tricks from some greedy investors, people who will never have enough money or control."

"I see." Enrique stared awkwardly and fidgeted with papers in his backpack.

Jack saw the distress in his eyes, a look he'd seen before, among brilliant scientists outside of their laboratory. Enrique was a sick man with a big secret and Jack was as curious as a kid on Christmas morning.

"Would it be helpful for me to expand?" Jack asked.

"Would you? I know my way around the laboratory but the corporate world is a mystery." Enrique leaned forward.

"And your world will forever be a mystery to me. But those two realities are important because that is why it all works."

"It is?" Enrique leaned even closer.

"Everything begins with a breakthrough. Without people like you, people like me have nothing to do. And your breakthrough has no value until it successfully moves from *concept to practice.* Without people like me, your baby could die, be stolen or be lost forever."

Enrique pushed his backpack to the side so nothing was between him and Jack. "In the laboratory, I search for solutions to problems. I begin with a hypothesis and I test it in a controlled environment. When I step out of the lab, I see chaos, uncontrolled variables everywhere."

"In business, we learn how to operate with most things out of our control."

"And this is what makes me nervous."

"I understand. But that is how the world functions. We engage human resources that are variables. We have production processes that are variable. Regulatory hurdles are always moving and markets and distribution around the world change constantly."

"My feelings are correct, yes?"

"Not completely. If we have game-changing technology, we not only have the variables, but we also face the greatest obstacles."

"That is going the wrong way, Jack."

"Game-changing technology threatens to make obsolete the most entrenched interests in the world, the established profit streams. Battle lines are drawn. The market leaders will do ANYTHING to hold their positions."

"This will be a problem." Enrique slouched back on the sofa.

"There are sharks in my world. They are big and they are always circling the entrepreneur boat. The killer sharks are the corporations with business risk. And there are the private interests of investors and governments."

"Sometimes my lab seems to be the safest place to be…I have heard the stories. How would you get my idea to market in this world?"

"If your discovery is a game-changer, I would assess the market opportunity, identify and nullify the associated risks, build protection and optimize control. If we do all of those right, profits will be beyond your wildest dreams.

"I am speaking in very broad terms. At the moment, I have no idea what you have accomplished. You may have something intriguing with little value to the marketplace. A game-changer must be relevant to have value."

"I see." He spoke with his eyes closing and opening.

"Enrique, are you…" Jack watched him close his eyes. He would let him rest for a while. His complexion was chalky. His tissue-paper-thin skin displayed roadmaps of red and blue capillaries and rainbow bruising. His leg and arm muscles were emaciated, hanging on the bones. He was retaining fluids in his ankles and calves—congestive heart failure. His abdomen was bloated on an otherwise skeletal body. Enrique could die today!

■ ■ ■

His eyes were not completely closed. He could see Jack assessing his physical condition.

You are smart enough medically to know my systems are beginning to fail. You're wondering if this sick guy is going to be around much longer. Should you invest time, money, your name and life in some concept or discovery when this guy is heading out of the picture? Yes, you should. You have always been my first choice, even though I had to test the waters with our government. I never expected them to come through all the red tape and clandestine crap. I think you have seen enough. It's time to set the hook. I'll pull you into the boat come December, only six months out…which I will need. Enrique opened his eyes and sat up.

"Well, thank you for that short nap. I hope it was not too rude."

"Not a problem at all, Enrique."

"And thank you for taking time to educate another scientist on the modern business world."

"I hope I was helpful."

"May I ask what you know about my world…Anti-aging Medicine?"

"I would qualify as a humble student."

"Can you give me a sense of your knowledge base in the field?"

"Sure. I have read a great deal about Anti-aging and life-extension; the 1976 Gordon/Kurtzman book, *No More Dying, the Conquest of Aging and the Extension of Human Life, The Life Extension Revolution* by Saul Kent,

1980, and Roy Walford's 1983 book, *Maximum Lifespan.* I took a look at Harman's research on the free radical theory of aging and longevity. I enjoyed Kenyon's study on manipulation of the daf2 gene that doubled the lifespan of a roundworm; fascinating. *The Prospect of Immortality* by Robert Ettinger was also an excellent read. I have looked at the Anti-aging industry, talked with geneticists, evolutionists and molecular biologists. I have only read about a third of the scientific publications and peer reviewed papers."

"What is your early conclusion from your journey, Jack?"

"Today, I see opportunity in genetic engineering and stem cell research. I would hold off on nanotechnology, cryogenics, brain emulation or therapeutic cloning, too early stage for me, although there could be a breakthrough at any moment to change all that.

"I was pleasantly surprised to learn most molecular and cell biologists believe the turning point is near, a trigger being when we learn what most of our genes are doing and the proteins they produce. Once we get there, lifespan extension would be a reasonable expectation."

Jack leaned forward. "And the work of David Sinclair is interesting; the possibility of the chemical *resveratrol* activating the SIRT1 gene is exciting."

"Some believe the SIRTI gene is involved in controlling lifespan. So you are impressed with David Sinclair?" Enrique watched him think…a genius for sure.

"Intrigued may be a better word. I like what I've read about his work and believe they are onto something…

"My instincts tell me Aubrey de Grey is the man to bet on. The Cambridge University geneticist is a true visionary. His proposal in the late 1990s seemed to be the appropriate research goal: *Strategies for Engineered Negligible Senescence*, development of regenerative medical procedures to repair age-related damage to maintain youth. As a business man and novice in the field, I have a gut feeling this should be the common thread that can unite efforts."

"Did you know the average human lifespan in the 1600s was thirty years of age?"

"No," said Jack.

"Today it is seventy-six. In four hundred years we have extended the average lifespan 250 percent. In the 1600s, getting sick and dying at the age of thirty was considered normal. It was death by natural causes."

"I don't believe people knew much about bacteria, contamination or infection. They probably did not eat properly either." Jack held his empty glass up and kept his eyes on Enrique.

"Actually, the primary killer was contaminated water. The separation of drinking water from sewage was a real problem back then."

"You would think doing that would be obvious."

"You grew up in a world with safe drinking water, refrigeration, vaccinations, antibiotics, sterilization, surgery, blood transfusion, vitamins, preventive medicine and much more. From the perspective of people in the 1600s, they could not begin to imagine a world with those things. Their friends and families died around the age of thirty, so they figured they would too. That was THEIR normal."

"And we are doing it again, aren't we?"

"Homo sapiens, bipedal primates, human beings...we are not complicated creatures." Enrique spoke as he looked past this world with a magnanimous gaze.

"The older I get, the more I can appreciate those words." In those few seconds, Jack got a glimpse of a man who had been where no others had gone.

Enrique refocused. He gathered his papers and jammed them into his backpack, his process not affecting his train of thought. "You would think we could learn from the past. People in the twenty-first century are as narrow-minded as those in the seventeenth century. Today, we are convinced getting old and dying like Grandma and Grandpa is the natural process...the way of the world...can't talk them out of it."

He closed the clasp on his backpack and perched on the edge of the sofa. Their eyes locked, both with their private thoughts. Enrique put his hands together like the Pope before a blessing. "Maybe we believe things are inevitable today because we just don't have the capacity to know better."

"I'm a little confused. Are you ending our meeting?"

"You will need some time." Enrique gripped his backpack with both hands.

"Time for what…?" Jack expected at least a peek, a snippet, something.

"Time for what I am about to say, Jack."

"Enrique, I'm a big boy. I can handle a rejection."

Enrique leaned forward, waving for Jack to meet him over the teakwood table. With faces inches apart he whispered, "I can stop the aging process." He looked around the TAO Lounge and said in a softer whisper, "…and I can reverse it, too."

Jack was frozen. He showed no sign of comprehension. Enrique had seen that vacant stare before, in the mirror the day of his discovery, the day he realized he had discovered a biogenic secret. Cellular immortality could change everything.

"I will show you what no man has seen." Enrique got to his feet and strapped on his backpack. He put his hand on Jack's shoulder and looked into his vacant eyes. "You will need time to process the significance of my discovery and how you would take such a find into your shark infested world. If you agree to be my partner, we will meet on December 8, in Memphis. That is six months away. Set it up and let me know. If I don't hear from you…well, I will assume this venture is not right for you."

"I agree…I will."

He watched the dying cancer patient navigate a path out of the TAO lounge doubtful the good doctor could survive the rest of the day, much less six more months.

Jack drank scotch until 2:00 a.m. The gorgeous waitress in the skimpy outfit hoped for a date, but he was in another world, his mind running wild.

If Dr. Enrique Medino accomplished what he had claimed, the world would never be the same. I would commercialize the most significant breakthrough since the first creatures crawled from the seas and walked upright.

Could it be? My God…could it?

CHAPTER NINE

"There are many, many different components of aging;
we are chipping away at all of them."
Robert Freitas
Inst. Molecular Manufacturing

8 December 2004

In six months, Jack Bellow and Enrique Medino would meet a second time in Memphis. There would be detailed discussions on the biotech breakthrough and *proof of concept* with verifiable laboratory results acceptable to a body of his peers. Enrique would separate "known" from "remaining unknowns" and provide estimations of time to resolution with a statistical analysis of probability for success. The process was a minimal requirement to validate the technical aspects of the opportunity.

The analysis would be a deep-dive review of stand-alone strengths and range of opportunities, critical pathways to markets and a preliminary outline addressing product development, regulatory hurdles, commercialization, key risks and anticipated capital requirements. Only then could corporate structure and ownership be negotiated. Depending on the assessments, only then could the decision to work together be made. Jack had been through the process a hundred times.

He made all arrangements and to his surprise received confirmation from Dr. Medino. He was still alive! They were to meet at the Crescent Club in east Memphis at 7:00 p.m. Jack was an hour early, standing in the bar looking out the window with his second bourbon and water. He tried to manage his excitement. Time always dulled the senses; it was too good to be true.

"Excuse me, Sir, is anyone sitting there?" asked the stranger pointing to the table next to Jack. After six months, he'd considered the ramifications of an immortal society: economics, politics, energy requirements, food, housing, education, transportation and more. How would life be valued or devalued? Would punishment for killing an immortal be an eternal life sentence? Could the planet support a population that only grew? If so, for how long and what might be the trade-offs and consequences?

Jack turned from the window, slightly irritated by the interruption. A well-dressed man stood a few feet away, unfamiliar, a new club member or guest. Out of habit, Jack quickly screened new people into one of two categories, friend or waste of time. This man was a polished professional, mid-forties, nice tan and athletic build with a shaved head and excellent shades, a very popular look for the premature balding guys nowadays. Jack picked-up on the expensive *Brooks Brothers* suit, diamond cufflinks and silk designer tie. He concluded the man was a financial guy, maybe a banker or stockbroker, and certainly a potential future investor—friend category, of course; Jack would be gracious. "I'm sorry, did you say something?"

The stranger was pointing to the vacant table and vacant chairs next to Jack. "I'm so sorry to disturb you, Sir. Is this your table? Or may I have it?" he asked with a pleasant smile.

Jack heard the words and saw the lips moving, but his heart and mind had already returned to that other place; he could not stop thinking about Enrique's last words at the TAO Lounge: *I can stop the aging process...I can reverse it, too.* If that was true, nothing would be the same. Virtually everything and everyone in the world would be impacted in some way. The search for the "fountain of youth" had been going on since man realized his mortality. Had Enrique truly found it?

Jack had left Las Vegas and continued his marathon research. He wanted to know all he could about the state of the art of Anti-aging Medicine. He was astounded by the enormous body of credible science that openly anticipated significant extension of the human lifespan. He learned that many already recognized the feasibility of immortality. The leaders in the field believed the human genome was close to being fully understood because of advanced computers and the merging of the biosciences.

"Sir, I can see I have disturbed you. I am sorry; why don't I just sit somewhere else." He turned and started to walk away.

Jack came out of his world and politely grabbed the gentleman's arm. "Please, I am sorry. I had something on my mind, please excuse me." Jack smiled as the man turned back to face him. Obviously, he was a weightlifter, with biceps hard as a rock.

"I don't have a table. This one can certainly be for your party," Jack said, as he turned from the window to move to the bar.

"Jack, it is good to see you again."

Jack stopped and turned. He never forgot a face—he thought. "Do I know you?" Jack asked, as he went through his mental *Facebook*.

"Oh, yes. You know me. We met in Las Vegas."

Still drawing a blank, "I am sorry and embarrassed. Please accept my apology. I must be having a senior moment. What company are you with?" Jack asked with greater curiosity.

The stranger walked up to Jack. "I am not with a company, yet. I was hoping maybe you and I could do business together...Jack Bellow."

Silence, the stranger smiling...Jack's puzzled face turned white. He forgot to breathe; his vessels constricted and blood left his head. Jack's heart pounded louder than the muffled sounds in the bar. The room was darker—Jack was leaving for a while.

The stranger had no trouble holding the six-foot-four, two-hundred-thirty pound man as he slid a chair under his butt. Jack's knees buckled and he collapsed onto the seat. The stranger stayed while help arrived. He held Jack's shoulders to the back of the chair. Jack's head hung like a rag doll, his glassy eyes dilated.

"I'm sorry to do this to you," he whispered. "But it had to be this way." Jack's eyes rolled back. He was gone.

"We don't have a lot of time."

■ ■ ■

"The finitude of human life is a blessing for every human individual."
Leon Kass
President Bush's Council on Bioethics

"There is no known social good coming from the conquest of death."
Daniel Callahan
Bioethicist, Hastings Centre

Jack was breathing normally. He lifted his head like a prizefighter after the knockout blow, color returning to his face. He looked to the man that kept him from falling. "Promise me you won't ever do that again...Dr. Medino."

They both smiled and then laughed. Both understood the significance of the moment. "Now that I have your attention, I can make that promise." Enrique winked and patted Jack on his cheek like a son. "Let's get a steak. I'm famished."

Enrique helped Jack to his feet and they went to the dining room. He ordered steaks. He would give Jack more time to process—the miracle.

Did you? Jack thought. *Did you find what every man has thought about in his life? Some have searched but all have dreamed? Did you find a way to stop the biological clock?*

It was the night he spent with Galileo, Newton, Pasteur, Edison or Einstein. If Enrique Medino had truly discovered immortality he was the greatest man to ever live. Jack had to know more.

"Enrique, I am ready to learn. I have seen my first miracle…but what exactly am I seeing? What are your discoveries? How did you get here?"

Medino sipped ice water and transformed; eyes sharpened and face tightened with disciplined focus as he opened the door of his complex world. Like a lion trainer, he seemed to command the elusive answers that he had pursued throughout a lifetime. They were now under his control but still trying to escape.

"In 1984, after a decade of genetic testing with stem cells and somatic cells, I formulated a compound-mixture with a singular goal: stabilizing the human cellular environment to optimize the protection of DNA and the replication process. I called my compound-mixture *Life2*."

"A compound-mixture?" asked Jack.

"Yes. A compound is a material in which atoms of different elements are held together chemically and cannot be separated. A mixture combines two or more materials without chemical reaction and can be separated back to the original components. *Life2* is a combination."

"I see."

"*Life2* is a complex formulation, fourteen elements compounded and a three-component mixture, each ingredient with a specific purpose.

"The TGO-STASIS program was an assessment tool I created. Each *Life2* element performed as expected, but combined, the outcomes were all over the board. I needed to assess 3,457 formula variations to have a chance at achieving my combined objectives…a chance…a long shot."

"I assume you ran formula variations against likely outcomes and the computer spit out 3,457 compound-mixtures, correct?" asked Jack.

"Yes, exactly. The program model took a year to build. The specialized somatic cell testing program began. *Life2-mod-1* was my first…only 3,456 to go."

"And you still might be a million miles away from a desired result."

"Exactly…so is the life of a researcher." They laughed at the conundrum.

"This summer I was alone in my lab on campus, a perfect time to load my most recent test data. I used the Vanderbilt mainframe because it was big, fast and secured. After analyses, I download, save and then delete."

"Thank God," said Jack.

"That night I loaded *Life2-mod-2777* data into the TGO-STASIS model; same procedure as always, but this time something odd happened."

"Something odd?"

"Something new; the twelve-somatic-test-panels showed robust cell replication in all sectors, including the S-panels and X-panels."

"And that means?"

"The S-panels are senescence cells and the X-panels are expired cells. The *Life2-mod-2777* formulation worked on all somatic cell types. It also worked in the worst case conditions, cells dying and dead."

"Is that when you knew you were there?"

"No. I conducted routine audits, resampled and retested a dozen times. The *Life2-mod-2777* formulation always gave the same results. It performed perfectly for all 4P12S areas."

"Ok…and 4P12S areas are what?"

"I'm sorry, Jack. I had to create a language. '4P' denotes four primary areas important to protecting DNA and optimizing the cellular environment for continuous replication: Telomere Maintenance, Oxidative Stress Reduction, Glycation and Helix Supercoiling."

Life2777 resurrected the earlier state cellular environment? I will need to go back to school to fully appreciate what you are doing." Jack waved off the wine. "Scotch on the rocks with a twist, please."

Medino smiled. "I'll give you the basic foundation to navigate tonight."

"Please do."

"We are composed of billions of somatic cells. They are diverse and specialized. Over our lifetime most are replaced several times. Skin, hair and blood cells are replaced continuously. Heart, liver and kidney cells are replaced thousands of times. Brain cells are never replaced—we have all we are going to get when we are born."

"I understand the process is necessary for our survival since we need to move out damaged and malfunctioning cells."

"Yes, it is accomplished by cell replication, mitosis. In the last ten minutes, we replaced 50,000 cells. At the moment, I am replacing cells much faster than you." They smiled at the extraordinary significance of his simple statement.

Enrique fidgeted with his linen napkin as he spoke, folding and unfolding it with great care between thoughts. "I had very basic questions when I started. Why can one somatic cell live longer than another? Why do they reach a point where they can no longer keep up? If the heart cell could be replaced as often as a skin cell, would hearts be stronger...longer?"

"Enrique, I think the logical answer to that question is yes."

"I agree. That would be the logical answer. With that thinking in mind, in the beginning I had to settle on key, critical assumptions and then constructed my hypothesis. That is what we call scientific method."

"I understand."

"Number one critical assumption: the *earliest* genetic environment in any somatic cell line is an ideal environment for the protection of DNA and the replication process."

"Ok."

"Number two critical assumption: *earlier* genetic environment in any somatic cell line has more lifespan and provides best performance."

"Yes…and your hypothesis?" asked Jack.

"The resurrection and maintenance of an earlier genetic environment for any somatic cell line will extend lifespan and optimize performance of the cell, tissue, organ and organism."

"You have just defined the somatic cells of a newborn," said Jack.

"Exactly. To be immortal, the objective is to maintain the biology of birth."

"Such a daunting task."

"I found in my research that sometimes stimulating the CREATION of that ideal cellular environment was possible, but other times LOCATION of the youngest cell environment in the area was sufficient."

"Quick question: does the accumulation of replication variances over a lifetime have anything to do with disease and degenerative conditions, aging and death?" Jack held his cup as the waiter poured the coffee. While watching Enrique he stirred a spoonful of sugar…no more scotch.

"I think to some extent, but it is more complex."

"What exactly does *Life2777* do?" Jack loosened his tie and leaned closer.

"It stimulates the natural cellular biology to restore and maintain telomeres. It tightens the DNA double helix coil. It repels free radicals and blocks glucose molecules from damaging DNA. This appears to be enough. *Life2777* seems to stop the dominos from falling."

"Incredible, Enrique."

"*Life2777* launches a life extending biogenic process."

"I understand."

"Jack, we must keep my personal use of *Life2777* between us until we have accomplished our business objectives."

"Enrique, how is that possible? The incredible change in your physical condition is visible to all; it is a miracle. People you know will see right away," Jack said.

"Yes, it is a miracle. That is how my progress is being rationalized today. Remember, the traditional healthcare practices do produce miracles every day. I am a traditional miracle that happened to beat pancreatic cancer. Oh yes, I diet and work out religiously too."

"Does your wife buy it…your family and friends, and how about your oncologist, do they all buy it?" Jack whispered as he put his napkin on the table.

"Yes. They all do. There is no other explanation."

"Actually, I am pleased to hear this, because over the months since we last met, I've come to understand that the ability to turn back or slow down the genetic clock must stay under wraps for many reasons."

"Where do we go from here?" Enrique looked at his watch and then around the room. No one was in earshot…which was good.

"You move into my place and we work night and day."

"My bag is in the car." Enrique started to stand but Jack waved him back down.

"Enrique, everyone will come after us. Our government could justify taking your life extension discovery—a national security risk…other companies…and more."

"I remember when President Clinton announced that the human genome sequences could not be patented after several companies poured millions into R&D to get a protected position. Later the *UCSC Genome*

Bioinformatics Group released the first working draft of the human genome to the entire world on the *Internet*." Medino was flustered. He patted the sweat from his forehead and leaned back with the eyes of a helpless man fearful of being robbed.

"As a businessman I will never forget it. The NASDAQ biotechnology sector lost $50 billion market cap in two days. A lot of U.S. companies and investors lost millions. I guess I never thought about what the scientists…the discoverers…lost."

"Our trust."

"Enrique, I promise you that your discovery will not be stolen. I have had six months to think about that, and I am pretty good when I focus."

■ ■ ■

"Most people who enjoy life can't get enough of it.
Those who claim they don't want to live longer than 'natural'
will go to the ends of the earth to cure themselves of cancer, heart disease and
injuries when they get stricken. Modern drugs, surgical techniques and
diagnostic tools are life extension technologies that few refuse."
Unknown

They would spawn the most powerful, evolutionary tsunami on the planet since fire. By the end of January, Jack would be up-to-speed on all relevant aspects of the Medino's life extension breakthrough. He would know the range of applications from least earth-shaking to most magnificent potential—all critical for the development of the strategic plans; there would be two—a published and a private.

Jack would engineer a most masterful business plan to protect and introduce to the world market unprecedented life-extending medical treatments. They would be prepared for hostile takeover attempts from threatened corporations, private interests, governments and covert operations. They would expect offensive strikes as soon as word got out. The incursions would be aggressive and sustained. Knowledge of the new science would turn anyone into a potential enemy. The risk of losing the technology was great; the risk of losing their lives, greater.

Enrique moved into Jack's penthouse that night. They were together every waking moment for the next eight weeks. Jack's place was atop the Exchange Building in Downtown Memphis. The private elevator opened on the twelfth floor to a spacious reception area: ten-foot ceilings, cream walls with modern art, white sofas and plush arm chairs, brass lamps and large plants next to a half dozen windows with a panoramic view of the Mississippi River and Memphis skyline.

Behind the reception desk was an impenetrable glass wall running the width of the floor. On the other side, the walls were populated with awards, recognitions, issued patents and capitalization events, a half billion raised. Passage through the thick glass doors was electronically controlled and laser protected. Beyond the office suite on the west side of the building were Jack's well-appointed living quarters. He would give Enrique the east half of the twelfth floor for his Memphis office and residence. A condo in Nashville would be his primary home; there would be continuing R&D at his farm in east Davidson County.

On December 21, 2004, two companies were formed; the *Life2 Corporation* and *BelMed Research, LLC*. Bellow and Medino equally shared ownership of both. By January 31, 2005, Medino would retire from Vanderbilt University Medical School and Bellow would exit all other business interests.

As agreed, Jack invested $10 million and would serve as the president and chief executive officer of both companies. Enrique transferred all intellectual property to *BelMed* and would serve as the chief technology officer and medical director, All research and development would be conducted at the secured complex on his farm in Davidson County, outside of Nashville. The *Life2 Corporation*, headquartered in Memphis, Tennessee at the downtown Exchange Building, would release Series A Preferred Stock to raise $50 million in working capital. The investor meeting was scheduled for March 15 in Memphis.

Sometime in January 2005, a meeting was held in Destin, Florida. Seven high net-worth medical technology investors were covertly alerted to the formation of two biotechnology corporations by the world renowned entrepreneur, Jack Bellow, and an unknown molecular biologist and geneticist from Vanderbilt, Dr. Enrique Medino. They thought it odd a man dying of pancreatic cancer had interests in forming two biotech companies. Even more curious was that Jack Bellow had invested $10,000,000 of his own money. Jack never used his own money!

The sharks were hundreds of miles away, but they smelled blood in the water.

March 1, 2005

Dear Prospective Investors,

Through the *Whiterock Bank of America* (or WBA), *Life2 Corporation* (or the COMPANY) is offering 10,000,000 of our shares of Series A Preferred Stock, solely to accredited investors, as defined under Rule 501 under the Securities Act of 1933, at a purchase price of $(___) per share. We reserve the right to increase or decrease the number of shares of Series A Preferred Stock, to approve or disapprove each investor and accept or reject any subscription in whole or in part, in our sole discretion.

The *Life2 Corporation* cordially invites you to attend a meeting with the Founders and Executive Management March 15, 2005. You will join a select group of private investors at the Crescent Club for a presentation of the company and discussion of the investment opportunity that will close April 1, 2005 at 5:00 p.m. CST.

The company was formed in December 2004 to enhance the quality of the human life experience through the development of innovative solutions. On February 15, 2005 the *Life2 Corporation* entered into an agreement with a proprietary Research Group obtaining the exclusive rights to develop and commercialize a non-invasive biotech solution for the treatment of osteoarthritis, the number one degenerative condition affecting an aging world population.

The *Ossi2™* product received CE Mark, cleared for European commercialization later this year, and the PMA-IDE application has been approved by the FDA with clinical studies in the U.S. scheduled to begin the first quarter of 2006. The *Ossi2™* product has been shown to restore articular cartilage in six months for level one and two osteoarthritis patients.

The investor meeting will be at the Westin Room at the Crescent Club in east Memphis. The reception will begin at 5:00, the business meeting at 6:00 p.m. and adjourn at 7:00 p.m. with founders and management team available until 9:00 p.m. (Schedule Enclosed)

Tiff Hansen, Executive Vice President of *Life2*, Inc. will contact you personally to arrange delivery of the *Life2* Private Placement Memorandum (PPM), or to remove you from the list of selected investors at this time.

Jack Bellow

President/CEO

CHAPTER TEN

15 March 2005

In one hour, $23 billion would be represented by those around the polished walnut conference table in the Westin Room at the Crescent Club, three months after Bellow and Medino formed the *Life2 Corporation* and right on schedule for the $50 million needed for the first phase of their veiled business plan. They would offer twenty-five percent of the company to a select group of high-net-worth, private investors. There was no room for institutional or venture capital money—which came with shark teeth. No time to play.

The *Life2* Series A Preferred Stock Offering would close quickly. Invitations to the dance were successful; the six targets were coming and some political trash tagging along. Jack was the master at managing investor motivation. Someone had to believe enough for everyone else; only then would immeasurable risks be taken.

Bluff City Butcher

Investors	Net Assets	Subscriptions	Goal
Albert Bell, Jr.	$12 Billion	$03 Million	$10 Million
David F. Jones	$05 Billion	$02 Million	$10 Million
Rudolph Kohl	$03 Billion	$10 Million	$05 Million
Henry Bishop	$01 Billion	$15 Million	$05 Million
Glenn B. Johns	$01 Billion	$15 Million	$05 Million
L.D.Fleming	$01 Billion	$05 Million	$05 Million
	$23 Billion	$50 Million	$40 Million
Timothy Loman	$30 Million	$02 Million	Reject
Charles Dunn	$20 Million	$02 Million	Reject
Nicolas Heller	$10 Million	$01 Million	Reject
	$60 Million	$05 Million	$0
Management			
Jack Bellow	$250 Million	$10 Million	Pass
Tiff Hansen	$50 Million	$05 Million	$05 Million
Dennis Glaser	$35 Million	$05 Million	$05 Million
Enrique Medino	$10 Million	$01 Million	Pass
	$345 Million	$21 Million	$10 Million

Their primary objective was to look like every other medical startup business with an understandably narrow focused technology. Rather than launch "LIFE-EXTENSION" day one and lose control, *Life2* would solve one medical problem that was interesting and lucrative enough to attract $50 million without the deep dive investor inquisition. Only Jack and Enrique knew the money raised would be used to put in place the strategic infrastructure and controls for the ultimate global release of the most significant discovery of all time. On this night, billionaires expected Bellow to oversell an unproven but promising orthopedic technology.

They would begin with heavy hors d'oeuvres and abundant alcoholic beverages to stimulate the standard business rituals: enthusiastic greetings, artful mingling, positioning and anticipation. The agenda would be predictable. Jack would welcome investors, introduce the company, talk about the technology and explain how it fit unmet needs. He would sell the investment opportunity and introduce Enrique Medino. Like all scientific gurus, Medino would speak to investors from the stratosphere; they would smile and not understand a word. Later, Jack would translate and drill down the PPM.

At the end, the corporate attorney would remind investors that all preceding information may be untrue and should be disregarded or interpreted at their sole discretion, and all forward-looking statements are subject to change, and best efforts may not be enough to avoid catastrophic losses.

By 8:00 p.m., $50 million was committed and only two sharks got in the pool.

PART THREE
FOUR PATHS CONVERGE
2008

CHAPTER ELEVEN

5 November 2008

"Gentlemen, thank you for coming again; a lot has happened since our August meeting. It appears Adam has a growing interest in me and my family. I do believe this fellow is working up to killing all of us."

Albert unfolded a handkerchief, touched his forehead and placed it on the edge of the desk. "We are only in November and there are two more killings—Panther McGee and Raymond Munson—that seem related. Tony has a half dozen, Elliott thirty or more and Carol Mason has found a dozen and is just getting started with the collaboration. Seems to be gaining momentum. I asked you here because it is time to share all the pieces of the puzzle that I have."

Elliott and Tony have been waiting for this moment. Revelations from the August meeting established the fact that Albert has had a twenty-five year history with the Bluff City Butcher. What does he know?

"I asked Max for help on what I thought was a personal matter. We met first in July and then again in September. His findings took him to Carrollton, Texas, north of Dallas, where they uncovered startling information. I want you two to have this. Max, please…"

"Albert, we have not spoken since my report. Is everything on the table?"

"Yes, Max…everything."

"Ok." He downed his drink, walked to the popping fire and lit a cigarette. After a few puffs he tossed his match and turned to Elliott and Tony. "In July, Albert asked me to locate a woman from his past, a Miss Betty Duncan." Max looked for the words that could minimize embarrassment, but Albert would have none of it and jumped right in.

"I had an affair in El Paso with Betty Duncan, December 1967, through February 1968. At the time, I had been separated from my wife for twelve years. Before the final divorce papers were signed there was a reconciliation. Please, continue, Max."

Elliott and Tony showed no reaction to the exchange.

"Albert went to El Paso in April 1968, to properly end his relationship with Miss Duncan. Before he could speak she informed him that she was pregnant. Albert's news regarding the recent change in his marital status was disappointing but accepted. Shortly thereafter, Miss Duncan disappeared and all efforts to locate her were unsuccessful. My firm learned Miss Duncan gave birth to a boy in Pecos and eventually relocated to Carrollton, Texas. She married Harry Tucker in 1972, and lived at the Silver Horseshoe Mobile Home Park.

"Something terrible happened in 1982, still unresolved. Betty, her alleged husband Harry, a Texas Ranger and friend of the family, Ken Stahl, and Betty's son disappeared. All personal belongings were left behind except the son's clothing. According to the police report, Tucker's pickup truck and the Texas Ranger's vehicles were gone.

"I flew to Dallas last week and met with the Carrollton police to go over the case file. Since we're talking about something twenty-six years ago, none of the homicide boys that worked it were around anymore."

"Get anything?" asked Tony.

"The filed police report said the property was cleaned up. The inside of the mobile home was like an operating room; been washed ceiling to tiles with Clorox and water…still in the bucket under the sink. And the dirt around the mobile home had been raked…only a few footprints and zero tire tracks."

"And the exact date they went missing?" asked Elliott calmly.

"October 17, 1982."

Tony sat up.

"I know that is an important date to you gentlemen, but there is more. Last week my team went out to sweep every square inch of the property with the most sophisticated equipment available. All hell broke loose when our people got under that mobile home; we picked up on something and started digging. Five feet down we came to the top of a skull…it was time to call the Dallas County Medical Examiner's Office. They worked it like an archeological dig and uncovered three skeletons."

"Do we have them identified?" asked Tony.

Max lit another Chesterfield and talked with smoke coming out of his nose and mouth. "I got the report from the Carrollton police this morning and just shared it with Albert." He passed around a copy.

"Through dental records, CPD identified Harry Tucker and the Texas Ranger. They were unable to get a positive ID on the third skeleton because they did not have DNA or dental records for Betty Duncan. However, the person put in that hole was a female of medium stature, and early reconstruction work fits Miss Duncan. A review of all missing persons in the region six months on each side of the date came up negative."

I know Gilgamesh has Betty Duncan's DNA. I wonder if they have gotten close to this dig yet, thought Albert.

"Betty's son is unaccounted for to this day. The CPD believe the boy snapped, killed everybody, and ran off."

"Max, show the picture."

"What are we looking at?" asked Elliott.

"This is a Polaroid taken July 4, 1982. Gentlemen, this is Betty Duncan's son. He is fourteen and his name is…Adam."

"Oh, my God…I did not see that coming," said Tony as he studied the kid in the picture. "We are looking at the Bluff City Butcher…the author of your love notes, Albert."

Elliott did not react. "Do we have a cause of death on the three?"

"There were identical puncture fractures on top of each skull."

"I see." Elliott took a closer look at the boy. He saw more than he would share at the moment. His demons were stirring; he had to keep control.

"We interviewed an elderly couple that lived in the mobile park in 1982. They heard about them going missing but didn't know anything. They told us Betty had been raped in 1974 and rarely went out after that. Adam was pretty much abandoned after that. They said he started living under the mobile home; the kid was five. Harry left only to work and buy groceries. Adam was alone except weekends…he went to work with Harry at Sanderson's Meat Processors. Harry was a butcher."

"Holy mother of God!" Tony looked at Elliott. "What else?"

"Adam was kicked out of school October 3, 1982. That was two weeks before he disappeared."

"And what happened at school?" Tony stood up and joined Max at the fireplace.

"Adam attacked a teacher with a knife, cut off his finger."

"I'm not surprised," said Tony staring into the fire.

Max sucked down another Chesterfield and threw the butt where Tony was looking. "I think this last bit of information will answer the rest of your questions."

"Ok, thrill me."

"Adam went after his English teacher…Raymond Munson. Apparently, Adam had a learning disability that went undiagnosed and therefore untreated. He was dyslexic. He struggled all through school because nobody cared enough to notice or evaluate him."

"Damn, the system screwed him," said Tony turning to Elliott.

"When Adam discovered his problem on his own, he blamed his English teacher for not doing his job…for letting him suffer."

Elliott was processing far ahead of the others. He was analyzing Adam's mental stagnation and emotional destruction. With calm focus he asked, "What do you know about his experience at the slaughter house?"

"Tucker took him most weekends, from the age of five to twelve. We met with people retired from Sanderson's. They had no idea that was happening. It broke every rule in the book even back then. They said in the '70s and '80s they processed a hundred head of cattle on a Saturday. Harry Tucker was the one that hung them by their back leg, stunned them and cut their jugulars…exsanguination."

They all sat in silence; the making of a serial killer was laid out in front of them. Adam Duncan was the Bluff City Butcher…And Albert Bell's son.

Adam left Texas October 1982. He started killing in Memphis one year later, thought Elliott. *He knew Albert Bell was his father and Philippé Ramirez was a connection to his 1968 roots. But how did he learn this? And how did he get to Memphis? He was fourteen when he left the mobile home park. Someone helped him clean up, bury the bodies and move the cars. Someone brought him to Memphis.*

Adam was not alone.

Tony's cell vibrated and he stepped out of the room to take the call.

Max took the stuffed chair next to Elliott, who was deep in thought. "What is your opinion of this Bluff City Butcher?" he asked.

Elliott's head was turned away from Max as he stared into the fire. Albert got up and stood next to the desk, crestfallen and with a troubled look.

"The Bluff City Butcher is a physically gifted, psychopathic genius that must kill. He is the most dangerous man I have ever encountered."

"That says a lot, but why the most dangerous?"

"You must understand what we are dealing with. This man is at the very top of the food chain. He is the meanest and smartest beast in the jungle, Max. He is a lion with the brain of Einstein, smarter than his prey, and he needs to kill to feel alive. The Bluff City Butcher has easily killed more than a hundred people and he is just getting started. I am afraid that he is unstoppable."

Tony rushed back into the study. "I've got to go; we have an officer down. It's happening now."

Albert rushed up to him. "Can you tell us anything?"

"High speed chase…they cornered a white van on the bluff." Tony looked directly at Elliott. They both knew who was driving. "It rammed a wall and rolled halfway down. They found one of our guys next to the van, cut up pretty bad, barely holding on. We have people combing the area. The driver of the van is on foot. And there is more…"

"What are you not saying?" Albert held his shoulders, their eyes inches apart.

"Carol Mason was there. She was attacked in the old *Landry's Seafood* parking lot on the bluff. I don't have details except that the attack was five minutes after our guy went down a few blocks away. Albert, her car is torn up bad. My partner had to let me go. I don't think she made it."

"I am going with you." Elliott went out the door first and Tony followed.

■ ■ ■

Carol struggled with the emerging puzzle. *Surely I am not the first to figure this out. Sumner has to be guarding information, and officially Wilcox has to be unresponsive and Albert said he would keep his distance. Do they already know what I have? Could they have even more?*

Working alone had always been her style, but the MPD collaboration was riskier than usual: too many blindsides. If her theory was correct, the psychotic serial predator out there had been around for maybe twenty-five years, outsmarting a lot of people. *If I get closer than the others, the Bluff City Butcher would have plenty of opportunities to kill me. Is it possible he is the one following me? Is that monster the one I could run into sooner or later…maybe even tonight?*

The first day at the *Tribune* she had noticed the old, white van following her. A failed attempt to paint over the Busy Bee Plumbers logo made it stand out. The van was always parked across the street from the *Tribune* in front of a vacant lot. She saw it outside the *Peabody Hotel* on Second Avenue and other places.

Tonight she was in a hurry leaving the *Peabody*. At the valet stand she saw the white van again…idling, dark windows and smoke. She turned away when it registered. Choking on her spit and trying to act natural, she felt a thousand thoughts collide. *Who is in that van? Am I getting too close? Is it the Memphis PD watching me? Is it the serial killer? My God, is the serial killer really the Bluff City Butcher…driving, for God sake?* She had to find out. It was parked in her path out of the *Peabody* driveway. The valet slid to a stop. She got in and adjusted her mirror. The van lights popped on. *"What are you doing? Don't leave yet."* She put her car in gear and circled the courtyard to exit onto Second Avenue; her headlights would point at the van. *Maybe I can flood the cab and see you…whoever you are.* Carol eased up onto the sidewalk from the *Peabody* driveway. The climb was enough to lift her lights into the front seat of the van now three lanes over. *"Oh, my God…!"*

The tires were smoking and screaming. It shot from its space into traffic, clipping two cars. Grabbing anything to write with, Carol pulled up her skirt and scribbled LHK 244 on her leg in scarlet lipstick as she watched three cars get pushed off the road and the van squeezing through and racing past Beale Street. Three squad cars shot by with lights spinning and sirens blaring. Carol got in line. She was in this thing. She would follow close enough for a visual but far enough to be out of the way.

More squad cars converged from all directions as word got out. Carol hung tight behind the first three, her *BMW* flashers suggesting she had a reason to be involved. She turned on her police scanner…the volume was perfect. *I'll just monitor until it's time to bail…*

227…Code 9 …we have a 10-57 …late model, white Ford van running south on Second at Beale…Code 3 pursuit

10-14 on a Tennessee License…*Lincoln*, Henry, King…two…four…four…over

HQ…Copy that…

HQ…10-16 …over

227…stolen…why am I not surprised…over

227…Code 20 on South Main at Vance…(inaudible)

227…Code 30 …van hit squad car at intersection of Talbot at South Main…MPD upside-down spinning…possible injuries…over

HQ…Check that…EMT on the way…over

Copy that…227 here…10-60 anybody…over

554…hello people…10-60…G.E. Patterson at South Main…happy to assist…over

227…554…appreciate assistance…now would be a good time to park sideways and get out of your vehicle…you should see us right…about…now…over

Holy Mother of God…can't give a brother some lead time…

554…checking in…how we doing 227?…over

227…sorry about your vehicle…you got him turned…van heading north…South Front…need to turn him west…Code 9 at Butler…anybody…over

998...three MPD and Fire Truck blocking South Front at Butler Avenue...over

227...copy that...if can...push van west on Butler...over

998...no time...here he comes...over

998...van went west on Butler...see you behind him...good luck 227...over

HQ...we have officers converging 227...where do you want them?...over

227...block north of Vance and south of Carolina...I am pursuing from the east...about ten car lengths back...bluff will block van on the west...we should box him there...over

HQ...copy that...over

227...approaching Tennessee Avenue...tighten Code 3...over

227...10-12 Holy Shit...van rammed brick barrier...rolling down bluff toward Riverside Drive...get traffic blocked on Riverside...over

495... Riverside shut down five minutes... no peds in the area...we're good...over

227...Code 8 ...227...going down bluff on foot...injuries likely...over

227...approaching van on side halfway down bluff...over

227...nobody in the van... repeat no...(inaudible)

HQ...10-13 ...over

HQ...227...10 13...over...

HQ...227...10 13...over...

HQ...227...10 13...over...

HQ...Code 30...Tennessee at Butler...bluff... over

HQ...Code 30...Tennessee at Butler...bluff... over

Talbot Avenue was where Carol gave up the chase; she was struggling to keep up and it was getting messy, squad cars spinning upside down along the way. She left the chaos and drove to the 200 block of Wagner

Place on the bluff, north of everything. There was a vacant lot. She remembered it was once *Landry's Seafood Restaurant.* She parked at the southwest corner, her black *BMW* blended into the shadows of the only thick shrubs in the area.

If her stalker got out of the van and made a run for it, she figured, there would be only two logical ways to go, north or south along the crest of the bluff. She cracked her window, turned everything off and sank in her seat into the even darker shadows of the *BMW* interior.

If you avoid the police and your escape route takes you five blocks north I'm in the perfect spot to see you. Really, who am I kidding? The odds of that are infinitesimal, a stupid long shot. What am I doing here?

Carol turned off her scanner after the van rolled down the bluff and before the police found their comrade butchered unmercifully—left for dead—the assailant on foot. She sat in the vacant parking lot seconds away from starting her car and leaving when she heard sounds, running hard and fast on the bluff, feet pounding the ground, legs cutting through tall brush, and panting like a race horse on its last turn. Her stalker was coming.

He was looking at her and she didn't know. Carol was glued out the side window, peering through a small opening in the thick bushes next to her car. She was focused, watching the south, trying to distinguish between swaying foliage and human movement. She was certain he would appear. But the sounds had stopped. *Did I miss you?*

The front hood of her car hit below his knees. She barely turned her head and saw him standing there. He was huge; she froze. He was a black silhouette on a dark sky, his long coat and long hair lifted with the wind gusts, massive arms at his sides and something hanging from his left hand. Carol prayed that she blended into the dark car interior. *Am I invisible to that monster...that thing? My car would be no defense if it wanted me.*

She sank deeper in her seat and leaned forward just enough to see above his waist. *What are you?* His muscular torso faced the car with his legs anchored like rooted trees unmoving in the wind. His head aimed south to the sirens. Hot breath blasted into the cold night air. It had a long, sloping forehead, overhanging brow, an edgy nose and chin, and then the straight, horizontal jaw line went to his thick neck.

His head jerked from the south to the car like a wild animal picking up a scent or a demon picking up thoughts. Either would be fatal for Carol. It looked down at the car as if for the first time and then looked where Carol would be seated. He knelt, only bending his legs…nothing else. He placed his open hand on the hood, still eying Carol. *The car would be hot and it knew the car is mine. What are you going to do with that information?* Carol's hand was shaking as she reached for the ignition but the keys were gone…she'd pulled them out to kill the courtesy lights. They were somewhere on the passenger seat—she did everything wrong.

Did fate bring her back to Memphis to be killed by the monster of urban legend? She was twenty yards from the place where it all began; Landry's was Captain Bilbo's in the '80s. When he raised his left hand she saw for the first time the butcher knife with the ten-inch blade. It was him, the knife-wielding giant written about in 1983, in *The Memphis Tribune.* He was four feet away. The Bluff City Butcher was on the other side of a quarter-inch piece of glass.

Maybe if her cell phone had rung a few minutes later the light would have never revealed her presence and everything would have been different.

Maybe if she had left the keys in the ignition and had locked the passenger door everything would have been different.

When the butcher knife came down with the force of ten men, piercing the metal hood, and when he pulled the knife to his chest with pure rage, there was little left for Carol Mason to do but scream.

The monster jumped on the hood and plunged the knife through the roof of the car. Carol's cries of desperation were muffled by the excellent soundproof features of her *BMW*. The sound that did manage to leak out was lost in a cacophony flowing from a busy city and the music on Beale Street just a few blocks away.

CHAPTER TWELVE

"It is our illusions that create the world."
Didier Cauwelaert

Tony got from the Bell estate to the bluff in seven minutes. Traffic had been rerouted from the five block area. The place was flush with spinning lights and screaming sirens and crawling with Kevlar jackets, helmets and raised weapons. In twelve minutes, six officers were seriously injured, one officer knifed and near death, four squad cars totaled and there was over five million dollars in damage to city and private property. Although no one was saying it out loud, the knife attack on the bluff raised the possibility they had their rare shot at the Bluff City Butcher. The high speed car chase evolved into armed brigades searching the bluff. Police headlights and spot lights were crisscrossing the night like a giant, illuminated spider web. Nothing could escape...except maybe the Bluff City Butcher.

Wilcox pulled up and stopped on the edge of the parking lot busy with police, fire and EMTs. Carol Mason's demolished *BMW* was in the corner surrounded by flood lamps and CSI agents documenting and inspecting the bizarre damage. With his car running, Tony rolled down the window and a young Memphis police officer approached.

"Evening, Detective Wilcox. I think they need you on the bluff down at Butler."

"Right, but first tell me what you got going here."

"We have a mess."

"Ok, give me the facts without the color, Officer Bentwood," said Tony while reading the name plate. Elliott opened his door and stood in earshot with one foot in the car; he would leave if he felt medically compromised…that was the deal.

"Yes, Sir. Well, Miss Mason's *BMW* was parked in the southwest corner of the lot. We believe the guy found her in the car and went crazy. He pierced the hood and tore the metal with a knife and pounded on the car. He climbed on the hood and stabbed at Mason through the roof of the car. He got her in the head, Sir."

On that note, Elliott shut the door and left. Tony watched him walk across the parking lot while halfway listening to Bentwood. He saw Elliott stop next to Mason's car with his head down. He had told Tony in October that he held back information from Carol Mason…information on the Butcher, that she had absolutely no idea what she was up against. Tony knew he would blame himself.

"Sir, should I wait a minute or so?" asked Bentwood.

"No, sorry, keep going. You said he stabbed her in the head. When did the M.E. remove the body?"

"There is no body, Sir. Miss Mason is far from dead."

Startled, Tony looked from Elliott to the officer. "What are you saying? Are you telling me Mason survived?"

"Oh yes, Sir. He got her once, a small scratch on her forehead. Miss Mason is fine. She is with the paramedics in the back of that ambulance. They are patching her up, nothing serious. She is a little upset they won't let her out until they finish all their checks. Sir, I don't mind saying, she is a knockout." Tony didn't hear the rest.

Unbelievable, she survived the Bluff City Butcher. "So, she made it out of that demolished *BMW?* I'll be damned."

"She said he nicked her head and she scooted as far down in that seat as she could. Apparently she bumped ON her headlights by mistake and then thought to start hitting the horn."

Tony smiled. "I'll be damned…"

"She made all kinds of ruckus. Our luck three squad cars were cutting across Wagner Place at the time."

"Did they see the guy?"

"No, Sir, nothing…just the demolished car sitting there…they couldn't believe it when Miss Mason crawled out."

Detective Harris pulled up alongside Tony. "I found you. Sir, we need to get to Butler. Our guy died on the bluff. They want us on it before anything gets screwed up. Will be easier for you to ride with me—I've got a shortcut."

"Shit…the bastard got one." Tony jumped into Harris's car and tossed his keys to Brentwood. "Give those to Sumner. Tell him I will catch 'em later at the *Peabody.* And, thanks for the info, Brentwood."

Elliott was standing alone next to the *BMW.* The officer triggered the emotions that might awaken his demons. After this, he was ready to give in to it all. He killed Carol Mason by not warning her. *The Butcher stabbed through the roof of the car and got her. He only needs one shot. Why did I hold back when I had a chance to warn her? What kind of man have I become?*

"Is this what I have to do to get your attention, Dr. Sumner?"

Elliott turned. She emerged from the chaos of flashing lights and running guns. She was the most beautiful girl he ever… *Is this Carol Mason?* His heart raced with new feelings. *She survived the Bluff City Butcher and she is stunning.* He tried to hide his personal feelings as he scanned her beautiful body medically. Her arm was in a sling and hand wrapped in gauze. She had a two-inch white bandage taped on her forehead and was missing a sleeve of her blouse. There was blood on her skirt that was ripped above the knee. Her nails were intact and there were no wounds on her arms or hands. She must have put on lipstick and combed her long, blond hair. She was smiling; her green eyes sparkled as she tossed her long, blond curls over her shoulder. Her resilience was refreshing, contagious. She was wearing heels, had long, shapely legs and perfect figure.

Say something brilliant; it has been five long seconds of staring. "So…I see you decided to let him live, Miss Mason." He stepped closer and she, closer to him. They enjoyed the opening and the view.

Carol had seen pictures but they did not compare with the up-close-and-personal. She always admired his accomplishments and reputation in a dangerous world, but now she was getting lost in his icy-blue eyes that looked down on her from his chiseled face and assessing his handsome frame in a pinstripe suit, loosened tie and open collar. He was a man with presence, projecting raw strength, depth of wisdom, and he carried empathy in his eyes. He had a dash of silver in his sideburns and his dark brown hair was in perfect disarray. She could smell him…unique…dreamy.

"Elliott, I saw him," she said with her big eyes melting his heart.

"And who is him?" He managed to get out four words and sound normal.

"Elliott, you need me." *Oh God, that could be taken a number of ways. But really, do I care? I don't think so…*

"This is not a game we are playing, Carol. This thing you saw is dangerous. It has been on a twenty-five-year mission and has consistently demonstrated an ability to accomplish its goals effortlessly. You are in way over your head."

She is so beautiful! What is the matter with me? Why am I thinking like this? Get control, Elliott. Concentrate.

"I am not a school girl looking for something cool to do, Elliott. I have a job to do just like you, and I can take care of myself. You can drop the macho approach. It is demeaning, and…you called me Carol." *Ok, I have never felt like this before*, she thought as she got even closer to his face…and he to hers.

"Excuse me, but you called me Elliott first." *That sounded mature.* "Therefore, I assumed we had progressed in our relationship and were moving to a first-name basis, and I have no macho cards to play. I am just being me. A top investigative reporter that did her homework would know that I have a PROTECTOR personality; it is a big part of why I am going crazy. I care about others WAY TOO MUCH. I am sorry if that offends you. I will try not to care about you, Carol…Miss Mason…Miss Carol Mason." *I think that is the first time I've ever felt flustered. What is that all about?*

"Elliott…you're right. Let's not fight. I take it all back."

"You do?" *That's new too.*

"Elliott, I saw the Bluff City Butcher. He stared at me from four feet away. I saw his face. I saw his body and his strength. If you want details you better make room for me at the table. I don't believe there are many people alive, including you, that have actually seen this guy. And what are you doing in Memphis anyway? You have been missing? *And I have been worried about you for reasons I did not understand until just now.*

"I'm helping a friend."

"Thanks for all the detail, Elliott."

"Look, maybe you have a point. But I was going to talk to you anyway, just to keep you alive."

"Well, that was big of you."

"Seriously, I thought the Butcher got you tonight. You were on my mind since our telephone call in September. I should have warned you then. I felt responsible for…"

"Elliott, that is so sweet, but you need to stop blaming yourself for all the tragedy in the world. You can't save everybody. Life is complicated and too short. Fact is that you have already done more than your share to make this world a safer place. You should think about all the lives you saved by catching fifty serial killers…don't think about the ones you couldn't save. The bad guys win sometimes."

"Thanks, but I do need therapy." They laughed. "You want to get out of here?"

"Yes, but my car is broken." They looked at the *BMW* and smiled.

"Right. And I don't have a car so I guess we walk…should be safe now."

Officer Brentwood interrupted. "Excuse me, Dr. Sumner. Detective Wilcox asked me to give you his car keys. He had to go to the other end of the bluff where the van went over the side. He said he would catch up with you later at the *Peabody.*"

"Ok…thanks."

"We are in luck. I have a fast car with a siren." Elliott was flirting. He liked Carol. *I can't remember the last time I really wanted to be with someone.*

"I'm at the *Peabody*. I can drop you at your place to rest or we can get a coffee or a shooter…your call."

"Are you kidding? I couldn't sleep if I tried, and there is no way I am going to pass up an evening with the great Doctor Elliott Sumner."

Elliott rolled his eyes and smiled halfway. *I feel like a kid with a crush.* "I think you use the term 'great' way too loosely."

"I live at the *Peabody*, too. Let's go there." They left the *BMW* and headed for Tony's unmarked.

"By the way, what is LHK244?"

"I do believe you have been looking at my legs, Doctor."

"Well, I couldn't help but notice that…"

"You are a genius, Elliott Sumner. You know the answer to that question, and I am certain you know more about me than a lady would want you to know. But, no guessing weight…got it?" *He is so handsome…*

"I wouldn't dream of it," Elliott said, holding back a smile. *She has maybe two percent body fat…please…you're perfect…*

Carol slid her arm through his…bicep was a rock; they walked the rest of the way to the car in a comfortable silence. *I feel safe…*

At the *Peabody*, after the third glass of Pinot Noir, Carol told Elliott the more shocking details of her last minutes with a monster; how he found her and the uncontrolled rage as he considered his options, measured conditions and came in for the kill. Carol described her desperate attempt to get under the steering wheel. Elliott felt her fear as she relived the Butcher's hands peeling back the metal roof and his eye looking in the hole, the smell of urine and feces and sweat. She was trapped and he was determined. She said her knee hit the ON button and the lights broke the terror in half…maybe she had a chance. Then she started to pound on the horn and the police were there in seconds. The Bluff City Butcher was gone…but where?

The man that towed Carol's *BMW* from the parking lot that chilly November night had squatted three feet from the most vicious serial killer in the country. Even if the Memphis police looked closer they would have missed the master of concealment. The monster rigidly clung to the branches deep in a cluster of the thick bushes next to Carol's car. At 3:45 a.m. the bluff was quiet again. The Butcher left the bushes and slipped into the early morning river mist.

CHAPTER THIRTEEN

"Boldness is a child of ignorance."
Francis Bacon, Sr.

6 December 2008

Albert Bell and Carol Mason walked into the main conference room at the Memphis Police Department. As set forth in the *Cold Case Collaboration Agreement,* after today *The Memphis Tribune* was free to use any information presented—of course, at their risk.

The facilities were like those of other metropolitan law enforcement agencies: white walls, gray linoleum, fluorescent lights and the smell of fresh coffee. Flanked by the American and Tennessee flags, the wood podium displaying the MPD seal stood in the front of the room. A dozen rows of stainless steel tables and chairs were already full; the buzz started the moment the Bell patriarch entered, You don't see billionaires often. Police Director Collin Wade was next to the seal; he welcomed Albert and politely acknowledged Carol Mason, the unproven outsider.

She was surprised to see Dr. Sumner; he smiled professionally from the back of the room the moment their eyes met. Detective Wilcox stopped to give his regards to Albert and Carol. He sat with Elliott in the back.

Dr. Henderson Bates was on the front row with his nose deep in a case file. He was in green scrubs and a white lab coat with "Shelby County Medical Examiner" embroidered in red over a pocket tight with pens, rulers and little gadgets. Next to him was Dexter Voss in an inappropriate, expensive three-piece suit. Others in the room were quietly waiting with only eyes moving—the note takers.

Director Wade started the meeting as stragglers found seats and the buzz died down. "We are honored to have a great Memphian with us today, Mr. Albert Bell." The room applauded long and loudly. Albert nodded. "We also have a new friend with us today. Carol Mason is one of the top investigative reporters in the country…now on the payroll of *The Memphis Tribune*. Welcome to Memphis, Miss Mason." If the dribble of applause was an indicator, she would need to suck it up. She was on course for a bad day.

Director Wade looked down at his notes and then up to the pensive crowd. "In July I met with Albert Bell to propose a joint venture that would bring together resources and expertise of the public and private sectors to benefit the Metro Area. Our vision, to build a community that watches out for all citizens, including those lost to us over the years. *The Memphis Tribune* and Memphis Police Department launched a collaborative review of a decade of unsolved homicides; these lost citizens can never be forgotten. They must be represented. Maybe we can make a difference, with more eyes and more effort.

"Miss Mason comes to our city with substantial credentials. She came to launch this important initiative on September 1, 2008. If you are in this room you are cleared for confidential information. According to agreements, Miss Mason will report on the first hundred days." He turned to Carol. "We look forward to your presentation on the Midsouth Cold Cases of 1995 to 2005."

Carol stepped to the podium suffocating from the deathly silence. All eyes were on her. She looked at Albert Bell; he winked. She was ready.

"Thank you, Director Wade. *The Memphis Tribune* shares your vision, your hopes and your enthusiasm. And thank you again for your assistance in obtaining the case files and cooperation of the Metro Area law enforcement agencies. Today, I am pleased to bring new and important information to your attention. I will talk about nine deaths out of the first one hundred and eleven reviewed, cases that merit immediate attention. This morning there are no rules. Ask questions at any time."

She opened her thick leather binder stuffed with organized dog-ears. "We looked at unsolved homicides, suspicious and traumatic accidents and suicides unwitnessed, missing persons of interest and violent deaths ruled 'undetermined.' Our target decade had three hundred and seventy-eight cases that qualify for review in this collaboration. The first group was composed of fifteen accidents, twenty suicides, twenty-six missing persons, fifty unsolved homicides and one undetermined death."

Carol began with the '95 Buford Forrester death in Blytheville, ruled accidental drowning. Then she reviewed the '96 abduction of R.L Thornton in Millington that changed to a homicide six years later when his remains were found in the shallows of the Wolf River. Next, she covered the bloody details of the '97 suicide in Hernando, Mississippi, when Ted Morgan supposedly plunged knives into his eyes. Then she presented the details of a '99 farm equipment mishap that killed William Delmar in Marion, Arkansas. The bizarre accident left his bloodless corpse in the middle of a corn field without a pancreas.

Carol methodically guided the room through the most questionable traumatic deaths researched to date. She went into graphic detail. Harvey Barnfield of Desoto, Mississippi, a truck driver, was killed by a knife; he was almost decapitated sitting behind his steering wheel at a truck stop. In '02 Trenton Brent was found in his garage, decomposing on the front seat of his Mercedes. Suspicious circumstances led to an *undetermined manner of death ruling*. She reviewed the '03 Bartlett, Tennessee homicide;

Chris Black was found in a hotel room missing his heart. She presented the '04 Germantown homicide; Jackson Woodall was found dead in his swimming pool, his skin taken from his back, chest and both thighs. The last case of the nine presented was the '05 homicide in Collierville. Gordon Wilton was the victim of a home invasion. The only thing taken was his digestive system, from the mouth to his anus. Wilton was bathed, sutured and put in his bed. He was found weeks later because of the smell.

Director Wade interrupted. "Miss Mason, I do not mean to disturb your flow but you have taken us through nine cases; accidental deaths, suicides and unsolved homicides. Do you reach conclusions soon, and will you share new findings? Do you have recommendations that will help the Metro law enforcement agencies?"

"Yes, Sir. I have new findings, conclusions and recommendations to share today. How helpful they are will depend on a number of factors we can discuss next." The room was quiet. Carol took the audience's temperature. She had to make a decision: hold back the real bombshells for another day or hit them hard with the horrible facts. Her eyes met Elliott's. She could see that he knew her struggle. He dipped his chin once. She knew what to do.

"The nine traumatic deaths presented have common threads. They are homicides of the worst kind; these people were hunted, captured, tortured, harvested and executed. Deaths thought to be suicides and accidents were carefully staged. They were low profile eliminations or precision harvesting events for unknown purposes. Great effort was made to hide each kill from the world. The nine were killed by one."

Whispers drifted across the room. Tony stopped chewing his gum and leaned forward. Dr. Bates put down his file for the first time all morning. Dexter Voss had an odd grimace on his face, nervously shaking his foot. Wade continued to hold his chin and stare, but was now moving a finger over his lip in contemplation. Carol pushed forward.

"What are some of the common threads that link these cases? Let me list a few for you now: (1) traumatic, unwitnessed deaths, (2) happened on October 17 in different years, (3) each had body parts carefully removed or destroyed, (4) they lost their entire blood supply, (5) death by surgical use of a knife and (6) there was a circular puncture wound at the top of the skull, all with the identical dimensions.

"AND why is the head trauma significant? Because, the puncture wound was strategically positioned to inflict specific and diabolical damage. A line drawn from the entry site to the midbrain at the base of the skull intersects large motor control centers in the brain. Damage to these areas renders the victim helpless. They are aware of what is happening to them, they feel the pain, but they are unable to move or make a sound. An ice pick was used…pushed into the skull to scramble the brain, then followed by exsanguination, death and tissue harvesting."

■ ■ ■

They underestimated Mason. She was just getting started and expected the director to move to the safest ground when faced with the most horrific nightmare of his career and lifetime. But the fog of denial was lifting. It was a new day.

"Miss Mason, if you don't mind, I have observations I would like to share, and then questions for you," said Director Wade.

"Of course...please go ahead." She was saving the knock-out punch. The next few minutes would determine her next moves.

"Miss Mason, I see how you have linked these deaths, but based on experience there is a greater likelihood they are not related. Allow me to share my point of view."

"Please do, Director." *Interesting power move, probably how he climbed the ladder. He is taking me to the hallowed halls of Collin Wade University, where all great minds learn the great secrets of the universe…please.*

"When someone dies traumatically they often lose a lot of blood and that is often the cause of death. Also, people die all over the world everyday. Those that die on the same day are rarely connected. Almost 100 percent are unlinked. Now, I would agree the head trauma you describe is of particular interest and merits the scrutiny of the medical examiner. Trauma to eyes and organs in tragic accidents and aggressive suicides rarely mean Dr. Frankenstein sent Igor." The room laughed. Carol didn't. "I have seen damage to bodies that was so horrendous that an untrained eye could not identify a single organ. Only a doctor would be capable of such assessments, not a policeman or a newspaper reporter."

"I understand your points, Director Wade. Let me say to you today—and be very clear about it—I took each point you raised and many more into consideration every step of the way. I have no interest or desire to create something that is nonexistent; that is no good for the MPD, the *Tribune* or the community. Our shared objective is to solve cold cases. The facts and the evidence I presented today came from months of work by highly qualified and properly motivated law enforcement personnel across the Metro Area. The only thing I was able to do was look at those facts on a broader plane. Director, the facts speak loudly."

"Miss Mason, I am Dexter Voss with the FBI. We met in September at the director's office; I believe it was your first day on the job."

"Yes, Mr. Voss. I remember." Carol was unimpressed. *I wonder what the white elephant in the room has to say. What is the FBI doing in a local police meeting anyway? No offense, but Elliott's presence gave it away before you, Voss.*

"I have a comment and question. The accidental deaths and suicides presented today are suspicious. I congratulate you on your work. They could be homicides and should be reopened. But what are you really saying? Is it your theory that one person is randomly killing people in the Midsouth…an ice pick in the head, taking their blood and body parts?"

Voss made it sound silly and absurd; there was light laughter. Carol waited for all heads to return to her so she could watch the smiles melt from their faces. After she saw the Bluff City Butcher on the hood of her car, she began to understand evil was real and a monster was out there. People usually dismiss what they don't understand and can't explain. That much she knew for certain. With her new knowledge of the danger, she felt a responsibility to bring people along as soon as possible. There was no time to waste.

"The short answer, Agent Voss, is yes." *That title should irritate the wise ass.* "A real monster killed these nine people; I'm sure of it. And when I am done with my part of this collaboration, I fully expect to find thirty or forty more kills hidden in the Metro system, all attributed to the same killer." Carol flipped to the back of her notebook.

"Let's look a little closer at the facts. Director Wade, the knife work on these victims was precise and duplicated. Each slice of the flesh was accomplished with a single, uninterrupted and controlled depth movement. The tip of the steel always found the left carotid artery and then the jugular vein and then the right carotid artery. The left-handed killer moved the blade from his right to his left, the cutting edge of the knife on each wound pointed to the victim's right. The angle of neck wounds were consistently delivered by someone six-feet-five-inches tall. The cuts through flesh and bone were like a hot knife through butter…the killer was stronger than the average man, more like ten men. The puncture wounds were always in the same place. Allow me to emphasize that point…exactly the same place. Yes, loss of blood is typical with traumatic deaths, but complete and total exsanguination is a procedure, not an accident or a common occurrence. The nine victims I brought to your attention today were killed by a single very sick and demented person. The body parts were carefully removed and most surgical wounds were meticulously sutured post-op."

Carol took a drink of water in a quiet room. She was very good.

"Mr. Voss, allow me to further clarify. I am saying one person killed these nine people over the decade reviewed. I am saying this killer has been active for twenty-five years…and, Agent Voss, I am saying this serial killer is still out there."

"With all due respect, I think that is a stretch. You are taking your theory, shaky at best, into the realm of ridiculous. This is the real world, not Hollywood," said Voss.

"Let me ask you a question, Mr. Voss. How long has the FBI been looking for this guy, my hypothetical moving to 'the realm of ridiculous' guy?"

The room broke into laughter. Voss and Wade were dancing and it was beginning to be obvious. They had no intention of showing their cards, but they wanted all of hers. "I'm sorry, but we have yet to establish what guy you think we should be looking for, Miss Mason," replied Voss, dodging her question.

"Do the names Buford Forrester, R.L. Thornton or Teddy Morgan mean anything to you, Director Wade or to you, Mr. Voss?" asked Carol.

"No, nothing comes to mind," said Wade.

"I agree, I have never heard their names before today," said Voss.

"Do you recall the 1983 kidnapping of Sabina Weatherford? Do you recall the killings on the bluff the following night? Four young men were attacked by a large man with a knife; three died and one survived. The Memphis police chased a large man onto the Harahan Bridge; he jumped. They never recovered a body." Carol glanced at Elliott, he approved and she finally got the dynamics, why Elliott and Tony were holding back, policy and old-school thinking that needed to change.

Wade approached the podium to retake control of the meeting, but he stopped half way and turned to the group. Holding the back of his neck he spoke. "Most of us know about the tragic disappearance of the young Weatherford girl and the triple homicide on the bluff in 1983, Miss Mason. We also know a man could never survive the fall or the cold, turbulent waters of the Mississippi River. It soon became an urban legend. The Bluff City Butcher was the boogeyman of the Midsouth, Miss Mason. The Bluff City Butcher stories grew over the years. He was behind every unsolved, brutal death, every missing person and all unexplained tragedies in the region. He is our shadow in the night. We don't need to stir that pot anymore. It would be unfair to the community."

Voss stood up next to Director Wade. "That is true, Director Wade. I believe Miss Mason has fallen into the trap by starting down a path in her research and saw it gain momentum like a snowball rolling down a hill getting bigger and bigger. Subconsciously she looked for a serial killer and then assembled random facts to fit."

They did their best to diminish her credibility and her findings. They berated her intelligence and dismissed her experience. Carol was about to close her notebook, maybe do battle another day, when Elliott Sumner raised his hand.

"Yes, Dr. Sumner. Do you have a question or would you like to join in with Director Wade and Mr. Voss?"

"I have a question, Miss Mason. What is the significance of the three names you asked Director Wade and Voss about…the three men they never heard of until today?" asked Elliott. "I believe you said Forrester, Thornton and Morgan."

The room was silent as they watched Dr. Elliott Sumner speak. His international credentials and unparalleled success hunting the most dangerous serial killers around the world earned him incredible respect. When Elliott finished his question all eyes turned to Carol Mason at the podium. She saw something in Elliott's eyes and knew what to do.

"Buford Forrester died October 17, 1995. He was the owner of the

Captain Bilbo's Restaurant in 1983, the place where the three boys were killed on the bluff. R.L Thornton was a Memphis Police Officer. He was killed October 17, 1996, the first responder that cornered the Butcher on the Harahan Bridge. Teddy Morgan was killed October 17, 1997. He was an employee at Captain Bilbo's. He helped the only survivor and was the only one interviewed on the news that night." Carol closed her notebook to a quiet, still room.

Several jumped to their feet and ran out of the room. Suddenly, everything was clear and everyone knew it. Wade was turning white and Voss red.

Elliott winked…done.

"Gentlemen, the Bluff City Butcher is alive and very busy. He has followed me on-and-off since I arrived. On November 5th, I was within a few feet of this monster. I watched this angry man destroy my car like it was a toy. It wanted to kill me desperately.

"You are predictable to him. Director Wade, I urge you go public with this information; educate and warn this community. Something has changed in this killer's world…it is on some new path, no longer satisfied with killing and hiding. I predict many more people are going to die in the Midsouth by the knife of the Bluff City Butcher."

"Obviously, we are listening to you and we have concern a serial killer could be in the Midsouth. But we are not prepared today to say it is the Bluff City Butcher of 1983. We will study the cases presented immediately," said Director Wade. "I ask you to continue your work and please, do not go to the community with claims that can only create more unrest and fear that could only complicate things. We will make an announcement when we address all related concerns, I promise you that."

Elliott was now standing behind Carol. She watched him speak. "Collin, we know what we are up against, whether you want to accept it or not. If you continue to minimize or disregard what we are telling you and you put more people at risk, I fail to see how I can be of help here. The time has come to change tactics. If Mason is left out of the loop and you are unwilling to change your approach in twenty-four hours, I am finished here. The people that die from this day forward are on your hands."

"Dr. Sumner, I understand your position. I need some time to consider all that has been presented. I hope you will continue as we complete our internal review."

Albert Bell put his hand on Elliott's shoulder; they were both men of presence and stature. Elliott sensed Albert wanted to give Wade more time to digest and process the reality of the moment. "Collin, I told you we would be privileged to have Carol Mason in Memphis. She climbed the mountain of the forgotten regional death cases without help, preconceived notions or bias. She has confirmed the Bluff City Butcher survived the Mississippi River and has been killing in the Midsouth ever since. The MPD protocols and the tactics employed over the years have failed. Now, we have valuable information and urgent recommendations from experts. The sooner you get Carol Mason in the loop and take new steps to catch this killing machine, the better for all of us.

"And as a citizen of this community, I can tell you this: I would want to know there is a dangerous predator loose in the area so I could protect my family. You can not possibly be everywhere. If you wait too long and more people die, they will get rid of all of you if they don't tar-and-feather you first."

Voss waited alone in Wade's third-floor office. He stood at the edge of the curtain and watched Mason and Bell fold themselves into the limousine. As they pulled away, his pen snapped, getting ink on his hand and expensive suit. Mason's progress was unanticipated, and now Wade would change strategy. The new information could not be ignored and that created problems for Voss.

The FBI never treated him with the respect he deserved; Voss was the only one smart enough to put it all together. He knew why the Bluff City Butcher took body parts, and for whom. After Voss single-handedly screwed up the government negotiations with Dr. Medino and lost access to his life-extension research, the FBI made it very clear that his career was over; he would grow old in Memphis. Voss went rogue in 2005. With all the changes Wade would need to weigh, Voss had enough time to take care of loose ends.

CHAPTER FOURTEEN

"The man who can keep a secret may be wise,
but he is not half as wise as the man with no secrets to keep."
Edgar Watson Howe

22 December 2008

He became irrelevant…obsolete. He was the radio talk show host on fire in the eighties but went from red-hot to hot-head and was tossed out of the biggest stations from New York to L.A. Jimmy Doyle was more trouble than he was worth, and there was plenty of talent to pick from back then.

Twenty years later he found humble. He spent ten years in a bottle, five in jail and five selling billboard space in Phoenix. The time had come to change his ways; the plan was simple, change the attitude and beg for a job in second-tier markets. Memphis was the seventh city on the list. He would keep pitching until he got a gig or died—no more billboards.

The now humble fifty-five-year-old liberal with dyed hair, a bald spot and potbelly finally got a nibble. He was incensed to learn his age and combative history were the main reasons he got the shot—all that changing for nothing. The WKRC station manger was looking for an old-school radio personality to host a new, contentious talk show in Memphis. He wanted an experienced, pugnacious personality to stir up things in the bluff city. Doyle came back; he was in fashion again.

Doyle had two gifts: he was both a master of discourse and quick on the uptake. He could learn anything once, but like a bumblebee going from flower-to-flower, he forgot the last topic the moment he left it—perfect for talk radio.

Barry Branch, he called him Bear, was the other half of the equation, Doyle's only friend and his program director. Bear was a human *Google*. Whatever topic Jimmy wanted to talk about, Bear had a pile of the most relevant information on his desk the next day. He kept Jimmy current and on track.

He had no problem going back to being an asshole! Doyle got the job at WKRC in Memphis the fall of 2006. After a year, the show was a hit. His in-your-face '80s style mellowed enough to be perfect for the *Talk of Memphis:* a call-in, open forum, six days a week, six to midnight show that syndicated in 2008, adding sixty stations nationally.

The West Tennessee Chapter of the American Academy of Biotech Research held its '08 meeting and awards banquet in Covington. Doyle was invited to do a live broadcast of the *Talk of Memphis* from the grand banquet reception hall where Dr. Enrique Medino, Chief Technology Officer of the *Life2 Corporation,* would receive a special honor for his pioneer work, *Advanced Genetic Manipulation for the Treatment of Osteoarthritis.*

For the first time since the formation of *Life2* in Memphis, Dr. Medino had agreed to an interview. He would be the only guest of the *Talk of Memphis* and it would precede the awards banquet. The reception hall accommodated fifteen hundred people standing. Doyle had the ideal setting to masterfully milk Medino on his ground-breaking research. Long time rumors running amok claimed the brilliant geneticist had discovered the secrets of biological immortality. Doyle was on a mission to find out.

ON AIR - LIVE

"HELLO MIDSOUTH PEOPLE…a cold December 22 on the way to the end of a great 2008. The time is 7:04 p.m. Central. I am Jimmy Doyle, your host, and you are listening to… the *Talk of Memphis*. (Music)

"Today, ladies and gentlemen, WKRC 1190 is on the road again. I am honored to bring you this edition of the show live from the Southern Banquet Hall in Covington, Tennessee.

"We are guests of the West Tennessee Chapter…American Academy of Biotechnology Research…their annual meeting…

"But I will be brief on opening comments because we want to get right to our very special guest…we only have him for fifteen minutes.

"My friends… *Talk of Memphis* dedicated this month to the *Emerging World of Bioscience in the Midsouth*," said Doyle in his perfect radio voice.

"We have spent time with the shakers, the bakers, the inventors, the doctors and even the very special patients looking for new medical solutions.

"I am pleased to report that we have much to be proud of… our great community is actively participating in the biotechnology global megatrend.

"Your friends and neighbors are looking for solutions in oncology, urology and orthopedics, cardio-vascular and organ transplantation today.

"I am incredibly honored to have our guest, ladies and gentlemen."

Jimmy reached over and shook hands with Dr. Medino as they clipped a mic to his lapel. He sat a few feet away with a humble smile. They were surrounded by 1,000 people wearing tuxedos and formal gowns. Jimmy Doyle had their most honored guest sitting in the center of his world, the place where he was the master; he would make history this night!

It could have been the center ring at Madison Square Garden on fight night! The show was airing in sixty-four cities across the country, live. They were the glowing ember in the center of a dense forest of educated wealth and influence.

"I am so pleased. the *Talk of Memphis* is privileged to have with us tonight the eminent Dr. Enrique Carlos Medino. Ladies and gentlemen, Dr. Medino is the Chief Technology Officer and co-Founder of the *Life2 Corporation*; global headquarters in Memphis, Tennessee…the great city on the bluff."

The audience in the hall applauded.

"Dr. Medino is an accomplished professional. He is a medical doctor, once specializing in obstetrics and gynecology. Prior to that he received his Bachelor of Science Degree in Advanced Organic Chemistry and Cellular Biology from UTEP and Master of Science in Molecular Biology from the University of Texas, and he received his medical degree from Southwestern Medical School and later, PhD in Genetics from Vanderbilt in Nashville. Our guest is a physician, researcher, visionary and pioneer. I am honored to have you on the *Talk of Memphis.*"

"Thank you, Mr. Doyle, you are a kind man."

"Doctor, I have you a very short time. I hope you won't mind if I get right to the heart of the matter, areas of great interest to our listeners, your esteemed colleagues and the world."

"Yes, that would be all right with me, Mr. Doyle."

"What is the *Life2 Corporation* working on now?" Jimmy threw his slow ball first. He would wait for the perfect time to send his change up, the one Medino should let go by, but will want to hit out of the park.

"Yes, of course I can do that for you. *Life2* was formed in 2004 by me and my partner, a very special businessman and respected entrepreneur, Dr. Jack Bellow. Our company is working on genetic-based solutions for the improvement of the quality of life. Our first biotechnology solution only took thirty years of research."

The crowd laughed.

"We have new answers for the non-invasive treatment of osteoarthritis."

"That is a prevalent and disturbing degenerative disease of the aging musculoskeletal system, painful joints like the knees, hips and spine," said Doyle.

"Yes. A common factor is the degeneration of cartilage."

"Can you educate us, Doctor?" asked Doyle.

"Yes. The joint is where bones meet and motion is permitted, bones articulate. At the end of each bone is a rubbery tissue called cartilage that is lubricated naturally. Over time these surfaces become damaged and wear away, exposing the bone. When bone rubs on bone we have pain. This discomfort then limits motion. Eventually, we can lose mobility. This aging process is called osteoarthritis and is the number-one degenerative condition affecting our aging population and even younger people that have joint injury."

"I see. What do we do now to treat osteoarthritis?" asked Doyle.

"It depends on the stage of degeneration. Early stage can often be treated with aspirin and exercise, but it generally progresses to the next stage, where pain is so great the treatment may require aggressive pharmaceuticals and injections. When that no longer works, mobility is lost, because the pain is too great. The joint must be repaired or replaced. This is a surgical procedure to resurface the articulating joints," said Medino.

"And why is that solution not good enough, I mean why would we want to avoid joint resurfacing or joint replacement surgery?" asked Doyle.

"First, it is a major surgical procedure. We would like to avoid major surgery if possible, especially as we get older; anesthesia, operating risks, possible infection, long recovery and enormous expense. A hip replacement can cost $100,000 or more. Second, the artificial joint replacement does not restore normal function. It allows the joint to function, but you are limited. Third, all implants fail at some point. It is a race; will the implant fail or will you die first? My point is that when the implant fails there is more major surgery, more aggressive reconstruction and increased risk to patients who are now even older and frailer. I think we can do better."

"I see, and what does *Life2* biotechnology hope to do, Dr. Medino?" asked Doyle

"Wouldn't it be nice if our body could fix the problem? Wouldn't it be wonderful if our osteoarthritic condition just went away without doctors and medicine and surgery?

"Wouldn't it be nice if your joints felt like they did when you were young?"

"The simple answer, Doctor…yes, yes and yes," replied Doyle while raising his hands for a little love from the audience. They clapped hands as if the first act of a Broadway play was over.

"At *Life2* we will soon offer a biotechnological solution that will eliminate the need for pain medication and surgery. We have learned how to talk to the cartilage cell that is no longer functioning as it was intended."

"The cartilage cell that is damaged or sick or dead?" inquired Doyle, somewhat leading the witness.

"An outside force—like disease or injury—can cause a cartilage cell to malfunction; we call this *necrosis*. There are internal forces that cause cells to fail too. We have names for these conditions; *apoptosis* is programmed death; the cell has a mechanism that says *'time to stop'* and everything shuts down. And, we have *senescence*, which is when a cell loses the *ability* to replicate or repair itself."

"So, your biotech breakthrough helps deal with those words you just said?" Doyle was going for the laugh and got it.

"Correct, we deal with those *words*," said Medino with a smile as he got more comfortable as the center of attention.

"Your biotech solution—the genetic solution—talks to these dying cells and somehow convinces them to act young again?" Doyle tried to sound simple. He was pulling Medino into his little trap, but it was still too soon to spring it.

"Today we will avoid making claims. *Life2* is in development phase. We want to learn about the patients we can help. We will find out what cells we can talk to…or convince to act young, so to speak," said Medino with a serious tone.

Jimmy scratched his head for effect. "Can you say today that *Life2* knows how to talk to cartilage cells? Or why would investors put $150 million in the game?"

"Yes, you are correct. We can talk to cartilage cells," said Medino.

"If *Life2* can restore vitality to a cartilage cell, wouldn't it follow that you are close to doing the same with other cell types?"

"Yes, we are close, Mr. Doyle."

"So, if we can keep cells from aging, does that mean the person would not age? Is that how that works?"

"Again, in the simplest of terms, that would be a correct statement."

"Do all cells have limited life spans?" asked Doyle as he referenced carefully choreographed notes that only he could translate.

"Yes, bodies of all living organisms are composed of billions of cells. We call them *somatic cells*. They specialize and become heart, skin, and hair, liver and so on. Some replicate, create new cells, millions or thousands of times and some hundreds, some fewer and some never, like brain cells."

"We are replacing our cells already?" asked Doyle.

"The average child between ages eight and fourteen replaces between twenty and thirty billion cells each day."

"Wow, I didn't know that."

"Everyday we produce billions of new replacement cells. From the beginning of my studies and research, I wondered why some somatic cells replicate thousands of times and others only hundreds or never. What if all cells could replicate thousands of times indefinitely?"

Doyle had Medino right where he wanted him. The fine doctor was back in his lab, tackling a problem, reliving a search for revolutionary solutions. *Medino may talk about his REAL breakthrough on the radio…this could be my time to shine!*

"Leonard Hayflick published his work in 1965. He talked about the *Hayflick Limit*, the number of times a normal cell population will replicate before it just stops. Geneticists and molecular biologists have been looking for ways to extend or eliminate *Hayflick Limit*. We have been approaching the phenomenon from several directions," said Medino.

"You figured it out for the cartilage cell. It seems to me you are in the best position to apply your Anti-aging biotechnology to other somatic cells."

"Yes. Your statement is logical. I am the first there," said Medino.

A hush moved through the reception hall. Doyle could not believe what just happened; Medino confirmed his osteoarthritis breakthrough was an Anti-aging biotechnology breakthrough. But it was a soft declaration. They had changed the Hayflick limit.

Jack Bellow and the entire *Life2 Corporation* had dodged that worm hole of discussion since inception. On day one the world tried to tie their work to Anti-aging Medicine. Jack wouldn't allow it, and Enrique was kept away from the media.

I don't think he knows what he just did, Jimmy thought. *I will push a little more; he is eating up the attention. There is nothing like the admiration of peers, tuxedos and a glass of wine! After all, if I discovered how to extend human lifespan years ago and was still keeping it under wraps, I would explode for sure. I would want all the credit and accolades that were coming to me. Medino is human!*

"Has there been any progress in the field of Anti-aging Medicine?"

"Yes. In the last decade there have been great strides in understanding the human genome, where genes are, what they do and how they relate to one another. We are learning how to manipulate genes, alter participation in a biological process and turn them on and off."

"Is that how the *Ossi2* product works?"

"Yes."

"I see." *He did it again. OH MY GOD! What is he doing? The world is listening. He might as well give it all up now.*

"Many conservative molecular biologists, geneticists and researchers believe we are ten to twenty years away from stopping the aging process."

"Your biotechnology somehow allows a cartilage cell to stay young. So it seems to me you stopped the aging process in that cell."

"Yes, it does that," said Medino.

Ok, that was big, must keep pushing. "I have done a little homework. If all our somatic cells begin as stem cells, then it would be logical that your remarkable discovery could empower all somatic cells to live forever, and then people could live forever. Dr. Medino, you could be the father of life extension…or even immortality."

Would he bite? Would he take this tempting pitch and smash it out of the park in front of his peers…his hometown crowd, for God's sake?

"Well, I think the first objective of the research is to slow the aging process. The second is to stop the aging process and the third is to reverse the aging process."

"Doctor, you are modest. Your landmark breakthrough in orthopedics is already at stage three. Your associates understand your accomplishment. That is why they are all standing with you tonight!"

Will he take that bow now? Over 1,000 people in the room. It was so quiet you could hear a mouse peeing on a cotton ball.

But the director of the AABR stepped in and gently tapped Dr. Medino on the shoulder and whispered into his ear. Medino said, "I'm sorry, Mr. Doyle, Director Grouse has just informed me the banquet hall is ready and I am to invite everyone to enter the dining room at this time."

Jimmy was stunned. His best pitch stopped over the plate in midair. "Yes, Sir… I understand, Sir, and I thank you for giving me your time this evening." *I had the interview of the century and was stopped at third base. The buzzer went off.*

"Mr. Doyle, you are a good man. I look forward to visiting with you again someday. It has been my pleasure."

The room erupted into applause as both men stood to remove their microphones and earpieces. But Doyle had to take one last shot; he couldn't stand it. The room transformed into a soft buzz as people began to flow away...abandoning his show.

"Dr. Medino, before you go..."

■ ■ ■

But the lights in the reception hall slowly dimmed. Moving tuxedos, flowing gowns and sparkling jewelry stopped and turned back. Bear turned on the spotlight that illuminated only Dr. Enrique Medino, and they clipped on his lapel microphone.

"Before you go, Sir, allow me to speak for the fifty million people all across this country glued to their radios at this very moment." He watched eyes light up and another hush roll through the crowd. "Dr. Medino, you are a humble genius, a treasure to all humanity. You are a modern day Copernicus...Newton...Einstein. Sir, you may be the greatest pioneer, trailblazer that has ever lived. Doctor, you have found a way to renew and extend the life of a cartilage cell. YOU ARE THERE, SIR."

The room was still. Bear dimmed the banquet hall lights even more, increasing the celestial mood surrounding Enrique Medino. This was the moment. Doyle just threw his best pitch and Bear got everything right.

"DNA has always been immortal. I discovered one way to maintain the cell biology in one cell type to allow DNA to do what God intended: to make life happen."

The room erupted. The house lights went bright, Medino smiled and melted into the swarm. He was gone and Jimmy Doyle just got the FULL attention of the WORLD.

"You heard it here first, ladies and gentlemen, on the *Talk of Memphis*, Dr. Enrique Carlos Medino has spoken honestly and frankly about the huge meaning of his discovery now focused on eliminating osteoarthritis. Yes, you heard Dr. Medino say, and I quote: '*DNA has always been immortal. I discovered one way to maintain the cell biology in one cell type to allow DNA to do what God intended: to make life happen.*'"

Within minutes sound-bites from the *Talk of Memphis* would be picked up by every major network, global communications entities and the *Internet*. By morning, the world would know about the *Life2 Corporation* in Memphis, Tennessee. Everyone would know Dr. Enrique Medino believed he was on the path to the fountain of youth or that he had already dipped his toe in the waters of immortality.

Jimmy Doyle was officially back.

■ ■ ■

The WKRC bus was almost ready to roll. Jimmy went outside for a smoke. It was 9:00 p.m. and everybody was at the banquet. Staff was closing down the mobile broadcasting equipment and loading the bus, and Jimmy wanted to be alone.

He sat in the moon shadow off the building, the front parking lot. That's when he saw the two vans on the other side of the highway and two guys moving jugs from one to the other. The westerly wind hit Jimmy in the face; he smelled kerosene.

They moved around suspiciously in their black pants, black long-sleeved shirts and black knit hats, looking like typical cat burglars. *Just like the stupid movies*, he thought as he puffed away. *Crap like that never really happens.*

He could even see their faces. One looked familiar. *Who are you, man?...I know you from somewhere.* It wasn't until the WKRC bus got back to Memphis later that night that Doyle remembered the guy was Dexter Voss, the FBI man he'd met at the police fundraiser in the summer.

Voss was a pretty cool guy. He was probably on some undercover raid in West Tennessee, some covert FBI assignment, he thought.

After the passing thoughts, Doyle was tired and just let it all go. He did make a note for Bear: *lay out a program plan for a show with area FBI. People would want to know what local FBI does all day—and night—to protect us Midsoutherners.*

Jimmy Doyle was awakened by the phone around noon the day after his incredible Covington, Tennessee show. Bear would never get him up after a late running show unless it was important. "I need you to go outside and get your newspaper. Or you can turn on the local news, now." Bear spoke in monotone. He knew Jimmy would think his clearest if he was not too upset.

Doyle didn't like any of this from the start. He sensed something was not good; something very big…was not good. Doyle slammed down the phone, pulled on his pants and ran outside. Too tight to subscribe, he commandeered his neighbor's paper from their driveway. It was all there…on the front page!

The Memphis Tribune

December 23, 2008

Staff Reporter

Medino Family killed; Fiery Car Crash on Austin Peay

Crash Kills Five in North Memphis—December 22, 2008. Around 11:30 p.m. an automobile traveling south on Austin Peay Highway left the road at a high rate of speed north of the Pleasant Ridge exit. The vehicle went down a steep embankment, through a small wooded area and into an open field where it collided with scrapped farm equipment.

According to witnesses, shortly after the crash the car burst into flames. The driver and four passengers were pronounced dead at the scene by the County Medical Examiner's Office. The deceased are Dr. and Mrs. Enrique Carlos Medino, Mrs. Ellen Hernandez (mother of Mrs. Medino) and their two children, Bryan (age 23) and Martha (age 25) Medino.

The Medino family was returning from a medical banquet in Covington where Dr. Medino received a special recognition award from the *American Academy of Biotechnology Research* for pioneer work in genetics and the treatment of osteoarthritis. Dr. Medino was a guest on the *Talk of Memphis* radio show hours before the tragic accident that took his life. He said his work opened doors into the emerging field of Anti-aging Medicine. Medino is a co-founder and the chief technology officer of the *Life2 Corporation* headquartered in downtown Memphis. His partner, Jack Bellow, President/CEO, was not available for comment.

An inquest will be held later today to rule on cause and manner of death. The Shelby County Medical Examiner's Office had no comments. The accident is under investigation by the Shelby County Sheriff's Office. Anyone who witnessed the accident or has information they believe could be helpful is asked to contact the Sheriff's Office at this time.

CHAPTER FIFTEEN

5 January 2009

Carol drove to Little Rock, Arkansas, to meet a most reliable source. Her window of opportunity was narrow; the contact was heading out of the country and the package was too sensitive to drop in the mail.

The Cold Case meeting with the Memphis PD confirmed she was out of the loop. She concluded her status would not change for a while and she had no time to sit on the sidelines. It was abundantly clear she provided more information on the developing nightmare than the MPD or FBI. Either they had minimal or they were hiding all of it. The time arrived; Carol would take their information any way she could!

She met her source at a mall. The transfer was smooth. She drove around Little Rock making random stops. Once confirmed she was alone, Carol checked into the downtown Hilton and chained the door, closed the curtains, and tore open the thick brown envelope containing the inch of papers. The half-inches of docs were separated by two black metal clips. The cover note said it all: *"Mason, not easy to get hold of…this is a piece of a multi-year cover. Some scary shit…They don't want*

*this on the outside—COMMUNITY STAMPEDE CONTROL." She
destroyed the note and read the front page.*

CONFIDENTIAL
Memphis Police Department
Homicide Division and Investigation
HD.54736.2008
Raymond T. Munson, 73/W/M
HOMICIDE
Detective Antonio D. Wilcox
October 17, 2008

Carol had hoped for only a few pages of the Memphis PD investigation
report on the Raymond Munson homicide, but now she held the
complete copy. At last, she had the details on the Public Library killing
on October 17, 2008, that were guarded aggressively. Before reading the
detailed sections, she flipped to the second report with equal enthusiasm
and great curiosity. She was shocked to see she also had the complete
medical examiner report in her possession.

CONFIDENTIAL
Shelby County Medical Examiner
INQUEST
Raymond Travis Munson - DOD 10/17/2008
Henderson Bates, M.D.
Date of Report: 10/24/2008

Carol got comfortable, cracked open bottled water and took a few big
swallows. Thank you, Little Rock PD, she thought with a smile. Her
source was the best. He was an insider with an attitude. *I don't know how
you did it, my friend. Memphis went to great lengths to keep this one under
wraps. Someone really screwed up letting it out the door.* Carol slipped off her
heels and settled back for a good read, first the medical examiner report.
The *Introduction Summary* was the place to start:

CONFIDENTIAL

SHELBY COUNTY MEDICAL EXAMINER OFFICE
10/24/2008
Inquest: 14327.45.5677
Name: Raymond Travis Munson
DOB: June 12, 1935
POB: Dallas, Texas

Occupation: Retired: Prof. English: U of M, SMU-Dallas-TX, NTSU-Denton-TX

Medical Examiner:Henderson Bates, M.D.
DOD: October 17, 2008
TOD: 0100 CST e
Pronouncement: 0530 MPD CST

Cause of Death: Primary: Acute Exsanguination
Secondary: Oxygen Deprivation

Manner of Death: Homicide
Inquest: 14327.45.5677 Homicide

Inspection/Autopsy Summary: 73/W/M estimated height 185.42 cm, weight 96.162 kgm, of normal stature, found in sitting position with arms suspended by wire-cable binding attachments from both wrists to ceiling fixtures and around chest, abdomen and chair. Healthy, well nourished, Caucasian male typical aging conditions; signs of arthrosclerosis, osteoarthritis, all other unremarkable. Trauma observations: deep lacerations to frontal and lateral aspects of mid-neck, severing carotid arteries and jugular vein, also penetration wounds to the groin-thigh region, severely perforating both femoral arteries with estimated accumulative blood loss rate/volume: 50-60% of available supply <30 seconds, 70-80% of supply within <60 seconds and 90-97% within 180-300 seconds. Multiple body parts harvested and taken from the scene. Not recovered at time of report. Missing body parts include; two eyeballs, two ears, nose, tongue, larynx, two hands, two feet and heart. All harvest sites were thoroughly cleansed (lavage) and trimmed and sutured. Detailed findings: pages 12-75.

Remarkable Observations: No visible defense wounds, suggesting deceased was subdued-incapacitated simultaneously. One pair of 06.35 mm. circular burn marks found lateral posterior aspect of neck; subject marks consistent with those produced by electrical shock or certain tazing devices. One circular puncture wound of 003.0 cm. diameter found at the superior aspect of coronal suture with cranial penetration and a singular, perpendicular track of equal dimensions and diameter running from entry wound through cerebellum cortex and ending precisely in the central portion of the parietal lobe. Wound consistent with those created by a heavy duty ice pick. Subject puncture wound occurred hours prior to clinical death and would be expected to inflict large motor muscle paralysis consistent with removal of certain body parts prior to exsanguination and/or clinical death. Detailed observations: pages 77-119.

Next, the Summary Review & Recommendations would tell her once and for all if Wilcox was playing games or pushing the truth down the collective throats of top brass:

Memphis Police Department
Homicide Investigation
Summary Conclusions & Recommendations
MPD 12033.788.2010
Investigator: Detective A. D. Wilcox
Name: Raymond Travis Munson
HOMICIDE

This carefully planned, torture-mutilation homicide revealed a depth of rage rarely observed and marks a likely beginning of a random "public killing spree" in the Midsouth region by an experienced predator and serial killer. The October kill was highlighted by the selection and removal of certain body parts and presents more information about the killer and the victim. SK likely knew this victim and held him accountable. The torturous removal of body parts prior to death and the choice of body parts for harvest were personal and symbolic. The body part removals symbolically left the victim without senses and abilities. These selections may directly relate to the incident(s) that occurred between victim and SK at a time in the past and therefore may hold the key to identification and apprehension of SK. Body parts harvested included: sight (eyes), hearing (ears), smell (nose), touch (hands) and compassion (heart). The removal of the larynx, tongue and suturing the mouth closed may represent loss of speech. Amputation of feet - taking away mobility or freedom, removal of stomach (?) and hands (?), the M.O. of capture, incapacitate (stun), exsanguinate, cleanse, dress and exhibit matches M.O. partials of other unsolved traumatic death cases. BCB is primary suspect in the Munson homicide.

BCB LOW PROFILE activity suspected in Midsouth region since 1983 and under continuous investigation by MPD and FBI, the Munson homicide would be a significant change in that it is a HIGH PROFILE kill. This suggests BCB has moved to a new, more aggressive level of desire. BCB mental derangement, anger and advanced killing skills suggest a rapid escalation in HIGH PROFILE kills in the Midsouth region can be expected. The level of activity has the potential of making BCB the most dangerous and prolific serial killer in the 21st century.

Critical Observation:

THE SYMBOLIC MUTILATION-KILL OF R.T. MUNSON ON OCTOBER 17, 2008, IS INTENDED TO SEND A MESSAGE TO AREA LAW ENFORCEMENT; THE BLUFF CITY BUTCHER IS GOING PUBLIC. THE TIME TO EDUCATE THE PUBLIC HAS LONG SINCE PASSED.

When she finished it was clear to her the MPD and FBI had either been out of touch with reality for some time or something else was going on. The Bluff City Butcher was unlike any serial killer she had studied. He was a raging, psychotic killing machine on some sort of mission, and the local law enforcement was getting bad direction from the regional FBI office. Everything she presented in November was applicable to the Munson case; everyone knew it but her…and maybe Albert. Agreement or not, it was time to go public with or without the MPD.

■ ■ ■

9 January 2009

In the Midsouth, an inch can shut down everything. The snow started to fall around noon; businesses closed early and schools sent kids home. The forecast said four to six inches, but the problem would be ice. Typical borderline freezing temperatures would transform a Midsouth winter wonderland into an ice skating rink with bumper cars.

Carol took I-40 east to Memphis. She would get home around 8:00 p.m. if she skipped dinner. She failed to factor in the steadily worsening conditions, and the slow progress gave her too much time to think about the Bluff City Butcher. She was convinced she must get the MPD to go public immediately.

Every town in America had its ghosts and goblins. There was always the haunted house or the witch in the neighborhood. The mysterious stories were often old and rarely written, all word of mouth, creatures that lived on the dark edge of the imagination between the real and the unknown, hard to believe but hard to completely deny. Growing up in Germantown, she was eight when the Memphis urban legend was born; a small girl kidnapped and three boys killed on the bluff in '83, knifed by a stranger who jumped off the bridge and drowned in the river. When she returned to Memphis and joined the *Tribune* the Butcher came up again; she was skeptical, had filed it away with Big Foot, Werewolves and Vampires. But now her organized world was in total disarray. The Bluff City Butcher was her first real monster. How could she ever get used to knowing something was out there that wanted to kill her? She felt like the kid afraid to look under the bed. This time there really was a monster waiting for her.

That night last November was scary. It looked inside her. The headlights poured over its dark, glistening skin and the fat, throbbing vessel sticking out of its squared, steel forehead seemed ready to burst. The Butcher swung its long, sweat-soaked hair out of his eyes and looked into her soul with a vicious hatred.

The thing plunging a knife into her car was beyond a psychopath on hallucinogenic drugs. It moved with the agility and strength of a young wild animal, sure footed and comfortable in the night. It could pivot and leap in any direction in a fraction of a second. It was alert. It showed no fear. It revealed a discerning intelligence and evil mission. That night it was angered; it would have to wait to kill Carol Mason. Why else was the Bluff City Butcher stalking her?

The lights of the Memphis skyline were almost visible on the horizon through the thick, falling snow. Carol was almost home. It had been two months since her encounter; the face of the Butcher was hard, stark and determined. It wanted her dead that night. *Did it forget about me? I'm the least of its worries. But now only two are alive that saw him: Marcus Pleasant and me. It killed everyone else.*

The Munson homicide validated her theory. Before Munson was put on display, the Memphis PD could continue business as usual in accordance with time-tested policy and procedures: low profile pursuit and reduced community awareness to prevent panic and distractions so limited resources could focus. Now the Bluff City Butcher had showed itself. It was going public; everyone was forced to deal with the denial fed by deep-seated fears…turns out there is a BOOGEYMAN out there after all.

The Hernando de Soto Bridge was icing over in spite of the sand and salt. Carol was crawling onto the slippery mess in a single line of traffic. It was 9:00 p.m. and could take another hour to cover the last few miles to the *Peabody*. Then the cars stopped. She sat on the bridge, her needle on empty. Gigantic snowflakes transformed the Memphis skyline into rainbow circles on her windshield; they disappeared with each pass of the blades. She shifted into park, killed the motor and accepted her fate— weather ruled.

It was after 10:00 p.m. when she pulled into a crowded *Peabody Hotel* driveway. She saw the line waiting for valet service and decided to park her own car. Carol was in too deep when she realized the weather had knocked out the hotel garage lights. When she got to the second level she saw one open spot…pulled in and turned off the car. With the lights off she could have been on the dark side of the moon. The locked passenger door popped open. A man got in the seat next to her and stuck a gun in her side.

Carol froze. She could not scream because she'd lost her breath. The gun was jammed in her ribs pointing up to her heart. She kept her eyes straight ahead to avoid seeing her attacker; maybe he would let her live. He was big and breathing hard, bad breath. Without a word, he reached over and his large, cold hand swallowed hers and removed the car keys.

My gun is in my purse in the backseat. My mace is buried in the side door panel; I may be able to find it. My martial arts training didn't cover sitting behind a steering wheel. Carol assumed she would be raped, beaten and robbed. But she might survive if she did not look at her attacker. Her heart was beating in her ears. The gun was pressing harder and the breathing was labored. She couldn't move. Then she realized it was not a gun. It was a butcher knife.

■ ■ ■

"Are you going to kill me this time?" Carol asked.

"Yes," said the Bluff City Butcher.

Oh, God! Carol kept looking straight ahead into the dark, desolate cement bunker. *Why didn't I stop and back out when I saw the lights were out?*

"If I wanted, it would be over." The tip of his knife inched her skirt up her leg to the top of her nylons where it stopped on her skin like a bee sting. She winced and felt a drop of blood roll between her legs. His mouth was close and his breath hot; each word moved her hair. He could see in the dark, like an animal. He was able to take her keys and stopped her reaching for her mace. She felt his eyes on her. *None of the Butcher's victims were sexually violated; they were mutilated and unmercifully killed. Will I feel the knife. Is this real?*

"I am different, and I am the same." He grabbed her left leg above the knee as he spoke. His thumb moved onto the inside of her thigh. She felt the controlled strength in his long fingers that could crush her knee like an eggshell. *What is he saying? What does he mean?*

"I am evil, and I am good," he said as if trying to convince her. "I am certain, and I am lost." He removed his hand from her leg. She pulled her skirt over her shaking knees. *This is how he does it—a ritual. Rants and raves over the victim, works into a rage and then plunges the ice pick into the head. He carries the crippled body to a place where he can savor cutting the throat, the bleeding and the harvesting.*

"My life should be told."

Does he want me to tell his story? Are the words threads of a chance to survive this moment? She started to turn toward the Butcher. *Does this monster have a conscience? Are there fragments of humanity?* Carol asked herself. *Why does the Bluff City Butcher want his life told?* Her chin met an unmoving finger. She forgot and made the fatal mistake. She looked at him.

The knife flew to the base of her ribcage, penetrating her coat and blouse. It stopped sinking into her after it broke the skin and was wet.

"Please, I heard what you want—your life to be told. I can help." Carol prayed her words were enough to slow the wild man's rage. But reality took hold. *Why let me live? Many died like this…begging. I am nothing to you except the one that got away, that saw you. Animal rules are black and white, unemotional. You have killed everyone that has ever looked at you…except me and the one boy on the bluff twenty-five years ago. Any chance I had is gone now.*

CHAPTER SIXTEEN

Carol never felt the knife or heard the question; she was in shock. By the time the lights screamed around the corner, the Butcher was standing in front of the car, ready to disappear. In a stupor, she lifted her head and saw him slide his knife under his belt and close his long, black coat. Tears filled her eyes, blurring the image; she blinked and he was gone. And then, she was gone.

Is this what death feels like?

The screaming engine, smoking tires and steaming headlights slid to a stop, flooding the *BMW* and the surrounding spaces with unbearable white light. She must be dead because there was no more terror, no pain and she felt safe and she heard the voice of the only man she ever loved…wanted to love…but never got the chance.

A loud noise, her door popped open. She was leaning back in her seat with her head limp on her chest. "Carol, thank God I found you." He checked the surroundings as he knelt and put his gun into the ankle holster. His car was smoking behind him with the door open. He was at eye level, his face close. He saw blood. "Honey…Carol." He reached to her abdominal wound; it was minor but her heart raced. She was on the edge of hypertension-induced shock. She was semi-conscious.

Both hands were fused to the steering wheel. He touched her arm; she flinched, gripping even tighter. He scanned the surroundings again and then whispered, "Carol, you are safe now. I'm here, I will protect you." Eyes still closed, she let him move her hands from the wheel to her lap and he gently pushed hair from her eyes. "Darling, you are not alone anymore. I am here with you and you are fine." He held both her hands in one and rubbed her neck. He saw that the passenger door was broken off the hinges and knew who was watching from the black of the garage.

Carol opened her eyes and turned to Elliott. She tried to speak but nothing came out. She saw something in Elliott's eyes she had never seen in a man's eyes before…and she smiled. "Elliott, you came for me."

He took her gently in his arms, kissed her lightly on the neck, feeling her stiffen and then relax. Their eyes met again. "Yes, I came only for you. Let's get you home."

He turned on a few small lamps in Carol's suite, covered her with a blanket and started a fire. She passed on the coffee. They took three shots of whiskey together and sat quietly reliving the ordeal in the garage, their newly exposed feelings, and watching the snow drift into the city. She held onto his hand. They weren't ready to talk…just feel. Each struggled with their feelings and the uncertainty of their worlds. Did they make the other more vulnerable to death by the Bluff City Butcher? Could they have a normal life together? Questions they'd never thought about before. Carol drifted off, her head nestled in the tender spot beneath his chin.

■ ■ ■

In an hour she was much better. Elliott said she rediscovered her stolen confidence and blind courage. After her ordeal and the hour to rest and think about her feelings for Elliott, she kept returning to the same place…when she was faced with certain death she saw only what was important in her life…the hidden feelings she had for Elliott.

207

Wherever it took her was right. No more hiding from life. But she needed a little help getting started. Minutes later, that help would come.

How could he miss fresh blood on her dress? She was wounded on her leg and had completely forgotten about it...in the chaos and her weakened state. But the injury was unknown to Elliott. In his protective, attending physician mode, he jumped into action, sliding off the sofa to his knees and lifting Carol's dress high above his head in search of the serious wound that escaped him...another Bluff City Butcher game. Elliott would never forgive himself if his failure to treat Carol's injury put her life in danger. How could he have missed it?

Upon closer inspection, Elliott found a small scratch on her otherwise gorgeous leg. Embarrassed, he tried not to linger on his knees with his head deep under her dress, although the view was breathtaking. As he gathered his thoughts and attempted to tidy up on his way out, he lifted his chin and cleared her hemline to begin his feeble explanation; he was met with her lips. She pulled him close and held him tight. Every feeling of passion they secretly held ignited the moment.

I fell in love with you the moment our eyes met that November night on the bluff, she thought.

Elliott undressed her with the aggressive and deliberate passion that aroused her wildest desires to have all of him and to give all of her. She opened his shirt and spread her hands across his muscular chest, feeling the beat of his powerful heart as they kissed wildly and tenderly. He explored her total beauty with his mouth as she playfully undressed him and climbed over his chiseled body with her luscious sensuality. They made blazing, passionate love. He caressed her soft, firm curves and she reveled upon his hard body as they were lost in a pleasure they could have never imagined. Their eyes were continuously searching the endless depth of their new love as they shared their souls for the first time.

I will never see life the same way. Elliott experienced the exponential power that flowed when two became one. *Is this what has been missing in my life? Does pure love bring clarity of purpose…another miracle of life as spectacular as the merging of DNA and creation?* Elliott carried Carol into the master bedroom, where they held each other close and shared tender love through the night.

I will sleep on your chest and memorize your heart. Once she'd found love, nothing was more important. Everything was possible.

When I hold you close I feel a new strength that denies my demons access. Elliott felt the edges of something that might give him back his life. Although he was a genius, he knew he did not understand the power of love.

■ ■ ■

"Do you want to talk about last night?"

Carol was barefoot. She climbed onto the sofa with her coffee and sat Indian-style next to Elliott, looking at him mischievously over the brim of her tilted cup. The morning sun was breaking through a sliver of the drawn curtains. Most of the four inches of snow would be gone by night. She kissed him. They were wearing only white terrycloth bathrobes. She let him peek.

Listening to his heart, he recognized he was crazy about her. Carol was intelligent, industrious, feisty, caring, gentle, playful and even more gorgeous in the morning after waking up.

"What is your question?" she asked.

"I think we should talk about last night." But she was in a playful mood.

"Last night on the sofa, all night in bed and, oh yes…all morning too. Are you sure you want to focus on just last night?"

Elliott pulled her to him and kissed her long and hard. When they broke she was dreamy-eyed and speechless. He smiled. Her head fit perfectly in his shoulder, where she could secretly watch him, his strong jaw bone and his gorgeous blue eyes looking at the fire. "Elliott, what is wrong?" she asked as she sat up and their eyes met.

"I think it is time. We need to talk about your visitor last night."

For ten hours her thoughts were occupied by overwhelming feelings for Elliott and unconscious avoidance of reliving the terror in the *Peabody* garage. Carol was far less prepared for the discussion than she could have known. Her familiar fears and frustrations were now hopelessly entangled with a paralyzing, near-death experience and her elevated desire to live a life with Elliott.

He watched her slip into the moment as the smile left her face and her eyes went blank. Again, she felt the weight of cold steel on her thigh. It moved up her leg. It was going into her stomach. The pain was coming. Then she died, she thought. Now, she was back in her suite and the anger was building; how could they put her in that position, twice? Then she went with it.

"My boogeyman, sure, let's talk about my imaginary visitor, the one no one will talk about because it is an urban legend, it is fake."

Elliott watched her slip in and out of her reality; anger was pent up and building as she navigated the fear, the tragedy and the trust. Now she could erupt.

"The Bluff City Butcher came for me last night. You know…the serial killer that Albert Bell, Tony Wilcox and you HAVE NOT BEEN HUNTING FOR TEN YEARS. The small-time, serial killer the Memphis police HAVE NOT BEEN HIDING FROM THE PUBLIC FOR GOD KNOWS HOW LONG. That's the one I was with last night.

"I have been kept in the dark and now you want me to tell you about the monster that pulled the door off my car, like it was popping a top on a can of Coke. You want to know about something everyone denies; the giant that has awful breath and his hand was on my leg ready to pop my leg out of its socket like a doll. It stunk. It was oily and wet and dirty. He spoke to me like an educated man, only a few words at a time. He knew he was stronger and smarter than everyone. The Bluff City Butcher said he was good and he was evil, and he wanted his story told.

"But I can't do this anymore, not now, especially not now, because I love you and I don't want to ever lose you, and no one will admit this thing is real...but me. I don't want to fight people...to keep them alive...anymore."

He reached over and touched her arm. She was trembling. *I would have been concerned if you were in denial or unwilling to let it out.* "Anger is good. You are a healthy, strong lady." Elliott swallowed her in his arms.

I never imagined how big my love could be, and how important it was for me to have a man in my life...a man that made me feel safe for the first time in my life.

"I think we are now officially a couple," said Elliott tenderly.

"I'm sorry. I don't know where all that came from."

"I'm glad you vented your anger with me, Carol."

"Elliott, I have been with that serial killer two times. Somehow I managed to stay alive. I don't think I can survive another one."

"Something must change." Elliott sat up.

"We have each other now; maybe that is a good place to start."

They made love and spent the rest of the day in their robes, sharing their life stories, their hopes and dreams. Elliott told Carol about his gifts, how they give him strength and how they threaten him. He told her that he almost took his life and how she touched his heart at the right moment on that September night when they spoke the first time. He said he knew then she was special to him. They talked about the Bluff City Butcher, Elliott's long history and Carol's discoveries. That day they got closer than they thought possible.

As the last snow melted by the next January sunset on the Mississippi River, Carol and Elliott had shared in a day more than most get around to in years.

"How do you know Albert Bell?" asked Carol.

"I met him in August this year, shortly after the Panther McGee autopsy. I have known of him most of my life."

"Really? How?"

"Albert knew my stepparents. Alberto Bella—his grandfather and the creator of the Bell empire—came to Texas in the early 1900s and set up cotton farmers on the Great Plains, financed irrigation, committed to cotton crops. The Bell patriarch held a meeting in El Paso around Christmas every year with the Texas Cotton Farmers. I went one year; Albert was there."

"Have you ever been suspicious about Albert's interest in the Bluff City Butcher?"

"Suspicious is not the word. I have been curious. Now, I understand."

"What do you know now that allows you to say that?"

"November 5, 2008, the night you chased the Butcher on the bluff, Tony and I were meeting with Albert and Max Gregory at the mansion."

"Who is Max Gregory?"

"Albert's friend, retired CIA, runs a private detective agency—Spyglass. Albert asked Max to find someone for him. Max found a whole lot more and Albert thought he should tell someone. Tony and I were sworn to secrecy…but it's time you knew."

"Ok."

"Albert had an affair in El Paso in 1967. Before you react, he had been separated from his wife for twelve years. When Max said Betty Duncan, I looked at Albert. I think the man still loves her to this day."

"Albert Bell is a man in control. How does he go twelve years honoring his vows and suddenly cross the line?"

"Maybe he met the girl of his dreams. When he returned to Memphis, his estranged wife sought marriage reconciliation. I assume Albert agreed because he thought it was the proper thing to do. He later visited Betty Duncan to break it off and learned she was pregnant. She disappeared. All efforts to find her, and the child he fathered, were unsuccessful."

"Did he have children with his wife prior to the '68 affair?" asked Carol.

"No. He had a daughter in '73 and a son in '82."

"Was Betty Duncan pregnant with a boy?"

"Yes."

"Reconciliation after twelve years, and on the heels of an affair and pregnancy, is no coincidence."

"I agree, but who had something to gain? Albert's daughter, son and wife are deceased. Albert is alone and Betty Duncan dead...or definitely missing."

"How do you know Betty Duncan is dead or missing?"

"There is a connection, Carol. We have identified the Bluff City Butcher. He is Adam Duncan...Albert's illegitimate son."

CHAPTER SEVENTEEN

*"God shows His contempt for wealth by
some of the kinds of persons he selects to receive it."*
Unknown

5 February 2009

The iron gates at the entry of the old Brent Estate were taken down the first week of February 2009. The county put up the new signage in front of the foreboding stone wall on Pleasant Ridge Road, just east of Austin Peay Highway;

WELCOME
North Substation Shelby County Sheriff's Office
NOW OPEN TO THE PUBLIC

The mansion and surrounding twenty-five acres were donated to the county seven years after Old Man Brent's death. He was a strange man that did odd jobs around town and lived in the woods until he saved enough money to buy some cheap land in DeSoto County, north Mississippi. His eventual wealth had nothing to do with intelligence, work ethic, or character and everything to do with dumb luck. He kept buying and selling land until the day *Walmart* wanted some. He seemed to have the kind of real estate that fit their expansion model.

They found him August '02 in his eight-car garage, lying in vomit on the front seat of his Mercedes. The garage was locked from the inside, keys in the ignition and gas tank bone dry. Toxicology confirmed cause of death was carbon monoxide poisoning and oxygen deprivation.

He was found a week after he died. The garage was a giant oven that baked him under the hot Memphis sun. It looked like a suicide, but no note and no history of depression. The decomposition and wealth factors made it impossible to rule out homicide. The M.E. ruled *undetermined manner of death;* needed more information. Two years later, nothing new. The case was filed unsolved, another Shelby County cold case.

Sale of the Brent mansion and surrounding acreage proved to be a problem: the impracticality of the mammoth structures, its rural location and the declining real estate market. In October of 2008 a donation strategy was adopted by the estate handlers. They wanted to close the books. The Shelby County Sheriff's Office wanted a north substation. They took a look. A deal was struck. G.E. Taft wanted the new facility operational February 1, 2009. He was the new sheriff in town; it was ready on schedule.

■ ■ ■

On the other side of the long, foreboding stone wall was a crumbling, one-lane asphalt road level with thick Bermuda grass and long narrow piles of raked leaves. Shrouded by fifty tall oak trees on each side, the little road crossed an open field of fresh cut hay and white sunlight to the front doors of the Pleasant Ridge North Substation.

The enormous Victorian mansion was surrounded by manicured lawns in winter brown, tall elms and endless hedges. Sweeping porches, sculptured pillars, ornate spires, tall black shutters, multi-paned windows, polished brass knobs and hinges, moss-covered brick, etched glass and slow moving porch ceiling fans made the *first encounter* a journey back in time, to an era of southern plantations and the simpler life in the early 1900s.

The Shelby County Sheriff's Office seal was on prominent display at the front steps of the mansion, right after the ominous metal detectors. The tall oak doors opened into the substation's main reception area, a large room with dozens of windows on three long walls and shiny wood floors that matched the library paneling. The room was loaded with green leather chairs left behind by Brent's representatives. The slow moving ceiling fans twenty feet above ran year-round but had little impact on the thick dust hanging in the air since the turn of the century.

The mansion's interior was remodeled to accommodate the basic operational and administrative needs of the sheriff's office. The first floor was remodeled to efficiently process people and paper; traffic tickets got paid, questions got answered and everything below a felony got handled. Felons were held and transferred downtown each night. No one went into the basement; the dark, dank space beneath the house was a catacomb of dead-end halls and dirt rooms with spiders, rats, snakes and other vermin, mostly uncharted waters, rooms and passages that did not exist on any architectural drawings on file with the county. The place was useless, just like the attic that was another place of little interest to anyone, at least not now.

The sharp, pungent smell of onion made its way into the sheriff's office through a cracked window. From the second floor G.E. watched the mowers glide effortlessly over the grounds of his new home away from home. Wearing his favorite tweed coat, he looked more like a college professor than a county sheriff. He was elected by a wide margin, getting a majority of both the black and white vote. That was a rare occurrence in the Midsouth. But Taft was able to cut all the barriers with his honest approach to all issues and commitment to every member of the community. He had the support of all sectors of the county and was backed by his good friend Albert Bell, the beloved owner of *The Memphis Tribune*. Taft said if Albert would run for sheriff he would step down and sleep at night.

At the beginning of his second year he lost Sophia to ovarian cancer. His wife of thirty-five years felt bad one morning. She died five weeks later, never had a chance. Soon after, G.E. started sleeping nights at the office; home alone was too hard. He would fall asleep with case files, reports and newspapers scattered about, sometimes balanced on his stomach and other times in his hand. One night in early February, G.E. fell asleep with the Medino files and some newspaper clippings.

It was the first week of business for the sheriff in the new substation. The sun was just coming up and G.E. Taft was standing at the window with a fistful of news clippings. He turned from the window and broke the morning silence with his firm, gruff voice. *Crash Kills Five in North Memphis...December 22, 2008.* Everyone in the open office sat up in their chairs to listen. *"Around 11:30 p.m. an automobile traveling south on Austin Peay left the road at a high rate of speed north of Pleasant Ridge Road exit...."* At the end of the article G.E. peered over his latest pair of *Walmart* reading glasses. His eyes scanned the room as he reached for his favorite coffee mug. Both deputies were looking at him intensely. The administrative staff was back to busily shuffling papers. After he took a large swallow of black coffee he replanted the mug on the windowsill and watched the mowers disappear into the garage where Old Man Brent killed himself eight years ago. "This one smells real bad, gentlemen. Have we made any progress over the past thirty days since that so-called accident?"

■ ■ ■

Marty Pilsner was the best deputy in Shelby County, but his introverted country demeanor kept him back. G.E. didn't miss much. He knew Pilsner better than Pilsner knew Pilsner. That is why Pilsner's desk was only twenty feet away from his office door.

Gerald Bon was the new kid on the block. He was Pilsner's rookie partner who got good scores on all his tests and had the highest IQ in the department. Gerald was a Greyhound puppy looking for a rabbit. He needed to be raised right or he would chase anything that moved.

Marty's long, skinny body was completely hidden behind the stack of files on his desk. He was bent forward with his nose almost touching the paper as he studied the last case report. He cleared his throat and answered the sheriff's question.

"We have gotten down the road on this one, G.E. but it's a real puzzle needing more work, Sir."

"Go on."

"If you will remember, December 2008 we had a bunch of problems with the scene."

Pilsner lifted his nose out of the file for the first time and jumped when he met G.E. leaning over his pile a foot away. "Hell, yes, I remember…damn it, Pilsner…a lot of peculiar things we damn sure did not share with the press…or anyone else, for that matter."

Pilsner had no reaction. He was startled, like when you spill your coffee or drop a cigarette between your legs while chasing a felon, but he was used to G.E.

"Sheriff, another vehicle was involved. Someone ran Medino off the highway with determination. We can separate farm equipment scratches and dents from the mystery car."

Pilsner sucked up a match with his Camel. "We have a first set of skid marks two hundred yards from where Medino left Austin Peay. We have a second set of skid marks fifty yards out that run solid all the way to the launch point. Medino had both feet on his brake those last fifty yards and we still estimated speed at almost seventy when he became airborne."

"What else?" asked G.E.

"We have witnesses that saw the fire start in the field that night."

"The Medino family sat in the car in the field, entangled in the farm equipment, for about thirty minutes before the fire began."

"What are you saying, Pilsner?" asked G.E. with his eyebrows almost touching and Gerald Bon inching his chair closer.

Pilsner took a long drag off his short cigarette and started talking with smoke coming out of his mouth and nose. "We got us a homicide, Sir."

Pilsner butted out his cigarette and lit up another one. "Sheriff, the timing is what got me wondering. How could a car sit almost thirty minutes and then burst into flames? It is possible under certain conditions I am told, but unlikely. So we checked it out. We spent time with the boys down at the fire station on Front Street—the arson boys. We all went to the scene. They concluded no way the car fire was spontaneous; it was set by someone."

"Shit, I felt it," said G.E.

"Sir, in spite of the high speed trip off the road and the final collision, Medino's gas tank and gas lines were intact—zero leaks. Lincolns are tough cars, Sir. We had it hauled to the county lot for a thorough inspection. I just got the full report. Sheriff, that car had more than a half tank of gas even though the thing looks like a 5,000 pound piece of coal. Most of the fire was in the interior of the car."

"What's the burn evidence telling you?" asked G.E.

"We believe the fire started after the crash near Dr. Medino in the driver's seat. We think someone could have been making sure Dr. Medino was dead."

"Did you get a make and model on the mystery vehicle?' asked G.E.

"The paint has been identified; 1989, 1990 and 1991 Ford…used for utility vehicles and pickup trucks."

"What have we learned from the medical examiner's autopsies?"

"The M.E. passed…no autopsies, only did full body x-rays, external body inspections and collected fluids for toxicology."

G.E. took his glasses off and slid them into his breast pocket, his eyes staring out the window. He had a big problem. "Keep me posted, gentlemen. This one stinks."

"Yes, Sir." Pilsner nodded at Bon.

A few minutes later Pilsner heard G.E. on the phone with the medical examiner. A meeting was set in an hour on the Medino Family HOMICIDE. Standard protocol was full autopsy on accident victims— the M.E. didn't do his job. The evidence showed that Dr. Medino was killed by professionals and the family was along for the ride.

G.E. would have the bodies dug up.

CHAPTER EIGHTEEN

*"All that is necessary for the triumph of evil is
for good men to do nothing."*
Edmund Burke

2 March 2009

By order of the Shelby County Medical Examiner, five muddy coffins arrived at the morgue on Madison Avenue at 5:35 a.m. Sheriff Taft and Deputy Pilsner beat everyone from the cemetery in spite of Monday morning traffic; they were sipping coffee at the back doors when the unmarked county vans pulled up, each carrying a member of the Medino family. Taft was livid when he discovered Bates failed to do autopsies on accident victims in his damn county. He'd demanded the Medino family be dug up and autopsies performed with Dr. Elliott Sumner present.

Pilsner banged on the metal doors. They rolled up with the rhythmical clanging of an old roller coaster climbing its first hill. Henderson Bates was waiting on the other side in his surgical scrubs and a frown. The sheriff did a lot of ass chewing on Bates, who didn't like any of it.

The morning behind the county morgue was dark, cold and damp. The mood was somber but courteous and efficient. With few words, five heavy coffins were moved from the vans onto the loading dock and each placed on heavy-duty flatbeds. The Medino family was checked into the system and rolled into the refrigerator. Each family member would stay in their sealed coffin until it was their turn. One at a time they would be wheeled into the "decomp-room" with laminar airflow and ultraviolet and antimicrobial lighting. The smell of a decaying, burned human corpse was unmistakably terrible and the embalming fluid burned the eyes.

Henderson Bates was a forensic pathologist from the Tennessee Medical School program. He had limited exposure to bizarre homicides; didn't see many weird ones in the Midsouth over his tenure, unlike big cities. He was already used to Elliott Sumner poking around his county and, deep down, he knew he needed the help, even though Sumner was fifteen years his junior and intimidating.

"Before we get started, Sheriff, do you want to say anything?" asked Bates.

"Yes. On December 22, 2008, my deputies responded to a terrible car crash on Austin Peay Highway. The car was burning in a field—no chance of anyone surviving that inferno. No one ever imagined the Medino family would be executed that night! Here we are today, the family taken from their resting place, because we have evidence the *Lincoln* was run off the road and a fire may have been purposely set sometime after the car came to rest. We want some smart people to look at the forensics and tell us what they see so we can catch the bastards."

Bates looked at Sumner. "Shall we begin with Enrique Medino?"

"Certainly, Doctor." Elliott pulled on gloves and adjusted his mask and mic, his brain already humming; he was a precision machine in the world of forensics. Elliott glanced over at Carol in her scrubs; she looked fantastic. She winked through her plastic protective visor. He drew the strength he needed to hold his demons off another day.

"Ok, Billy, release the hounds." The assistant broke the seal on the casket and popped open the lid. The room filled with the pungent stench of burned and rotting tissue mixed with the stinging bite of embalming fluid. Observers gagged and eyes watered, but no one puked this time. The day was young. "Caldwell, hit those HEPA fans on high for a few minutes," ordered Bates, like a captain of a ship turning into battle.

As the disturbing odors hung, the coffin was opened the rest of the way with the expected creepy, squeaking hinge. Although the room was full of educated people, it gave them all willies. The burned body had been sealed in an airtight box underground for sixty days. The fungal, bacterial soup was thriving, driving the natural decomposition process.

Medino's body was lifted from the coffin and placed on a gurney. One arm disconnected and was set on his legs. After a full body X-ray, Medino was moved to the autopsy table under the bright lights surrounded by a wide array of surgical instruments and power equipment. Pictures were taken as Elliott examined the body, dictating external observations. Clothing still fused to the skin was removed and prepared for microscopic examination.

"Dr. Roberts, thank you for coming. Can you educate us on the burns that Dr. Medino sustained?"

"Certainly, please give me a moment." Roberts leaned over the body with a magnifying glass and started dictation. He moved from midline of the abdomen to chest to arm, neck and head. He walked around the table and repeated the process, then legs and feet, talking continuously into his head-mic. When he arrived back at the starting point, he turned to Dr. Sumner. "I would like to hold my final comments. You are the forensic expert, Sir."

"That will be fine." Elliott knew Roberts was uncomfortable. He had never been at an exhumation. Elliott saw the tiny crystals, silica granules and rainbow, an oily residue, carbon powder and oxidized iron flakes. He processed incoming data against his robust data base, twenty years of accumulated knowledge on burns. Elliott's eidetic memory flowed through endless mental notes on burn research, noteworthy cases, electrocutions, thermal and chemical burns, combustibles, flammable materials and motor vehicle fires. Like a pro, he spoke articulately and touched Medino every step of the way to create the formal audio and video record. Witnessing the knowledge and technique of the best in the world, he knew, could become an awesome experience for everyone in the room.

"The fire was not produced by the vehicle. Dr. Medino died from something other than the burns he received. The injuries from the accident were incidental as well." The room was quiet. Medino's body had already told Elliott everything he needed to know. The rest of the time was for the benefit of the others. He spoke slowly and precisely.

"A flammable liquid was introduced on the driver side window and ignited. This took place a short time after the vehicle came to rest in the field. The burn patterns cannot be misinterpreted; the science is known and predictable. The most severe burns sustained were the greatest distance from all other sources of vehicular flammables. That is illogical; therefore, other flammables were introduced another way."

"Then how can gasoline be associated with the fire?" asked Bates.

"Gasoline is not the combustible that caused this fire and Medino's burns."

"I don't understand, if not gasoline…then what?"

"Kerosene," said Elliott, as he turned to Dr. Roberts, "Kerosene."

"Exactly, Dr. Sumner, I concur," said Roberts. "I could barely smell it through the decomposition and embalming stench, but it is there."

The M.E. realized he'd botched the Medino case in December; he was embarrassed that five homicides almost got by him. It was time to set his personal feelings aside and to get to work. They cracked Medino's chest and methodically inspected, removed and sectioned each organ. Sumner offered to do the cranial and Bates agreed. Soon Elliott validated the last piece of the puzzle, information he was looking for…but with surprises.

"We have a cause of death," said Elliott.

His cranial dissection skills were flawless. With his scalpel, he made a ten-inch incision from above the right ear, around the back of the head at the base of the skull to a point above the left ear. He inserted a surgical spatula to separate the subdermal connective tissue from the boney skull. When done, he pulled the scalp forward and folded it over the face, pulling it down below the nose like removing a Halloween mask from the back of the head.

The skull was circumferentially cut with a power saw and the top portion lifted off, revealing the brain beneath the thin, translucent covering—the dura-mata sheath. Elliott held the skull cap to the light; the photographer zoomed in for the close-up. A small, circular penetration fracture was on the coronal suture, measuring 3.175 mm in diameter. He pointed to the dura-mata and matching puncture wound.

"Dr. Bates, I will need a nine-inch probe," asked Elliott with gloved fingers pointing to the heavens.

"Billy, give Dr. Sumner the disposable probe set."

He inserted. "As you can see, the tip of the probe reaches the midpoint of the brainstem, penetrating several vital sensory control centers including large motor—arms and legs—cardiovascular and the respiratory control centers." With a laser pointer Elliott highlighted the centers on the digital image for the record. "Note the dime-size shadow at the base of the wound track in the brainstem; it is fluted."

"What does that mean?" asked Sheriff Taft as he leaned over Elliott's shoulder.

Bates, who had been uncharacteristically quiet for the last ten minutes, answered. "That means the device used to penetrate the skull and reach the brainstem was pistoned, moved up-and-down repeatedly at varying angles. The action scrambles brain tissue—disrupting and damaging. The killer wanted to be certain everything shut down."

"Dr. Medino was alive after the accident. When the *Lincoln* came to a stop in the field he was conscious, pinned by the steering wheel. He saw his killer."

"I am certain an ice pick was introduced after the crash, paralyzing Medino. He was aware of everything but unable to move when he was doused with kerosene and set on fire," said Elliott. "I suspect you will find identical wounds on each member of the Medino family." Elliott left the probe in place and stepped back so Bates, the official M.E., could take over.

"Sheriff, there is nothing new here. The Memphis PD and FBI have been adequately informed since December 2008, on what we think we are up against, right, Agent Voss?" asked Carol accusingly.

Voss harrumphed, "That is 'Director Voss,' and I would say we have…"

Taft interrupted. "Pardon my French, Madam; I have no beef with you or Dr. Sumner. But this shit has got to stop." G.E. gave up on containing his immense irritation at the dimwits all around the Memphis mystery. "I have stayed in the background long enough waiting for Director Wade and his boys to do something. Voss, you should be ashamed; the FBI in Memphis has been useless as tits on a warthog for years. The time has come for some old-fashioned police work. Keeping this Bluff City Butcher a secret from the people of Shelby County is bullshit. Our job is to protect them, not use them as bait, for God sakes."

Taft turned to Elliott. "Doc, can you and Mason give me and Pilsner some time today to get up to snuff? We have got to get going on this thing with or without the God Damn Memphis PD. We have some ideas. If they have a problem, Shelby County will take your contract over and pay you double. And Miss Mason, I like the way you kick ass and take names. Albert will let you do whatever you think needs doing."

"Tonight good?" asked Elliott.

"Yup. When and where?" asked Taft.

"Sheriff, I will call your office on that," said Carol.

"Good. Voss, you need to tell the Feds we ain't waiting anymore for the magic. From now on you are along for the ride."

"Yes, Sir. I will pass that on," said Voss.

"Tony, I don't blame you, buddy. But you need to tell your boss G.E. is getting into this now. I recommend you boys GO PUBLIC on the Bluff City Butcher before I do. You tell Wade to call me with questions. The Medino family is not going to die in my county without a lot of shit hitting the fan."

Elliott and Carol left the decomp-room, doors swinging behind them as another casket rolled by them.

"Are you all right, Elliott?" Carol asked as he put his arm around her waist and she grabbed his hand on the way to the car. They stopped when they were out of earshot.

"That was not the work of the Bluff City Butcher. Something is going on around here and we need to find out fast."

The Memphis Tribune

Memphis Police GOING PUBLIC: Serial Killer in Midsouth

March 17, 2009

Carol Mason

Memphis, TN – Today the Memphis Police Department held a press conference to inform the community a serial killer was in the area. Director Collin Wade said the killer may be linked to unsolved homicides in the Metro Area. MPD would not specify how many cases.

Wade said the FBI has been involved. "A substantial amount of resources are directed to apprehending the killer and we urge Midsoutherners to be calm, cautious and vigilant." Wade and other police officials would not answer questions, citing police policy with ongoing investigations. When reminded "cold cases" are not active investigations, Wade had no further comments.

A Midsouth killer, tagged the "Bluff City Butcher" by the media in 1983, attacked four men wielding a large knife. Three were killed by the stranger, who escaped, jumping off the Harahan Bridge. A body was never recovered. City officials reject the sensational treatment of a common criminal and discourage others from fanning public fears, causing unfounded panic and despair. They had no further comments on the Urban Legend that has captivated Midsoutherners for 25 years and would not say how long they have been looking for the serial killer.

In related stories, *The Memphis Tribune* and Memphis PD collaborative review Metro Area Cold Cases from 1995 to 2005 is near completion. Sources close to law enforcement say privately the findings are connected to the serial killer in the area.

■ ■ ■

ON AIR - LIVE

"Welcome back, ladies and gentlemen. I am Jimmy Doyle and you are listening to *Talk of Memphis,* W K R C…eleven…ninety on your A. M. dial. It is 8:35 p.m., March 17, 2008.

"Ok…I have Dennis in Midtown. You are on *Talk of Memphis.*"

"Hello, Mr. Doyle. You know, with all this talk about a serial killer in Memphis I have a friend that is a Memphis cop and he told me the FBI has been looking for this guy a long time, several states. They think this serial killer is linked to a hundred killings, and none of this is public information. The FBI has regular meetings with the police to update them so they keep their eyes open. They think the guy has lived in the Midsouth a long time."

"Did your friend say when these meetings with the FBI took place?"

"Yeah, they do two a year."

"Two a year? How long have they been doing them?"

"Well, my buddy has been a cop six years and he said they were doing them before he got there."

"Best kept secret. Thanks, Dennis in Midtown. Ok, hello Linda in Germantown. You're on *Talk of Memphis.*"

"The Dennis guy just on the phone said the police and FBI have been looking for this serial killer for over six years and bodies are stacking up. If they don't find this animal soon, there will be people leaving Memphis. I am scared to death! I cannot believe law enforcement kept something like this from the community it is supposed to protect."

"I'm sure there are many people out there that share your concern, Linda. But you know it is pretty much standard procedure for the police to pursue serial killers behind the scenes."

"No, that is news to me and I don't like it at all. They are supposed to protect us. How can that happen when they don't tell us about danger in our midst?"

"Well, you don't have to like it but it is a fact. Going public with information on a serial killer can make things worse. The police never want to educate the killer on what they know nor do they want to motivate more killing. Going public can produce copy cats and generate useless leads that take limited resources away from the real police work. The list of negatives is substantial," said Doyle.

"Their way doesn't work! Look how long these killers get away with it and look at how many innocent people are getting killed. The local police and the FBI need to rethink what they are doing to protect us."

"James in Olive Branch, you're on *Talk of Memphis* with Doyle. What say you?"

"I got one question for you, Doyle. If a lion got out of the zoo and your neighborhood was a mile away, would you go jogging that night?"

"No. I would probably refrain from jogging days too," said Doyle.

"That's the point, Doyle. The people running the zoo aren't telling you the damn lion is loose. You cannot make that basic safety decision to deal with the unsafe condition; a simple act of jogging may get you killed! People at the zoo never have the right to keep such dangerous information to themselves. If you are mauled by the lion, they are responsible."

"Victoria in Bartlett, you're next on *Talk of Memphis*. What do you have for us?"

"I have a question, Mr. Doyle. Do you think there are serial killers that have killed a hundred people? Or is that just more urban legend stuff?"

"Well, I have read about a few over the years. But I think a serial killer is too stupid to kill so many times without being caught."

"Jeff in Memphis, you are on the air."

"Where can I learn more about the Bluff City Butcher urban legend? It was interesting the police never used the name in their press conference this morning. I guess they think the Butcher is bullshit."

"Actually, Jeff, it is probably the opposite. The police avoid use of such names or tags to avoid scaring people. The last thing they want is all of us running around in fear."

"Do you know the urban legend, Mr. Doyle?"

"Yes. In '83 there was an incident on the river bluff. Four guys were attacked by a large man with a large knife…three died that night and the man with the knife jumped in the river and was never found. Everything after that is a ghost story. Does it exist?"

"I go the other way. I think we show an arrogance when we deny the existence of things we don't yet understand. The best position to take on the unknown is to consider the possibility, be cautious and learn."

"Well said, Jeff. Along those lines, I invite all my listeners to tune in tomorrow night. My guest is the only man alive who stood face-to-face with the Bluff City Butcher that night in 1983 on the bluff. He watched three of his friends die by the knife of the urban legend.

"Why was he allowed to live? What was the Butcher like? He has lived out of the country alone with these answers and more…for twenty-five years. He is back to tell his story…against the wishes of the Memphis PD and FBI. Tell your friends and be sure to tune in tomorrow night."

"Ok, we have Vicki in Tunica. You are on *Talk of Memphis.*"

"I missed the beginning of the show. Did you cover the police press conference?"

"Yes. We touched on it, why?"

"Well, I don't think I'm alone on this, but that was a joke. They must think we are idiots. They are so LAME to say they are looking for someone possibly linked to a few unsolved deaths in the Midsouth."

"What is your point, Vicki?"

"What is my point…ARE YOU KIDDING? It is 2009. I have more information on my *iPhone* than the MPD, or they are still playing games with the community. Right now, there are more details on the

Bluff City Butcher and unsolved murders across five states on *Facebook, Twitter* and *Google.*"

"Ah ha…that's right, the communication age is upon us," said Doyle.

"No offense, Mr. Doyle, but you are showing your age."

"Well, I am an old fart, Vicki in Tunica. But I am into this big time."

"Mr. Doyle, we are dealing with a sick serial killer that has been around here a long time. The top people in the field of forensic pathology and criminology have weighed in on this monster. The world-renowned serial killer hunter, Dr. Elliott Sumner, profiled the Bluff City Butcher ten years ago. Sumner described this one as a REAL MONSTER. The most dangerous human predator he has ever encountered, that has possibly killed more than any in American history."

"I always say my audience is the smartest in the world. Thank you, Vicki."

"One comment…the Bluff City Butcher may have other names in other places over the years. When it recently showed itself in Memphis, Dr. Sumner came out of retirement and is in Memphis working with the police. He now believes Memphis has always been the Butcher's home. I suggest you get Carol Mason from the *Tribune* or Sumner on your show. Goodbye."

"Goodbye, Vicki. I have time for one more call. We have Adam in Atoka. What say you, Adam?"

"Marcus cannot talk on your show."

"Excuse me?"

"No Marcus," said the caller.

"No Marcus. Why, Adam in Atoka?" asked Doyle.

"No Marcus…or you will be in this. You will meet my anger, Doyle."

"What in the world are you saying? Excuse me…Hello. He's gone. That was a strange call, ladies and gentlemen, no idea what just happened…and we are out of time.

"Ok, remember to tune in tomorrow night to hear from our special guest, the only man alive that saw the Bluff City Butcher. This is your host Jimmy Doyle signing off. Thank you for listening, goodnight everybody."

He hit seven toggles down and one toggle up, *Talk of Memphis* was off the air and uninterrupted classical music would drift over the airwaves until 5:30 a.m. and then the morning show would take over.

What in the hell was that last guy about? Doyle thought as he pulled together his pile of notes and references. *Nobody knew Marcus was the guest except me and Bear. The guy came to me after the press conference, wanting to talk on air. The only way was if his name was not used in the promo. But still, it would be difficult to find. That's what the Adam guy did, the prick. Damn, I hope Marcus didn't hear.*

"Hey, Jimmy, very good show; you're the master." Barry Branch was always pumping up Doyle's ego as the self-appointed program director, just one of his many useless responsibilities.

"Hey, Bear, what was that last caller all about?" asked Doyle.

"Hold on, Jimmy, you have a visitor coming your way. I will shut some things down and see you in a few."

His broadcast studio door opened. "Mr. Doyle, I'm Detective Wilcox with Memphis Homicide." Tony closed the door behind him.

"Why are you here?"

"Your last caller. Mr. Doyle," Tony frowned and pocketed his badge.

"The weirdo—Adam in Atoka—what about him?"

"Adam called me on my cell after he spoke on your program tonight."

"Shit, is Adam a cop messing with me?" asked Doyle.

"No, far from it." Tony moved in closer to Doyle.

"What in the hell is going…"

Tony raised his hand and cut off Doyle. "I'm going to say things. I can only ask you to keep this confidential. But understand that I will deny everything and you will look stupid, got it?"

"Fuck…you are scaring the shit out of me." Jimmy stood up.

"I'm sorry, but sometimes things in this world are complicated. Being here puts me in conflict with my direct orders, but if I were in your shoes I would want to know what I have to say."

Doyle sat down. Beads of sweat rolled from his sideburns. His armpits were already soaked. "Fuck…ok, this conversation never happened. I tend to cuss when I am against the wall…ok?"

There was a soft rap on the door then it opened. Tony did not take his eyes off Doyle. Alex Harris leaned his head in the room, unwilling to commit his entire body to what was going to happen next. "Alex?"

"Yes, Sir, Alex here."

"And?"

"It's him, for sure," said Alex.

"Thank you, Detective Harris. Please keep people out for a while."

"Yes, Sir." The door closed with a soft muffle…a soundproof room.

"Oh, SHIT, what the fu, fu, fu."

"Mr. Doyle, you were talking to the Bluff City Butcher."

"Adam in Atoka is the Bluff City Butcher?"

"The name Adam means nothing. It was handy, that's all," said Tony knowing Adam Duncan was the Butcher. "The very real Bluff City Butcher was on the phone with you tonight."

"How do you know?"

"We have his voice print. We got a match, just a confirmation of what we already knew the moment I got the call on my cell. Mr. Doyle, we have been looking for him many years."

"The Bluff City Butcher is real?" asked Doyle. "I knew it."

"Yes, unofficially."

"But why is he calling me?"

"He listens to the radio. We monitor talk shows as part of an effort to understand behavior and next moves."

"Why is he interested in me?"

"If you allow Marcus Pleasant on your show the Butcher will put you and your friends on his list to kill."

"And he has done that before?"

"Oh, yes, and there is little we can do to protect you."

"Thanks for the heads-up, Detective. You are a good guy to take a risk to let me know. I do understand rules, although I don't follow many, but I do know what they are." They both laughed and stopped abruptly.

"This is a tough situation. I wish we could put Marcus on the radio so people could get the truth. But it just is not worth risking your life."

"Well, I may be accused of many things, Detective Wilcox, but I am not letting some halfwit, sick prick control my life."

"I don't think this is something you want to mess with, Mr. Doyle. The Bluff City Butcher is dangerous."

"I am sure he is dangerous."

"He has killed more people than you can imagine and their deaths were horrific, excruciatingly painful and prolonged. This demented monster enjoys what he does. In the strongest possible terms, I advise you to cancel Marcus."

"Cancel?"

"Marcus understands that he will be committing suicide by coming on your show. Mr. Doyle, he has had twenty-five years of torment. He cannot take it anymore. He is willing to give what is left of his life hoping the Bluff City Butcher makes that one fatal mistake."

"You want me to cancel the biggest show I could ever have? The one that will get me the national attention I deserve?"

"Mr. Doyle, I record my calls." Tony pulled out his cell phone. "I want you to hear this."

"*Yes.*"

"*Hello, TONY.*"

"Long time, no hear, BCB. Where have you been?"

"Busy."

"Did you hurt the Medino family?"

"No."

"It looked like your work."

"I watched…I will cut up the weasel on the fourth of July."

"Time to stop this, BCB…let me get you help."

"No. I like it. Others need help."

"Why the call?"

"No Marcus show, tell the fat mouth running the show."

"Why should that bother you?"

"I will butcher Doyle and show him to the world. He gets one chance."

"I am going to find you."

"I will find you when I am ready."

Tony closed his phone and slipped it into his pocket. Doyle was white and wet. "You heard the voice of a very sick serial killer. Mr. Doyle, you do not want to get his attention. We have had a dozen specially trained undercover agents on this for a decade. So far, this guy does whatever he wants to do and we can't stop him."

"What makes him unstoppable?" asked Doyle.

"He is a demented genius. He is a psychopath with an IQ way off the charts. He is physically superior to men…animal-like strength. The Bluff City Butcher is a homicidal anomaly—a beast with brains."

"How does a genius become a serial killer?"

"They tell me intelligence has nothing to do with crazy."

There was a knock at the door. Tony stood up. In walked Branch. "It's late. Are you guys about through?"

Tony turned to Jimmy Doyle and extended his hand. "Mr. Doyle, thank you again for giving me a few minutes to meet you. I am a real fan. Your show is fantastic, good for Memphis, and thanks for letting us listen to the nut on your tape. We will do our best to make sure he is not a problem."

"I appreciate that, Detective. I guess we all have to deal with the crazies from time to time. Please come back to see us anytime." Jimmy did his part. Bear had no idea what went down behind closed doors.

Why should both of them be petrified?

It was after midnight. Doyle was threatened by the Bluff City Butcher and his car was the last one in the dark station parking lot behind Beale. He walked a convoluted line to stay under the working flood lights. He felt eyes. His heart was thumping. Once he was safely in the car, doors locked and the backseat confirmed empty, Doyle's confidence started to come out of hiding. By the time he got to his apartment he was not allowing some sick bastard to tell him how to run his show.

By morning, Doyle had the script completed for his national promotion of the *Marcus Interview*. Bear would tape promo spots and feed them to sixty-four radio and TV stations, *Internet* and communications networks. His promotion would make it very clear to the Bluff City Butcher: someone would tell his story...the one who had seen the sick bastard face-to-face.

■ ■ ■

> *"During times of universal deceit, telling the
> truth becomes a revolutionary act."*
> **George Orwell**

18 March 2009

He was up twenty-four hours straight. He walked into the station directly to the broadcast booth and briskly slammed the door behind him. All eyes were on Doyle; he was not talking.

His coffee mug was filled to the brim next to the microphone. He dropped an armful of papers on his desk, *America's Serial Killers* on top. With eyes closed, Doyle sat, sipped and psyched-up.

He was scared.

A knuckle rapped on the glass. Eyes opened…five fingers in the glass…four, three, two, and one…

ON AIR

"Hello everybody, this is W K R C 1190 on your AM dial. It is a Wednesday, March 18, and the time is 5:58 p.m. in Memphis, Tennessee…the City on the bluff next to the majestic Mississippi River.

"Welcome to… *Talk of Memphis,* the number-one radio talk show in the Midsouth, and you know me…your host Jimmy Doyle. Are you ready for another scintillating, electrifying and illuminating night of discussion, my friends? We have a lot to do tonight and we will waste no more time.

"Our Memphis Police are going public with old news, friends. Yesterday morning a five-minute MPD press conference had the full attention of our community. They tell us that they BELIEVE we JUST MAY HAVE a serial killer in our midst, but they can't tell us what they know…an active investigation.

"Let's see what we already know and add that to all the helpful information we received from our police department who ARE SERVING AND PROTECTING.

"We know a serial killer has been in the Midsouth since 1983. We know he takes people randomly at night and kills with a butcher knife. We know he takes body parts. Now, add it to the information we received from the MPD; *cannot find it, cannot catch it, cannot talk about it.* Well, our conclusion is simple. The serial killer is very sick, very angry and very intelligent. I suggest the Memphis police could begin by calling this serial killer by his correct name: Bluff City Butcher! Once they admit to the

OBVIOUS, I would suggest they change strategy because IT AIN'T BEEN WORKING FOR TWENTY-FIVE YEARS NOW.

"Everything we know about the Bluff City Butcher we get from urban legend. How do you separate THIS TRUTH from the available information sources that are dealing with things like *Big Foot, the Loch Ness Monster, the Headless Horseman*, and the Boogeyman? Why is law enforcement leaving us with that crap? Because they think we are unable to deal with reality.

"Ladies and gentlemen, I am tired of being treated like a child. I am tired of public servants not serving; instead, they're making big decisions without consulting me.

"Their job is to serve and protect this community. Sharing vital information when danger is imminent is expected. Yes, their job is to catch the bad guys, but we are not their bait tackle box. Damn it to hell, I expect…I demand more from city servants.

"I challenge the Memphis Police Department, Shelby County Sheriff's Office, the medical examiner's office, city and county mayors and Metro Area law enforcement agencies to call me right now. Deny one single thing I claim to be true about this serial killer. My phones are open and I am waiting…the whole damn Midsouth community is waiting.

"I challenge law enforcement to rethink their strategy, devise a new one. The Bluff City Butcher is winning.

"Midsoutherners, the lion is out of its cage and the zookeepers have not told us for a very long time. How many of us must be eaten alive before we are given all the information SO WE CAN HAVE A LOUSY CHANCE TO SURVIVE THIS UNVBELIEVABLE, HORRIFIC NIGHTMARE?"

"Are you near a radio?" Tony called Elliott from headquarters.

"Yes, I'm with Carol, have Doyle on now; sounds like he passed on your advice to back away." The radio program, on in the background, went to commercial.

239

"I guess it was a good idea to leak to a public venue; otherwise, change in strategy would take another year at best."

"Maybe this will stir things up, get the changes we need and save a few lives."

"Elliott, Doyle figured out what I was doing. He is a stand-up guy putting himself out there like that. He understands the risks."

"My father told me a long time ago that life was all about preparation for those few moments that come along that matter. This moment belongs to Jimmy Doyle. And he knows it. He is a good man."

"But the price is so great, Elliott."

"Tony, we make those decisions every day. Jimmy Doyle understands the price and has decided it is worth it. I respect him for that."

"I will catch up with you tomorrow."

"Later." He called his partner.

"Yes, Sir?" answered Alex.

"I want three undercovers on Doyle's back twenty-four-seven starting now, and it would be best to keep this low profile. Keep it from Doyle."

"Sir, I'm listening to 1190. Three of our best are at the WKRC station in various obscure roles with eyes on Doyle." Tony smiled. Alex was starting to figure things out on his own. He closed his cell and turned up the radio.

"Yes, we should be in fear for our lives. Yes, we should have our questions answered by law enforcement. The time has come…citizens in a community are not to be used as sacrificial lambs when danger is here.

"We are in the dark because this serial killer is far worse than anyone imagined; it is a killing machine, a predator walking among us like a lion in a herd of elk searching for the next one it will take. I say hell no! I am going to run like hell until I cannot run, and then I am going to kick like hell until I cannot kick, and then I am going to pray that when the lion is at my throat the rest of the herd comes to trample that lion to death.

"PEOPLE, I have a very special person with me tonight. He is the only man who saw the Bluff City Butcher twenty-five years ago and lived. *Talk of Memphis* is where you get the information that matters. He has spoken with law enforcement, done his duty, but he is going a step further; he is talking to the community. This is Jimmy Doyle. We will be right back."

Doyle flipped the toggle down; the "ON AIR" light box went out. The staff at the WKRC station crowded around the broadcast booth glass, applauding. The whistles and cheers felt good, but Jimmy knew he'd just signed his death warrant. Wilcox needed someone to step up because his hands were tied in the political machinery of the city. The time was right for Doyle. He figured if the Bluff City Butcher had a list, he was probably already on it, with or without Marcus Pleasant on his show. He pretty much was on everybody's shit list.

ON AIR - LIVE

Four…three…two…one…"And we are back, ladies and gentlemen. Tonight, *Talk of Memphis* has a special service to perform. We have with us the man who survived the city's first encounter with the legendary Bluff City Butcher.

"Tonight, a man's walk down a very dark road in his life will be difficult to hear: his losses, his terror and his pain. Why would he do it? Why relive this horrific nightmare with millions of people on a nationally syndicated radio show…and why now?

"Marcus Pleasant believed the Bluff City Butcher died when he leaped off the Harahan Bridge, dropped a hundred feet and crashed into the turbulent waters of the Mississippi River that fateful night in 1983. The only way Marcus could live his life from that day forward was by letting the river carry away the unimaginable evil he witnessed.

"But the suspicious events across the Midsouth changed his mind. He heard enough to know the Bluff City Butcher survived. The twisted

241

predator was stepping out of the fog of urban legend. The Midsouth was his *killground* and he was UNSTOPPABLE. Marcus, now a retired Navy Seal living in Baltimore, came home to tell his story, because maybe knowing what is out there can save lives.

"Ok, here is how this is going to work, ladies and gentlemen. I am holding calls for a while. Tonight, Marcus will tell his story. Along the way, I will ask questions that I think you may have. When we are finished, Marcus will decide if he will take questions. Marcus agreed to two sessions, one tonight and the second on our next program; you will call in with your encounters and Marcus will separate fact from fiction. He believes others have seen this guy, but their information is getting lost. Ok, let's begin."

He sat in the chair across from Doyle; the microphone was positioned so he could talk normally and lean back comfortably.

"Welcome, Marcus, I am very pleased to meet you," said Doyle.

"Thank you for having me, Sir. I must admit that I got cold feet this afternoon. I am good now."

"Marcus, please call me Jimmy." Doyle watched as Marcus nodded. "Let's not waste any time. This is your moment. Please." He turned on Marcus's microphone.

"I saw the man the first day Memphis knew something real bad had come to town. I guess I saw him before they gave him a name."

"You are referring to the Memphis urban legend. Is that right?"

"Yes. I guess it is urban legend to you and others—I get that. To me and my friends the Bluff City Butcher is a real monster."

"Yes, we are certainly detached from your reality. Go ahead, Marcus."

"It was a Monday night, October 17, 1983. I'd had my twenty-third birthday and joined the Navy earlier that month. I hooked-up with friends at Captain Bilbo's, a decent restaurant on the bluff, good bar at night. Anyway, it was supposed to be a going away party; I was leaving for San Diego in a few days and then shipping out to the Persian Gulf for a two-year tour. We got the table out on the back deck where that Weatherford girl sat the day before…before she was kidnapped."

"That would be Sabina Weatherford, the five-year-old child taken off the deck of Captain Bilbo's the prior Sunday morning. They never found Sabina. Please continue."

"Well, Sir, we were drinking beer, talking and cutting up some and looking at the Mississippi River…the barges, and the sun slowly dropping and stuff. It was the end of a nice day. And then it started, rustling weeds and all, noises on the bluff in the tall grass. Cory wanted to go check."

"Go ahead, you're doing great," said Doyle as he adjusted his mic.

"Well…we were talking about the kidnapping and the man they described in the news…all kind of spooky but also interesting. We were getting drunk and I'm not proud, but I smoked a lot of pot that day, so nothing really mattered much to me.

"I came back from the bathroom and my friends were gone. I saw Teddy carrying three beers into the weeds on the bluff. Well, maybe twenty or thirty minutes later, when I had not heard from them, I started to worry they would freeze if they slept it off out there."

"Is that when you went looking for them?"

"Yes. I went into the weeds. There was a path, matted grass, and then…" His head dropped, turning side to side…NO. Thirty seconds of silence on a radio broadcast was suicide. Jimmy's instincts said wait. When it came to radio, he was always right. He knew *Talk of Memphis* was going into homes across the country; the syndication deal was hatched in November. He understood that people despise evil and Marcus was the good guy against evil…that lived. Jimmy's audience would wait for Marcus—the victim—because they were there for him this time…and they were dying to hear more about the monster.

"Take all the time you need, Marcus. I know this is hard."

"I'm sorry. I don't like what happens next. I've kept it in a place that I stayed away from for a long time because I…"

"Marcus, you are with friends now. Ladies and gentlemen, we will be right back." Doyle cut for commercial.

He did something unheard of; he told Marcus to stop…call it a night. Jimmy saw what it was doing to Marcus: the tremors, sweating and gasping for breath. Doyle could not put another human being through it, not even for ratings. He told Marcus to sit there and pull himself together. It was over. When Marcus was back in control he could get up and walk out of the broadcast booth and go back to Baltimore. He was done.

ON AIR - LIVE

"And we are back. Ladies and gentlemen, I am sorry. We cannot continue with Marcus tonight. He has been through the ringer already. This is far worse than I had imagined…the price this man is paying…again…it is too much to ask. I am sorry, but…"

Marcus reached over and turned on his microphone. "I need to tell my story." His eyes said he was not leaving. He'd carried the terror and pain alone too long. He wanted it out of him tonight. He wanted to help Memphis and help himself. He would tell them about the predator on the bluff and then he would leave Memphis forever.

"Ok, Marcus…the microphone is yours." Doyle could almost see people across the country stop everything to hear the man who survived a hideous serial killer. The twisted roots of the Memphis urban legend would be pulled from a dark hole and held up to the light.

"I saw the big man with the black ponytail, wearing a long coat. The Weatherford girl was sitting next to him and two of my friends—Cory and Roger—had their backs to me. Teddy was not there…not so I could see him, that is. The Butcher saw me right away. I slipped and fell on my back looking at him. He just smiled. He was not worried about me. He was in control.

"He had a knife in his left hand. It was a long knife, ten…twelve inches, and the shiny blade was fat…it flickered in the light…the sun was half down. His eyes stayed on me the whole time. I froze. Everyone was watching him. Nobody was moving." Marcus stopped talking again. He was shaking. He ran his hand over his military cut and a rooster tail of sweat caught Doyle's attention.

"Marcus…"

"The knife…I see a blur. His arm goes down, up fast…but my friends are in the way. I can't see. Then he lifts him up."

"Who does he lift up, Marcus?"

"Teddy. He holds him by his hair and lifts him up."

"Is he trying to get away or calling for help?"

"No. He is…"

"Unconscious?" asked Doyle.

"His mouth is moving. He is trying to say something. His eyes are open but he is not looking anywhere."

"He doesn't see you, Marcus?"

"No…Teddy is dead. He didn't have his body anymore."

"Oh, my God." Jimmy turned aside and threw up in a trash can.

Marcus was mumbling in a daze. "I couldn't move. I turned my head away and then he was standing in front of me with Teddy's head. I couldn't look at Teddy. I looked at HIM, the biggest human being I ever saw: mad eyes in thin circles of dirty white, nostrils opening and closing, grey skin peppered with black and blood and black hair…tied in a knot."

Marcus got up. The image was more than he could take. He had put that monster in a dark place for twenty-five years. Now, he'd let it out and it was bad.

"I saw the knife stuck in the ground next to me. I could reach…but he was watching me. He smiled and held his hand up. Like a bolt of lightning, it passed my face. I was cut—my nose—like a bee sting. I was bleeding. He leaned over me and smelled me…memorized me. I waited to die." Marcus was done: exhausted, breathing hard and soaking wet.

"Marcus?"

He never heard the question. "I opened my eyes and he was gone. They were all gone: the girl, Cory, Roger and Teddy. I was drenched. I thought it was water. It was blood."

"Marcus, let's stop," said Jimmy.

"I lost three friends that night. I don't know why he left me. I wish he had killed me, too."

"Marcus…"

"I've got to go, NOW." He jumped up and left the broadcast booth…all eyes on him as Jimmy Doyle's voice vibrated out of the speakers at WKRC.

"Memphis…Marcus has left the building. This has been a very difficult time for a man who has carried a terrible load for so many years. What he said is more terrible than anything I could ever imagine living through. There are many who believe the monster he described, the Bluff City Butcher, is out there right now.

"I sincerely hope Marcus Pleasant benefits from the hell he just went through. And I pray the total story gets out there soon so we all have a chance against this darkness that has fallen on our city.

"This is Jimmy Doyle and the *Talk of Memphis*, wishing all of you a safe journey. Goodnight, everybody." Doyle hit the toggle and the music piped through the station speakers. Marcus was booked for two nights. Doyle didn't expect him to show again.

CHAPTER NINETEEN

19 March 2009

Albert Bell phoned Director Wade and Sheriff Taft at 4:00 in the morning. They came to the mansion immediately. They all agreed a meeting of the people involved must be held before the end of the day.

He called each name on the list and offered a limo to pick them up at 5:00 p.m. Albert was not surprised everyone was available and most accepted his offer for a limo. He simply told each the truth. He had an unexpected visitor in the early morning hours; the Bluff City Butcher had left a letter, and their name was on a list.

The limousines crossed the grounds with motorcycle security alongside. They rolled to the front doors of the Bell mansion; each guest was met and escorted to the east room. Taft, Wade and Wilcox had arrived earlier.

Guests were seated at the long conference table on an oriental rug centered in a square room. The twelve-foot ceilings, antique-white walls and tall windows draped in blue and gold lace curtains gave the spacious environment an inviting ambience. The slow moving ceiling fans and colorful oil paintings of Midsouth landmarks framed in brushed gold were spaced tastefully around the room. Fresh cut flowers in giant urns stood at the corners, releasing a summer fragrance.

Charles Dunn and Timothy Loman walked in with Nicolas Heller, three high-net-worth investors heavily involved in the *Life2 Corporation*. They took three seats at the far end of the table. Tony Wilcox entered with Colin Wade, G.E. Taft and Dexter Voss; they sat near the middle. Jimmy Doyle and Dr. Bates sat next to Taft. Jack Bellow, the president/CEO of the *Life2 Corporation,* did not acknowledge the presence of the investors—Dunn, Loman and Heller. He sat at the opposite end. The last to enter were Elliott and Carol followed by Michael Bell and Albert, who took the open seat at the head of the table.

The sun was down. It was already a dark and cold night. No one was talking. All eyes were on Albert. He carried a black leather valise that was now on the table in front of him as he sat and politely nodded to each guest. Small crystal pitchers of ice water and glasses on linen on sterling silver trays lined the center of the table. At twelve of the thirteen seats were black leather binders with paper and pen. Everyone watched as Albert poured a glass of water and took a swallow, his eyes looking over the rim, moving up one side of the table and down the other…again. He confirmed everyone's presence and signaled William at the double doors. The overhead lights dimmed and the doors closed with a soft muffle.

"Good evening, everyone. Thank you for making this assemblage possible on short notice; your time here will be well invested." He spoke with the substantial confidence of a man who long ago became comfortable with his enormous power and responsibility.

"Two days ago we learned a dangerous serial killer was loose in the Midsouth. Earlier today a foreboding communication was delivered to my front gates, a message from our formidable adversary, a message in which everyone in this room was named." Albert took another slow drink of cool water and studied faces. Most were engaged and some were not, but even if they could comprehend the grave danger lying ahead, and even if they took every possible precaution Albert knew most of the people sitting in the east room would die horrible deaths. There was little anyone could do to stop the Bluff City Butcher.

"In the early morning hours, I met with Memphis Police Director Collin Wade, Shelby County Sheriff G.E. Taft, Midsouth Regional Director of the FBI Dexter Voss and of course the Shelby County Medical Examiner Dr. Henderson Bates. We agreed the information I came to possess must be shared with all involved as soon as possible."

A big screen television monitor descended from the ceiling as Albert continued. "This morning an envelope was discovered by my security team; it was wedged in the main gates of the estate." The monitor stopped five feet from the floor and flickered on; the high definition color picture of the front gates to the Bell estate came into focus. At the lower right corner of the freeze-frame was a date/time indicator: 03/19/2009…03:26:00.

"This is where we begin. This particular motion-activated security camera is located on the north side of Walnut Grove directly across the street from our entry, as you can see." The video started, the time indicator advanced in seconds. At the 03:26:32 mark, a shadow moved into the lower left quadrant of the screen with the gates in the background. Immediately the auto-focus zoomed in, finding wet, coarse, long black hair, a head turning as it moved closer, and then an eye inches from the camera lens, an eye now centered on the big screen in a sea of blacks and grays. It was a thin band of white encircling a thicker band of grey encircling a dilated, black pupil with a small fleck of white glistening in the very center, a reflection of the small white light in the base of the camera. The eye jerked left and right, up and down and stopped, as everyone watched. The pupil contracted to half size.

The camera was discovered in the knothole of the oak.

The image on the big screen was jarred three times, and then struggled to refocus. Through the shattered lens the shadow took shape as it bolted across Walnut Grove to the front gates and then disappeared to the west.

"Gentlemen and Miss Mason, this video is the only recorded image of the Bluff City Butcher. Before I continue, Mr. Voss, please," Albert passed the remote.

"Thank you, Mr. Bell. Yes, this is the only known video observation of the Bluff City Butcher, the serial killer that we have been seriously hunting for twelve years. It has eluded cameras and eliminated those people who have seen him, except for two: Miss Mason is one of those lucky people and we are pleased she is with us tonight." Voss acknowledged her presence respectfully.

"You just saw twenty-six seconds of the Bluff City Butcher. You may think you saw nothing or very little when in fact you saw a great deal. We now know what we are up against."

■ ■ ■

"Seven seconds of the back of its head, nine of an eye, four of the camera getting beat on and six seconds of a dark blur sprinting across Walnut Grove, passing the gates to the mansion and disappearing west into the darkness." Voss looked around the room, knowing the information he would share was only part of what they were able to learn in Washington.

"Mr. Bell allowed me to get this video to FBI headquarters in Washington DC for analysis. As agreed, I am going to share information with you and ask that you maintain confidentiality."

He advanced the video to a series of frozen frames. "Our enhancement methods are proprietary. However, I can share some end products. From this video, we can calculate that the Bluff City Butcher is six-five and weighs two-hundred-fifty pounds with less than one-percent body fat.

He is a robust forty-year-old Caucasian male of European descent with black hair. He is atypically strong and able to move faster than any human has ever been measured."

"Excuse me, Doyle here." He raised his hand. "You expect us to believe you can tell how strong and fast some guy is by looking at a night video for a few seconds?"

"Not just a video, Mr. Doyle," said Voss. "We were able to measure strength by conducting compression analysis of the pulverized tree trunk that held the camera that the Butcher hit three times. Recreation of comparable damage required an equivalency force of ten men. We don't know how the Butcher physically accomplished the damage, but we are certain our measurements and calculations are accurate. Regarding the speed of the Butcher, that was determined by analysis of the video. It was a simple calculation of time and distance. The Butcher moved from the oak tree, across Walnut Grove to the gate, and left camera view in 6.32 seconds. We know the distance covered and determined he sustained an average speed of 29.7 mph. To go from a dead start he had to achieve a top sprint speed of 37.8 mph. The fastest recorded sprint speed of a human is 27.79 mph. The Bluff City Butcher is moving 10.0 mph faster. At first we did not believe it. But it has been confirmed by our top gait-analysts in Washington DC."

Voss advanced freeze frames to the Butcher in flight almost upright and from behind. "We have no frontal views. If he was walking down the street in Memphis today, we would know him only by his size and muscularity. He would undoubtedly cover up and could hunch over to blend into a crowd, especially at night with a long coat."

He advanced and zoomed in on the Butcher. "In this frame, the knee-length coat flares open as he leaves the gates to the west. On his belt are three sheaths containing three items of interest. Enhancement analysis allows us to identify these items. One is a ten-inch butcher knife.

Another is a seven-inch ice pick, and the third is a four-inch razor. Each has a black pearl handle." Voss sat down as the monitor advanced to the eye of the Butcher, exactly where Albert wanted it to be. As important as it was to transfer information, everyone in the room must grasp the deadly reality of what was in their life.

"Thank you, Director Voss," said Albert. "Now, what could be in the envelope the Bluff City Butcher delivered to me this morning? What is so important to this killer?" Albert looked around the table; they were listening intently while looking at the Butcher's eye freeze-frame on the screen behind him.

"It is hand-written," said Albert as he removed three dog-eared, crumpled, stained and partially burned parchments, each protected in a plastic bag to preserve for forensic analysis. He read aloud;

"Albert Bell, you get the letter. You will be last. Nothing can change what I confess or avow. I take at will and I leave in darkness. I am alone again. My wants change again. You tell those who will die. I will watch life leave each, and like the others before them, they will thank me at the end for what I do not do.

"My guardian is gone. I know why and I know who. I am what you know, but others hide their demons. I want pieces of them.

"I will take the voice of Doyle and leave the body for a world to see that I am real and I am here. He will be my first but others will be a part of him.

"I will take your brother next and feast upon his liver when I want. He has the ire of a number two, the jealousy and greed. He must go. He is my number two.

"A worm of putrefaction and corruption living on the flesh of others, Heller will be skinned like the snake he is and hung in Shelby. He is my number three.

"Loman is an overeducated hyena, a treacherous and stupid animal that has lost all rights to oxygen decades ago. He loses his lungs, my number four.

"Dunn is more swine than human. The fat man feasts on the weak and will lose his over-indulging digestive system from mouth to anus, my number five.

"*The FBI loses a man for proprietary and confidential reasons known only to him, and it is just. Voss is my number six.*

"*Memphis police will lose their best man because I need his eyes more then they know. Wilcox is finally mine, number seven.*

"*Bellow must go for purposes he will know only at the end, my number eight.*

"*Sumner must go for reasons he may already know, my number nine.*

"*Albert Bell, you must go for reasons you will not believe. I will share when death is near. You are my number ten and…then it will be known to all who I am.*"

He set the document down and leaned back in his chair. The room was dead. G.E. Taft spoke first. "Thank you, Albert. As this sinks in, I will remind everyone that this information cannot leave this room. I am sure I speak for Collin Wade. An active investigation is underway; this is extremely sensitive evidence. I will add there are people in this room whose names do not appear on this list; Carol Mason, Dr. Bates, Director Wade and me. However, we are here because we are intimately involved and understand our risk is as great, list or no list. We are all in the way of the Bluff City Butcher."

Collin Wade got up from his chair. "I concur with Sheriff Taft a hundred percent. We face a very dangerous killer. We have no idea why he chose you other than what his words say on this list. We are confused by the target selection; a radio personality, businessmen, investors and law enforcement. His organ harvesting plans have some symbolic meaning but overall this letter gives us little to go on. I will ask Dr. Elliott Sumner to comment. He has been hunting the Bluff City Butcher for many years and knows him best."

After the letter was read, Elliott was reminded of the victims and all the evil he'd battled in his life. His heart began to race. He could lose control. Carol moved her leg under the table and touched his gently. They looked at each other. His heart slowed and he regained control. No one knew his struggle but them.

"He is unlike anything I have ever hunted. He has been killing for twenty-five years for reasons that evolve. The Bluff City Butcher has killed over a hundred people in six states. So far, he has been unstoppable."

Loman jumped up and glared at the law enforcement officers at the table. "This is crazy. If you cops could do your damn jobs we would not be in this mess. Why can't you catch this sick bastard?"

"Mr. Loman, I suggest we all stay focused. We are not playing the blame game. No one is here tonight to explain to you the enormous complexities of hunting a genius serial killer in a modern world, a subject on which I am certain you have nothing to contribute. The Bluff City Butcher has chosen you for a reason—a reason only you would know. If you can figure that out, maybe we can help you. Otherwise, your death is imminent. You will be another unpredictable kill, I'm afraid, Sir." Elliott had compassion but tonight that would contribute little to saving lives.

"I have no idea why that piece of vermin wants to cut out my lungs," said Loman as he looked around the room. Dunn and Heller looked away and down. Elliott picked it up. There was something there, but the three would probably take it to their graves.

"Each should think about the words the Butcher used when talking about you. Is there a clue that could help in your protection or our tracking him down?

"The Butcher has been successful avoiding capture because of unpredictability and keeping a low profile; he hid his kills—suicides, accidents and missing persons. Now he is going public, with high-profile kills, seeking recognition. As you learned tonight, this serial killer is different. The BCB possesses superior physical skills. As I just alluded to, he also has a genius IQ. He stays four or five moves ahead on unpredictable kills."

The meeting continued for an hour with little progress on deciphering the Butcher's words and targets. Everyone decided to stay in town; location was not a deterrent. The meeting adjourned.

"How do you think it went?" asked Carol when they met at the *Peabody* lounge later that evening.

"As good as could be expected," said Elliott. Carol reached over and touched his hand, sliding her thumb under his shirt cuff. His eyes met hers immediately.

"I have something I must tell you, Elliott."

"You do?" He set his drink down and put his hand on hers.

"I wanted to tell you at the mansion but the time was never right. I thought once we were alone it would be better…easier, but it still feels…strange."

"We tell each other everything, remember? You are a professional and I care very much for you personally. You can tell me anything and it will be fine." Elliott pressed his leg to hers and she smiled and then got serious.

"The Bluff City Butcher was in my headlights, five feet from me on November 5, 2008. I saw his face clearly. I did not hallucinate or let fear overtake me to the point that I could erase that picture. Elliott, I know his face…perfectly."

"I know you saw the Butcher that night. Every detail of your description that night, I remember. What are you trying to say, Carol?"

"Elliott, the man I saw that night was Jack Bellow. He is the Bluff City Butcher."

■ ■ ■

20 March 2009

"Do you expect Marcus to show tonight?" asked Barry as he entered the seedy second-floor office on South Main above Pandora's Hair Salon. WKRC put them there a few years ago; it was meant to be a temporary location.

Jimmy looked up briefly to acknowledge the arrival of his portly program director and then returned his eyes to the book in his lap. "You know, Bear, I didn't think so at first, but I have a good feeling about our man Marcus.

"What do you mean?"

"Marcus is Navy Seal—100 percent military—he spit shines his wallet, for God's sake."

"Ok, so what?"

"Marcus gave his word. He will show up or be dead somewhere." Doyle flipped the last few pages of his fourth book on serial killers, the one about the hunters.

"It says in this book that Dr. Elliott Sumner is the biggest and the baddest. That dude is personally responsible for taking off the streets fifty of the meanest serial killers in the world over the last ten years. He only had to kill twelve of the bastards because they were trying to kill him, like the shark out of water biting everything in sight."

"Yeah, I read about him too. I think I would listen to anything that guy had to say, if you know what I mean."

"Barry, I have got to tell you what happened to me last night."

"It sounds confidential." He sat on the sofa across from Doyle and lit up a cigarette. "Ok, what?"

"Bear, I was called to a private meeting at the Bell mansion. They sent a limo to pick me up and one hour later the limo dropped me at my place."

"No way," said Bear choking on his smoke.

"There were a dozen people there."

"Who was there?"

"Elliott Sumner, for one, the bad ass I just read about. He was the most successful homicide investigator in the whole damn world, almost 100 percent success rate when he gets after your ass. The Bluff City Butcher is the only serial killer he can't seem to catch."

"No shit?"

"This book says he's been hunting the Butcher for ten frigging years."

"Ok. What about the meeting? What was it all about?"

"The Bluff City Butcher wrote a letter and delivered the damn thing to Albert Bell. There was a list of people he is going to kill next. I'm on the top of the list."

"No way, Jimmy! You've got to leave town now."

"No. That won't work. Location has never stopped this bastard. He has killed in six states. He finds you."

"Then you have got to stay protected twenty-four-seven."

"They had a video of this guy, Bear, a fucking genius and superhuman physical stuff—runs fast, jumps high, climbs higher, strong—stuff like that."

"Jimmy, he is just a man, not a magical monster," said Bear.

"Don't ask me how, but the FBI evaluated a video of the Butcher and examined a tree trunk he pounded to break an embedded camera. They did compression analysis and calculated his strength was equivalent to that of ten men. Shit, the damn thing has been clocked running thirty-seven miles per hour. The fastest human in the Olympics was clocked at twenty-seven."

"Are you shitting me?"

"No, I swear to God, I am telling the truth."

"What can they do to protect people on the list?"

"They were open and honest about that. The cops cannot do much because this serial killer is so smart and so unpredictable. In the letter he said he would take my voice and show my body to the world."

Barry got up and paced the small office. "This is unreal. Are you messing with me? This guy is a freaking demon from hell. Why is he so ticked-off at you?"

"In the letter he said I did not listen to him; I put Marcus on the radio. This demented bastard has killed more than a hundred people. Dr. Sumner said the reason he is so hard to catch is because he is a genius and he kills randomly."

"Is that it? Shit. I cannot sit still. I am going to go crazy. I am going out. I have some errands. Do you want to come with me?"

"No, I need to finish reading this before the show. If I don't see you back here, I will see you at the station. The Butcher is not going to grab me in broad daylight."

"Right, that's good. Ok, I will hook up with you at the station. Going forward, we stay in crowds until they catch this sick animal," said Bear.

"Ok, I will see you tonight." Jimmy looked back at his book as Bear left.

He went out the door, keyed the deadbolt and headed down the narrow staircase. The only light bulb in the hall was out, so he was forced into a dark patch at the bottom of the stairs. The front door was just a few steps away. He could feel his way along the wall. No one used the back door because mops, buckets and rubber trash cans always blocked the exit and the back alley was overgrown and nasty. If the light had worked, Bear would have seen everything in the back was neat and organized. He would have also seen the chain hanging off the back door. When he made it to the front door he opened it and the light of day poured into his face. That's when he saw the large shadow next to him, and the door closed.

When Jimmy left an hour later he felt his way down the dark hall too. If he had screwed in the only light bulb he would have seen all the blood on the floor. He didn't even notice his red tracks on the sidewalk on the way to the studio.

CHAPTER TWENTY

21 March 2009

Elliott called Tony from Bellow's penthouse atop the Old Exchange Building; he went to voice mail. "You got Tony Wilcox, leave a message; I'll call back when I can."

"Elliott here…you need to get to the Exchange Building, 9 North Second Street, at Court. I'm in Bellow's penthouse with two bodies. It's a long story."

They were sitting at Bellow's dining room table with the good china and silverware. Both were wearing business suits with white shirts and ties. They were missing their heads. Officer Starnes, the night watchman for the *Life2 Corporation* since the inception, was at the desk in the lobby. He recognized Elliott from the papers and let him go up to the penthouse. Elliott thought he got the call from Jack Bellow, the voice on the phone. He said to come to the penthouse as fast as possible or someone could die. When he got there, the glass door was ajar so he could go into the secured offices and Bellow's private quarters. That's where he found the bodies.

Elliott's phone rang. "Hello, Tony."

"What did you do, Elliott, kill two guys and you're trying to cover it up?"

"Very funny, are you almost here?"

"I'm parking now. You want me to call the boys or talk a little first?"

"You can call the boys. We don't need sirens if you have the pull. I can assure you, as a doctor, the two guys I'm looking at have left this world. Get forensics up here; this one Bates needs to come see himself."

"Ok, see you in a couple. We will have five minutes before the place gets crazy. Hey, Willie, this place will be crawling in a few minutes, you good with that?"

"Guess so, Detective. You need anything from me down here?"

"Try to keep the media outside." He waved as the elevator doors closed.

Tony walked in on Elliott processing. "Is this what I think it is?" asked Tony as he walked around the table looking at the two well-dressed, headless corpses.

"Yes, if you think it is the work of the Butcher," replied Elliott. "The heads were removed with one sweep. He has done that before, usually when he's in a hurry or the victim is a secondary target. He is getting ready to tell us something…big in his world."

"What's he want us to think about?" asked Tony.

"It's safe to assume he wants us to wonder why the dead guys are in Bellow's penthouse. And how did they get up here? They didn't just walk up here all dressed up with no heads," said Elliott.

"You think?" Tony was patting down the pockets of one of the deceased.

"BCB did slip a note down the esophagus of both. I wasn't going to open presents until you got home."

"And they said it would never last." Tony pulled a wallet from one's back pocket and started picking through the contents.

Elliott pulled a leather case from his breast pocket and removed long, narrow tweezers. From his other pocket he removed disposable gloves and three tightly folded plastic bags. "You never know when the need will arise."

"You laboratory geeks kill me," said Tony with a smile. "Go ahead. Do your magic, Doctor."

Elliott removed the first note; he unrolled the eight-inch tube and read it aloud; *"Hello, Elliott and Tony. This is the beginning. I know you had a good meeting at the mansion. I will work from my list. This one is for Doyle…they will join each other soon."*

"'They will join each other soon'…means something. Did Doyle have a partner or close friend that you know about?" asked Elliott.

"Yes, a partner. We got a call from Doyle this evening. His program director did not make the 6:00 p.m. show, a guy named Barry Branch."

Tony put the contents of the first wallet on the table. "Well, I guess BCB wanted us to know. Here is Barry Branch's driver's license."

Elliott placed the first note in an evidence bag and went fishing for the second. He had it in seconds. *Me again…How did I know you would open me second? Tony, I told you I did not want Marcus talking about me on the radio. I told Marcus twenty-five years ago to stay away or I would send him to his friends. Do you wonder why I let him live? He was going to tell everybody tonight…too late."*

"Marcus Pleasant never made it to the *Talk of Memphis* tonight. They were less worried about him because he had been through so much the night before," said Tony.

"Before people start arriving I have to tell you something off line. Carol met Jack Bellow at the Bell mansion this week. First time she'd ever seen him."

"Right…and?"

"Tony, she saw Bellow on her car that November night on the bluff."

"Bellow is the Butcher? Are you kidding me?"

"I'm not saying that exactly."

"Then what are you saying?"

"Let's consider the possibilities. Carol is a professional observer. I am sure she saw Jack Bellow, or someone that wanted to look like Jack Bellow."

"Ok, I'm listening. It is something I never would have thought about. I guess we need to be wide open if we are ever going to figure this guy out."

"Did you look at Bellow? He is six-five easy, and probably weighs close to two-hundred-and-fifty pounds. He is in incredible physical shape."

"It's a giant stretch for me," said Tony. "How does a man do such horrific things to so many for so long and in a parallel life achieve great success as a top executive and renowned entrepreneur?"

Elliott placed the second note in a baggy and sealed it. He removed his gloves and put them in the third baggy and left all three on the table for the forensic team. "I know it is crazy. What if the Butcher wanted her to see the image of Bellow that night? Now we are in Bellow's home with two butchered bodies. Why? I have never seen Carol so sure of something. Bellow is in this thing somehow, and we need to figure it out."

"It is getting murky. Add to this the Medino family killings. The head trauma was BCB modus operandi. That connects the triangle Butcher, Bellow and Medino. Why are they associated, for what purpose?"

"Tony, the Medino death was staged. Have you seen the final M.E.'s report?"

"The director is still sitting on it."

"It was staged to look like the work of the BCB, but the puncture wound is the wrong size. Only insiders know, and whoever did this screwed up by using the wrong ice pick. We keep this quiet until we figure out who benefits from Medino's death."

The elevator doors opened and half a dozen badges got off.

"Medino was important to the Butcher. He must have seen the execution."

"His needs were changing. On November 22nd there was no turning back."

"He is going to do something with the heads, isn't he?" asked Tony

"Yes, and it is going to be big. I will see you later." Elliott stepped back. Memphis police, the CSI team and the medical examiner filed into the room.

■ ■ ■

The headless bodies were taken from the Exchange Building in black crash bags, protected from both the heavy downpour and news cameras. The inquest was set for seven in the morning. Bates had another long week and still no one had been crossed off the Butcher's list.

Tony and Elliott met at the WKRC parking lot to finish their discussion; they would tell Jimmy Doyle his missing program director had been found. There was no reason to give details; decapitation was a traumatizing image. Tony had orders from Wade to sit on the Marcus Pleasant death for a while. The killing of the survivor of the 1983 killings on the bluff—where it all began—would throw gasoline on flames of fear and desperation already spreading across the Midsouth. But Tony owed Jimmy more. He would tell him about Marcus, too. Elliott would take the heat if there was any.

You could see the entire floor from the glass entry. Behind the etched WKRC logo was a beehive of activity on a late Saturday night—people, papers, phones and computers. Everything stopped when Tony and Elliott were spotted; their wet hair and dripping coats stepped onto the floor to a frozen sea of wide eyes and statues. Nothing was said as they navigated the desks to the owner's glass office strategically positioned the farthest from the front doors; the "walk of trepidation" was the bad part of the job. As they approached the office it emptied except for the boss standing behind the desk—white as the driven snow. The station manager came in behind and closed the door.

Jimmy Doyle was on air in the broadcast booth when the manager appeared on the other side of the glass, signaling for a commercial break. The March 21, 2009, edition of the *Talk of Memphis* went off air due to technical difficulties and a tape of a prior show—better days—took over. Doyle was escorted to the owner's office.

"Is Bear dead?"

"Yes, Barry Branch is dead," said Tony. He looked at the owner and station manager; they got the message and left immediately. "Jimmy, sit down…please."

"Was he killed by the…?"

"Bluff City Butcher? Yes, he was."

"I knew it. When Bear missed the Friday show we looked all over for him. I called. He never answered. I left messages until his voicemail box was full; that lousy son-of-a-bitch serial killer. Bear was not on his fucking list. Are you sure?" Doyle held his head in his hands, his fingers spread and palms over his eyes.

"The Medical Examiner will do the autopsy tomorrow. We are sure," said Tony. Elliott sat quietly, studying Doyle unlike any other silent observer.

"How did he kill him?"

"A knife…he lost a lot of blood," said Tony.

"Oh, God, why kill Bear? He was a harmless, big guy. Damn perverted freak."

Tony leaned toward Doyle on the sofa next to him and whispered, "There is more you should know." Doyle lifted his head. "This cannot leave here." Doyle nodded. "Barry Branch and Marcus Pleasant died together."

Doyle fell back on the sofa and looked at the ceiling as he fell endlessly into the abyss. "That Bluff City BASTARD killed Marcus Pleasant, too? After twenty-five fucking years he still had to kill…shit. How sick do you need to be to carry a fucking grudge that long?"

Doyle sat up and looked at Elliott for the first time. Up until then he was emotionally unable to acknowledge anything except Wilcox and the nightmare. Doyle's eyes were wet and red. His hands shook. His shirt was soaked.

"Jimmy, I want you to meet Dr. Elliott Sumner."

Elliott was sitting in the brown leather chair on the other side of the room, legs crossed and long arms draped on the chair arms. His eyes were sharp and his chiseled face revealed concern but strength. When their eyes met, Elliott nodded.

"I know who you are, Dr. Sumner. I saw you at the Bell mansion. You are a serial killer hunter. The Bluff City Butcher has toyed with you for more than a fucking decade."

Elliott let it go. Jimmy Doyle spoke the truth. "Yes, that's me, the one and only." He saw Tony's slight smile before the head turned. He always enjoyed it when someone tugged on Superman's cape. It made him human.

"Do you remember me, Dr. Sumner?" asked Doyle.

"Yes, of course."

"Of course you do. You have a fucking photographic memory."

"I am sorry about your friend. I wish I could tell you something that mattered."

"Thanks. I know. I'm going to miss that big guy…a lot."

"If it means anything, we will keep at this until we get him. And one day we will get him." Elliott had to defuse hostilities between them before he could effectively ask the questions that would help. He needed Jimmy Doyle to completely trust him and to relax or the planned interview would be useless.

"Thank you, Dr. Sumner. I guess I can appreciate this guy is a real oddity. I'm sorry for taking a cheap shot, before."

"We are fine. Your comment was accurate. The Butcher has toyed with me for years. He is my nemesis, always a step ahead, a breath away."

"I read that you captured or killed around fifty serial killers in the last decade, far more than all the law enforcement agencies combined, including the FBI."

"Don't believe everything you read, especially now-a-days. There were a lot of good people like you involved. I was just the one they wrote about."

"I also read that you carry every one of those sick bastards in your head—your photographic memory—a relentless reminder of your haunting experiences and the reason you had to leave the business. Shit, man…that must be an awful thing…to see the sickest bastards in the fucking world everyday…and all the poor people like Bear that they took away. You probably feel their pain too. I cannot imagine what Bear went through and all the others…alone and…."

"It is a difficult profession, but it is much harder for the victims."

"How do you keep from going nuts?"

"Is this an interview, Mr. Doyle?" asked Elliott in a gentle tone.

"Oh, sorry, not appropriate…just rambling; if you guys don't find this monster soon you are going to have to look at my pale, naked body next." They smiled. "I'm on the top of the asshole's list, and if that's not motivation, well the hell with you both."

They all had a good laugh, one they needed. The mood lightened even though gloomy burden of the recent kills hung in the room.

"Jimmy, as you know we are dealing with a highly intelligent homicidal maniac. He has maintained an advantage by killing randomly. The list is the first time we have held his plan in our hands. I suspect he had some form of guidance before. I believe he is now working completely alone and his needs are changing."

"How so?"

"The Butcher moved from low-profile, random kills to high-profile, targeted kills."

"Now we can sit and wait for him, right?" asked Doyle.

"Well, you would think so, but he still controls a lot of variables."

"For example, killing Bear and Marcus…variables, he was messing with you guys on his way to me?"

"Yes. Mr. Branch's death is about you. But, Mr. Pleasant's death is more about the Butcher. Something happened between them on the bluff in 1983."

"Jimmy, do you know Jack Bellow?"

"No. Why do you ask?"

"We found them in his penthouse."

"That is strange."

"Do you know anything about Jack Bellow?" asked Elliott.

"Yes, I think everyone knows Bellow is the president of *Life2 Corporation*. Those guys are working on biogenic stuff that is mind boggling. Did you know I was the last person to interview Dr. Medino before his death?"

■ ■ ■

"Tell me about Dr. Medino and the last night you spent with him in Covington."

"I can tell you he loved all the attention. He was what I call a very good interview; I could move him easily because he was playing the crowd that surrounded our live show in the reception hall. It was his big night. He was getting a special recognition award for his pioneer work in genetic engineering and biotechnology solutions." Doyle leaned back and started to relive that great night for radio like so many times before.

"I know you answered questions for the Shelby County Sheriff's Office and the Memphis police following the accident, but I'm interested in the odd, peculiar moments, your personal, off-the-wall observations, the kind we all make but rarely share because we think they are insignificant, silly or stupid. Do you understand?"

"Yeah, I got yah. Let me think a sec. That was a busy day. Dr. Medino was chomping at the bit to brag about himself. I was able to get him to admit publicly that he was closer than anybody to solving the immortality, or life-extension, puzzle. My personal observation, Medino was closer than anyone will ever know. He probably found some secret, maybe in 2004 when he hooked up with Bellow, the business brains of the operation. I think Medino was dying to tell the world but knew he had to roll it out the right way. It's hard to keep a secret."

"Ok, good. That's what I am looking for, your gut feel, the passing thoughts and judgments you personally made that night. Let your roving mind's-eye speak." Elliott rested his open hands on his knees and let his shoulders drop as he spoke. Doyle took the same position and closed his eyes a few seconds. Tony could see Elliott's powers of suggestion were working.

"I can tell you this; it hit me right away that Dr. Medino was the smartest guy I had ever met. I felt that way immediately. It was how he spoke, the depth of his ideas. He seemed to struggle to communicate with mere mortals.

"His concepts and his world of thought are so far beyond us that he struggled to find the words for others to see or understand. That interview…I felt like I was sitting with Albert Einstein. Or, that I was a child."

"Good, interesting, an Albert Einstein aura and he solved the 'immortality puzzle' and he was hungry for recognition."

"Yeah, I know it sounds crazy but those kinds of thoughts were flying through my pea brain at the time. I don't normally share it because it can get bizarre, like when I went out to have a smoke that night and thought I saw cat burglars."

"You saw cat burglars?" replied Elliott without moving. "Go with that. Relive it. Tell me exactly what you saw and thought. You're sitting down with a cigarette…"

"Yeah…I was killing time, waiting for my crew to finish packing the bus to get back to Memphis. I was outside sitting in the shadows with a smoke. I noticed two white vans on the other side of the highway. There were a couple of guys dressed completely in black…thought that was odd…like in the movies. They were moving jugs from one van to the other. I counted five. That was when I smelled the kerosene, a light breeze in my face; it had to be coming from them."

Tony sat up and Elliott's eyes widened…same page as usual. Doyle had no idea what he was saying. Elliott's artful interview techniques were the carefully honed assets of a remarkable investigator. He could transport people to a time and place and stimulate their deep memory processes, the portal to 100 percent recall that few know how to tap. He developed the technique when he discovered interrogation triggers the opposite; it numbs the senses with fear, paranoia and mistrust. Elliott could essentially hypnotize without the use of the swinging watch and the snap of fingers when it was over.

"Very curious, you could smell it," said Elliott, encouraging more.

"At first I was suspicious, even hid my cigarette so they would not see my burning ash. It wasn't until I got back to Memphis that I remembered one of the guys I saw. Then I figured it was probably some undercover deal and none of my business."

"Oh?"

"A covert government operation or something."

"Why did you think that?" asked Elliott casually.

"It was an FBI guy…Dexter Voss. He kept looking in my direction, but I don't think he saw my cigarette. Anyway, I assumed it was our tax dollars at work."

"What else?"

"That's all. I went back inside a while and then we got on the bus and took off."

"And what about the two white vans?"

"Gone, I thought, at first. But they had just moved them off the edge of the road…over by some trees with their lights off. You really had to be looking or you would have missed them."

"Did you tell this to anyone else?" asked Tony after getting the 'ok' nod from Elliott. He was done.

Before Jimmy could answer the door opened and the station manager rushed into the room looking for Detective Wilcox.

"You said I would have the opportunity to talk to staff about Barry." He turned on the TV. A picture of Branch was in the corner of the screen, a reporter was standing in front of the Exchange Building as two zipped crash bags were loaded into the M.E.'s van. The words on the bottom of the screen said everything: *The Bluff City Butcher Gets Two More.*

"Oh shit, here we go." Tony pulled out his cell. *At least they don't have a picture of Marcus Pleasant up there,* he thought.

"To answer your question…no one," said Jimmy. "You're the only ones who know this."

CHAPTER TWENTY-ONE

"What is play to a cat is death to the mouse."
Danish Proverb

8 April 2009

Pictures of the three-headed man hanging from the Hernando de Soto Bridge were all over the *Internet* before the police could reel in the sick, pathetic joke—perfect for *YouTube*. Someone thought it would be fun to scare people weeks after the Memphis police released information a serial killer was in the area. Waking up to local news coverage of a three-headed dummy swinging ominously fifty feet above the Mississippi River was funny to some but disturbing to most Midsoutherners. No one has three heads; it was stupid.

Just days after the Memphis PD press conference there were two high-profile deaths; *The Memphis Tribune* suggested linkage to the Bluff City Butcher. Local law enforcement and city officials discouraged crediting the acts of common criminals to the urban legend; their long standing policy of silence had done its damage. Their credibility was minimized. Only after the provocative ramblings of a regional radio talk-show host and the persistence of an investigative reporter at the *Tribune* had any information started to flow to the community at risk.

Every day over 50,000 vehicles crossed the Mississippi River at Memphis on the Hernando de Soto Bridge. The six-lane structure was three football fields long and rose a hundred feet above the largest river on the continent. On the morning of April 8, 2009, a river pilot pushing a line of empty barges north approached along the east bank like so many times before. This time would be very different.

As the hidden sun painted the morning sky, a dark object descended from the bridge in measured increments like a fat spider leaving his web for the day. The river pilot struggled to make sense of the potential obstacle; he zoomed in with his camera phone. Over the years he had seen unusual things, but this was the most peculiar.

The three-headed dummy was incredibly life-like but a pitiful attempt to harass riverboat traffic. And the sign on its chest made no sense: "I NEED A PIECE OF YOU." The river pilot videoed his approach, sent it to *YouTube*, for the hell of it, and tried to ram the "river piñata." It was just out of reach.

The 911 call was made when the "hoax" crossed over the stern of the long-run river boat. Six squad cars, a fire truck and ambulance got to the top of the rope in six minutes; TV traffic choppers got to the bridge in two. Live coverage of the three-headed joke ran on every Memphis channel, and the unfolding oddity was snapped up by the networks: *more breaking news following bizarre developments in the Bluff City Butcher story coming out of Memphis.*

Local news condemned the elaborate prank and described it as a twisted effort to play on the fears of the community. Reporters encouraged anyone with knowledge of the jokesters responsible to step forward. Obviously, no one would and every station in Memphis kept rolling as the repugnant curiosity continued to unfold and immensely helped the ratings.

A nation watched as firefighters hoisted the man-sized dummy to the bridge. But when it reached the railing three of four let go of the rope.

The one left holding was pulled perilously close to the edge before others standing by grabbed the line and saved the day, all caught on live-TV. The second time the dummy made it to the bridge railing one of the three heads fell off and rolled wildly, scattering some of the crew. It was carefully recovered and placed with the now two-headed dummy. All morning, commentators floated their theories without facts, attempting to explain what was unfolding. Everyone was tense because there was always the risk of terrorist acts, booby-traps and the unknown in a crazy, unpredictable world.

When the paramedics covered the dummy with a sheet, the news media was confused; still no information from the bridge. When the white tent popped up and the Shelby County Medical Examiner van pulled onto the Hernando de Soto Bridge escorted by spinning lights and sirens, everyone knew something terrible was happening before their eyes. The three-headed dummy was no hoax!

Was it a freak of nature? Some carnival sideshow act that committed suicide? Or was the oddity killed and put on display? Or was it a sick message from the Bluff City Butcher? Memphians wanted to know, and now a national audience was watching what was billed as the works of possibly the most horrific serial killer in American history, the monster that brought the world-renowned forensic investigator out of retirement.

The Bluff City Butcher wanted his story told on primetime.

Nobody knew this was Act One. Elliott got the call at sunrise; the message was brief. *"Guess who went for a walk on the bridge."* He recognized the voice. BCB had been busy last night. Elliott kept his old phone number for the Butcher for times like this one. Maybe he would make that fatal mistake Elliott hoped for. But ten years later, he was still waiting. Elliott flipped on the news; it was on every channel.

Tony called. "Doyle is missing."

"That's not good."

"Our guys saw nothing. When they heard the crap on the Hernando they busted down Doyle's door…he was gone…very little blood."

"How?"

"He took him out the back window. The Butcher climbed a twenty-five foot brick wall to the third floor window. Shit, Elliott, how could the Butcher scale that?"

"He works out. See you on the bridge," said Elliott grabbing his coat.

"Are you going to tell Mason?"

"She's in New York on a long shot, thinks Albert's daughter was killed by the Butcher up there."

"I thought she died on nine-eleven…she was in the tower."

"Carol says no. We'll see," said Elliott.

"She probably knows about the Hernando anyway, it's gone viral…*YouTube.*"

"The Butcher is running the show. We're public, Tony."

"Doyle would like that."

"He would." They both knew Doyle was on the bridge.

They pulled up to the white tent at the same time. One lane was shut down; traffic was stacked up ten miles east and west on I-40. They had to get their looks and move everything to the county morgue; the flow of commerce on the major artery crossing the country had to be restored. Field Agents, CSI and the M.E. were in the tent finishing up when Tony and Elliott opened the flap.

■ ■ ■

It was Jimmy Doyle. His throat had a five-inch vertical wound neatly sutured. Bates confirmed the larynx was gone, as the Butcher had promised, and the carotids and jugular were neatly severed; Jimmy was on empty, total exsanguination. There was no other trauma except the obligatory puncture wound on top of his head and the surgical attachment of heads to his shoulders.

Barry Branch's head was sewn by the neck to Doyle's left shoulder. It had been frozen…was thawing out and starting to stink. The head that fell off belonged to Marcus Pleasant. A metal rod protruded five inches from Doyle's right shoulder. The rod was hammered to the groin. The wounds confirmed Doyle had been alive for the experience.

Elliott quickly examined the body and two heads, looking for any clues to take him one step closer to the Butcher. He found trace blood on the rope—missed by CSI. It could be the Butcher's. Doyle's clothes were washed and dried but there was trace dirt on the lateral left leg, medial right leg and left shoulder, dirt different from the surroundings, dirt picked up prior to the movement of the body. CSI might narrow areas of interest, perhaps figure out what part of the county the dirt came from.

"Are you done yet?" asked Tony.

"Yes, I'm good." Elliott mentally returned to the world of mortals.

"We're good here, guys. If the M.E. is done, you can move them to the morgue. Put the body and the heads in one crash bag. Media has seen enough bizarre images for one day," said Tony as he hit speed dial. His partner had another long day coming.

"What's with the sign? What do you think, Elliott?"

"It's new." Elliott was still processing and running scenarios. "The Butcher is confused, not sure what he wants."

"Talk to me, Elliott. Step away from the light," Tony chided.

"Sorry. We touched on it the other day. Somehow he is connected to Dr. Medino. When that man was killed on Austin Peay—possibly by a rogue Dexter Voss—the Butcher completed his change. I am dealing with the same methodical killing machine, but now he is on some mission and I don't know where it is headed."

"What does the sign around Doyle's neck mean?" asked Tony.

"*I need a piece of you…*is not the Butcher talking."

"How do you know?"

"The Butcher never *needs*, he only *wants*. That is his core struggle. He found himself in a world that he has never understood. Now, without his surrogate guardian—Medino—he is more lost, more desperate than ever...than since his childhood." Elliott's phone rang. "Excuse me."

Tony couldn't miss the broad smile on his friend's face. "Go ahead, Elliott, I got this. We will catch up later."

Elliott stepped out of the tent and walked to the railing. "Hey, good looking." His heart raced even though she had been gone only one night.

"Elliott, I see there is an incident on the Hernando Bridge. Did the Bluff City Butcher strike again?"

"Yes. He got Jimmy Doyle this time, number one on his list."

"God, and he was protected 24/7, right?"

"The Butcher went through a window, twenty-five feet straight up a brick wall."

Carol's voice went to a whisper. "I am sorry, Elliott. I am sorry for Mr. Doyle. He really led the way to get the word out to the people on the Butcher. He is the one that lit the fire under the Memphis PD. That makes three in three weeks. Elliott, are we ever going to stop this monster?"

Elliott saw a tuft of hair snagged by a bolt jutting out from the bridge railing where Doyle had been hanging...it was long and black. He waved at a field agent and pointed to the railing. "Please collect that hair sample, possible Butcher...get me a DNA profile STAT."

"Yes, Sir," said the agent. He carefully collected the sample for processing.

"Where are you, Elliott?"

"I'm on the Hernando de Soto Bridge playing detective with Tony. Hey, I have a helicopter in my face right now. You near a TV?"

"Actually, I'm standing next to one in the lobby of the New York Hilton and yes...I can see you standing there all handsome and virile."

Elliott winked at the camera. "That's for you, beautiful, my sensitive side."

"Thanks, you big showoff. You just gave the nation a wink, and they are talking about you. Gee, Elliott…these people think you hung the moon. They say it is wonderful to see the *Western Sherlock* back. Your presence means the BCB is the real deal."

He smiled and looked at his watch. "When do you get home? I like you a little and might want to sip a Pinot and just look at you."

"I love you too, Elliott. But I don't get back to Memphis until tomorrow night. Remember, I am meeting Max in Destin to close some loops on Sheila Bell's very suspicious suicide back in 2001."

"You think she was murdered?"

"Yes. But like the Medino death, it could be the work of others…with a motive."

"Ok. Be careful, young lady."

"When I get back we have a lot to talk about."

"Heck, I had something else in mind."

"I have a lot more in mind. See you soon, handsome, and you be careful too."

The Memphis police couldn't stop the runaway train. City officials met an hour after the bridge reopened. The city mayor made his expectations crystal clear: Memphis Police were going public today. The press conference was set to start in an hour—in memory of Jimmy Doyle—full disclosure from this day forward. The people of the Midsouth were going after the Bluff City Butcher together. Maybe a few million eyes and ears could make a difference.

CHAPTER TWENTY-TWO

"If you believe in something, no proof is necessary.
If you don't, none is sufficient."
Unknown

8 April 2009

Following an emergency meeting with the mayor and city council, Memphis Police Director Collin Wade agreed the time for full disclosure had arrived. A press conference was scheduled two hours after they removed Jimmy Doyle's body and the heads of Pleasant and Branch from the bridge. They would tell Memphians the terrible truth and the world would be watching. Director Wade had some opening comments but it was decided Tony would be the face of the MPD on the Bluff City Butcher case.

The podium stood outside police headquarters in the courtyard facing Main Street. Crowds were building behind barriers normally used for parades and celebrations; this time the mood was somber, uncertain and terrified. The press was assembled. Suits with headsets, TV cameras, sound booms, flood lights, cables and satellite dish trailers were set to stream the breaking news across the country. The shocking events on the Hernando de Soto Bridge that unfolded before millions was now the hottest drama in the country since the "White Bronco California" road trip.

Wade tapped a microphone in the cluster as a trolley rambled by like a big box of loose bolts ready to fall apart and scatter. Heads turned to watch the commotion move down Main; the familiar sounds helped ease the tension. Wade didn't want to be here; his wet, beaded, balding head and fisheyes were huddled behind the podium, doing little to instill confidence, but his scripted words would save him as they had so many times before. He cleared his throat into the microphone and smiled inappropriately.

"This has been a difficult day for all Memphians. We got up to a reckless and inconsiderate prank, a hoax beyond imagination, but then it got worse. We discovered the hoax on the Hernando de Soto Bridge was a vile, perverse and horrific killing put on display."

Whispers flowed across the courtyard.

"On the morning of March 17, 2009, we held a press conference to report a serial killer in our area. We urged vigilance. Standard police procedure limited public disclosures on the active investigation, a *best practice* designed to keep information from the perpetrators and to accelerate capture. Following the cruel, vicious actions of a very sick individual, everything changes today. To best protect our citizens, we operate with full disclosure."

The crowd buzzed.

"The serial killer we are pursuing is the Bluff City Butcher."

The crowd erupted. Caterwauling rolled down Main Street, chasing the clanging trolley. Shock spread from the city across the Midsouth and into a country as radio, TV and the *Internet* informed everyone instantly. The first official acknowledgment of the existence of the Bluff City Butcher sent chills down spines everywhere. The beast had stepped from the fog of urban legend. He was a living monster and he was loose in the city…the Midsouth…the world.

The Bluff City Butcher forced the city's hand—they had no other choice. Director Wade felt the significance of the moment and gained confidence that what he was doing was right.

"This demented killer is responsible for the tragedy on the Hernando de Soto Bridge. These chilling developments have changed how the Memphis Police Department will remain true to our mission: to protect and serve. The dreadful conditions we face require this change in our tactics. Pursuit of this pathetic killer can no longer be undercover. It must be public. We are all in this together. The Bluff City Butcher is going public and so is your Memphis Police Department."

He hoped for a rousing round of applause, but the crowd was silent. Nothing could have prepared them for the collision of emotions; a real monster in their midst that wanted to and could kill any of them at any time.

Director Wade folded his notes into his breast pocket and faded away.

Tony stepped up to the podium without notes. His stature had an immediate calming effect; his deportment presumed respect. He was a man that understood the battle between good and evil. His eyes confirmed he was capable, strong and fearlessly determined. He looked over the crowd. The courtyard was hushed except for the detail of photographers capturing the moment.

"I am Detective Wilcox."

He had their attention.

"At 6:10 a.m. we received a 911 call from Captain Otis Dodson, a long-run barge pilot pushing north along the east bank. Captain Dodson reported the incident on the Hernando de Soto Bridge as it unfolded predawn. From his boat he watched an unidentifiable object descend from the bridge directly in his path. Captain Dodson took a closer look and saw what appeared to be a three-headed body spinning at the end of a rope above the water. He concluded the object was a stuffed dummy, a joke, a harassment effort aimed at riverboat traffic.

"At 6:16 Memphis Police, Fire and Paramedics were on the bridge. At 6:24, subject dummy was pulled onto the Hernando. We realized at that time we were dealing with a victim of a brutal homicide."

Tony gave the crowd a moment to comprehend the startling information. He felt sure his next words would drive home the shocking reality of a gathering darkness in the Midsouth that would endanger everyone. His next words would merge the nonbelievers and the skeptics with the suspicious and the believers. All eyes would open at the same time and see the hell that he and other experts had been facing for years. It now had descended on the region.

"The dead man on the Hernando de Soto Bridge is Jimmy Doyle, the WKRC radio talk-show host of the *Talk of Memphis.*"

The shock rolled through the crowd; bewilderment and anguish were soon replaced with sheer terror.

"This is difficult to hear, but you must know what we are up against. That can make you and your family safer."

The crowd settled down.

"Jimmy Doyle was taken from his home last night. He was killed by the Bluff City Butcher. Mr. Doyle suffered multiple stab wounds; his throat was cut and he bled to death. The M.E. will complete the autopsy today and officially rule."

Tony paused to drink water; the crowd was silent and stationary.

"The heads of two decapitated homicide victims discovered on March 21, 2009, were attached to Jimmy Doyle's shoulders. Barry Branch, a WKRC Radio employee and program director for Jimmy Doyle, was one decapitation victim. His head was attached to Mr. Doyle's right shoulder. The identity of the second decapitation victim has not been given until this moment. Ladies and gentlemen, the head of this second decapitation victim was attached to Mr. Doyle's left shoulder. It is Marcus Pleasant."

As expected, the crowd erupted. His interview on the radio was in the news.

"The sign hanging around Mr. Doyle's neck said, *'I need a piece of you.'* This threatening message must be taken seriously. This serial killer takes body parts from its victims for purposes unknown. We believe this message is saying no one is safe."

"How long has it been out there?" someone yelled.

"The Bluff City Butcher has been in and out of this area since 1983. Pursuit by the FBI, state and local law enforcement and specialists has been focused in six states: Texas, Arkansas, Mississippi, New York, Florida and Tennessee."

"So the Memphis urban legend is true?"

"The man that kidnapped Sabina Weatherford October 15, 1983, and killed Cory Fortis, Roger Kent and Teddy Rosser two days later; that date—October 17—is significant—was named the Bluff City Butcher. He jumped off the Harahan Bridge and was never seen again. There have always been suspicions, but now it is clear to everyone he survived the river and has been killing ever since. Yes, the Memphis urban legend is true."

"What changed it for you?" asked a well-dressed man on the front row.

"Three people: a world-renowned serial killer hunter, an English professor and an investigative reporter."

"Detective Wilcox," an attentive man began, "thanks for taking our questions. I am worried for the safety of my family. I could live with this alone, but I have a wife and kids that are in danger. What must I know about this serial killer that might help me better protect my family?"

Tony leaned to the mic. "You and your family are why I am standing here today. My advice is simple. If you were on a safari in Africa, you would learn about the predators around you and seek information from an experienced guide. You would properly arm yourself. You would give up the walks at night…feeding time. You would sleep with one eye open and your family around you. Basically, you would accept the reality that you are surrounded by things that want to kill you. A walk to the front yard for the newspaper could be where the lion pounces…you must take precautions and always be ready. The Bluff City Butcher is the lion in our neighborhood. He is smarter than you. And he is hungry."

A voice deep in the crowd yelled, "Does this sick freak kill people randomly?"

"What may appear random to us may in fact be targeted by the Butcher. We currently estimate he has killed over a hundred people. We know his objectives have evolved recently. However, it is possible we will find the majority of his kills are somehow related."

"What do you mean by random and targeted?"

"Mr. Doyle was targeted. Barry Branch and Marcus Pleasant were not targeted…they were collateral killings."

"Do you know why Mr. Doyle was targeted?"

"Honestly, no. We know the Bluff City Butcher did not want Marcus Pleasant on the Doyle radio show, but that is not enough reason for me. I think there is something else going on there. If we figure it out, it may take us to the Butcher.

"Can you tell us how he kills?" asked a young lady in the front row.

"Yes ma'am. The Butcher is patient. Once he finds his victim he waits for the perfect opportunity to strike. He has a process: stun the victim, cripple them so he can do what he wants: torture, exsanguinate, harvest organs and hide the body. Lately he has modified the last step; he puts the victim on display.

"Let me give the news people a chance for a few questions and then we will get back to the community. We will stay here as long as it takes to answer your questions. We are changing our tactics dramatically. Your knowledge and awareness are vital to our efforts to better protect you and to stop this serial killer."

"Detective, Jim French with NBC. Based on the Memphis urban legend, the Bluff City Butcher has been around a long time. He has killed and avoided capture for at least twenty-five years. Who knows the most about the Bluff City Butcher? Can you tell us about the BCB: his appearance, what makes him different, his strengths and possibly his weaknesses, if he has any?"

Tony saw Elliott at the edge of the crowd, talking on his cell. "Those are important questions. The man who knows the Bluff City Butcher better than anyone else in the world happens to be with us today." Tony pointed in his direction. "Dr. Sumner, could you come up here and take a few questions…please?"

■ ■ ■

Reluctantly, he agreed. Elliott moved through the crowd with a sure-footed gait, his head above the sea of tentative faces that opened a path all the way to the podium. He stepped up to Tony and whispered, "Thanks, brother." They gripped hands. His arrival was broadcast live across the country. The major networks interrupted scheduled programming with breaking news out of Memphis, Tennessee. Beneath his close-up streamed: *internationally acclaimed forensic pathologist and premier serial-killer hunter, Dr. Elliott Sumner, comes out of retirement to hunt the Bluff City Butcher in Memphis, Tennessee.*"

"Check three o'clock…rooftop," whispered Tony.

Elliott turned to the bank of microphones, TV cameras and a sea of anxious eyes. He dipped his head once in respectful acknowledgment and scanned the area, including the janitor with the mop positioned high above the hullabaloo at three o'clock. He turned briefly and cleared his throat, looking at Tony, "…*not a problem.*"

The crowd grew quiet.

"Hello, I'm Elliott Sumner."

"WE NEED YOU, ELLIOTT SUMNER," a lone voice echoed from the courtyard.

Elliott seized the moment to calm with soft humor. "Sometimes it is good to be needed, my friend. I don't know if this time is so good." A ripple of relief surged down Main, cutting the edge off the tension.

Elliott got serious. TV cameras zoomed in and the national audience began to feel the gravity of the moment; the world renowned specialist was their only hope against an unstoppable monster terrorizing the Midsouth.

"Yesterday, only three people alive had ever seen the Bluff City Butcher. Today, there are two, and I am one. For a long time, hiding was important to this serial killer. He wants to GO PUBLIC now. Well, today I will shine a bright light on him so all will know what we are hunting.

"He is six-foot-five-inches tall, weighs two-hundred-fifty pounds, with a brawny build. He has a gray, unshaven face, sharp jaw, thick brow and deep-set black eyes. His long, black, oily hair is tied in a knot; the ponytail drops to the small of his back. He wears a black leather coat that hits below the knees, a dark shirt and dark pants and boots, size fourteen.

"This predator is uncommonly strong, the equivalency of ten men, and he is uncommonly fast, with top speed measured above thirty miles an hour. He has a twenty-five to thirty foot leap and easily scales flat vertical surfaces. The Butcher is nocturnal. He hunts in the dark and is adept at blending into his surroundings: shadows, alleys, stairwells, bushes and crowds. He stands as still as an oak tree in a wind storm and moves as quiet as the wind. It has been my experience his presence is only given away by a peculiar smell.

"HE IS A PSYCHOPATH AND A GENIUS. Yes, he is physically superior, but it is his mental superiority that makes him the most dangerous killing machine I have ever encountered. He is smarter than his prey and, so far, his hunters."

"What about his knife?" someone yelled from the crowd.

"He uses a ten-inch butcher knife. He can dismember a victim with one pass. His razor-sharp blade moves with incredible speed, power and accuracy."

"Doctor, I am Bill Pate with ABC News. How can it be that a genius intellect can also be a serial killer?"

"Intelligence has little to do with insanity. Regardless of IQ, you can be predisposed with psychopathic tendencies. If such a person is placed in a dysfunctional environment, those inclinations are further accentuated. The Bluff City Butcher is the product of a perfect storm: biological and environmental breakdowns."

"Why should we fear this serial killer more than any other?" asked Pate. "FBI Behavioral Sciences division estimates there are 400 active serial killers and that number is growing."

"Mr. Pate, Detective Wilcox spoke of a safari: life in a jungle surrounded by animals that want to eat you. As the people in Africa adapted to their world, we must adapt to ours or be eaten alive. Today we have one animal that is smarter, stronger and faster than all the rest. We must find and destroy him or he will kill us, regardless of our defenses. The Bluff City Butcher has already killed more people than any one animal in the modern world. He must be stopped." Elliott turned the podium over to Wilcox.

In north Shelby County a thumb pressed against the TV screen, covering Detective Wilcox's head. The Bluff City Butcher managed a slight smile although the reason escaped him. He felt the heartbeat through the screen as he pushed his gnarly toes into powdered dirt and sweat dripped from his scarred, muscular chest. In the distant haze were battered books in a stinking pile of refuse; *Gray's Anatomy, Webster's Dictionary, The Bible, Einstein's Life* by Isaacson, Michener's *Texas, Dalai Lama* and classics like *War and Peace, Moby Dick, Gone With the Wind and Huckleberry Finn.* He'd read them all and hundreds more. Always with the same reaction: he felt nothing.

In eight hours he would take Michael Bell and skin Nicolas Heller. The sirens woke him up. He was dreaming. He will get all of them, he reminded himself. *They know who they are.* But now he wondered if the sirens were coming or going.

■ ■ ■

11 April 2009

At 9:37 p.m. Officer Cannon got the call, a body hanging in a tree. The Collierville police dispatcher gave him the address; a vacant lot on a side street off Byhalia Road north of Poplar Avenue. The dispatcher said a homeowner walking his dog saw someone hanging in a tree. *Probably another suicide,* Cannon thought. He'd had only one homicide in Collierville over his six-year tenure, but tonight his twenty-three years with the Memphis police would come in handy.

He was closest to the location; Cannon made a U-turn on Dogwood and hit on lights and siren; ETA three minutes. His heart rate, blood pressure and facial expression never changed as he raced to the death scene, weaving through traffic on Houston Levee, and then shooting east on Frank Road with one thought...*poor son-of-a-bitch.*

The ambulance got there seconds before Cannon. They had just dropped off a patient a few blocks away when the call came in. As Cannon rolled to the edge of the property he could see the shadow twenty feet off the ground near the center of a tree at the back of the lot. He saw that the nearest streetlight was about twenty-five yards away. The homeowner that called 911 was an old guy in pajamas and slippers with an old dog on an old leash. *If he had not been waiting for the dog to finish taking a long piss he probably never would have seen a thing. Or maybe the guy is the Bluff City Butcher in disguise,* he laughed to himself. Cannon credited his sense of humor for keeping his sanity over the years. There had been so much talk of the BCB that everyone was getting punchy.

Cannon parked diagonally, blocking the side road about ten yards from the edge of the property. He called for back-up just to keep traffic and media out of the immediate area, even though he knew suicides were rarely covered. People in the neighborhood were looking out windows and standing on their porches watching the excitement, but the middle class rarely got in the way.

Although Cannon was in his mid-fifties, he still looked like he could stop a bull with one punch. Truth was, his aching joints made getting in and out of the squad car an intolerable ordeal. He put his hat on and walked toward the tree with his clipboard and flashlight. Now it was all business; this was his death scene and the poor son-of-a-bitch was going to get everything from Officer William Cannon...old school.

The emergency medical technicians knew their roles; one was getting things ready on the ground and the other was heading up the tree to check vitals. The dead guy was hanging by the neck not moving, just gently swinging in the breeze. The climb was arduous but the young EMT moved like a monkey with his eye on a new coconut. He reached the victim about the time Cannon's light found both of them, which turned out to be a bad idea; he fell out of the tree. Fortunately, his descent was broken by a few branches and Officer Cannon. Both sitting on the ground with the light still on the body they could see there was no need to check vitals. The man was deader than dead.

Cannon called for more back-up, Collierville homicide and CSI. His next call went to his old friend, Tony Wilcox. He thanked the witness who called and sent him and his dog home. Cannon was pleased the old guy didn't have his glasses. *EMTs would probably be loading the old fart onto the coroner's wagon with the guy in the tree.*

The victim's glossy pizza neck was stretched to its limit, like taffy. The battery cables were looped under his jaw, tied at the back of the head and looped up around a tree limb. The neck was the weakest link, but it did manage to hold onto the two-hundred-sixty pounder. The man had been skinned from his neck to the ankles and wrists. When his raincoat opened they saw the raw, bloody muscle, tendons, ligaments and the yellow adipose tissue. The feet and hands were amputated, body fluids dripping from the sutures.

The neighborhood block was closed to through traffic after Wilcox and Sumner pulled onto the scene. Cannon waved them in and they met at the base of the tree for a recap. A forty-foot perimeter was set—everything by the book.

"Hey, Billy, how are you?" said Tony with a friendly smile.

"I'm good, Tony. I'm real good. Sorry to get you out of your warm bed tonight."

"You know I never go to bed. Billy, this is Elliott Sumner. He has been…"

"Say no more, Anthony, the *Western Sherlock* is known. Seriously, it is good to meet you, Dr. Sumner. You have done more to make this world safe than anyone could ask of a man. Guys like me appreciate guys like you," said Cannon with a firm grip.

"Thank you, Officer. We are in this together." They all looked up at the victim swinging in the tree. Cannon gave the rundown; Tony and Elliott took off their coats and climbed the tree.

After rifling through coat pockets he found the ID. "We've found Heller." said Tony.

"We sure did. Does he live out in this area?" asked Elliott.

"Yes," Tony yelled down to Harris and tossed him the ID. "We can send a car to his house off Winchester. Maybe that is where the Bluff City Butcher did his work. Let's send a team."

Elliott had his penlight out, examining Heller's head. "Give me some time up here before we cut him down."

"You got it." Tony climbed back down.

Elliott was alone with Heller and the Butcher. *It is your work, no doubt. Give me an unexpected advantage. That's all I'm looking for now. Your dissection work is meticulous; removal of the dermal layers without disturbing the underlying muscle or adipose tissue demonstrates your skills, but who taught you this? Was it Enrique Medino? You carefully rinsed off Heller at the end; I see he was on his back at that time…maybe on a gurney somewhere.*

The cranial puncture wound is in the usual place, the carotids and jugular are sliced open with a single pass of the blade and you dissected the feet at the ankles and hands at the wrists. The stubs sutured as always: U.S.P #2 non-absorbable nylon, vertical mattress stitching and packer's knot, and the Knot of Isis. You left me nothing new...so far.

At midnight the body was lowered to the ground and placed in a crash bag. As they pulled the zipper up a teal Ford pickup was waved through and directed to a parking spot in front of the property. A tall, lean man wearing jeans, a white shirt and black cowboy hat met with Officer Cannon at the curb.

"Who is that?" asked Elliott.

"They found Heller's brother. Said he would like to come out now. Cannon knows the guy; said he could handle it."

The paramedics were ready to move the body when Tony got to them. "Men, can you give us a minute? We have a family member."

They looked over at Officer Cannon and the man in jeans; he removed his hat and dropped his head. Cannon put his hand on the shocked man's shoulder. They turned and walked to the tree. The paramedics unzipped the crash bag a few feet. A tearful positive ID was made.

The M.E van pulled away as the fog crawled into Collierville. Tony followed them to the county morgue.

The fog was thick, beading on the windshield enough to make the wipers necessary and adding to the already difficult situation. The rusted teal Ford pickup struggled to stay on the road; he tried to keep his left tire on the centerline snaking through the back hills of west Tennessee. Merle headed north on Mt. Pisgah to his sister's place in Fishersville, but this night the road had more curves than before and was taking forever. Even though it was late and Mary would be in bed, a phone call was out of the question. Merle wanted her to hear it from him in person. *Our successful brother is dead—Nicholas is in HEAVEN.*

Elliott was driving in the same fog but heading west on Poplar to the *Peabody* downtown when he got the phone call he was expecting. The Bluff City Butcher didn't want to chat. He was brief. "Heller is in HELL and Michael is with me. Three down, seven to go."

CHAPTER TWENTY-THREE

25 May 2009

"I'm not comfortable meeting with an FBI Agent," said Loman.

"He called us. We just sit and listen," said Dunn. He looked up and there was Voss, navigating the tables, heading their way.

"Hello, gentlemen." He walked through the Crescent Club as if he owned the place and took the seat at their table nearest the window. "I hope you haven't been waiting long." Over his career Dexter Voss had conducted hundreds of meetings like this one; he scared the hell out of people and then gave them one way out: something for him. Voss could always count on the greedy, cold hearted bastards taking the most expedient path—their personal preservation was valued above all else, even their mama.

They had dinner and light conversation: world events, Memphis sports and the weather. Loman was uncomfortable, Dunn wary and Voss presumptuous. The dinner arrangements were made by Voss; he had secured a private room for after-dinner drinks and more candid discussion. After they were seated behind closed doors with brandy in hand, Voss wasted no more time. He'd sized up Loman and Dunn long ago. The FBI had their eye on them and Heller since the Tennessee United Bank & Trust scam; a Mississippi Congressman was killed a year later, 2003. Strangled.

"We've been watching you for a while. Looks like your buddy Heller is off the hook now, thanks to the Butcher skinning him in April." Voss laughed. Loman squirmed. Dunn stared like the cold blooded killer he was.

"Watching us? What does that mean?" asked Loman as he choked on his brandy.

Dunn sipped with shifty eyes on Voss. *If the FBI had anything, dinner and drinks were definitely not standard operating procedure for booking felons.*

Loman was not as bright—Voss started with him.

"Mr. Loman, you killed Mr. Bishop in Destin." He spoke as if he was telling him where to find the bathroom. Loman didn't move. Voss leaned back in his chair and watched a bead of sweat escape his hairline. The next one to talk would lose.

"Are you crazy? Bishop was a guest at my beach house the night he died, but I didn't kill the man. It was a private meeting of *Life2* investors. Bishop disappeared. Hell, he took an ill-advised, late night walk on the beach alone. We didn't know he was missing until he didn't show up for breakfast the next morning. I have witnesses on my whereabouts that night and I told everything to the Destin police.

"Save it for your attorney. We have you on video stabbing the poor guy twenty-seven times. Loman, we have you running up to him and we can count each time you plunged your knife into the man."

Loman turned white and slumped back in his chair. Dunn still didn't react.

"Bishop was still moving when you rifled through his pockets and dragged him into the surf past the sand bar. You pushed him out in the

Gulf and stayed there to make sure he was drifting in the right direction to go out with the morning tide—shark bait. Did I miss anything, Loman? The poor bastard didn't agree with your *Life2* takeover scheme so you killed him. I have met some sorry-ass business people over my life, but you are scum. You enjoyed every minute of it.

"The nights are dark in Destin. That wasn't me. It was someone else."

"You are a real prick, Loman." Voss held up his *iPhone* with the video running and sound. "What is really sad is when Bishop called you by name and begged you to let him live. He promised he would stay out of your takeover scam. By then you had stabbed him twelve times. I believe we can hear your special words now. *'Fuck off…I never liked you, Bishop….'* I think that will get you the customary lethal injection, you useless prick."

"Turn it off, asshole," said Loman. He downed his brandy with the same look in his eyes he'd had when he killed Bishop. The quaint meeting room was quiet.

"Ok, Mr. Dunn, now you. My goodness, you were a bad boy too." Voss laughed hard with his back to both of them as he poured another brandy. For effect, he took his time looking out the window at the cars swishing by in the light drizzle. "Lawrence just deserved to die. Isn't that right, Mr. Dunn?"

"Yes. He did deserve to die," replied Dunn with an arrogant tone.

"I see. Well, then you should be acquitted for your role in the rightful execution of a criminal; judge, jury and executioner. You have nothing to fear from me."

"Mr. Voss, I appreciate you have extensive resources and capabilities at your disposal, but I was nowhere near Mr. Fleming when he died and I have no traceable connections to anyone who could have been involved."

Voss had figured Dunn would be more of a pain than Loman, but he knew how to handle the various personalities and defensive tactics. This was Voss's life.

"Mr. Dunn, do you really think I would have you here tonight if I did not already have your balls in a vice grip?" he asked calmly as he approached Dunn in his chair.

"I have no idea what you think you have, Director Voss. But I have no time for these games. I am going to call it a night."

Voss grabbed Dunn's throat with the speed of a rattlesnake and lifted his fat head up. Dunn's fat body followed. Voss turned his head to Loman. "Don't move or I will kill you next, you piece of shit!"

Loman had no plans to move. Dunn was in the barrel now.

"Dunn, it is people like you that make me sick. You think you are better than everybody. You think the world belongs to you and we are all in your way, a nuisance." He tightened his grip. "Fuck Fleming. You had him killed and we have all we need to put you away. But that's not what we are so pissed-off about. You killed a United States Congressman. The poor guy was re-zoning a parcel of land that you owned. It would have cost you a couple hundred thousand in taxes. So this one you did on your own. You did it like I am doing you now, you fat punk. You strangled the short Congressman with your hands as you pinned him under your fat ass."

"I'm choking. I can't breathe! Please." Dunn could do nothing against Voss's strength. He started to pass out.

Loman watched with a sick grin. Voss dropped him back into his chair.

"What do you want?" asked Loman as Dunn struggled to recover. Voss straightened his tie, brushed off his suit and took a seat. He looked at both with contempt.

"What do you want from us, Voss?" asked Dunn, rubbing his throat.

"For your transgressions to go away you are going to do something for me. You guys are going to kill Jack Bellow."

"Kill...Jack Bellow?" Loman jumped up, spilling brandy on the carpet.

"Why kill Bellow?" asked Dunn as he loosened his tie and unbuttoned his shirt, desperate for air.

Voss had them. "Let's just say Jack Bellow is more than he appears to be."

"What is he?" Loman didn't really care to know the answer and Voss could tell.

"That, you need not be concerned with."

"If we do this for you, what is in it for us?"

"Loman, you are one dumb prick. You're in no position to negotiate."

"I meant to say, if we do this for you, can you do us a favor?"

"Better. As I said, your past transgressions go away."

"That's all you got?"

"You are a greedy bastard. Ok, how about I throw in the *Life2 Corporation* with covert assistance: the undetectable adjustment of assets to give you the leverage you need for a legal takeover. That could be in place in five or six months. I know a group of you high-net-worth slobs believe the time has come to take the company public and Bellow is in your way."

"You can do that?" Dunn asked, soaked from over-exertion.

"Yes, we can and we will. I want Bellow dead. I will give you to June 25th. If he is still walking around after that, your incriminating videos will be planted where you least expect and search warrants will be issued. They will be admissible in a court of law and your asses will be owned by the Tennessee State Prison System. Or I may have you both killed."

Loman looked at Dunn. They both looked at Voss and smiled. "Is a week fast enough for you?"

■ ■ ■

Leaving the Crescent Club—and nightmare meeting with Voss—Loman walked alone to the parking garage. He was on a very important phone call, making arrangements to have Dexter Voss killed immediately.

Negotiations went well—only three times the going rate. $300,000 included running the body through a grinder and feeding it to the Mississippi River catfish. But in all his excitement, Loman completely forgot he was the next name on the Bluff City Butcher's list.

The *Dodge Sprinter* was parked next to his *Volkswagen Phaeton.* All the overhead lights in the garage were functioning except for one, but Loman didn't notice. He started his car remotely upon entering the garage. When he arrived, the dark image between his car and the large van was not a pillar. He only had time to look up.

The Butcher speared Loman's skull with a single, precise thrust as he had done so many times before. The ice pick found the mark; Loman's arms and legs locked. The Butcher had five seconds to remove the pick, wipe it off and slide it back into his belt—Loman's legs went limp on schedule. He put him in the back of the *Sprinter* on the dissection table; no need for restraints or gags. Loman was already losing control of his bowels and the twitching was almost over. He would stay alive but was not going anywhere anymore.

The Butcher left the *Sprinter* and Loman in the garage, the appropriate sticker prominently displayed on the rear bumper made it all possible; vehicle registration and parking renewals were handled online. The Butcher picked up Loman's cell and borrowed his car. He would return everything shortly.

Within the hour Dunn called Loman's cell. *"Don't talk. Pick me up at Salsa's now. We need to synchronize on taking this asshole out tonight."*

From behind a pillar in the shadows near *Salsa's Mexican Restaurant,* Dunn watched Loman's *Phaeton* enter the parking lot. It stopped and he got in. His first mistake was not confirming the identity of the driver. His second mistake was only looking out the passenger side window as they departed. Dunn never got a chance for a third. The crashing blow to the back of his head rendered him unconscious for the rest of the night. However, he would wake up in time for the removal of his digestive system. Loman had it much easier. He would die the moment his lungs were yanked from the gaping chest wound.

It was all in the letter. There should have been no surprises. A box containing a digestive system and pair of lungs was delivered to Albert Bell's front gates. DNA confirmed the owners. This time all cameras pointing to the gates were pulverized, but Albert was pleased his guards were spared, the three found unconscious in a pile behind the quaint stone guardhouse.

■ ■ ■

3 July 2009

Voss recruited for his covert operation a man named Phillips, who, he knew, was a disgruntled FBI information systems tech. If there had been any other way, he would have taken it because he hated computer geeks, especially the stratospheric caliber of geek employed by the bureau—so smart about technical matters but so dumb about everything else.

The FBI had no reason to think Voss knew about the bugs they had secretly planted in his rental house—they'd been there since 2005. But Voss knew the FBI was suspicious and he was pretty sure they were looking for a way to nail him. For years he pretended like he didn't know. That morning, Phillips flew to Memphis under an assumed name. He came in the side door of the stand-alone garage behind Voss's house, out-of-view of covert cameras and directly into a bug-free environment swept long ago.

"What do you mean there is nothing on it?" yelled Voss as Phillips tried to explain the condition of the Medino hard drive.

"You told me everything was perfect six months ago when you examined that hard drive. You said the ingredients and formulas for the *Life2* compound production were complete and the specialized treatment regimens were laid out in detail. We were good to go in December 2008. What are you telling me in July 2009?"

"The hard drive you took from Medino's farm was processed like every other hard drive the FBI acquires. I ran all the diagnostics by the book, the way we would run any hard drive to get around security software and to avoid traps that could compromise data recovery. I copied and transferred Medino's database to the FBI mainframe, into our secret lockbox, according to our plan, and I saved another copy off line. The detailed formulations and treatment regimens were in code as expected, to be broken later. YES, I did validate all data transfers, and YES, I saved the Medino database in three separate locations," said Phillips, running out of breath and pacing back and forth on the paint drop cloth spread out on the garage floor.

"Then why, six months later, is everything gone?"

"Medino's security was sophisticated. The standard FBI diagnostics triggered some unknown stealth virus that was deeply embedded in his database. At the 140-day mark, the bomb went off. His virus was awakened and consumed everything in ten seconds. Medino had stuff the FBI had not yet seen. The man was not fooling around. He wanted to keep his information secret."

"But you copied his shit onto the FBI mainframe in our secret area. How did you lose that data?"

"The Medino virus traveled with his data. Really, this is my world. There is nothing we can do now. The Medino database is gone. His hard drive is toast. His security system did what it was intended to do. We need another plan," said Phillips.

Voss had no other plan. His decision to get the hard drive was unsanctioned and covert—his retirement program. He was going to negotiate his billion dollar deal with the federal government. Phillips was supposed to be the brilliant computer geek that could successfully navigate the Medino security and move the "Anti-aging technology" database to a secret lockbox deep in caverns of the FBI computer system; they would never think to look there. It was genius.

Phillips had lost everything: Medino's database, precious time and Voss's confidence. The discussion was over. The silencer was already screwed on the dirty gun sitting behind the coffee can. Phillips didn't see it coming because Voss shot him in the back of the head. He rolled his body in the paint drop cloth and tossed him in a dumpster behind apartments on Poplar later that night. If there were FBI mainframe loose ends, it would explain Phillips' sudden disappearance.

Dexter Voss, an FBI agent for twenty-five years, had been the Director of the FBI Midsouth Regional Office for five years. Although it sounded special, it was a subordinate sector and his last chance. Now, Voss had screwed up too many things, but he didn't care. He was in his own midlife crisis; he'd divorced his third wife and left kids in Newark and Baltimore without looking back. His life in Memphis was work, the gym and one-night-stands.

He was never surprised at assignments that came across his desk. He lost count of the UFO investigations. Big Foot, vampires, ghosts and zombie sightings were always popular, along with the invisible Communists or little people living in the woods waiting to take over the country. Then there were the bizarre inventions: antigravity mechanisms, five-hundred-mile-per-gallon carburetors, cures for cancer, drug sniffing crickets, mind reading spectacles and blood substitutes that stimulated superhuman strength. In June of 2004, when someone claimed they held a key to immortality, Voss just booked the meeting like a dental appointment and drove to Nashville.

The assignment came to the Memphis field office directly from 935 Pennsylvania Avenue, FBI Headquarters. They always arrived as an embedded message in the designated spam of the day. Voss was directed to get with Dr. Enrique Medino, a short trip to find out if the Vanderbilt geneticist had something of interest. They met at a Starbucks in an obscure location east of the city.

If he had paid closer attention in 2004, he would have avoided the need to kill him four years later. When Medino introduced himself Voss almost laughed out loud; the man claiming to hold a key to immortality was almost dead. Only Voss's twisted mind would enjoy the irony—and visibly express it.

Medino explained his battle with pancreatic cancer and the chemotherapy that was killing him. He talked about his research and said he'd solved the puzzle three months ago, after three decades of testing theory. Medino told Voss he would be 100 percent cured in six months, but Voss had stopped listening at hello. For him, the meeting was another wasted day with a dreamer.

Medino told Voss his biogenic solutions were applicable to all somatic cells regardless of age, sex, race or medical condition. Because his treatment regimen replaced most damaged cells with younger, healthy cells, disease-free life could be possible, and he believed the biogenic induced process could go on a very long time.

Voss was impressed with Medino's brains—probably a genius—but he was not buying into any of the "immortality" mumbo-jumbo. When he heard the proposition he was certain Medino was a nut. The offer of exclusive rights to the U.S. Government came with three requirements; (1) Medino would get full credit for his discovery in the form of a national monument, national holiday and a life enrichment research facility, (2) following proof of concept he would receive $1 billion tax free and (3) after mutually agreed success targets were hit, Medino would receive an additional $3 billion tax free.

Voss told him they were definitely interested—as he always did—and that he would get back with him soon. Once in Memphis he filed a report rejecting the validity of Medino's claims.

■ ■ ■

December 8, 2004

Six months later Voss was on a hot date with a high-priced prostitute—dinner at the Crescent Club and an athletic sleepover later; he had saved up a long time for the one big night. By chance, from his corner table in the main dining room he could see Jack Bellow sitting at the far windows, looking a bit anemic and his eyes locked on his guest. From behind, Voss could tell the man was middle-aged, sporting a crew cut, tan and a build like a wrestler: thick arms and shoulders. When the man turned his head, the profile was familiar. It bugged Voss the rest of the night.

He never forgot a face. *Who is that stranger in my town?* At the end of the evening they got up to leave and walked by Voss's table. Bellow waved and kept walking. The guest slowed a bit, made eye contact, dipped his head once, smiled and was gone. The man's arm muscles were well defined in the tight fitting suit coat and his white shirt was pulling at the buttons on his chest but not his belly, which was flat, and the man walked with a bounce in his step, as if ready to sprint. The whole picture was driving Voss to drink until Murray, the club manager, passed through the dining room. Voss couldn't take it any longer and asked Murray about Jack Bellow's guest.

"That was Dr. Medino out of Nashville," said Murray.

"No, I think you are mistaken. Dr. Medino is a much older man, and I believe he is battling pancreatic cancer. I had an occasion to meet him this summer; he was near death."

"Nope. You just saw Dr. Enrique Medino. He beat cancer and is a proud SURVIVOR. He believes it was a miracle. Ever since he went into remission he has been dedicated to working out daily and eating right. He looks great." Murray scraped the bread crumbs from Voss's table linen and smiled at the hooker.

"I don't know. He sure didn't look like the Dr. Medino I met."

"I understand the shock. When Jack Bellow saw him the first time in the bar tonight, he collapsed, fainted, for God's sake. Medino caught him on his way down, held up the 230-pound man with one hand and moved a chair under him with the other. He stayed with him until help arrived. It was unbelievable. I guess Jack saw the sick Dr. Medino too and was shocked to see him the way he is now."

Voss was not feeling so good. The elevator ride down made him even worse. He paid the prostitute and puked in the bushes as the taxi pulled away. After gathering himself, he went back up to the Crescent Club to drink. It appeared Medino had actually found a key to life-extension. That was when Dexter Voss realized his career was over.

Murray, the undercover FBI plant, watched Voss on the monitors from his office while downloading the audio-video feed from table seven. He prepared the encrypted file for transfer to a top-secret location in Washington DC. This time he got some quality stuff; Medino spoke in detail of his biogenic breakthrough and Bellow laid out the most likely business strategy. A few times Murray had to visit their table to move items blocking audio feeds or fisheye lenses. They thought he was keeping the wine flowing but he was keeping the show rolling.

Murray leaned back in his chair with a smile; the Crescent operation went well. *It took several years to get in a position to manage this club and also to get Jack Bellow to have his Medino meeting here, a place where everything could be monitored.* The FBI had been watching Medino on and off for more than three decades and used Dexter Voss for the 2004 meeting in Nashville—strategic; they couldn't send the heavyweights from DC or the validity of the Medino Project would be elevated and outside covert interests would become an even greater problem. The December dinner confirmed what the FBI had suspected; Medino finally had a reproducible event. The government would start putting a package together while moving Voss out of the way.

CHAPTER TWENTY-FOUR

4 July 2009

He never smoked but decided anything he did now was probably not going to kill him—the Bluff City Butcher was coming for him. Dexter Voss was one who knew why his name was on the list; he'd killed Dr. Medino.

He imagined it almost exactly the way it happened. He was alone in the backyard of his crummy rental house in the crappiest part of Memphis. The neglected, overgrown neighborhood with its tight, empty alleys provided the perfect network of shadows. Dogs were always barking and cars squealing and neighbors didn't care what went on next door. Dexter made it as easy as possible for the Bluff City Butcher to make his move.

The fourth of July was just another excuse to take a day off. For reasons Voss couldn't fathom, people liked to sit around lighting firecrackers, drinking beer and cooking on a grill. He was fine sitting alone on his plastic patio furniture on his crumbling cement slab, holding a glass of aged rum and looking at his shitty backyard—his own little Brazilian rain forest. A few bottle rockets crossing his airspace were celebration enough. But this time was even more special. He was getting drunk because his luck had finally changed.

The first glass of Neisson Rhum was dedicated to Jimmy Doyle, the poor bastard freaking-out at the Bell mansion, number one on the Butcher's list. Doyle was dead. Voss drank one glass to Doyle and wondered if he was still alive when the Butcher hammered the steel spits into his shoulders down to his balls. The medical examiner said both metal rods managed to miss vital organs and blood vessels all the way to the iliac crest.

The second glass was raised in memory of Michael Bell, Albert's little brother. Michael was forever number two in life; the Butcher made him number two on the list. When he was taken, everyone else on the list could bend over and kiss their collective asses goodbye. Michael Bell had more protection than a sitting U.S. President. Now, he was gone and they were all waiting for his body to show up somewhere terrible. The second glass of Neisson went down smoother than the first. Voss was feeling better already.

Heller, Loman and Dunn—numbers three, four and five—were brutally dissected exactly as the Butcher promised. Voss despised the rich bastards. They had so much, yet it was never enough. Voss was the opposite; he was given so little and even that was taken away from him. The third glass of rum was for the three jerks sitting in hell.

Now, it was Dexter's turn. The Butcher wrote; *"The FBI loses a man for proprietary and confidential reasons known only to him.* Voss is number six."* How did the Butcher find out it was him? No one was around when Voss forced Medino's *Lincoln* off Austin Peay. No one was around when he rammed the ice pick in five heads, poured the kerosene and lit the match. But now his backyard was dark. Superman was sitting alone on the patio, and everything was in place. Dexter Voss was FBI. *Make your move, you freak.*

When the glass touched his lips he sniffed the rum and opened his eyes. The Bluff City Butcher was standing a few feet away. He had finished circling. Dexter swallowed and set his glass on the patio table next to the folded newspaper. The serial killer was much bigger than Voss envisioned and the face was hard, angry and still.

"Are you going to talk to me before you kill me?" asked Voss, professionally impressed that the Butcher got so close without detection. "Was Medino your friend?"

The black eyes narrowed, the nose wrinkled and the brow dipped.

"Was Medino your Guardian?" Voss kept the murderer's attention as he moved his right hand down the arm of the chair, his fingers inches from the loaded and cocked Colt he'd put under the newspaper before sundown. The barrel was pointed perfectly.

"You hurt Medino," said the Butcher through the slit in his lips.

Voss had practiced the move hundreds of times before; he was good. The FBI training required 1.2 seconds to grip a loaded weapon less than ten inches from an opened hand, aim and shoot. Voss could do it in 0.8 seconds.

"The FBI made me stop him. They control me. They would kill my family if I didn't do as I was ordered. They said stop Medino." *I know your voice. I know who you are,* he thought as he tried to see more of the Butcher's face that was half in the shadows.

My God, Jack Bellow is in disguise. Damn, he is one sick bastard. The Medino connection makes sense. The jaw line and chin and nose and now the voice, I cannot believe what I am seeing. "You are Jack…fucking…Bellow."

"You are a dead fool."

Voss never had a lucky day in his life until the Fourth of July 2009. The bottle rocket zipped into his backyard, exploding ten feet behind the Butcher's right shoulder. His black eyes moved for a fraction of a second. Voss gripped the gun perfectly and got one round off, through the newspaper and in record time.

The Bluff City Butcher was hit between the eyes…a perfect shot…unbelievable. He dropped like a giant oak in the forest.

Really, you were never that bad. You were just a sick man with a knife.

Voss would never forget the most perfect moment in his career as an FBI Agent. It was like hitting the impossible three-point shot at the buzzer or crossing the finish line a tenth of a second ahead of the fastest man in the world.

The kick of the gun hurt his elbow, a sharp pain, but that was ok. The sweet smell of burnt gun powder stung his nostrils. The explosion rang in his ears. Then the muffled sounds of Midtown came and stayed a while. It was as if he'd left the world and was reentering the atmosphere. Everything was in slow motion and everything was perfect at last. Finally, he had a plan that worked.

Like a well trained professional, Dexter Voss had lured, distracted and waited for the perfect moment. Now, he was the one who had killed the most dangerous serial killer in American history. Dexter Voss killed the monster that the famous Dr. Elliott Sumner could not catch. Now, Dexter Voss could go back home and get the respect he deserved from the Bureau and his family. The Medino debacle and all his other failures would be forgotten because Dexter Voss had stopped the Bluff City Butcher.

One shot. But what did I do with my gun?

■ ■ ■

The FBI got to the house before the Memphis Police knew anything. The bugs caught the whole thing. They swept the place clean before placing the anonymous 911 call on a disposable cell. Detective Wilcox was the third car to pull up. The police squad car in the vicinity was first and Elliott was second; he was waiting for Tony out front.

Tony, arriving last again, was frustrated. "How did you get here before me?"

"I'm just smarter than you," said Elliott. That took the chip off Tony's shoulder.

"Funny. I think Voss surprised all of us."

The patrolman met them at the front door and walked with them through the house to the backyard patio. "There was no need for paramedics."

The death scene was different. The crumbling cement patio was red with blood. Dexter Voss was sitting in a plastic chair, his right arm missing at the elbow; it was lying in the grass, his hand holding a gun. The severed arm was obviously the first pass of the Butcher's knife. The second pass sliced a five-inch gash across the neck, much deeper than usual, his head hinged back. The last thrust of the knife traveled through the center of the heart and out the back of the chair.

Tony circled, careful to protect physical evidence, and knelt to sniff the barrel. "He got one off, Elliott. I think Voss managed to piss-off the Butcher."

"Do you remember what Doyle said the night we found Branch and Pleasant at Bellow's penthouse?" Elliott spoke while processing the scene methodically.

"You mean, about seeing Voss in Covington?"

"My caller said Voss confessed to killing Dr. Medino."

"Do you think the FBI is in this somehow?" asked Tony.

Elliott pointed to the patio table and held up a finger as he felt under the edge. He removed a small listening device and handed it to Tony. "No, I am sure Voss was rogue, working on his retirement. This kill is another Butcher message. He doesn't like the FBI."

Elliott winked.

"He shouldn't take it so personal; that's what you get when you kill and cross state lines." He dropped the device in the bottle of rum; then they explored the death scene separately.

After the medical examiner and the forensic team arrived, Elliott and Tony met at Barksdale's for a cup and to share notes without the FBI listening.

"My caller was talkative." Elliott waved off a menu. "Just coffee."

"How so?"

"Voss got a shot off that almost hit him."

"That explains the mess; the Butcher is usually such a tidy serial killer."

"He watched Voss hide the gun under his newspaper before dark and then waited for Voss to drink four tall glasses of rum."

Tony sipped his coffee. "Hmmm, so he was stalking in daylight and waiting hours for the right moment to attack. We always assumed he traveled at night."

"I suggest you have your people go back over recent kills and look for security cameras in the general vicinity, looking eight hours before time of death and forward from that time."

"Agreed. What else we have?" Tony punched numbers on his phone.

"The Butcher waited for Voss to fall asleep before he approached. He stood there for a long time. I wonder what he was doing."

"How did you reach those conclusions? I saw where he was standing, but how do you know how long he was there and that Voss was asleep?"

"You saw the shoe impressions in the grass where the Butcher stood just off the edge of the patio, correct?"

"Yes…the bent grass."

"If fescue grass lies flat for more than an hour in the sun then it has been damaged. The Butcher's two-hundred-fifty-pound load crushed the grass for at least five or more minutes. Less time would have simply bent the grass and it would spring back to normal.

"Ok, good. I will buy that, but you said Voss was sleeping. How did he manage to get a shot off at the Butcher if he was sleeping?"

"Something snapped him out of a drunken stupor; a firecracker or a mosquito bite, a dream or even a single spoken word that was important to him. In a split second, Voss saw the Butcher and executed his plan, filling in the story around the shot. Voss believed he had an open shot at the Bluff City Butcher and his FBI training took over from there. I will bet Voss convinced himself he was victorious before he died. Again, all this happened in seconds, the imagination filling in all the empty spaces."

"Elliott, you're good, but really, how do you know Voss just woke up? Maybe he was never asleep in the first place. Maybe the Butcher stood there ten minutes and they talked and then the Butcher killed Voss."

"It's possible, but unlikely."

"Why?"

"Well, follow the logic. If I was Dexter Voss, I don't think I could grab a gun and get a shot off, get my arm cut off, get my head cut off and take a knife in my chest with my feet casually crossed at the ankles. I was half asleep and drunk," said Elliott.

"Damn, I missed the feet," said Tony.

"But more importantly, who was the Butcher talking to for five minutes?"

"Someone was with Voss and the Butcher?"

"Voss was asleep. The relationship was with the Bluff City Butcher."

"Elliott, the FBI must be in this somehow."

"Remember, the FBI was exploring a deal with Medino in 2004. Voss met with Medino before Jack Bellow. Sources confirm Voss fell out of favor. He blew the deal or he was being used by his superiors in some covert way."

"Why would an orthopedic biotechnology be important to the FBI?"

"Medino had something more."

"Ok, but what science could get the attention of the FBI?"

"Tony, the man was a top geneticist going to Anti-aging conferences. You heard his December interview with Doyle."

"You believe that stuff? You believe extending life is really possible?"

"Yes. It is possible. The sciences are accelerating and merging. Computers allow for millions of calculations necessary to understand the human genome, biochemistry, molecular biology and—soon—what controls life and death. If a cell can be programmed to turn off, it is only logical to conclude it can be programmed to stay on, to keep making new, healthy replacement cells. We know that DNA is immortal."

"If Medino found a key to life-extension, I would assume that would be important enough for governments and private interests," said Tony.

"The FBI would take a lead role because such technology would be viewed to be a national security risk. Or possibly a special, top secret agency," said Elliott, as his mind advanced theories on *Gilgamesh*.

"But why would they kill Medino?"

"I think we can safely conclude Voss killed Dr. Medino. He probably stole the technology—software, hardware, formulas, codes—and thought he could sell it on his own to a government, but something went wrong...recently. That would explain why he got drunk and waited for the Butcher. I believe Dexter Voss was inviting death. He was a broken man; his personal life was falling apart and his career with the FBI pretty much over after screwing up the Medino deal."

Tony held up his fingers, half-an inch apart. "That would explain the bugs too."

"The FBI swept the house for Medino's property—or a treasure map—then called it in to the MPD. The Butcher called me when he got where ever he stays. It's got to be somewhere in Shelby County."

"So the Butcher did someone a favor last night by killing Voss," said Tony, rubbing his head. "Do you think he is taking direction?"

"It's one possibility we need to keep on the table," said Elliott.

"If you held the secret to immortality, what would that be worth, Elliott?"

"Countries have gone to war for less. Extending human life two, three fold or more is a world-changing event. Tony, anyone could be involved in our little mystery now. I used to think we were only after the Bluff City Butcher. I'm starting to think it could be something even more."

CHAPTER TWENTY-FIVE

"I know one day I'll turn the corner and I won't be ready for it."
Jean-Michel Basquiat

4 September 2009

He had trouble believing fifty-eight days ago Dexter Voss was killed in Midtown. Wilcox was getting tired of looking over his shoulder; he was number seven on the list for a visit from the Bluff City Butcher. Five of the first six were confirmed dead. Michael Bell was taken on April 11. His body had not turned up...yet.

Hanging Doyle off the Hernando de Soto Bridge accomplished two objectives for the Butcher: national attention and terrorizing half of the Midsouth community. The shocking, full-disclosure press conference that followed the incident was successful in terrorizing the other half of the community. Unfortunately, the Memphis police had no choice. New tactics were required to capture the demented predator.

The city of Memphis was thrown into unbridled panic and despair as Bluff City Butcher killings routinely made the news. After Doyle, Branch and Pleasant, the killing of three Midsouth millionaires and the disappearance of Michael Bell were devastating. When the Midsouth

Regional Director of the FBI was slain by the Butcher in his home, some Memphians had had enough. They packed their bags and left town.

In August, officials said four percent of the area population relocated permanently and seven percent left temporarily. Then the Munson family filed a class action lawsuit against the city. The downward spiral gained momentum. The Bluff City Butcher was beginning to change the very course of an American city.

Tony left the office at 6:55 p.m. feeling down. Maybe one good night of sleep would make all the difference. He would drive straight to his condo to crash early. Turning into his driveway, he waved to the shadow in the driver's seat of the patrol car parked across the street. Its wipers were on; it had been raining on and off all day. The MPD was watching Tony 24/7 now. Tony knew the guy out front would be relieved at 9:00 p.m. so he didn't stop to talk.

Tony pulled into his garage and closed the door with the remote. He turned off the car and just sat behind the wheel, rubbing his eyes, exhausted from constantly looking for something new, anything that could get him inches closer to catching the Butcher. But all the little things were starting to slip through the cracks; he had forgotten he was to meet Elliott and Carol at the *Peabody* for drinks at seven. It was unlike him.

Normally, he was observant, but the week had been long and all he could think about was falling into his bed. Otherwise, he would have noticed his front porch light was out. He would have checked and discovered the light bulb had been unscrewed. Once inside, he automatically locked the door, turned the deadbolt and hung the chain. Any other time Tony would have seen the drops of water on the marble entry leading to the bedrooms.

Nothing happened until he tossed his sport coat on the bed, took off his gun and hung it on the hook deep in his closet. When he turned back the cold steel, razor sharp blade swept across his chest; the burning, stinging pain instantly stole his breath. The blade passed one inch deep, clipping ribs like cardboard and opening the peritoneal cavity with a sucking sound. All he could feel on his way to the floor was his cell phone vibrating in his pocket.

Elliott calling from the *Peabody*.

The Bluff City Butcher took his time with Wilcox, wanting to keep him alive as long as the human body would allow. The second pass of the Butcher's knife opened his abdomen. Contents of his stomach oozed out and mixed with blood and feces pouring from the lacerated large intestines. The Butcher would save major arteries for when he was ready to take Tony to the edge—the end of living and the beginning of dead, He had plenty of time.

He watched and waited for Wilcox to break, to pass out from the pain. Tony's eyes stayed open and on the sinister eyes of the monster sitting on the edge of his bed. To speed up the process, the Butcher playfully pushed the blade into Tony's right chest cavity; the lung collapsed and Wilcox began to struggle for air. He fought to keep his eyes open as his lips tightened with a defiant determination. The Butcher watched curiously and felt nothing.

The sirens got louder but they were not coming to the Wilcox condo. The BCB had killed the policeman out front hours ago; Wilcox should have looked closer. *Who would be concerned about a guarded, off-duty, big shot homicide detective?* he thought as he waited, leaning over number eight, watching for a hint of submission.

Tony was losing control. The punctured lung and blood loss were taking him down. He struggled to stay conscious, but he would know death was near when the pain stopped and his interest in this world left him. For the moment, he wanted to see the Bluff City Butcher's face. He wanted to understand how a man could kill so easily and so often. Would the eyes give him some answer?

The Bluff City Butcher sat on the edge of the bed, Tony on his back on the floor at his feet. The bedroom was dimly lit. Blood was pooling in his abdomen and streaming from the ten-inch abdominal flap onto polished wood floors each time his body fought for a parcel of air, another piece of life. His brain could no longer give instructions to his body. Tony looked one last time at the Butcher and felt the last sting of the blade deep in his belly. The black eyes of the demon finally revealed something…a primitive, prideful moment as his hand summoned death once again. The power was arousing.

The Bluff City Butcher smiled with one corner of his mouth as he opened his coat and removed the ice pick from his belt.

■ ■ ■

"Death knocks once, dying countless times."
Martin Dansky

The Memphis PD buried their top homicide detective and a seasoned patrolman on Saturday, September 12, 2009. The Bluff City Butcher had made sure Detective Wilcox died a slow and painful death. Although the community would never know the details, the message sent was chilling enough: not even the top cop on the case was safe. The officer watching the condo never had a chance. He was just in the way.

If there ever was a good day for a funeral it was the second Saturday in September. The Memphis police honored their own under a cloudless sky on a perfect seventy-two degree, low-humidity day in the Midsouth. The funeral procession began outside City Hall and went down Second Avenue to Beale, led by fifty silent squad cars, their blue lights spinning. Downtown sidewalks were packed and heads bowed as the black hearse passed in a sea of police officers, wearing full uniform, marching in formation, their hats over their hearts and their heads looking to the setting sun.

The procession concluded at Elmwood on South Dudley, the oldest cemetery in Memphis. Graveside services were held for Detective Anthony Wilcox and Officer William Hanson, standing room only. Over 200,000 Midsoutherners lined the streets that day. They were paying their last respects to the fallen and showing unending support for their Memphis Police Department, who were both humbled and reinvigorated by the experience.

Tony had solved hundreds of homicides in Memphis. He had an unshakable commitment to the rules of law and a person's right to be safe in their community. He was known for getting the job done. Sometimes his *Dirty Harry* approach got him in hot water with the top brass, but the city and county mayors and city prosecutor knew his heart and knew also that they needed a man like Detective Wilcox to take out the trash. After the two twenty-one gun salutes, everyone went home, saying Tony would have been proud.

On that fateful Friday night Elliott had had a bad feeling. Tony was ten minutes late for drinks at the *Peabody*. Like Elliott, Tony was never late to anything. When the second call went to messages, he knew the Butcher had him; they both had anticipated Tony's most likely kill site would be his home at night.

They got to the condo in five minutes, sirens all the way. When they broke down the door the Butcher crashed out of the bedroom window and fell from the second floor, hitting the ground in a dead run. Squad cars swarmed the area like bees protecting the hive. They fanned out and a containment parameter was already going up four blocks out. The canine squad, choppers and the TACT units were operational seven minutes after Elliott's call to Director Wade. Although it was dark, thermal imaging devices and the canine squad were highly functional. Memphis patrol cars crawled streets and alleys with spotlights and loud-speakers, warning residents the Bluff City Butcher was in the area.

Elliott was the first to reach him. Tony was lying in his blood, dead. Seconds would determine if there was a chance for him to come back. Elliott cocked back Tony's head, opened an airway, hit his chest and launched aggressive CPR as he ripped off his bloody shirt between compressions and blew air into his lungs. He saw the bubbling, bloody chest wound—pneumothorax—and pressed his palm over the hole to allow Tony to breathe. Miraculously, he responded. A gasp for air was followed with coughing blood and short, irregular respiration. Elliott found a faint heartbeat. Tony's eyes blinked and his body jerked as his body fought to live again.

He kept pressure on the chest wound and turned his attention to blood loss; the major flow was from the ten-inch abdominal wound. Elliott's anatomical expertise and honed senses allowed him to blindly reach into Tony's belly to locate the primary bleeders; there was one major. He pinched off the artery to the left kidney; it would buy him a minute at best—both hands were committed. He had done all he could do alone. He needed help or Tony would slip away.

If the Bluff City Butcher had Tony for five minutes, Tony would have a blood supply problem. When leaving the *Peabody*, Elliott called the special standby ambulance and spoke with his two hand-picked paramedics. They were instructed to pick up twenty units of O-negative packed red cells that were on hold at the Regional Blood Center for just such an emergency. The director of the blood bank would meet them on Madison Avenue a block east of the Baptist Hospital complex. They could grab the ice chests on the fly and be at Tony's condo four minutes later.

The place was a beehive, but everything moved out of the way, creating a path for the special medical team. They exploded through the front door with arms full and saw Sumner over Wilcox in a sea of red, one hand over a pneumothorax and one deep in his belly of blood; they knew immediately he was holding a bleeder. Mike Primeaux and Mike Hinton were the best in the city. Without words or wasted moves they went into action, one patching the pneumothorax and passing a surgical clamp to Elliott for the bleeder, and the other flushing blood clots and mucus from Tony's airway, bagging and taking control of respiration as he slid a bag of O-negative and transfusion kit to the doctor. They would push a unit in each arm and have a dozen more ready to go.

Tony's partner was the last in the condo. He closed the door behind him and moved to the dining room. Harris dragged the table into the kitchen with all the lights he could find, closed the blinds, draped bed sheets and started boiling water—the operating room was open for business. They moved Tony to the table, cut off the rest of his clothes and started another IV pushing Ringers Lactate. Tony's blood pressure was perilously low. Elliott blindly navigated the abdominal cavity in search of more bleeders and fatal lacerations. One by one, he located and surgically repaired each and then turned his attention to the damaged organs and other cavity repairs. Luckily, the heart was untouched. The intestines, stomach, liver and one kidney required attention.

Mike and Mike anticipated each of Elliott's surgical needs while they maintained CPR, monitored vitals, communicated changes to Elliott and pushed red cells, fluids and administered life saving pharmaceuticals.

Tony's condo was treated like an operating room. Elliott limited access to only three; Primeaux, Hinton and Harris. The two paramedics were battlefield ready and among the very few that knew what was likely to happen to either Tony or Elliott. Both anticipated the Bluff City Butcher's moves but could not be sure who would be first. Mike and Mike had been carefully prepared and for the last ninety days were ready to face the most impossible conditions. If it had been Elliott, they would have taken over for him…off the record. Elliott knew their capabilities.

He repaired everything he could find that was damaged by the Bluff City Butcher. They flushed and suctioned the peritoneal cavity, inserted drain tubes and closed. They bandaged and tightly wrapped plastic around Tony's abdomen and chest, administered a broad spectrum antibiotic and pushed blood bag number nineteen. They did all that was humanly possible to save Tony. But in the end the damage from the Butcher's knife was too great. Detective Tony Wilcox was pushed too far beyond the point of no return.

Elliott had done his best. He thanked the team for their heroic efforts and professionalism. The only thing left to do was to remove Tony's body from the condo and transport him to the Shelby County Morgue. They gently placed him in the black vinyl crash bag, zipped it closed and set him on the gurney for the somber ride out of the condo. Their heads hung low as they walked him to the waiting ambulance under the quiet lights of the local news media. For a moment all movement stopped and all heads dropped. The body was handled with care and reverence as they placed it next to the other crash bag; Officer Hanson had died hours earlier and was propped in his car. The Butcher was a patient...monster.

The back doors closed and the ambulance pulled away, no sirens and no flashing lights. Detective Wilcox and Officer Hanson would be transported to the medical examiner for autopsy—two more homicides. The bloody death scene would be processed by the Memphis CSI team for the next several hours. They would do everything twice because they had lost two of their own and the Bluff City Butcher got away. They hung their heads under the burden of pain, loss and another failure.

Elliott watched the slow ambulance turn onto Poplar and disappear before he returned to Tony's bedroom. He stood at the shattered window that the Bluff City Butcher crashed through one hour earlier. He saw where the Butcher landed, two-hundred-fifty pounds dropping twenty feet onto soft ground. But the tracks went back to the condo, ending at the thirty-foot brick wall...similar to the wall at Jimmy Doyle's place.

"Alex, can I see you just a minute please?" asked Elliott.

"Yes. What can I do for you, Sir?"

"He is in the attic," Elliott whispered. "Follow me." The Memphis police were gone. Only CSI agents remained, gathering the last of the forensics. Elliott and Alex pulled out their guns, turned off the hall light and opened the door to the attic stairs. The climb was quiet and dark. Their heads reached floor level, where they could see the open window above Tony's bedroom. There were stacks of boxes and covered furniture between them and the window.

Elliott reached for the light switch as Alex aimed his gun at the open window. When he flipped on the light, a sofa was sailing toward them. Alex emptied his gun in all directions before the sofa knocked them both down the stairs. They recovered and ran to the open attic window and saw the fresh blood on the sill.

"Alex, your boss would be proud. You killed a sofa and wounded the Butcher," said Elliott. They watched the BCB run into the dark night.

"Thank you." He holstered his weapon. "I'm just happy to shoot something, Sir."

The Memphis PD returned with dogs and picked up the trail. It was a straight line to the Memphis Zoo three miles away. But there was where it ended.

Later that night, alone in his car and on the way to Millington, Elliott allowed himself one smile. Tony Wilcox was taken to the Shelby County Morgue, but they wouldn't take him out of the ambulance. Everybody had to believe he died that night. Everybody.

PART FOUR
COLLISIONS OF LIGHT

CHAPTER TWENTY-SIX

15 October 2009

Carol Mason listened intently on her cell. "My preliminary came up empty, so far no *Gilgamesh*…anything. Are you sure our government is or was involved?"

Carol had assigned this little chore to one of her less used confidential sources in Washington DC.

"Yes. It was started in the private sector by the wealthy elite. The government got involved in '49, possibly the FBI," said Carol as she flipped through notes in her study. She'd left the *Tribune* at noon to work away from the eyes and ears. Instincts told her *Gilgamesh* was a keystone to the evolving mystery around the Bluff City Butcher.

"Why would the FBI have an interest in this *Gilgamesh* thing?"

"National defense," she replied.

"And what is a *Gilgamesh?*"

"It has something to do with genetic research." As a rule, Carol never gave sources more information than her sources gave her. Or else what's the use of the source?

"Ok, you believe *Gilgamesh* came in with the FBI in '49 and moved deeper into the government in '51, correct?"

"Correct," answered Carol while reading a new text message on her BlackBerry.

"Hmm, I wonder if the military got it. That would explain all the dead ends. No! The DOD is where I need to look."

"Great. Maybe you could look at the DOD and military. I can find you." Carol typed a reply to her text message concerning a registered letter that came for her at the *Tribune*. It was from Belmont Floral Services, her preferred D.C. source. They had a week head start. She sent a short text to her assistant, Jen: "COURIER TO ME AT *PEABODY* NOW."

"You know, if this *Gilgamesh* thing exists, it could be deeper in the system than I have ever been…for a good reason," said the source.

"When something is too important for Congress or sitting Presidents to know, I get real nervous. Who has the right to that kind of power?" asked Carol.

"You would be surprised what goes on around here."

"What do you mean?"

"I get to places in this crazy system. I look at changes in spending and utilities, use of office supplies, movement of personnel, death rates and other obscure data points. You would be amazed how many cell phones a new, top secret project goes through in the first week. Someone always leaves a door open somewhere and I walk into top secret projects all the time."

"That's why I come to you, Richard."

"I know. I am good, but this time you may have outdone yourself. I have been kicking around these halls for thirty years and have never heard the word *Gilgamesh*."

A loud knock at Carol's door drew her attention. "I appreciate your interest in helping me find the truth. Someone is at my door, gotta run. I'll find you in a week."

The young courier was standing in the hall with letter and pen. After he saw Carol, he added the smile for free.

She would never talk to Richard again. After they spoke he placed a call to an old friend, or so he thought, and asked the wrong questions. The last entry in his HR file was a 10/15/2009 request to use all accumulated vacation days; he never returned. Someone searched Richard's phone records that day. There was one call they couldn't trace. Carol always used a disposable phone when talking to her sources.

She had twenty minutes to look at the contents of the letter, fix herself up for Elliott and walk to the *Hard Rock Café* on Beale—dinner 6:30 p.m. Elliott had something important to talk about and now Carol had something for him. They shared everything now and were discovering they were a perfect fit in more ways than one.

She held it up to the lamp. The water stains on the flap were not aligned; the registered letter had been opened and resealed. There was nothing she could do about it except know someone was watching and they had the information. She tore open the letter and pulled out the single page.

A photographed table was centered—codified data in five columns and twenty lines. No reference was made to *Gilgamesh*. Whatever it was, it would require careful study: abbreviations for countries in column four were the only obvious thing that jumped out at her, but now she had to freshen up, grab her things and get out the door.

She left the *Peabody*, courtyard exit. The air was crisp. It was already dark but the walk to *Hard Rock Café* was short: South one block on Second, east two blocks on Beale. The Bluff City Butcher grabbed her at the turn. He took her the same night Jack Bellow disappeared…October 15, 2009. This time the phone call went to Albert Bell. The instructions were brief: *No police or Miss Mason is the next to swing from the Hernando. Tell the DOCTOR I have her. I'm sure he wants to keep her alive. Tell him to stay by his cell…ONE RING, ONE CHANCE.*

Carol had rounded the corner and walked into an iron arm; it closed quickly. The Bluff City Butcher pulled her in and wrapped her up like a boa constrictor; she was instantly buried beneath the black leather coat. Each move tightened the hold, taking more life from her lungs. The tip of the butcher knife was pressed against her side and the mouth of the Butcher was pressed against her ear. *"You can die or come quietly and maybe have a chance to live."*

She was petrified, unable to think, still struggling with the tightening hold. Soon she lost all of her air and ability to make a sound and fainted. The people on the busy sidewalk suspected nothing or cared less. They saw a man helping a lady into a van. It was over in twenty seconds.

The van turned off Jackson onto James north of the interstate. After the overpass it took a short right onto a seldom used dirt road to nowhere and the lights went off. It crawled into the woods and navigated the maze, taking a new path. After ten minutes of moaning shock absorbers, it found a shallow creek bed and moved to the end of the desolate ravine and into a ten-foot drainage pipe that was laid back in the 1950s when the Brent Estate was built a quarter mile to the south. The van was able to pass through the wall of dense foliage and climb into the pipe thirty feet where it parked behind a black *Dodge Sprinter*.

She woke up when the engine cut off, her head throbbing. She was unable to touch the dried, bloody wound because she was tied, gagged and hooded. The smell of sweat, vomit and urine was replaced with raw sewage the moment the door ground open. She felt the Bluff City Butcher's gaze; he snorted, spit, grabbed the rope around the knees, and spun her to an upright position. He put her in a canvas bag and threw her over his shoulder, her struggles futile. The door scraped closed and he ran into the hilly, wooded terrain. She passed out several times and lost all sense of time and direction.

She awakened and thought maybe they'd reached their destination. The Butcher stopped and leaned forward. She heard keys—*unlocking a door maybe*—then the rusted hinges, *maybe a shack where he lives.* He bent down deeper and they started to descend. Her heels were close to his head so she put all she had into kicking his face. After three solid blows, he dropped her to the ground. If she got the eyes she had a chance. The Butcher staggered, swiped his arm across his bloody nose and regained his footing. After a few bloody snorts he pulled the bag from the shrubs and hit her head again. This time she remained conscious. He dragged her down steps and across a dirt floor for an eternity, his bloody nose dripping all the way.

Time meant nothing. She was in dark silence. She had no doubt that the third time the Bluff City Butcher had her, it would be the last. She heard a girl crying somewhere. The muffled sobs changed into faint echoes and then there was nothing. *Was that real or imagined?*

He tossed Carol into a cage, still tied, the burlap bag over her head. Through the holes, she focused on a light bulb hanging from the ceiling. The musty room was big and mostly dark. Her cage was rusted, shoved into a corner next to dusty boxes and a mattress. She saw a stainless steel table on wheels pushed against an old washing machine and a big sink. A hose from the faucet hung to the floor with a shower head. On the wall were metal things: knives, cleavers, saws and hooks.

This had to be the Butcher's nest.

■ ■ ■

15 October 2009

Jack Bellow turned off Second Avenue onto South Court with a controlled fishtail, skidding to a perfect stop in his private space beside the old Exchange Building. It would always be the place where cotton and merchant fortunes were made and lost even though the *Life2 Corporation* had taken most of the twenty floors.

It was late and the unexpected cold snap had thinned the downtown sidewalks. He turned off the ignition, disconnected his cell charger and looked in the rearview mirror. Something moved in the park near the monument. He watched a moment longer, figuring it was probably nothing. He left his black *Lexus*, looking over his shoulder, and moved into the shadows of the building where he further checked the surroundings. With head down he went to the front entrance, realizing the weight of the moment. Everything must go his way.

The night watchman was behind the white marble reception counter on the south wall of the lobby. William Starnes had just finished his rounds and had sat down with a cup of coffee. He was about to peruse the security monitors embedded in the counter that were fed by a half dozen cameras in the building and selected downtown rooftops. He had been watching the black *Lexus* all the way from Washington Avenue, sliding around the corners and onto Second and then South Court, then the precision stop at the curb. He also saw the security alert flashing on his computer next to the monitors.

Starnes took a slow sip of his steaming coffee and entered his password with one finger; he was still not used to looking through the cheap reading glasses on the tip of his nose. He watched Mr. Bellow slip out of his car like some cat burglar and slink into the shadows of the building. *Now what could Mr. Bellow be up to tonight?* He took another sip and checked his computer; access to the urgent security alert posted at 8:00 p.m. was granted.

Over his six years at the Exchange he'd received three; one announcing the sale of the building and everyone's termination, the next from Jack Bellow hiring everyone. The third was bad: instructions to lock all ground entrances and secure the building. Jack's parents had been killed in a house fire in Dallas—arson. A message had been left for Jack at the fire scene; he would be next.

Jack had been in the office with no knowledge of a fire or the deaths of his stepparents. When they told him, they had to take him out on a stretcher. Jack was gone three months. He was never the same.

With his hand on his holstered Smith & Wesson, Starnes opened the coded file as Mr. Bellow approached the front doors. He read: *POST DATE 10/15/2009, TIME 20:00. CODE: LEVEL 3. EXTREME CAUTION, FORCE REQUIRED, DETAIN FOR MPD • JACK BELLOW PRESIDENT/CEO TERMINATION EFFECTIVE 10/16/2009, TIME 1700; BELLOW ACCESS TO LIFE2 PROPERTIES DENIED. ALL PRIOR RIGHTS AND PRIVILEGES REVOKED • POSES SIGNIFICANT RISK OF TAMPERING, THEFT AND/OR DESTRUCTION OF LIFE2 PROPERTY • BELLOW MAY BE ARMED AND DANGEROUS • PROCEED WITH EXTREME CAUTION.*

As Jack entered the lobby Officer Starnes got up from his chair, three-hundred-pounds of muscle on a six-five frame with a gentle face; fights never came his way on purpose. *Mr. Kohl said there would be days like this. When I retired from the Memphis police he said he needed someone like me to secretly watch out for Mr. Bellow. He always got me the jobs, keeping me close, and when he got me the security job in the Exchange Building I was the happiest because I could carry my gun, just in case. I've known Mr. Bellow for twenty years. But now, things are getting a little bit confusing. What did Mr. Bellow do that made these people say all the bad stuff about him?*

Jack darted to the private elevator. "Hello, Willie. How are you doing on this cold October night?"

"Good evening, Mr. Bellow. It's so hot in here I'm staying 'bout as warm as a frog on a lily pad in the sun." William started to move down and out of his marble fortress.

"Well, I am glad you're staying warm."

As Willie kept parallel with Jack, the counter in between, there was an uncomfortable silence. He cleared his throat. "Mr. Bellow, I'm surprised to see you tonight. Is everything all right? Can I help you?"

Jack recalled how he'd met Willie twenty years before. They seemed to run into each other all the time. When he bought the Exchange Building and saw that Willie was the new night watchman he started to put things together. For some reason Rudolph Kohl wanted Jack protected 24/7. He had met Rudy twenty years ago, a wealthy investor who took an interest in him when he enrolled at Harvard. He assumed because Kohl invested in his businesses he was protecting his assets. But lately it started looking like something more than that.

As they moved down the counter together, Jack saw the troubled look on Willie's face. *The damn internal Security Alert System. I bet the board sent an alert already. I bet those sons-a-bitches are blocking my access to the executive offices. But I have no other options. I'm going up one way or another.*

"No, I'm good, Willie." He stepped onto the elevator and hit the three. He was startled to see Willie standing a few feet from the open door with his large presence blocking most of the light and his right hand resting on the top of his holstered gun. They looked at each other in silence for three very long seconds and the elevator doors began to close. Officer Starnes reached out and stopped them with two fingers. Jack gripped the gun in his pocket. *I don't know if I can shoot you, Willie. Please don't test me.*

"Mr. Bellow, I need you to be extra careful tonight. It is just your luck I ran into you because, with all the recent downtown break-ins, I have been spending my time walking outside. I might be hard to find." Willie smiled and Jack nodded. They were on the same page. Willie took his big fingers off the doors. They closed. Jack swallowed and slid his employee card through the scanner; if it had been deactivated he would still be stopped, held on the elevator between floors until the Memphis police arrived. But it was the only way to get to the secured executive level.

As the elevator inched upward Jack thought about the series of events that got him into his mess. *My termination was a surprise. When Enrique died the preferred shareholders got control of the board and my elimination was imminent. I never even considered the possibility of my friend and partner dying in an automobile accident; he survived pancreatic cancer. He was the genius geneticist on his way to mastering immortality. And those greedy, low-life bastards that terminated me, their disrespect was expected but their words were even more telling. I will never forget them... "It was nothing personal. Thanks for getting us this far. EVERYONE IS REPLACEABLE...EVEN YOU, BELLOW."*

The time had arrived to implement the secret backup plan he and Medino laid out in the beginning. The *Life2* technology would not be lost to imbeciles.

Jack had everything in order. The single greatest breakthrough of all time was going with him. It would be lost to the arrogant and the blind. The technology Jack would leave behind would fail in year-four of the clinical studies; robust cartilage regeneration would stop.

Dr. Medino observed the phenomenon in 2005, and he immediately tracked down the problem and made the minor modification to his life-extending, biogenic formulation. I could not believe his reaction when he projected one failure event. He thought he was incredibly stupid to make such a mistake— instead of 304 peptide he used 403—simple human error. But the corrective action required a Medino or everything would be lost.

Prior to the first takeover attempt of the Board, Jack quietly terminated the *BelMed* contract with *Life2;* a small clause buried in the three-hundred-page document went unnoticed by the sharks. After tonight, Jack would have everything that mattered.

It was nothing personal!

■ ■ ■

The elevator stopped. Jack pulled the hammer back on the gun in his pocket. He had never shot a man, but now he had a reason. When the doors opened no one was there. He was on the third floor. He had got past the security system.

Willie was sipping coffee at his monitors. He watched Jack get off on three. Willie had found the operator's manual just in time to shut down the security system on elevator number one. Nobody would be messing with Jack Bellow tonight.

Jack entered the boardroom and sat down in his old leather chair at the end of the long conference table as he had done hundreds of times before, but this time it was late and he was banned from his company. He sat in the dark, looking out the window. Like a moth, he was attracted to the only street light; Second Avenue was a ghost town. A panhandler dragged a piece of cardboard through the light and into the bushes next to the building, probably bedding down for the night. Jack's mind did it again; *objects enclosed in a package may require some degree of protection from shock, vibration, compression, temperature, water vapor, dust, dirt, chemicals, biologics and more. Because permeation is a critical factor in the ultimate composition and design of a wide variety of packaging materials, including corrugated cardboards, each may contain...*

Stop now, he told himself with a smile. Jack had learned a long time ago how to control his eidetic memory. Maybe if he had known his biological parents he would have learned a few more secrets on how to manage his other gifts, the ones he never talked about to anybody.

Like Medino, Jack would probably miss out on the life-extension biotechnology they possessed. As expected, things getting dangerous. He pulled a pint of *Jack Daniels* from his coat, downed a third and set the bottle on the polished cherry table. With his eyes on the lighted area on Second Avenue, he savored the warmth of the Kentucky bourbon as it surged through his body, and he accepted the reality that

Gilgamesh was closing in along with other covert, private interest groups and foreign governments that would stop at nothing. Now, with Medino dead and the *Life2* corporate takeover public in twenty-four hours, each entity with a vested interest in the biogenic technology would make their move. Although Jack knew he had intellectual gifts that allowed him an unusually clear view of the future, he had no idea he was one of five people possessing the life-extending genetic anomaly. If he had known, maybe he would have made different decisions at the end.

Jack picked up the bottle, downed another third and waited for the next warm surge. His eyes adjusted as he looked around the boardroom and relived some of his most critical decisions that made the *Life2 Corporation* possible. He was immersed in the smells of the hundred-year-old building, his home for five years. In a strange way the familiar mix of mildew, old dust and new *Lemon Pledge* gave him added strength and resolve to protect Enrique Medino's breakthrough at all costs. He would make sure it got into the right hands: the only person alive he was sure would do the right thing.

The last of the bourbon flowed smoothly down his throat. Today he was shattered into a million pieces and each piece was shattered a million times more. He had nothing to hold onto in this world. He was on empty. His last connection to a civilized and productive existence had been severed by people he thought he could trust. They changed the rules and took advantage. They crushed what they could never understand: creation. The greedy, high-net-worth investors had one goal—steal his company. They took the last thing in the world that mattered to him…and they destroyed the possibilities. They would surely fail.

He used his cell phone to light the way into his office. A large oak desk was buried under a dozen distinct piles of documents. The oak credenza had a keyboard, three flat screen monitors and more piles. Two taupe sofas sat across from each other. Four stuffed oxblood leather chairs completed the four-sided sitting area, with brass lamps hanging from the ceiling at the corners and a smoked glass coffee table in the center. The wall with double doors into the main hall had built-in bookshelves to the ceiling, loaded to capacity. Jack had read each book at least twice. On the side walls were large, colorful paintings of Midsouth landscapes and Arkansas views of the Memphis skyline.

Jack turned on one lamp and went to one of the small groupings of pictures that hung on each side of the window above his credenza. Each picture had a story, a special time or person or place in Jack's mysterious life. He went to the least of them, a small black and white photograph mounted in a big glass frame, the back of a woman looking into the Grand Canyon. It was his only picture of his mother, whom he'd never met but often thought about. He had no knowledge of his biological father. There was a picture of his stepfather and stepmother, too. The picture of his mom was the only one mounted on hinges; it covered a small wall safe known only to Jack.

He worked the combination, opened the small safe and removed a palm-sized leather-covered box with $GILGAMESH$ embossed on the front. Inside was a specialized, encrypted, external storage device and booklet—alphanumeric-coded guidance document with a thousand characters on each of the twenty-five pages. The booklet cover had the only printed message: *"Tampering with device activates self destruction. Access requirements are multifactorial with alphanumeric, deca-code authentication. This device is lined with volatile plastic explosives and will kill the unauthorized attempt to open files."*

He'd set up the new administrator access sequence the day after Enrique Medino was killed. The FBI was getting close in June of 2004. In 2008, Jack was almost certain Dexter Voss had killed Medino and had stolen Medino's hard drive from the Nashville farm. The embedded beacon tracked the movement. Jack assessed the risk and remotely gave the self-destruct command when he knew Voss and his team were comfortable. The destruction of the hard drive would lead to the elimination of Voss by the FBI or a task force from *Gilgamesh*. His reports on how Voss died suggested *Gilgamesh* engaged the Bluff City Butcher, although he could be wrong.

Jack's only remaining task was to get the Medino device and codes into the right hands. He slipped the case into his pocket and went to the elevator; everything needed for the global production and dispensing of the *Life2* Medino Life-Extension Compounds were in his pocket and time was running out. Before the elevator doors closed his cell phone rang.

"Mister Bellow, the Memphis police are surrounding the building. I don't think I can help you out of this mess…too many of them."

Jack could hear a voice in the background demanding Starnes put down his phone.

"Willie, meet me at the 'hole' in five." Jack disconnected.

"Ok, Mama, I'll pick up bread and a dozen eggs when I get off." Willie closed his phone and stood up. He was a foot taller than the policeman with the big mouth. "Would you like to take my mama some bread and eggs?"

The officer backed away and joined the others on the elevators.

"Uh huh…I didn't think you wanted anything to do with my mama."

When the lobby emptied, Willie stepped inside the coat closet. The door to the basement was in the back, behind buckets and mops. He went down the narrow staircase built a hundred years ago and known by only a few. He was going to join Jack, who was already standing next to the old laundry chute from the third floor. He was covered in dust and cobwebs but smiling. Willie saw that he had the cover off the access to the sewer pipe under the building. If he remembered right, it came out somewhere near Poplar and Main…an alley, but he could be mistaken.

Jack was the first to speak. "Willie, I got a little favor to ask."

CHAPTER TWENTY-SEVEN

"A good plan violently executed right now is
far better than a perfect plan executed next week."
George S. Patton

16 October 2009

Killing time, Elliott memorized everything in Carol's suite. He had managed no appetite or sleep over the last twenty-four hours. His cell could ring at any time. He had to be ready. It was almost midnight. The Bluff City Butcher would save everything for the seventeenth.

His rental car was parked on Third with a full tank. He had a hunch the Butcher would give him a destination north of the city. If he was right he could cut at least five minutes and maybe catch the Butcher off guard. It was not much but the BCB always did his homework and Elliott had to go for every unexpected advantage possible. He was going into battle with an intelligent, psychopathic killer that made very few mistakes and had already demonstrated he was unstoppable.

On the other side of town, Marty Pilsner and Gerald Bonn found a few drops of blood on the cellar steps at the back of the sheriff's north substation. G.E. Taft would leave it to them to investigate and report developments. He was on his own secret mission and would not be deterred; *probably a bum living in their damn cellar anyway.*

Meanwhile back at Carol's, Elliott's singular focus was to keep his lifeline to Carol open, his cell phone. That's why he let all calls roll into voicemail. He would not risk tying up his phone checking on the mail, not with Carol in the grips of a monster. The Butcher was clear, *one ring or you lose Carol.* He held all the cards.

If Elliott had answered just one of the sheriff's three calls around midnight or checked just one voicemail message, things could have ended differently…on Mud Island.

Elliott willed each minute off the antique mantle clock. She even had a picture of them holding each other and smiling; it was an informal gathering at the Bell mansion. She was beautiful that night. Elliott couldn't remember ever smiling as much. He had never been happier in his life. And she helped him control his demons. Now, it was up to him alone.

■ ■ ■

Only two people knew there was a DNA match to the Bluff City Butcher. The tuft of hair found on the railing of the Hernando de Soto Bridge, probably snagged when the Butcher lowered Doyle over the side, had adequate tissue on the strands for DNA testing. Later, the blood in Tony's attic was another confirmation that the DNA profile belonged to the BCB. On October 12th, Elliott gave the lab a third hair sample; he said it was taken from Tony's condo. He lied.

They met privately on October 11th. Elliott explained to Jack Bellow the messy complications when two decapitated men were found at one's dining room table, regardless of innocence, lack of knowledge or absence from the country. Elliott shared the eyewitness account from a reliable source that claimed Jack was the Bluff City Butcher. After laughing at the absurdity of it all, Jack explained his reasons for resistance. DNA testing a president/CEO of a successful private enterprise that is preparing to go public would damage company valuation and harm investor interests. Guilty or not, the damage would be enormous; markets were driven more by emotions.

After dinner they agreed a confidential DNA test could work. Jack's DNA would be labeled as an "unknown" sample. Elliott would be the only one with the results and he would use his reputation to eliminate Jack Bellow from the list of suspects.

At 2:00 p.m. on October 15, 2009, Elliott called Jack. The test had been completed. Jack Bellow's DNA was a 99.9997 percent match to the DNA known to belong to the Bluff City Butcher.

"Jack, I think I can explain this; I know you are not the Bluff City Butcher."

"There must be some mistake, a mix-up of specimens or something. There is absolutely no way. This could destroy me and my company."

"I won't let that happen. It is important that we talk. The only explanation is that you are his twin brother."

"Twin…brother?"

"Jack, were you adopted?"

"Yes."

"We need to get together right away. I have a lot to tell you and some questions."

"I am going into meetings with board members now. They are waiting. Then we have a series of critical investor meetings that cannot be put off. My absence would be problematic. I can meet with you tomorrow, my place," said Jack.

"I will be there at 9:00 a.m. and we will get this resolved."

"Ok, Elliott. That's good. See you then."

■ ■ ■

Later the night of the 15th they said Jack Bellow was seen at *Life2* after hours. But the night watchman said they were mistaken.

Elliott had too much time on his hands the next night waiting for the Bluff City Butcher's call. *Why would Jack avoid me?* He thought. *Is it possible that somehow Jack is the Butcher, after all? He certainly is big enough and strong enough, but he did not display the psychopathic or typical aberrant behavior disorders when we had dinner. He is clearly a very intelligent man. But could he have a DUAL PERSONALITY condition so bizarre and unique that it is unknown to modern medicine? Was Carol right? Did she see through him all along?*

Elliott thought it was starting to get suspicious. *You were only a few blocks from Carol when she was abducted the other evening, the time you said you were unavailable to meet. DNA doesn't lie—Jack Bellow could be Adam Duncan. And your extensive travel could be a cover for killing.*

Elliott had a lot of time to run scenarios. The important elements in the mystery were lining up: Betty Duncan and Albert Bell...the affair and unknown births, Adam Duncan and the Bluff City Butcher...Alberto Bella and *Gilgamesh* and the FBI, Jack Bellow and Dr. Medino's biotechnology...and somehow Elliott and Carol were a part of the mystery. *Could the stakes in my battle with the Bluff City Butcher be even greater than I ever imagined? Is the common thread life extension?*

■ ■ ■

At 2:45 a.m., October 17, 2009, Elliott got the call he was waiting for. He answered in the middle of the first ring. "YES?"

"I got two this time. Get here at 3:15 and both live. Come early and I kill one. Come late and I kill two."

"Where?"

"Where we met a year ago."

Mud Island...the trail behind the NO BOAT LAUNCH sign...the clearing on the bank...how could I forget?

"I'm watching. You decide." The Butcher disconnected as Elliott stepped off the elevator and hurried out of the *Peabody* lobby to his car on Third. Mud Island was on his list of potential sites, but at the bottom.

That was why the Butcher chose it. Elliott could get there in minutes and possibly get that one unexpected advantage he would need to have a chance against the unstoppable.

He had a plan. He had been in tough positions with serial killers before, but this one would be different. This one was the most intelligent killing machine he had ever encountered.

And he had the girl he loved.

Elliott had to save Carol first. He could not allow anything to get in the way of accomplishing that primary objective. Then, and only then, he would try to take the BCB alive or dead. Sacrificing his own life may be the only way he could take the Butcher down.

As he accelerated up Third his command over the demons in his head began to falter, as if they knew he would not survive the confrontation with another one like them. He struggled to suppress their mounting interference and buried the images that had crippled him for so long. Without Carol, he was vulnerable. She was the light in his dark world. But now he was forced to work alone…again.

■ ■ ■

Sheriff Taft went into the city with his .44 magnum, double-action revolver stuffed in his pants beneath his sport coat. Earlier, Pilsner was passing by his office door and overheard G.E. talking to Albert Bell on the telephone. Ten minutes later G.E. was giving last-minute instructions and leaving for the weekend.

Over the years, Pilsner often went to the range with Sheriff Taft, most of that time while he was a deputy. That's how he knew G.E. was taking his big gun out. The 7.5 inch barrel on the *Model 629 Smith & Wesson* was a hard thing to hide on a short, round body; it would always poke out somewhere. Knowing he was packing didn't matter. Pilsner would never question the sheriff, especially on Friday, October 16, 2009. He had a good idea what G.E. was up to.

He was on edge all week. Everyone on the Butcher's list was dead or missing, leaving Elliott and Albert. It liked to kill on October 17th every year. In seven hours, its glorious day would arrive again.

They spoke at 5:20 p.m. Albert said the Bluff City Butcher called him directly; it had Mason and instructed Sumner to wait for a call, no police or she would be the next to swing from the Hernando Bridge. Jack Bellow's disappearance and Mason's abduction could only pull Sumner and Bell into the mix. G.E. told Albert there was nothing either of them could do but wait. When he hung up he got Pilsner. His orders were, *"Anything on the Butcher, call me. Otherwise, I am unavailable."* Then he closed his office door.

Alone, G.E. inspected each .44 magnum hollow point before sliding them into the six chambers of the largest American handgun ever made. He rubbed the gun down with a soft rag and a little linseed oil. Before he stuck her in his pants he leveled her on his lucky raccoon head across the room and said his customary prayer. *"Lord, I pray you give me the strength and the time to get off one clean shot. If you give me two, I will know you're standing next to me. If you give me three, I will know you're just showing off…amen. And tell Sophia I love her."*

G.E. fully expected to join his beautiful Sophia. As he pulled away from the substation he looked back and saw Deputy Pilsner in the window. They made eye contact and nodded. G.E. was leaving things in good hands.

There was nothing else to do on that Friday night, so Pilsner hung around the office after G.E. left. He wanted to catch up on paperwork and move some of the piles off his desk. That's when he came across the missing persons reports stuck in the wrong stack. Lost filings were a big deal. This time it couldn't be bigger; the two people missing were last seen on the grounds where Pilsner was sitting.

One disappeared in February and the other in April. Winston Jones was a day laborer. He worked a few times for *GreenWay*, the contracted groundskeepers for the county. Winston never picked up his paycheck. After two weeks, *GreenWay* called the emergency contact on his employment application and spoke to a cousin. The last time they saw Winston was his first day on the Shelby County Sheriff's North Substation job.

Pilsner could think of a lot of reasons why Jones disappeared; each was legal and a matter of choice. Most day-laborers were beset by problems: alcohol, drugs, misdemeanors, felonies. Some were perpetual drifters or bums looking for an easy dollar; when one came along they were gone. However, it was highly unusual for a day-laborer to leave any paycheck behind, although the case didn't merit a lot of investigational time.

The second missing person case made the Winston Jones case relevant. Hank Breslin also worked for *GreenWay*, but as a fulltime employee with a three-year work history. When Breslin didn't show up for his carpool, the *GreenWay* people on the job stopped and looked for him. They searched the entire north substation grounds and buildings, to no avail. They found Breslin's rake and one of his work gloves in a ravine behind the main building, the remodeled Brent mansion.

There were about ten minutes of daylight left, so Pilsner went for a walk on the grounds. He lit a cigarette and started for the back of the mansion, curious to see for himself where Breslin's glove and rake were located. The walk was longer than he anticipated; he had spent all his time inside and never fully comprehended the enormous size of the substation—"Old Man" Brent's mansion.

He was struck by the abrupt change in the grounds. They went from manicured landscape in the front and sides to neglected, wild growth in the back. Abnormally large, deformed bushes and dense trees were jammed together from the back edges of the mansion to the dark woods fifty yards away. The back of the mansion had no windows or doors. The ground sloped creating a small ravine along the back with thick brush and sticker bushes that would discourage anyone from entering. The back wall of the mansion was packed with giant juniper bushes and wild shrubs.

Pilsner was losing light so he hurried down the slope to the base of the ravine for a look at the area where Breslin's things were found. The ravine was the coldest, wettest, darkest and creepiest place on the property, a perfect home for an assortment of miserable critters: snakes, rats, big spiders and all the things Pilsner would shoot if they got close.

As he walked along the back of the mansion, just by chance he noticed some cellar doors deep in the junipers. They had probably been forgotten long ago. Another minute of lost light, and Pilsner would have missed them. He was standing where Breslin's rake and glove were found.

How did they get all the way down here? And what happened to his other glove?

Pilsner lit a cigarette and turned back to the cellar doors. Before his match went out, he saw the tip of a juniper branch above the doors, it was broken—an odd place for a damaged branch. *What could break a little, soft tip of a juniper branch? It was naturally protected and out of the way.*

He had one match left. His curiosity and relentless attention to details would not let him leave without looking closer. He lit his last match and leaned into the junipers. The broken tip of the juniper was pinched between the cellar doors above an old rusted padlock. He lifted the lock and held the match close enough to see fresh cuts on the oxidized metal around the keyhole. *This lock was opened recently.* As the flame moved to his fingers, he ran the flickering light down the center of the doors to a cement footing.

Before the match went out, he had seen enough.

■ ■ ■

"Hello, Mr. Anderson, this is Deputy Marty Pilsner with the Shelby County Sheriff's Office, North Substation."

"Great. Did you find Hank Breslin and Winston Jones?"

"No. I am sorry to say we have more work to do."

"I am very worried about Hank. He wouldn't just run off. I have known him for several years."

"Do you remember the time of day they disappeared?" asked Pilsner.

"Yes, Sir. Hank disappeared an hour after sunup. I remember because it was the day that Bluff City Butcher hung the radio guy over the river."

"That's helpful. What about Winston Jones?"

"Well, it was after dark. He left the group to go take a piss."

"Where did he go?" asked Pilsner.

"Back of the mansion; there are no windows and a lot of bushes."

"Did anyone go look for him?"

"No. His ride assumed he left with someone else."

"Do you store equipment or supplies in the cellar? Do you or your people use the cellar doors in the back of the mansion?"

"No, we keep everything on the *GreenWay* trailers. My people have strict orders to stay out of all structures."

"How can you be sure they follow those orders?"

"Violation is cause for immediate termination without pay. They all sign off on the rules day one. In all the years, I have never released anyone for going into a building."

"Maybe they see a cellar differently." Pilsner lit a cigarette.

Anderson was having a little laugh. "Deputy, I am sorry. I don't mean to be rude, but I can guarantee you nobody goes anywhere near those cellar doors in the back of that mansion."

"Why's that?"

"One night we were finishing some work on the north side of the mansion, right after sundown. One of our day-laborers came running from the back with his eyes as big as saucers. He was talking Spanish a hundred miles an hour. The translator said the guy saw a monster!"

"What happened?" asked Pilsner.

"He said a giant in a black cape floated out of the cellar, put a lock on the doors and ran into the woods as fast as a horse at full gallop. Ever since that night they all believe the ghost of 'Old Man Brent' lives in that cellar!"

"That is funny. Does the man still work for you?" asked Pilsner.

"No, he's dead," said Anderson.

"He is dead? How?"

"A few days after his vision, he was in a bar fight and got killed."

"Was he shot in a bar?" asked Pilsner.

"No. He was knifed, throat cut ear to ear. They said he bled to death."

"Did they catch the guy that did it?" asked Pilsner.

"They got the guy he was arguing with in the bar, but there were no witnesses to the fight that happened in the alley behind the bar. They found him the next morning."

"Ok. So at least they got the guy."

"I don't think so," said Anderson.

"Why?"

"Well, the work crew told me they put his brother in jail and don't even know it. He's an illegal alien using a fake name and social. The guy would never kill his own brother; they only worked as a team. One time I picked one to work and the other said, *"Dos por favor...de nada."*

"I see, Mr. Anderson. Thank you for your time. Check back with me in a week for an update. I have got to go. Goodbye."

Pilsner hung up and hit speed dial. "Gerald, come to the north substation, NOW. Bring your flashlight and your gun."

"Yes, Sir; will be there in three minutes, Sir."

"No sirens, no lights and no attention, son; right now it is just you and me. Park in front and meet me on the north side of the mansion. Gonna teach you lock picking."

After he hung up the phone Pilsner took out his gun, opened the roller and inserted six, thirty-eight hollow points. As a rule he never kept a loaded gun. At the cellar doors, just before his last match went out, he had seen three fresh drops of blood on the cement footing. Whatever was in the cellar was bad. He hoped the lock meant the bastard was out for the night.

CHAPTER TWENTY-EIGHT

The dream…He turns and sees the monster that escapes him for a decade,
the beast that kills a hundred, the pure evil known only by a few alive.
He sees his face: the gloom in obscurity and the moon in glass,
black eyes under a slanted brow. The desolation shows one feeling;
the corners of its lips are up because the knife is moving into Elliott's side…
a twisted blade, a piercing thrust and warm, wet legs…
the spinning, the explosion and incessant ringing above muffled sounds of life,
and then quiet. And when the peace comes none of it matters anymore.

17 October 2009

He made all the lights on Third; Island Drive was empty. He turned off his lights at a hundred yards, engine at fifty, and coasted. When the car stopped he popped the trunk, climbed out the window and skirted moonlight, running in the darkest shadows along the edge of the crumbling, weed-infested parking lot. Elliott remembered everything perfectly; 440 days ago he had met the Bluff City Butcher on Mud Island. Why his nemesis chose to return was just one more mystery.

Elliott passed the NO BOAT LAUNCH sign, eased into the brush and navigated the narrow trail, reaching the end seven minutes after the call. His early arrival should give him some advantage. He waited low and listened. Then he leaned inches and looked across the moonlit clearing. *No…please don't be….*

She was on her back, the same mound of sand at the river's edge where Sabina Weatherford had lain in a fetal position over a year ago. Now, long blond hair was draped over her face and shoulders and her white cotton dress fanned, capturing scant moonlight illuminating her lifeless corpse in the otherwise dismal setting. Her hands were gripping the handle of a butcher knife that protruded from her chest. Carol Mason was dead!

He gasped for air and stood up—nothing mattered anymore. He crossed the clearing, eyes fixed on his last reason to live, and he dropped to his knees, resting his head on her cold, rigid body. She was dead well before the phone call.

My demons are wasting no time. They are kicking down the doors in my head. I don't care anymore. Carol is gone and I have no more desire to fight for life. The swelling flood of pain and terror would soon overtake him, triggering the autonomic protective responses, the only fatal flaw in Elliott's unique system of enormous mental and physical gifts. He would soon experience the unsurvivable cardiac event predicted by Dr. Gilmore.

Killing Carol was illogical. The Butcher needed to hold onto something to control Elliott, to insure willing participation in the ultimate battle. After her abduction, Elliott's plan changed. He would offer his life for hers. The Butcher would take the deal to reduce the variables and grab another advantage. Only after Carol was safe would Elliott toss his gun into the river and face the Butcher's knife.

Why would you give away your leverage? Elliott was no longer a willing participant. He would die on his own. For the last time, he smelled her perfume and touched the lace on the dress that he had helped her pick out. In the darkness he broke her hands from the handle of the knife imbedded in her chest and then held them one last time—a quiet goodbye. *The pain is unbearable. The demons are almost in...I am ready to die now. But...Carol never wore rings!*

Did he make a rookie mistake? Was he so overcome with the big picture that he allowed his misery to fill in the rest? There was a ring on her finger, but everything else about the girl lying in front of him was Carol. He had not seen her face; it was hidden beneath her long blond hair.

I could not bear to look before, but I must now. One finger moved her hair from her face. It was her chin. It was her lips. But…it was not her cheeks, or her nose or her eyes. The dead girl was a double. She was not Carol Mason.

Stunned, Elliott struggled to hide his emotions. He had to look as if he was still fooled. He needed time to recover.

I feel your eyes. What is your purpose, so elaborate? You went to great lengths to find someone with Carol's physical attributes; to kill her, dress her in Carol's clothes and this presentation—I arrive early as you surely predicted and see only what you know I will see; my pain fills the gaps. I abandon my training, my plan, my caution and my purpose. You saw my love for Carol as a flaw and you used it to disarm me, to ensure your final kill when you wanted it. But now…you see I moved her hair! I have given away any advantage I may have had before.

When he looked up, it was too late. The trap had been successful; the large, silent shadow was leaning over him and the tip of the knife moving into his ribs for the last time. For the genius, psychopathic serial killer, it was vital that number nine die after number eight and before number ten. The Bluff City Butcher was ready to take Elliott Sumner's life and was not going to risk an error in the final hours. Now he could enjoy the kill he had been saving for years.

He allowed Elliott to look into his face one last time, the gloom in obscurity and a moon in glassy, black eyes beneath a slanted brow. The empty desolation revealed one emotion. The corners of the Butcher's lips were slightly up. At last he was ready to eliminate Elliott Sumner, the only man that ever challenged him.

Elliott had one more move—the plan. The tip of the Butcher's knife broke his skin and blood began to run down his side. Elliott yelled in the monster's face, "I NEED YOU NOW, WILCOX!"

He would think it impossible, a feeble attempt by a desperate man. The first reaction was what Elliott had hoped for: momentary distraction. The pressure on the knife eased, focus moved and the window of opportunity opened. At last, Elliott owned a sliver of time. When Tony landed on the Butcher's back, Elliott had no resistance turning the knife and plunging it deep into the Butcher's belly. The blade sank up to the handle and the blood instantly gushed from the wound and flowed down their legs.

In seconds, the Butcher relived the Wilcox death; they tried to save him but it was impossible. The Butcher had watched from the attic as they took Wilcox out in a black bag and laid him next to the other dead cop. He watched the ambulance crawl away, no sirens and no flashing lights. He watched the funeral procession down Second Avenue and the burial at Elmwood Cemetery.

Tony Wilcox is dead, thought the Butcher. *But who is on my back, pulling my hair and pounding my head? And what is that sharp pain in my stomach?*

■ ■ ■

At the condo in September everyone had to believe Tony had died; it was part of the plan. Heads were low when the ambulance pulled away, but inside a paramedic was hanging another unit of O-positive blood. Tony had lost more than he had in his body. Elliot made sure they transfused faster than it was coming out until he could stop all the bleeders.

Typically, the ambulance would make their delivery to the county morgue and go back into service. But these hand-picked paramedics took orders only from Elliott Sumner. After the morgue they had another stop to make. Twenty minutes later they were waved onto the Millington

Naval Base and escorted to a section known to few. They pulled up to a secret military medical facility.

Back at the county morgue, Medical Examiner Bates unzipped Tony's body bag and tossed the blood soaked towels and pillows into the incinerator. He opened a secret file and removed a completed set of autopsy documents with Tony Wilcox's name across the top. Bates initialed and dated each page and placed the official documents into the work-transfer folders to enter the forensic system. He then propped his feet and imagined the wounds as he dictated his complete autopsy of Tony's corpse. He borrowed tissue and body fluid samples from the surplus of the day—that wouldn't be missed—and prepared a Wilcox specimen rack for toxicology; anything less would raise suspicion.

Dr. Bates released the bodies before sunrise. Tony Wilcox was in a sealed cremation box, in accordance with last wishes. The appropriate documents with the verification/certification signature of the acting Shelby County Medical Examiner were attached according to protocol. The box would remain sealed and cremation would take place before the next sunset.

At the Millington base they checked Tony in under an assumed name. The base commander had the paperwork ready when they pulled up; Tony, alias John Trent, was a retired Navy man and the unfortunate victim of a one-car accident. He was sewn up at an ill equipped hospital in Mississippi. Only the base commander knew his true identity; he owed Elliott a favor and believed the urban legend.

They were hoping for six months but got only six weeks. The Bluff City Butcher made his move on Elliott by taking Carol Mason. Tony was cleared to participate, but his healing injuries would now limit the extent. He would not stay at home.

When Elliott learned Carol had been taken, Tony checked into the *Peabody Hotel* in disguise and with a pager. The moment the Butcher called to give

Elliott instructions, Tony's pager went off and he got into Elliott's trunk. Tony would stay there ten minutes after Elliott parked the car and departed. Tony's mission was to track down Elliott's position without detection.

Elliott needed to be on his own a few seconds at precisely the right time. They were sure the Butcher would savor the final moments. Elliott would call out to Tony Wilcox, who would stand up in some threatening manner—*the man I had killed, number eight, is back…is alive. What does that mean?*

But Tony had to ride the bull, injuries or not. He was determined to give Elliott all the time he needed, even if it killed him. The Bluff City Butcher's attention would be on him, for sure!

The Butcher peeled Wilcox off his back with one hand and threw him across the clearing and then threw Sumner at Wilcox. He looked down at his wound. By the time they had found their footing, the Butcher was pulling the knife from his gut and leveling his eyes on the two who would die that night. He was smiling as the blood flowing from his belly slowed to a trickle.

What is he thinking? He is seriously injured and Tony has a gun pointed at him, thought Elliott. *If he releases Carol, he gets me.*

The weight of the Butcher shifted to his back foot; knees were slightly flexed and shoulders dipped. He was ready to pounce.

"Wait," was all Elliott could get out. *The Bluff City Butcher could cover the seven feet to me before Tony could pull the trigger. He would use me as a shield and a second later Tony would be standing, holding his gun, and his head would be falling to the ground.*

"Carol…where is my Carol?" Elliott took another step toward the Butcher. "Let Carol go. Then you can have me."

But this was just another kill. Two men were no match even when the beast had a serious gut wound and a gun was pointing at him. Elliott's calculations were all wrong. The Butcher had no priorities and no sense of negotiation. Killing Elliott was no more important than killing a stranger. The BCB lured him to Mud Island with one objective…kill number nine…Elliott Sumner and anyone else in the way. The Butcher raised his knife in a ferocious blur of motion and bolted forward like a wild animal. There was nothing Elliott or Tony could do.

The explosion came out of nowhere. The Butcher stopped in flight and dropped to the dirt. They stood confused. The world slowed and all sound was muffled. They looked at each other and then to the brush behind them. The moonlight captured the cloud of smoke leaving the long barrel of Sheriff Taft's massive gun.

The Butcher jumped to his feet with a single burst of wild energy bringing him within reach of Elliott. The second blast knocked the Bluff City Butcher back to the river's edge where he stood, a dark shadow on the gray water of the Mississippi. His head was down, arms hanging and knife pointing to the ground.

Maybe the Butcher is confused. Maybe he has never felt pain before. Or is he considering his options? If he was dying Elliott had to take a chance or he may never find Carol. He was desperate and moved toward the Butcher to make a deal.

The third explosion was loudest and longest; the echo ran up and down the river forever. The Butcher stopped and then fell backwards into the dark water, where he was held on the surface, floating in stillness and peace, and was swallowed by the darker water sliding by Mud Island.

G.E. Taft walked into the clearing holding his gun in two hands, pointing to the sky as if in prayer. Before Elliott could speak he put his hand on his shoulder. "Son, we have Carol. She is alive, pissed-off and demanding to see you."

Elliott was speechless.

Taft continued, "And we have Michael Bell too, alive…unbelievable." He took a close look at Wilcox and his mouth dropped. "And what in the SAM HILL are you doing here? Are you one of them angels I've been hearing about, son?"

"No, Sir, but I do believe you are." Tony was holding his stomach. The bandages showed some blood seepage. He knew he risked more physical damage, but there was no way he was not taking a ride on the back of the meanest serial killer in the whole damn world.

Elliott aimed his penlight on Tony's abdomen and looked under the bandages. "You will live, partner. Just popped some stitches."

"Thanks, Doc."

They wanted to take the Bluff City Butcher back alive, but G.E. told them what they needed to hear. "You know he was going to kill you boys a minute ago. He was stopping for nothing. We had no options left. It is over. Justice has been served this night, gentlemen."

"How did you find us?" asked Elliott.

"Hell, I've been watching you ever since Brother Wilcox bit the dust. I smelled something was up. Sumner, I followed your skinny ass all over the damn city for weeks."

"I never knew that, Sheriff," said Elliot as he stepped into the water.

"Well, hell no…you didn't know…damn younger generation just doesn't pay attention…damn iPhones and iPads and technical stuff. Nobody opens their eyes anymore. In the future take a look in your damn mirror once in a while, son."

"Yes, Sir." Elliott fished around for the body and made Tony stay on the bank. "Tony, stay away. You get this water on that wound and you will get sick and die."

"Been there, done it." Tony laughed, holding his stomach in pain.

"Gentlemen, we've got one hell of a story to tell. You are not going to believe what Deputy Pilsner discovered," said G.E. while wiping off his .44 in the moonlight.

Elliott waded deeper into the river, up to his chest, but the body was gone. He had hoped it got hung up in something, but no such luck. The current was strong. Debris going by just a few feet out was getting sucked under.

"People don't know how bad this river can be. It looks peaceful from a distance, the Lazy Mississippi River, but all hell is breaking loose under that surface. Big is always bad, boys," said G.E.

"Where did you find Carol?" asked Elliott.

"In the damnedest place, but I have my orders to take you to her, not to talk."

"You're the boss, Sheriff, unless the mayor is in this too."

"No, and hell no, the boss said don't spoil this for her. She wants to see the look on your face. Miss Carol reminds me of my Sophia. Damn good lady, son."

Tony opened his cellphone. "Collin? Tony. It's all over. Come to the north end of Mud Island. Get boats out. The Butcher is dead, floating around out there now. He was shot three times. We saw him drop."

G.E. went to the dead girl on the mound. Tony joined Elliott next to the river and they watched. "I thought she was Carol. Do you know who she is, Elliott?"

"No. But I have her engagement ring." He removed it from his shoe and gave it to Tony. "This should help identify her."

G.E. was putting his coat over her like he was putting one of his daughters to bed. He would stay with her until the M.E. arrived. He would make sure she was identified and would talk to her family and the young man who loved her. G.E. knew what was important.

In minutes, Mud Island was swarming with police; flood lights buzzed all over the river in search of the body. Each hour that passed was 1983 all over again. This time they owed the community a body. This time they were not stopping until they found the Bluff City Butcher's corpse.

CHAPTER TWENTY-NINE

"Crime takes but a moment, but justice an eternity."
Unknown

Twenty Hours Later

"This is where I was put." Carol pointed at a cage. "They found Michael Bell in another room," she said while staring at her blood on the floor beneath her cage.

Without a word, Elliott put his arms around her from behind and guided her to another part of the room of wood-framed walls and ceilings and dirt floors. The place was lit up; portable flood lights were everywhere and electric cables ran through the labyrinth of tunnels beneath the north substation and out the cellar doors to giant generators rented by the county.

"The Bluff City Butcher brought me here from the woods."

Pilsner and Bond stood quietly in the background. G.E. and Tony stayed close to Elliott as Carol told her story.

"Excuse me, Miss Mason, we found the large drainage pipe where he kept the *Dodge Sprinter*, a half mile north of here. The big pipe was hidden behind a wall of thick foliage. We never would have found it if we weren't looking."

"Was the van there?" asked Carol.

"No," said Pilsner.

"That van should be on or near Mud Island," said G.E. looking at Bonn.

"We have someone looking now, Sir," said Bonn.

"I can't believe the son-of-a-bitch was under my ass the whole damn time. If it wasn't for Marty and Gerald we never would have found Miss Mason and Mr. Bell. These guys deserve all the credit. Damn good police work, Pilsner…damn good."

Carol squeezed between Gerald and Marty, put her arms around their waists and pulled them to her. "I can never thank you two heroes enough for finding me down here." Both men smiled, blushed and dropped their heads, acting as if they had never been so close to a beautiful girl.

Elliott nodded and extended his hand. "Marty, I am really impressed by how you followed a trail of hunches that began with a misplaced report and ended with a dangerous walk in the bowels of hell without wasting time or letting fear get in the way. I have been all over the world doing this and can tell you that what you did was special. You, Marty Pilsner, literally saved the lives of Carol Mason and Michael Bell. I am honored to know you."

For Marty Pilsner, recognition from the world renowned forensic investigator of the decade made his career.

They approached stainless steel tables on wheels next to a wall loaded with tools and surgical instruments. "The workshop," Elliott murmured.

"Can you tell us anything by looking at this setup?" asked G.E. while nervously cleaning his glasses.

"Very sophisticated," he said as he processed. "Many of the surgical instruments are specialized, used for delicate procedures." He picked up and examined one scalpel and continued. "Specimen collection," he looked in the expensive microscope, "and special slide-making equipment tell me this setup was for a medically trained doctor."

355

"What was this place used for?" asked Tony as he opened a rusted cupboard and removed a tissue culture flask containing a piece of meat floating in a clear liquid.

Elliott took it from his hand. "The tissue preservative solutions and transport supplies make this place primarily a tissue acquisition site. There were a lot of organs and tissue samples leaving here." With his eyes he followed an electric cord draped from the ceiling to a dark corner of the dirt room. "That ice machine and the packing materials mean boxes of organs moved out of here routinely."

"The doctor was doing surgery on people here?" asked G.E.

"Yes, I suspect a lot of organ and tissue harvesting."

"Did the Bluff City Butcher work on people here?" Carol put her arm through Elliott's as she stared at the cold stainless steel with brown stains.

"Maybe some, but I don't think this was his thing."

"What are you saying?" Tony looked back over his shoulder from the wall of grotesque instruments.

"As I said, a medically trained person was seeking specific specimens. Each had to be evaluated, properly removed and processed in a specialized way or they would be useless. I would assume, if the Bluff City Butcher was involved in the process down here, that he had some ancillary role: closing, suturing, cleansing, laundry and disposal of bodies."

"The tables on the far wall have restraints," said G.E.

"I'm afraid that surgery was performed on several victims at a time. The limited restraints suggest they were kept in a vegetative state...probably until they died."

"That would insure a steady supply of fresh tissues," Carol offered.

"But there is no evidence of effort to keep them alive long: no IV apparatus. There would be no other way to nourish or rehydrate in their condition," said Elliott.

"Was the Butcher...an Igor?" Tony grimaced.

"No. He was too intelligent and self-driven for a subservient relationship. I would bet the Guardian played the 'validation game' skillfully for a long time, giving him the attention, a purpose, and friendship he needed."

"Over time, the Guardian got more control, right?" asked Tony.

"Not control, the Butcher, no matter what, was going to kill. The Guardian plugged into that and aimed his kills for his needs," said Elliott stepping back from a large barrel with flies.

"Is that what I think it is?" asked Tony staying several feet back.

"Human bones." Elliott bent over and examined one rib hooked on the lip of the barrel. "Teeth marks!"

"Jesus...I feel like throwing up," said G.E. as they went into an adjoining dirt-floored room and Elliott kept talking.

"The Butcher was intellectually advanced but emotionally limited."

"That psychology crap makes no sense to me," said G.E.

"When his Guardian dropped out of the picture the Butcher went back to a singular purpose, the simple desire to kill. But selecting victims alone, without the direction he seemed to be getting for many years, was confusing. His purpose in his dysfunctional life had diminished once again. The loss of the thrill made him search for a way to get it back. The public display of his work was an attempt to get that feeling back. At least, that's my thinking at present.

"They were both perverse," said Elliott. "The Guardian needed fresh tissue and the Butcher needed to kill...a most dreadful symbiotic relationship.

"We may have what we need to identity this...Guardian," said Carol. All eyes turned to her. She led the group through a shadowed hole in the wall, debris piled on each side of its entrance. The narrow tunnel had been carved out of the dirt long ago; it was framed with old boards now covered in cobwebs. The tunnel opened into a large area with rock walls and was filled with dust-covered boxes. The air was stale—the smell of wet, moldy dirt. She carefully maneuvered around the numerous stacks of boxes to get to the other end of the thirty-by-twenty foot room. Under portable lights were some open boxes and a dozen files neatly spread out on a long folding table.

"Documents will be scanned into an official, electronic repository," said Carol to break the silence. "Right now they will be seen only by a select team and held in a secured area by the Shelby County Sheriff's Office."

"We hit the mother lode," said G.E. as they edged up to the table.

"These boxes contain an enormous amount of information. We are finding detailed information on victims of the Bluff City Butcher and the medical procedures for each." Carol handed a file to Elliott. He flipped it open and scanned the entire contents in seconds.

"This is set up like a patient file: name, residence, physical examination, date of abduction and surgical procedures, the organ-tissue harvesting record, death and disposal...and even location of the body," said Elliott.

"Did you see the dates on these boxes?" asked Tony. "They go back to 1965. This box appears to be the most recent...December 2008." Tony's phone rang. He took the call. Everyone stopped and watched. "They found the Bluff City Butcher. We need to go."

"Good. We can avoid a repeat of '83," said Elliott as he put his arm around Carol and led the way out.

"They're taking him to the medical examiner's office. Bates wants to get started as soon as we can get there. The media coverage of this event is from all over the country so be prepared."

Once outside, they scattered and took off in separate cars. Elliott and Carol broke from the group and got into Elliott's car, their first time alone since her abduction and his near death battle with the Bluff City Butcher. They immediately embraced and kissed passionately with their hands going everywhere.

"You know we have a little time to make love right here," said Elliott between hard, passionate kisses and wild groping.

"I need a lot more time for you than we could possibly have now. God, I was so worried about you, Elliott. I knew the Butcher was using me to get you. I was so stupid to walk to Beale." Carol held his neck tightly.

"That's just like you, thinking of my predicament, not yours. I love you, Carol."

"I know...and I love you, Doctor Sumner."

He started the car and they sped out the substation gates and onto I-240. They would be at the county morgue in five minutes.

"Did you see the watermark on that one victim's summary page?" asked Carol.

"Yes—*Gilgamesh*—and I saw the initials next to the pharmaceuticals listed in the patient history...I mean victim's history."

"What did you see?"

"E C M, of course."

"For a while, we've suspected Enrique Carlos Medino was the Guardian."

"Suspecting and knowing are two very different things. I went into the final battle believing I was the one with the best chance to stop the most prolific serial killer in American history. My purpose was to save you and destroy a serial killer. Now I discover the stakes are far greater than I ever imagined...possibly world-changing."

CHAPTER THIRTY

"A wise man proportions his belief to the evidence."
David Hume

20 November 2009

The meeting option went through Max. He was approached by an old friend in the CIA. The informal emissary suggested Max encourage his friends to attend. Unnamed high-level insiders were disturbed that a top secret government program could be in jeopardy due to inquiries sprouting from the Bluff City Butcher investigation and linkage to Dr. Medino. Actions would be taken. A courtesy meeting was on the table once. It would be off the record. Max was given twenty-four hours to confirm participation of Bell, Sumner, Mason, Wilcox and Taft.

Timing was the only good thing going for the courtesy meeting. The Bluff City Butcher was dead, the inquest completed and the archaeological efforts in the catacombs under the north substation had already identified one-hundred-twenty-seven victims in six states. The Shelby County Sheriff's Office was working with the FBI and several law enforcement agencies, providing locations of victims' remains. Because Jack Bellow had been confirmed by DNA testing to be the Bluff City Butcher and he allegedly killed five of the ten investors in his company, *Life2* Corporate assets were frozen. S.E.C. launched an investigation with six citings: illegal change of control, improper distribution of capital, conflicts of interest, illegal IPO, investor-tampering and insider trading. Through Max, Albert Bell got the group together for a decision on the proposed meeting.

"If these government people want a meeting they will need to fit our schedules," said Albert. "Elliott, am I missing anything?"

"No. If someone has a problem with an official investigation they need to come to Memphis and present their case. We are going to understand Medino's research and linkage to a twenty-five year killing spree regardless of government threats."

"Is everybody else ok with that?" asked Albert. They nodded in agreement.

"Max, tell your friend we will meet with them here tomorrow at 6:00 p.m. I recommend they send their top people."

"What possibly could motivate them to comply?" asked Max.

"Our meeting is a courtesy option, not a command performance. Their attendance will be in their best interest. They will have an opportunity to influence decisions to run a relevant story in *The Memphis Tribune* slated the following day: *"U.S. Government Complicit in Top Secret Life-Extension Research Linked to The Bluff City Butcher and 127 Deaths."*

The government saw the wisdom and accepted all—minor—adjustments to the suggested meeting plan. Three arrived at the Bell mansion in a limousine and were seated in the north dining hall, at the center and one side of the thirty-foot table. At precisely 6:00 p.m. a door opened and Albert's group entered and sat down across from the guests. Albert positioned himself in the middle and was flanked by Elliott and Carol on one side, Tony and G.E. on the other. Max did not attend. The meeting was cordial and mildly exploratory for ten minutes and then moved to the meat.

"Of course, our government is typically engaged in hundreds of top secret research projects at any given time," said Phillip McCormick, the slender middle-aged gentleman with a mustache, sitting in the middle of the three. From the start, he was the most engaging, the apparent senior member of the group, although titles never came up.

"Our national interests are best served when we acquire an advantage that is relevant in an ever-changing and dangerous world." Tom Slater sat across from G.E. and Tony. He looked away when he spoke, as if someone could see secrets in his eyes. His right ear twitched when he was being evasive. Knowing that could come in handy later.

"When government efforts are in the best interest of the people they serve, there is seldom controversy," said Albert. "The problems throughout history have come when a few tried to decide for many. Oversight helps to insure the people's interests are represented. I have heard your group is engaged in activities not known to our elected leaders."

"Well, I don't believe the..." McCormick started.

Elliott leaned in, cutting McCormick off, his silent presence projecting the strength of a more worldly man. "Gentlemen, we need to be direct. What do you know about Enrique Medino's research and linkage to the Butcher that you can tell us?"

"Dr. Enrique Medino was once a respected molecular biologist and geneticist with good research. Unfortunately, later in his life he resorted to trickery for personal gain," said McCormick.

Tony laughed. "How can you prove such a claim? The man is dead."

"Did you know Medino was dying from pancreatic cancer in June of 2004? Did you know six months later he miraculously recovered?"

"Yes, he was a proud cancer survivor," said Elliott.

"Remarkable, don't you think, Dr. Sumner? Have you ever seen such a recovery from pancreatic cancer?" asked Slater.

"No. I was surprised, frankly. But I had no reason to suspect he faked his recovery. Miracles do happen."

Slater slid a DVD to Albert. "I suggest taking a look at this when you can." William intercepted the DVD and disappeared. A screen descended from the ceiling and the video started to run as Slater spoke.

"Here you can see a very sick Dr. Medino greeting Jack Bellow at the TAO Room in Las Vegas on June 24, 2004. The man is death walking." They watched for a minute and it went to a second video. "Now, six months later, we see a healthy Medino energetically walking into the Crescent Building in Memphis, Tennessee…and here he is helping Jack Bellow into the dining room; notice he is holding Jack up with one arm."

"Mr. Slater, we have seen these videos before," said Albert.

"I'm sure you have; they tell the story Medino wanted to tell, the story Jack Bellow experienced firsthand. A cancer cure and life-extension discovered at last. Jack Bellow prepared his entire life to introduce the greatest breakthrough of all time to the world. He lived the Medino miracle. He was given his dream opportunity by the *Father of Immortality himself!*" The video ended with rolling lines.

"Is this all you've got, Mr. Slater?" asked Elliott.

McCormick whispered, "Jack Bellow was Medino's engine for the creation of personal wealth in the twilight years of his failed career."

A third video started to run. "This is security camera footage from the *Hilton Hotel* in Nashville. The date and time registry in the lower right corner…June 14, 2004, 7:10 p.m. CDT. You see a terribly ill Dr. Medino sitting alone on the sofa, his condition similar to that in Vegas ten days later."

"I think we all agree, that is Dr. Medino in the midst of chemotherapy at Vanderbilt Medical Center," said Elliott.

A second man entered the picture; it was a vibrant Dr. Medino. He passed an envelope to the sick Dr. Medino; they shook hands, talked and laughed together for another minute. The video ended.

"We have an imposter," said McCormick.

"The sick version of Dr. Medino was played by Alfred Canter, a small time community actor and patient at the Medical Center. Unfortunately, he died in January 2005. The poor fellow had no chance. He was afflicted with pancreatic cancer.

"Medino had a proposition for a dying man; an all expense paid trip to Vegas and one-day acting gig paying $50,000. Canter was weak and had nothing to leave his wife. He memorized Medino's bio and the biotechnology script in a day," said Slater.

"You can imagine Bellow's shock in Memphis the night he saw the real Dr. Medino, the man on steroids and growth hormone working out four hours a day."

"His lifelong research got nowhere. Time was running out and he was desperate. Enrique Medino would fool the top biomedical entrepreneur in the country. He had cracked the genetic code for immortality. They would form a private company and raise $150 to $200 million. Medino would transfer $50 million to a Swiss bank account and disappear."

The sheriff shook his head. "Interesting hypothesis, but let's get back on track. The question was: what do you know about Medino's research and his connection to the Bluff City Butcher? If you were watching him for thirty years, surely you knew about the Bluff City Butcher, right?" asked G.E. Taft.

"Yes, he failed, and yes we learned about the Butcher."

"How hard was it to watch him kill innocent people while you protected your covert surveillance operation?" asked Tony.

"Ok, it is fair to suggest covert government operations can be cold and callous. In this case, we failed to see a connection until September 3, 2008, the McGee homicide. We put McGee in Tom Lee Park so you could find him, along with clues we thought could help. Yes, we did protect our anonymity," said McCormick.

"You expect us to believe you watched Medino for thirty years and you missed a twenty-five year relationship?" asked Tony.

"Believe what you want, Detective Wilcox, but I will remind you that Dr. Sumner, the most accomplished forensic homicide investigative mind in the country, was fooled too. The Butcher and Medino were never seen together. Enrique came to Memphis twice a month and stayed at the Brent mansion. We had people watching the place...no Butcher," said McCormick.

"Have you guys ever seen the Bluff City Butcher?" asked G.E.

"Yes, the Panther McGee homicide. One of our agents on September 3, 2008, was tracking Medino as he attended a late dinner and was drinking with investors on Beale Street. Our man was parked on a side street watching the restaurant. He called in and reported a brutal abduction; a man with a guitar was beaten and pulled into a van. He followed."

McCormick looked down at his hands and bit his lip. "Our guy described him as a big six-five, two-fifty pounds, long hair, strong, dark complexion and wearing a long black coat. We found McGee and our man's right arm still gripping his gun in the grass. We never found our agent."

"I'm sorry to hear that," said Elliott. Slater and McCormick were visibly shaken. The third guy showed nothing.

"We put McGee in Tom Lee Park, closer to the police station, so they could get on it right away. And, yes, we stayed in the background."

"You should give us your agent's name before you leave. We may know how to find his remains," offered Elliott. The room was uncomfortably silent during the human moment amidst the high level chess game.

"Did you witness the Raymond Munson homicide?" asked Carol.

"No," replied Slater. "Our focus has always been on Medino. At the time we knew very little about a serial killer, and the link to Medino. We did spend time in October and November of 2008 trying to learn more."

"What did you find out?" asked Tony.

"Detective Wilcox, we found absolutely nothing until we thought to look into the background of Raymond Munson."

"Why check on him?" asked Tony.

"We saw similarity with Panther McGee. It was a horrible death, there was surgical work, the victim was on display and organs were harvested."

"Did you learn anything?"

"We learned everything you probably already knew for a long time; Munson was an English teacher at Carrolton Junior High. A kid came after him with a knife, cut off his finger in '82."

"How did you hear it ended?" asked Elliott.

"The boy went to jail for a day. They put him through some tests to understand why he got so angry, and confirmed he was dyslexic. But they also discovered he had a high IQ and some psychopathic tendencies."

"What happened to the kid?"

"Munson never pressed charges. Adam Duncan was kicked out of school. The Duncan family disappeared October 17, 1982. We read the CPD police report that concluded Adam killed his parents and a Texas Ranger. Our thoughts were that Adam became Jack Bellow and, secretly, the Bluff City Butcher. I guess now we all know that to be true."

The Feds are steering discussions in areas known to most, Elliott thought. *The time to take the meeting another direction has arrived.*

"Let's switch gears." Elliott pushed the meeting in a direction that would be most helpful and productive for them. "You knew about Dr. Medino's 'life-extension' research. Where did you think he was getting his fresh human tissue over all those years?" Elliott leaned into the table.

"We monitored his movements, mail, Nashville home, Vanderbilt lab and his Davidson County farm; we found nothing. We concluded his tissue supply had to be coming from the Brent mansion. But eighty-five thousand hours of surveillance showed the same repeating story; twice a month Medino arrived on a Friday and left on a Saturday or Sunday. He carried a small overnight bag and briefcase, both inadequate to transport organs packed in ice," said Slater.

"Even after Brent died, Medino kept going to the mansion twice a month. He was predictable; he always parked in the same place on the side of the house."

"You saw nothing?" asked Elliott.

"Nothing."

"I see."

"Then, after Medino's death, we took the opportunity to visit the Brent mansion for a closer look. We discovered loose stones in the foundation of the mansion. Dr. Medino was passing boxes of organs and tissue through the hole in the foundation into his side car window. I can assure you that we never picked up on that when he was alive. We did not know how the tissue would even get into the Brent mansion. We were sure it was getting to his Davidson farm somehow."

"A covert supplier?"

"Yes, sophisticated, but now we understand the Bluff City Butcher was bringing victims into the mansion through the woods in the early morning hours. He must have known we were there because we never saw him."

Albert cleared his voice and eyes turned to him. "What is your group doing that warrants such aggressive tactics with the Memphis Police Department, the Shelby County Sheriff's Office and the other accomplished professionals engaged on this special assignment?" asked Albert.

"Excuse me, please. I can take it from here gentlemen." The third government man spoke for the first time. "Thank you, Mr. McCormick and Mr. Slater. You may leave at this time…please."

Without a word, they stood, nodded politely and exited the room. They were escorted to their limo and were gone. A second limo had arrived during the meeting; it was cleared and sitting in the driveway fifty yards away from the mansion with the motor running. Three of Albert Bell's security guards were standing next to it with their hands resting on holsters. Three more hunkered in the woods with high-powered rifles, three beads on the tinted windshield, driver's side.

"I apologize for the cloak and dagger nature of these sorts of things. I am Owen Chambliss; I work at the pleasure of the President of the United States."

■ ■ ■

"Mr. Bell suggested we send our top people. I like to think that would be me." Chambliss laughed alone and then his face went flat. "My objective is one-dimensional. The United States government unquestionably respects the sovereignty of state, county and city municipalities. We have no intention of injecting ourselves into your affairs. I will tell you what I do for our nation and then hope to reach a mutually satisfactory arrangement."

Albert and Carol shifted in their seats and Elliott's index finger tapped quietly as his pupils narrowed. "You have a captive audience, Mr. Chambliss," he said.

"Thank you, Dr. Sumner. First, allow me to begin by apologizing for our aggressive tone at the onset. Our secret agency deals with entities outside our country, often people hell bent on destroying America. Our work environment has shaped our dialogue and tone. Sometimes we forget we are talking with our own people. We simply must do a better job with that." Chambliss looked away for a fleeting fraction of a second.

Elliott knew he was lying. "Apology accepted, please continue."

"My job is to manage the apex of our nation's top secret programs. Typically, the programs I see have developmental life-cycles that span generations. Most decisions were made before my birth or will be made after my death. The ideas, innovations and discoveries we nurture are beyond the knowledge and imagination of most people when they first appear on the horizon."

Carol's ire was wrapped in her tone. "And forbidden knowledge of our elected officials, isn't that right?"

"Yes, Miss Mason, sometimes a necessary tactic in a complex world. But these decisions were made by our elected officials and can change again." He smiled awkwardly.

Carol leaned forward and clasped her hands, her eyes staying with Chambliss's. "Since the beginning of time, man has pursued the unknown, searching for new ways to enhance the human experience. Why is your secret agency needed, really?"

"We were created to give the United States a better chance to protect early-stage innovation and discovery. The greatest advantages come when we are the exclusive owners of breakthrough knowledge. Never before has it been more important to advance and strengthen our position in the world." Chambliss shifted in his seat for the first time and looked Carol in the eyes. Elliott knew he was being truthful. Or, at least, he believed what he just said. "We are at the front end only…and then we pass it along."

"Can you give examples of past involvements?"

"Quantum theory, electromagnetism, splitting the atom, expansion of the universe theory, nuclear fission, space travel, stealth technology and the human genome, to name a few."

Carol unclasped her hands and laid them on the table palms down, all fingers pointing at him. "That's interesting. How about getting current, like us, Mr. Chambliss?" she challenged.

"The creation of self-replicating synthetic life, anti-matter, antigravity, self-perpetuating energy sources, artificial intelligence, robotics, time travel, psycho-kinesis and of course, life-extension and immortality, the reason we are together today." He continued with a renewed sense of strength in his tone and eye contact.

"I don't believe I need to go over the enormous benefits afforded the country that cracks the genetic code and masters immortality FIRST. I think we all know that country will control the universe for an eternity. Obviously, we would like it to be the United States."

Nobody moved. Elliott waited ten seconds. "What are you worried about?"

"Worry is not the word, Dr. Sumner. A missed opportunity for the United States is my concern. We must remain stronger than our adversaries."

He said MY concern—a slip maybe. "If Dr. Medino is the failure you seem to think he was, help me understand your continued interest in his work."

"In catacombs beneath the old Brent mansion, at *Life2* Corporate headquarters, Jack Bellow's Penthouse or the Davidson County farm, maybe one piece to the 'life extension puzzle' exists." Chambliss adjusted his tie and took a sip of water.

"What do you want from us?" asked Albert with a diplomatic tone.

"We want three things. First, turn down the volume on the Medino linkage to the Bluff City Butcher. Second, share all scientific information from the Medino, *Life2* and Butcher investigation. And third, leave the U.S. Government out of all communications and discussions; our inclusion only complicates things for you and for us."

Albert nodded. "Let's start with…why number three?"

"If the U.S. Government is associated with Dr. Medino and the Bluff City Butcher, Memphis will be crawling with agents from all over the world. They are very dangerous people. They will stop at nothing to get what they want. You could throw the Midsouth right back into another horrific killing frenzy, but this time there would be numerous killers with resources."

Albert looked to Elliott to take over. "Mr. Chambliss, #1 and #3 are reasonable and doable, but #2 is more complicated. There are attendant legal matters to address with regard to the handling of private property, assets owned by an American company and its investors. You can rest easy knowing all pieces to the puzzle owned by *Life2*, *BelMed*, Dr. Medino and Jack Bellow are protected and unavailable to the public.

"Our first interest is to solve the active—multiple—homicide cases. We have one-hundred-twenty-seven deaths in six states and we are just getting started."

"Dr. Sumner, our legal counsel has informed me that mechanisms are available to meet all legal requirements while allowing government access and review of relevant scientific information," said Chambliss, while fiddling with something in his coat pocket.

The fiddling says you're reaching. Elliott was cordial but firm. "I am confident what you have could be reviewed and put in place relatively fast if it is satisfactory to all with vested interests. Such decisions do assign personal liability. Therefore, we must be comfortable with the terms of the arrangement and the resultant exposures. By law, while engaged in an active investigation, we have a fiduciary responsibility that drives everything…as I am sure you know, Mr. Chambliss."

"Yes, but lost time jeopardizes our country's 'life-extension program' regardless of your efforts to maintain a protected and confidential operation." His voice cracked.

"I understand your concern," Elliott replied as he sat back in his chair. He was done with the meeting. The others leaned back with him.

"Respectfully, Doctor, I am good at what I do and can assure you that at this very moment our enemies know we are meeting, and if you have not already been, you are about to be infiltrated. Our country is compromised if one key piece of the puzzle falls into the wrong hands."

Elliott stood up first. The rest followed and then Owen Chambliss.

"We will implement #1 and #3 immediately. We will have our attorneys on call to meet with yours. A document could be in place allowing government participation in forty-eight hours, Mr. Chambliss. Until then, we will protect the rights of the owners of private property and we will continue with our investigation. Because the Bluff City Butcher crossed state lines, the FBI is fully engaged. Apparently your agency is no longer associated with the FBI or CIA." Elliott baited Chambliss.

"I must accept your proposal. Please understand, you underestimate what is coming your way! Our immediate involvement would bring the experienced guidance and robust protection you must have in the face of the lethal wave of covert activity. Our enemies will kill anybody in their way...ANYBODY."

Desperation leaked from his words as Elliott looked away and rounded the table with Albert to escort him out of the room. Tony, Carol and G.E. stayed standing at their seats with heads down.

Elliott put a hand on his shoulder, made eye contact and extended his hand. As Owen Chambliss gripped his hand Elliott asked, "What do you know about *Gilgamesh?*" and waited for a reaction. Surprisingly, Albert revealed the most; his head jerked, wide-eyed, toward Elliott. Chambliss showed nothing.

"Let me think; *Gilgamesh* is a word I've heard before, but where? I know. It was college, one of the first stories ever written: *The Epic of Gilgamesh.*"

"Ah...it's a story. What is it about?" Elliott asked as they stepped into the hall.

"I'm sorry; I don't recall. Oh, yes, it's about a king and gods. Why the interest?"

For the first time, Elliott saw some discomfort, a twitch in Owen's eyelid. "No interest, just curiosity, an unfamiliar word I came across recently."

Albert and Elliott walked Chambliss the rest of the way in silence. They shook his hand and stayed on the front steps as the odd little man disappeared into the back of the limousine and pulled away. At a hundred yards the limo reached the crest and dropped out of sight on the downward slope crossing the open field toward the iron gates on Walnut Grove.

Looking straight ahead Elliott asked Albert, "When are you going to tell me about *Gilgamesh* and the genetic gifts of the Bell family patriarch?"

Albert smiled slightly and, this time, did not flinch. Between the meeting hall and the front porch he realized that he was tired of guarding the family secret. And Albert had a growing concern it was somehow connected with the gathering storms.

"I guess that time is here." His mind pulled out the memory of his father and the silence back on that August day in Austin when he had asked the same questions. Now, standing on the front steps of his own mansion fifty-three years later, Albert was more than his father ever imagined. He was the true sage and Elliott the student.

When Albert turned to speak, a blinding flash of light lit the north sky, followed by a deafening explosion. They braced themselves, feeling the concussion and smelling the bitter fringe of a molten, gaseous inferno. They looked at each other and then the giant plume of thick smoke climbing into the sky just beyond the crest. Pieces of the limousine rained down on the property, some whistling by, cutting through trees and clanging down the cement drive and splashing in the ponds.

Owen Chambliss went out in spectacular fashion.

They watched as an unmarked drone with a fiery tail managed a tight figure eight, leveled ten feet above the ground and broke through the plume on a direct course to the front doors of the mansion, exactly where Elliott and Albert stood. They had seconds to react, but it was too little time. A jump to the ground would not avoid the destruction of the mansion and rocketing debris. They were doomed.

"It appears Mr. Chambliss was accurate in his assessment of the new dangers coming our way," Albert said hurriedly while stepping in front of Elliott.

"Not completely, Albert. Mr. Chambliss overestimated their ability to protect." Elliott firmly moved Albert to his side. With his arm around his waist they leaped off the porch into the dense shrubbery. Not much protection, but all they had. Lying face-to-face Elliott suggested, "I may have taken us from the proverbial frying pan." They both smiled, the drone seconds away and their fates sealed. Then the front door opened.

"What's going on out here?" Carol stepped out on the porch in time to see the drone approaching. She froze. "Oh, shit." Just as suddenly, it shifted course, an upward arc that cleared the mansion by twenty-feet. The sizzling rocket thrust swept the porch, lifted her dress and it was gone.

Carol saw only the tops of their heads in the bushes. Without a view, they were waiting for the explosion that was sure to come. "You men can come out now. I sent the bad rocket away," she teased.

After a bit of maneuvering, Elliott helped Albert back onto the porch and into Carol's waiting, helpful arms.

"I told you Miss Mason was special," said Albert. She winked at both.

The shared near-death experience was another bonding moment for Elliott and Albert. They continued to move closer together. The enormity of a missile attack on private property sent a clear message. The flow of adrenalin erased the conversation seconds before, but the topic of *Gilgamesh* would come up another time.

"What does all this mean, Elliott?" Albert asked as the mansion emptied behind them and the sirens grew louder.

"Another meeting in the near future, I would think." Elliott put his arm around Carol. "The question I cannot answer is with whom."

■ ■ ■

Two weeks later Max secured some classified information. "Yes, please put me through to Albert."

"Hello, Max."

"We have confirmed a drone was stolen from an Air Force base in Texas and it looks like an inside job, Albert. Not sure what that means.

"And there is nothing on a government *Gilgamesh Project*. No one is talking about the missile execution of Owen Chambliss. Albert, no one has ever heard of Thomas Slater or Phillip McCormick. This whole thing has fallen into a black hole. Be careful."

CHAPTER THIRTY-ONE

"The true mystery of the world is the visible, not the invisible."
Oscar Wilde

22 December 2009

Albert sat alone in the upstairs study, waiting for Max to call back. All he could hear on the phone was, *"It's important, will call when plane lands, five or ten minutes."* The rest broke up.

Quiet time was the last thing he needed. He sat by the phone, looking out the window as guests arrived and he struggled to come to terms with all that had happened in his disastrous life. He had lost a son, a daughter with child and a wife—all to a monster he created. He could not stop thinking that if he had stayed with Betty Duncan in 1968, maybe Adam would have taken a different path. The one-hundred-twenty-seven who died by the Bluff City Butcher's knife would be alive. And that mattered. *How can the errors of one man be allowed to destroy so many? I have searched all my life for one answer. Why was I born into a life of privilege? Why me?*

Two months had passed since the Bluff City Butcher had been killed on Mud Island. The twenty-five-year urban legend finally had come to an end. The city of Memphis could step out from under the cloud of terror and return to normal. *The Memphis Tribune* told the whole story. The

Butcher was a deeply troubled man with a name. Adam Duncan, alias Jack Bellow, was Albert Bell's illegitimate son. The painful truth would hurt many in the beginning but strengthen all in the end.

The gathering at the Bell mansion before the Christmas holidays was a time for those who'd fought the battle to remember and seek closure. Invited were all that had a role in ending the nightmare. From the Memphis police to the sheriff's deputies and medical examiner's office, paramedics, the Millington Naval Base team and members of the FBI, *The Memphis Tribune and WKRC*—all were now honored guests of the Bell patriarch.

The Christmas party was off to a good start. Everyone was early, a very good sign. They poured into the mansion with a refreshing, festive spirit. Carol and Elliott were enjoying one of the many fireplaces, chatting with Tony, his partner Alex Harris, and Michael Bell, who still needed to put on some weight after being caged for several months in the bowels of the Brent estate. Why the Butcher let him live would always remain a mystery. Wade, Bates and the new FBI Regional Director were conversing with Cole and Bradley by the Christmas tree in the grand entry. The Bell sisters were taking friends from the sheriff's office and the MPD on a tour of the kitchen where chefs were creating a special feast. Albert would be downstairs after his call with Max, and as usual, G.E. Taft was running late.

He pulled up to the mansion gates and waited for the guard to get off the phone. G.E. was not a partier, especially since he'd lost Sophia. He came because he and Albert were close and he was getting attached to Elliott and Tony, two bright young men with character and values. G.E. adopted Carol Mason as his only newspaper person and the granddaughter he never had, a role she fully embraced.

Carol had believed all along that Jack Bellow was the Bluff City Butcher. She saw his face that November night in 2008. Now, the DNA and the body they pulled from the river ended all doubts…for most. The Shelby County Medical Examiner had a full house for the historic event, the autopsy of the century. As expected, the corpse presented with the abdominal wound inflicted by Elliott and three large caliber gunshot wounds inflicted by G.E. Taft. The exit wounds eliminated any possibility of ballistic analysis. Because the body was in the water for almost twenty hours, tissue damage presented the customary hurdles. The M.E. ruled the head wound killed the Bluff City Butcher.

Sitting in his car, patiently waiting for the guard, G.E. thought about his third shot. He struggled to accept he'd hit him in the head. It just didn't seem possible. His first two shots hit their marks…exactly where he aimed: the left and then the right deltoid muscles without shoulder joint involvement. G.E. just wanted to wing the Butcher, slow him down and let him think, maybe give up. The third shot was aimed five inches above the Butcher's head. G.E. saw the corpse. He saw the entrance wound in the center of the forehead. Clearly he had missed his mark. Either he dropped his aim or the Butcher jumped up into the path of the .44 magnum hollow point, but that would require perfect timing.

After five minutes of sitting and waiting, G.E. politely tapped the horn. *Albert always had two guards but tonight there was one; maybe another one escorted a guest to the mansion. The guard didn't acknowledge the honk. He didn't even move.* G.E. knew immediately that something was wrong.

Under the steering wheel, he confirmed the load, took it off safety and got out of the car, looking in all directions. He approached the guardhouse. One was lying on the floor in a pool of blood and the other, on the phone, was tied to the chair, his arm propped and entrails hanging from his abdomen. Both guns were still in their holsters. They never saw it coming. Telephone and computer lines were pulled from the wall and a set of large bloody footprints went from the guardhouse toward the iron gates, one left open a few inches.

■ ■ ■

"I still don't get how Medino got control of Adam Duncan, alias Jack Bellow, alias the Bluff City Butcher," said Tony.

"Medino was obsessed with the concept of Anti-aging since his college days," said Carol. "He became an OB/GYN doctor to gain access to an endless supply of fetal stem cells for his private research; he kept the umbilical cord blood of his patients without their knowledge. Out of nowhere, Betty Duncan showed up at his clinic in Pecos, Texas carrying the first-male-born of the billionaire, the Bell family patriarch."

"And why is that significant to Dr. Medino?"

"He just found a way to fund his expensive research."

"How can you be so sure? That seems like a huge stretch."

"In the archives beneath the Brent Estate we found a file with the 1956 publications about Albert Bell and his installation as patriarch following the tragic death of his father."

"That's it?"

"In October of '68, when Medino met Betty Duncan, he paid $25,000 in legal fees to get a complete copy of the Bell family patriarch succession plan, the rules governing transfer of assets. This legal instrument was unique. It was created at great expense by the top law firms of the day, engaged by Alberto Bella in the early 1900s. He wanted a failsafe way to transfer enormous accumulated wealth across generations with the lowest exposure to loss, taxation and outsider manipulations."

"So, Medino gets this legal review and learns what?"

"The patriarch is the CEO of the *Bell Corporation*. As is the case with any business entity, the death of a CEO does not trigger new tax events or open new avenues for outsider interests. The installation of a new CEO is a business process. The same is true with the Bell patriarch succession plan. However, the legal instrument that Alberto had created insured the new CEO would always be a Bell family member.

He established the first-male-born prerequisite, without exception. It is an iron-clad control mechanism."

Stepping into the conversation, Elliott offered some insight. "Medino's research drove everything. This brilliant researcher was making groundbreaking progress—in genetic engineering—back in the 1960s, and he was already struggling with the funding. He knew his future financial needs would be astronomical. Betty Duncan dropped out of heaven—her child was his way into the future. In the early 1980s he was already underwater and had to try to accelerate his plan to access the enormous Bell family fortune. He had been keeping tabs on Betty and Adam Duncan over the years and knew exactly where to go and what to do. In 1982 he left Memphis for Carrollton, Texas."

Tony spit out his ice cube and set his empty glass on the silver tray going by. He asked for another and turned back to Elliott. "Are you referring to the time of the family disappearance: Betty Duncan, Tucker, the Texas Ranger and Adam?"

"Yes. Max's work and our reconstruction of Medino's lab notes recovered from the Brent catacombs. To follow the trail it is important to understand Medino's research required a steady supply and wide variety of fresh human tissue: heart, lung, kidney, liver, brain, endocrine glands, muscle, cartilage, bone and more. Medino was analyzing the genetic variances of specialized somatic cells. His notes from back then are eye-opening…his research way ahead of its time."

"What do you mean?"

"Medino was answering the question: why do some cells reproduce frequently and endlessly while others don't? His delicate genetic experiments required fresh human tissue, sometimes having to be no more than a few hours after death. Underground, or illegal, human tissue was cost prohibitive, and locating it fresh was next to impossible," said Elliott as more people gathered around.

"We have been able to confirm Medino phoned Betty Duncan on October 16, 1982, from a hotel in Dallas. We do not know what they talked about, but we believe he went to Carrollton the next day, which was Adam's birthday. We believe he arrived during or shortly after Adam killed his mother, stepfather and a Texas Ranger, although there still are a lot of loose ends. If we are correct with our 1982 assessments, this was the turning point for Medino: take Adam to the police or cover up three murders and take Adam with him to gain control of the Bell family fortune and the endless funding for his research."

"We believe Medino took care of everything," said Carol, "…the clean up, burying the bodies under the mobile home, getting rid of the cars and taking Adam out of Texas."

Elliott picked up the story. "Adam was traumatized, for sure. Medino cared for him and became his surrogate control figure, his guardian."

"And the Memphis connection?" asked Tony.

"Records at the Brent estate confirm Enrique knew Trenton P. Brent for years, a believer…a silent benefactor. Medino was working on the secrets of immortality and Brent wanted to be at the front of the line. It was easy for Medino to make arrangements for Adam to secretly live in the basement of the Brent estate; a friend of a friend with nowhere else to go. Maybe he even said Adam was hiding from the law. We will never know, but in return for the basement abode, Adam was to stay out of sight and take care of the grounds, which apparently he did for a very long time."

"Adam lived there most of his life while in Memphis, even after Brent died."

"We know Adam came across a stash of money," said Carol. "Brent was known for keeping large amounts of cash hidden on his property. We can confirm Adam found $4 million and assume Brent caught him in

August of 2002, when Brent was found dead in his garage. The cause of death was suffocation and carbon monoxide poisoning. The M.E. ruled manner of death 'undetermined'…another cold case."

"Hmmm…that explains the exhumation of Old Man Brent in November. You were looking for the cranial puncture wound," suggested Edward Cole as he leaned an ear into the conversation circle.

"And we found it." With a smile, Carol patted the editor-in-chief on the back.

Elliott cleared his throat and the circle turned their attentions to him exclusively. "I can accept that Adam Duncan is the Bluff City Butcher. I struggle with the concept that Adam Duncan and Jack Bellow are the same people." He respectfully and gently slid his arm around Carol's waist. "DNA cannot be ignored. There is definitely a match, but something is not right."

"What?"

"I don't know. However, I have learned to follow my instincts even when the facts say something very different. We often make the mistake of thinking we know everything."

"I have less of a problem accepting it." Carol rubbed Elliott's hand on her waist tenderly. They had debated the topic and knew each other's position well. "I know I saw Jack Bellow on the hood of my car and will never forget that face, the face of the Bluff City Butcher," said Carol. "And it is reasonable to conclude that Dr. Medino used that $4 million to get Adam the help he needed to pull off a dual personality scenario: private tutors, diction coaches, expensive acting lessons and he had seed money to start his first company. I am comfortable with the thought that Adam Duncan could pull it off. Remember, he was a psychopath and a genius."

■ ■ ■

Albert's private line rang in the upstairs study. "Max here, can you hear me?"

"Yes, Max. I hear you perfectly. I have you on speaker in the study. As you know, I have a house full of people and am disappointed you are not one of them."

"Is Dr. Sumner with you tonight?"

"Yes…downstairs."

"May I ask he be retrieved immediately?"

"Certainly. Hold on." Albert called William and gave the order. "Ok, Elliott is on his way."

"I'm in Dallas, catching the next plane to Memphis. We have a few minutes."

"If you are coming for my Christmas party you are going to get here when people are going home."

"You know I've never been one for crowds. A pack of Chesterfields and glass of vodka on the rocks is the extent of my holiday season." They both laughed.

Elliott glided into the dark study, surprising Albert, who was bathed in the only light and leaning over the speaker phone.

"Ahhh…Elliott, I have Max on the phone. He is in Dallas, hopping a plane to Memphis. Max has information to share and asked if you could join us."

"Elliott," crackled Max from the box, "hello, Sir."

"Hello, Max. It must be important if it can't wait for you to land."

"We don't have much time. Let me begin by saying I made a mistake. Some information I gave you is incorrect and it is significant. What I am about to share has been thoroughly confirmed. I stake my reputation on its accuracy."

"Max, what is it?" asked Albert, squirming in his seat.

"I told you Betty Duncan gave birth to a boy on October 17, 1968."
"Yes?"

"Albert, she had triplets…three boys: two identical twins and one fraternal."

"I don't understand. What are you saying, Max?"

"Elliott, you're a doctor, explain to Albert how this happens."

"Ok. A typical pregnancy is one egg, one sperm creating one embryo and making one child. On rare occasions, there are two eggs fertilized by two spermatozoa that form two separate and distinct embryos that develop into two unique babies…or fraternal twins. Technically they are dyzygotes…two fertilized eggs. Then again, on other rare occasions one egg and one sperm form one embryo that splits into two embryos. They then develop into two babies that are identical twins, technically called monozygotes."

"I see. Betty had three boys…one dyzygotic and two monozygotic," said Albert.

Max crackled in. "Two boys were given away a few weeks after birth. We have learned that they were placed on front porches of wealthy, unsuspecting couples in different cities in Texas. We found Adam's identical twin…his monozygotic brother."

"Where is he, Max?" Albert asked with his hands flat on the desk.

"He was given to Mary and Vincent Penland in November 1968. The Penland family was big in retail apparel. They were killed in a car accident Thanksgiving Day, a few weeks after finding the baby on their front porch. The Penlands had no family. They left everything to charity and their housekeeper, Greta Stoner. Greta kept the baby boy as hers. No one knew the Penlands even had a child. Greta Stoner had a birth certificate made and acted like the baby was hers all along. Greta married in 1971. Her husband adopted the boy. He was a gifted child. They gave him everything. His parents died in a suspicious house fire in Dallas, Texas in 2005."

"Max, who is he?" asked Albert.

"The couple that adopted Adam's twin brother were Greta and Mark Bellow. Your son and Adam Duncan's identical twin brother is Jack Bellow."

"Jack Bellow and Adam Duncan are identical twins?" repeated Albert as if he just took a punch in the face.

Elliott scratched his head. "That explains why Carol is so certain she saw Jack Bellow on the bluff, and I thought I saw him on Mud Island, and it explains the DNA match."

Max cleared his throat. "Jack Bellow's life is well documented. He was a very intelligent man with a long list of academic and business accomplishments."

Elliot mumbled into his lap. "We have Jack Bellow in the morgue, an innocent man. Adam killed his brother." His face was hardened when he lifted his head and looked at Albert across the desk. "That means the Bluff City Butcher is still out there."

"How can we know for sure who is in the morgue?" asked Albert.

"I let the DNA and other objective body-of-evidence override my observations and instincts. I dismissed all inconclusive forensics because I was fooled too." Elliott continued to make mental adjustments, moving at lightning speed through his databank of clues. "The night I fought the Butcher the knife was in his left hand. I turned it into his abdomen. When I examined the body in the morgue I expected to see the cutting edge of the entrance wound to his left but it was pointing to his right. I thought I made an error or perhaps the knife was held differently by the Butcher; it was a matter of seconds. I dismissed the anomaly."

"It also explains Sheriff Taft's third shot," said Max. "He has been adamant about aiming above the Butcher's head."

"The Bluff City Butcher did not die that night. He fell into the river and escaped once again, gentlemen. He put his clothes on Jack Bellow, duplicated his wounds and hung Jack in a quiet place on the river to be found. Another clever escape." Elliott leaned back in his chair deep in thought.

"Max, Betty had three boys. Two were given away. Do you know anything about the third boy, the fraternal twin?" Albert slipped on his glasses and opened a tattered file that had sat before him from the start.

"Yes, but first let me ask Elliott something. It may have some bearing. Elliott, what do you think Adam Duncan is trying to accomplish?"

"There are three possibilities. He is working for someone, he is simply continuing Medino's mission, or he is a serial killer alone in a world doing the only thing that he understands. I guess a fourth possibility could be some combination of these that we just don't get at the moment."

"Do you know why Adam taunted you over the years…why he must kill you?

"I assumed my overblown reputation was a pathetic challenge."

"Max, why must Adam kill Elliott?" Albert looked up from his light-flooded desk at Elliott sitting a few feet away in the high-back, leather armchair, the room bathed in edgy shadows. In the seconds of silence before Max could answer, Albert heard the whine of a single floorboard, the one he had stepped on a hundred times before. He knew exactly where to look.

He squinted to see and it took shape. The massive presence was silent and now standing behind Elliott. Only the eyes and long blade caught the light.

The speaker phone crackled alive. Elliott looked up and saw the reflection of the Bluff City Butcher in Albert's glasses. Max cleared his throat, unaware that his next words would be a death sentence for Elliott and Albert Bell.

CHAPTER THIRTY-TWO

"The wisest men follow their own direction."
Euripides

Albert saw him clearly. He was angry but unprovoked, lost but determined. He was a man and an animal capable of intelligent, deadly strikes in all directions. He owned the room…and his eyes said he knew it.

Albert jumped when Max's voice broke the silence…and the moment. Max answered Albert's question with six words. "Elliott is your first-born son!"

At the end of the last word, the Bluff City Butcher rested the ten-inch blade on Elliott's shoulder and touched a bloody finger to his mouth.

Elliott had not forgotten the smell of the monster on Mud Island, the smell that was missing at Jack Bellow's autopsy and the smell he detected the moment he entered Albert's dark study. But now, in a different way, Elliott would remember the smell as belonging to the brother he hunted but never knew.

For Elliott, the six words completed a lifelong puzzle that he had to let play out.

I always felt abandoned and alone. I too have been lost, but not weighed down by a psychopathic disorder and dysfunctional life experience. In an odd way, I understand who I am for the first time and why I will die at the end of the Bluff City Butcher's knife. I see Adam's confusion and I now understand his twisted mission. He never had a chance.

Albert had to get Max off the phone. He needed time and could not allow Max to deliver any more information that could enrage Adam.

"You have given us a lot to think about, Max. Let's say goodbye and pick up when you get to Memphis later tonight."

"Absolutely, Albert. I should arrive in a few hours. Goodbye." Max hung up and called G.E. Taft's cell to tell him the Bluff City Butcher was in the mansion.

There was a bloody trail of butchered guards and dead dogs from the front gates to the mansion. The extreme security measures of the Bell estate proved to be no match for the skills of the ruthless predator. Carol's investigations in New York, Dallas, El Paso, Destin and Memphis had pointed to the Butcher as the killer of Albert's entire family. Although there were holes and stretches, this visit would answer all questions. He would end the Bell lineage.

■ ■ ■

His presence was beyond Albert's imagination. Is this the person writing me since 1983? You could cut Elliott's throat, leap my desk and slay me before a single drop of blood flowed. In seconds you would have number nine and ten…but you would need to go back for number eight. Or would you be done? Or would you be starting…again?

As Adam approached his time to kill, Albert saw that his son was more animal than man. But maybe there was still enough man left for a father to reach.

"What is it that you need…son…really need?" Albert said "son" without thinking. It came naturally to him because he had known for months that Adam Duncan belonged to him.

But he revealed nothing. He stood firmly rooted, his brow relaxed but eyes dancing and his index finger on his left hand tapped on the shining blade inches from Elliott's throbbing carotid artery.

I can see Jack in Adam and Elliott in Jack and myself in all three. The two men before me are born of my seed, the Bell family seed of the privileged. They are so different; one accomplished, principled, a protector dedicated to justice. The other void of heart, unprincipled and dedicated to nothing but pain and terror. One son is a willing combatant of evil and the other son a willing destroyer of what's good. How could such extremes come from one man… from me?

Elliott felt the weight of the butcher knife on his shoulder but not on his heart. He looked across the desk and saw his father for the first time, a man he knew and admired, his jaw line, his thick brow and the same penetrating steel-blue eyes. *How could I miss this? The slight tilt of his head and squint of his eye; it is the same that Carol sees in me, she says, when I am solving a problem. But most important I see a good man, a gentle man, a giving man at a time of great personal discovery and nearing death. And these will be some of my final thoughts. That is good.*

Adam put his right hand on Elliott's shoulder and moved the knife to his neck. The blade nicked the skin; he bled. Once the phone call ended Adam's eyes stayed on Albert. *Was he studying me, memorizing me or trying to find himself in me to prove his existence?*

A drop of blood left Adam's shirt cuff. Another left his fingernails and hit Elliott's hand. There was the added odor of infection. Adam's October wounds were untreated—the river water—and Adam was dying. He answered Albert's question.

"I want for one day…" Adam stopped and turned his head. He heard something or smelled a danger. His senses were sharp. Elliott's eyes dilated. He too sensed something. Adam's eyes came back to Albert. He started again but this time finished. "I want for one day to feel I am not a mistake."

How could this heinous killer, this demented soul, this monster who watched at least one-hundred-twenty-seven people beg for their lives…how could he have any human feelings? Albert thought. *Were pain and loneliness the only emotions he ever felt in this world? Adam was neglected by his mother, abused by his stepfather, overlooked by his schools, used by Medino and abandoned by his father.*

Albert got up from his chair without a word, walked around the desk and up to Adam, who knew he controlled the room. Albert stood in front of the killing legend and saw the lost boy trapped inside the monster. Albert felt his son for the first time and acknowledged that Adam was terribly sick and alone in a nightmare.

Adam removed his hand from Elliott's shoulder and opened his stance to face Albert. Their eyes were even, their faces close. Each saw the other. Albert looked down and then back to Adam's eyes. They were standing in a pool of blood—Adam's blood.

"Son, this stops here. I learned I am your father; you are my son. Adam, I am the mistake, not you. When you were confused by this world I was not there to help you understand. I was not there to make it right for you. A father is the only man a son could always trust to help him in life. I made the unforgivable error of losing you, not being with you when you needed your father in a confusing world. Adam, I am sorry, son."

Albert put his hand on Adam's shoulder. Adam winced, not from the pain—he could handle pain—but because he'd never had his father touch him before.

The door to the study exploded open. Tony and G.E. rushed in, moving to the opposite side of the room, guns leveled. In the same instant Adam pushed Albert toward the door, easily lifted Elliott from the chair with one arm and pressed the blade of the knife to his neck. He threw open the balcony doors with such force they broke from the jambs and flopped to the floor. Snow settled in the room. Adam backed onto the balcony with Elliott in a death grip; he left no room for a clear shot.

From the floor, Albert pleaded. "Adam, this can stop now. I can help now. Please let me help. Everything I have will be used to help you with the rest of your life. Please trust your only father."

Carol rushed into the room to Albert's side. She then saw Elliott in the grips of the Bluff City Butcher, the monster she knew so well. Albert rose from the floor, joining Carol as she started toward the balcony.

"Carol, stop…do not come closer, please," ordered Elliott. "Everyone back off. Give Adam and me room and time." Carol looked confused, but she had learned to trust Elliott's judgment. She moved back to Albert and they stood together.

The guns were lowered and everyone stayed at the far wall of the study.

Adam stood like a statue. The night was quiet. Cold air poured into the room. His blood was soaked up by the fresh layer of snow at their feet. It would be over soon.

But Elliott felt the knife move slightly from his neck and Adam's weight shift onto his shoulder. He could feel the rhythmic shiver of septic shock; the infection was rampant in Adam's bloodstream. The Bluff City Butcher loosened his grip of the butcher knife and Elliott saw "it" clearly, on the skin flap between the thumb and forefinger, a place easily viewed when one wanted it viewed and easily hidden the rest of the time. There was a small tattoo—like on the stationery—the now familiar word, but its story still not known. The tattoo: *Gilgamesh.*

From the other side of the study they watched Elliott turn and speak to the Bluff City Butcher. His eyes dropped to the knife and back to Elliott. Then the Butcher spoke to him, their eyes locked but not hard, and they looked at Albert and back. The Butcher's words were heard only by Elliott, Albert and Carol.

"My brother, I don't understand feelings…I must go…now."

Albert took a step forward. Carol held him back. "Adam…Adam, I can help you if you will let me. I can help you, son. Please give your father one more chance."

Adam let Elliott go and spoke to Albert as if they were alone in another place at another time. "Thank you for this day…Father."

With arms spread and a firm look, Elliott entered the room to block all lines of fire. G.E. and Tony got the message and lowered their guns.

Adam's face tightened, his brows merged and his nostrils flared. He transformed into the horrific beast he knew so well, the place where he was safe. He opened his arms like condor wings, revealing bright red blood-soaked garments beneath his black leather coat. The wounds received on October 17th were raw and oozing with infection. He showed his strength one last time, defiantly raising his knife in a fanning blur and throwing it across the room with phenomenal accuracy, sticking it in the wall over Tony Wilcox's right shoulder. Neither moved. Their eyes met. He turned and leaped from the balcony into the winter night. He was gone.

Seconds later, the room emptied onto the balcony—the Bluff City Butcher was on the run again. Albert and Elliott knew differently. They would be the last onto the balcony.

There were thirty squad cars encircling the mansion, their high beams lighting the grounds and every officer with gun drawn. Every cop within five miles had responded to Taft's call for backup. The message that went out was simple, like Taft; *"We have the Bluff City Butcher at the Bell mansion…come help!"* But on that night guns would be holstered without a shot fired. There would be no chase and no more chapters written.

Word would eventually go out. The Bluff City Butcher was a real monster: a genius, psychopathic killing machine with no feelings and no conscience. Adam Duncan was a mentally disturbed, lost and lonely man who experienced only one meaningful moment in his life—the unconditional love of a father willing to give everything he had to help right impossible wrongs.

The Bluff City Butcher had the physical ability to easily clear the razor sharp spire atop the main entry to the Bell mansion. But when he left Albert's balcony that cold night in December he was Adam Duncan.

After all the boxes in the Brent catacombs were opened, they knew they had been hunting the most prolific serial killer in American history. Some would say the monster that killed so many was impaled by the spire while trying to escape an armada of police at the Bell estate. For those who were there that night, the end of the Memphis urban legend came when Adam Duncan found the strength to destroy the Bluff City Butcher.

He was the only one who could.

THE END

EPILOGUE

Sometime in the spring of 2010

Rudolph Kohl was riding in the backseat of a blue and silver *Bentley* convertible. Sporting a handlebar mustache, he had on his *Teddy Roosevelt, Pince-Nez* spectacles with single black lanyard. He parted his hair close to the middle. Rudy was stuck in a time long ago. He never liked flying and never got used to digital watches, computers or liberals, although he'd been a loyal Democrat or Progressive all his life. When he could, his preference was to relieve himself the old fashioned way, on a tree…and he often did.

As the *Bentley* pulled up to the Bell mansion, all he could think about was his Isabel. She loved the place. When he could see the spire through the trees, all he could think about was Adam.

Albert greeted him at the car, an unusual event for a person of Albert's stature, but he held a deep regard for the man he had known all his life.

They sat in the west garden. It was a morning in May but not yet hot and humid. The shade draped over the flagstone terrace. Where the sun found a way through the leaves, the morning dew was already gone. William made sure there was hot coffee, cold juice, blueberry muffins and real butter—Rudy's favorite. It was almost 9:00. It wouldn't be long now.

"I'm so pleased Adam let Michael live and Elliott too, for that matter," said Rudy as he settled into his chair, pushing a white linen napkin under his belt.

"I agree," replied Albert. *I remember my relief when I saw Michael. He was just a shell of a man. I thought I had lost my brother. And Adam let Elliott live. But do you really care or are you manipulating me again?* Albert opened his newspaper. His pent up anger was returning. He wanted to keep it in check.

"Did Michael go back to Florida to play with his toys?" asked Rudy.

"Yes." Albert kept his head in his paper.

"Albert?"

"What?"

"How long are you going to be upset with me?"

"I don't know." *That's it; I am not playing this game his way anymore.* "How about fifty years? That should make us even." He flipped the paper and snapped it into position, revealing his mood for the first time in years. He got some of Rudy's attention.

"I am sorry I didn't tell you, but I had no other choice." Rudy put a dollop of butter on a warm blueberry muffin and ate half with one bite while reaching for his steaming black coffee.

"How could you manipulate my wife? And how could you do that to me?"

"Albert, when your father died in that damn plane crash, I had to make decisions for the good of the family. *Gilgamesh* was a reality and your role, the role of a Bell patriarch, was pivotal."

"You could have sat me down and talked a long time ago. You made decisions about my life that were not yours to make. I lived the last fifty-six years believing my wife had stopped loving me the day my father died, the day she would never trust again."

"Albert, that's not all my fault. If you had been truthful with Sheila from the start I could have never convinced her to quietly back away. You were twenty-four, still struggling with the weight of the Bell family name, the wealth, the power and your role as the first-born male. Albert, you were nowhere near ready for any of it, especially for *Gilgamesh.*"

"You knew I was at the bottom when my plane landed in El Paso in December of 1967. I checked into the presidential suite at the *Plaza Hotel* and wanted to kill myself."

"Yes, we knew where you were emotionally. But William always kept a close eye on you. We wouldn't let you hurt yourself. I was sure you would work through your emotions. Deep down, you had to know how special you are. I was positive that you would leave El Paso stronger than you had ever been. At that point, we had to let you get there on your own."

Albert dropped the paper and leaned toward Rudy. He looked deep into his eyes, searching for every ounce of meaning. Albert needed to reconcile so much: his memories and interpretations of so many key events in his life that now defined him. *Was I truly diminished by the actions of this man? Were others hurt by the decisions he made and those that I made? Was my life like everyone's life, a unique collection of truths, lies and awakenings?*

"All this time I thought my wife had left me. I had not been with a woman for over a decade. I thought Betty Duncan was my miracle. The most beautiful girl I had ever seen wanted me. Now, forty years later, I discover she was employed by *Gilgamesh*. And I find out she is dead." He folded his paper and set it next to his plate, now committing to the discussion for the first time.

"Betty Duncan did want you. That was part of the profiling program."

"I guess they think of everything, don't they?"

Rudy stopped chewing. "I don't know what to say to make it better."

Albert didn't hear Rudy. "After I impregnated her they sure got me out of the picture quick. And I always wondered why my ex-wife wanted to reconcile our marriage the day after I had the greatest sex of my life with a woman I fell in love with the very moment our eyes met, the woman I think about every day to this day."

"We are very good at what we do, Albert."

"I had thought for years that I wanted Sheila back. I didn't know then that it was the memory I was clinging to. You killed the love for both of us in the first year of our separation. But somehow you knew if Sheila asked for me back I would come running. Didn't you?"

"Yes, we did." Rudy popped another muffin into his mouth as William refreshed his coffee and left the patio. His face tried to look concerned but Albert saw through it.

"Betty refused my financial support. She disappeared…

"My God, she had triplets! She had three boys and you still kept me out of the whole thing. She gave two of my sons away and she kept one…the damaged one. And I still don't believe I have that whole story. Adam was lost. He killed so many!

"A Mexican drug cartel, the reason Betty Duncan vanished in 1969. That was probably the most elaborate lie I have ever heard in my entire life." Albert fumed.

"I thought that was a bit too creative but the fabrication held up pretty good. Max Gregory was even fooled when he did his investigation for you last year. I was shocked that he found that trail and didn't see through it." Rudy pulled his napkin out of his belt and shook the crumbs onto the flagstone patio. A cluster of sparrows descended immediately. He folded his napkin, took off his spectacles and rubbed his nose.

"Albert, I am sorry for the lies surrounding your transition to patriarch. At the time, you were not ready for the whole story and time got away. I have been running around the world and watching from afar."

"Why Betty Duncan? Why not Sheila?" asked Albert with ire.

"Genetics," said Rudy. "Betty Duncan was the approved vessel."

"The approved vessel?"

"Yes. Betty was the approved vessel to complement the unique genetic makeup of the next generation Bell patriarch. Without her knowledge, Sheila was evaluated and it was determined that she was not suited. Betty Duncan was found after years of searching. She was the most ideal vessel for a Bell patriarch, the most comprehensively qualified vessel ever. That was why we felt good about the triplets."

"Rudy, I had three sons I never knew for forty years. How could you let that happen?"

"I am honestly surprised you didn't pick up on the similarities. Elliott, Jack and Adam were so much alike physically. Granted, you did not see Adam until the end. But the three of them were tall, athletic men with penetrating eyes, chiseled jaw lines, and the way they carried themselves was similar. Each had an incredible presence, something hard to define but when you see it…you see it.

"Albert, they were you in so many ways, but you didn't see it. You never asked. I thought you did not want to see, so I left it alone and time got away. You had a very busy life with your other children, with Sheila, and then tragedies that took them all away. I struggled finding the right time and the right way to tell you, and here we are."

Albert was leaning back in his chair staring well beyond the distant trees. "After I knew they were mine, I could see." *Maybe I was in denial.*

"As we anticipated, the boys had genius IQs, photographic memories and unparalleled analytical skills." Rudy sipped his coffee in thought.

"I think Elliott Sumner has the most advanced sensory systems of anyone. That man probably has even more gifts, probably finding them when he needs them. And I'll bet he is not looking for a one of them.

"And Jack, he was the perfect visionary. That man could see the future, and he acquired all the skills to get there and to bring people along.

"Adam could have been a world-class athlete; his physical attributes were closer to a wild animal than a man. But Adam had that terrible problem."

"I guess *Gilgamesh* didn't have all the bugs worked out," said Albert with his coffee cup under his nose and eyes on Rudy.

"We were late finding that recessive-trait in Betty's genetic profile."

"When did you discover the problem?"

"Seem to recall third trimester of the pregnancy."

"What happened?"

"Since there were three babies they waited until delivery and took blood from each baby. Elliott and Jack did not carry the trait. Adam did. The *Gilgamesh* protocol on such matters is very rigid—postpartum euthanasia."

"Kill the baby?"

"Yes. But Betty was very convincing. She would keep Adam under control and transform him into an asset. I guess we were all hopeful. You know the rest: she got raped, then the mental breakdown and emotional abandonment of Adam. He eventually killed her and a whole lot of other people. And then he came for you, Albert."

"I could have helped him. I was everything he needed but never got. All those innocent people would be alive today." Albert dipped his head, turned away, and brushed a tear from his cheek. "Those people...all of them are on us."

Rudy pretended not to hear or he was avoiding the topic of blame; Albert thought it was the latter.

"Adam's life will always be the greatest tragedy," said Rudy. "But now you have a son. I have been looking forward to this day—to meet Elliott. How are you two doing?" He glanced at his watch, although he had no place he had to be.

"We are doing fine. We are getting some time together when we can."

"Albert, it's been several months since he learned. How much time?"

Albert took a much longer sip of coffee to make Rudy wait. "Enough time."

"There is so much he needs to know, so much preparation, work. He should be living here." Rudy fidgeted with his silverware: picking it up, putting it down.

"Elliott Sumner is a world-acclaimed forensic pathologist in demand. He travels and handles numerous cases all over the world. One day he is pivotal in bringing the Bluff City Butcher nightmare to a close, the next day he learns he is the Bell patriarch and the next day he gets a call from Scotland Yard...the Serpentine Strangler escaped. What do you want me to tell you, Rudy?"

"Is he coming into this willingly...the right way?"

"I think so. Elliott understands his lineage and responsibilities. He is a strong man and a very successful man on his own. I am confident he will be an exceptional patriarch when that time comes."

"I know you wish you could have raised him. However, you are right; he has done well in his first forty-one years."

"He has his internal battles to work through. Carol seems to be the best thing that has ever happened to him. She is giving him the kind of strength that is not programmed into you."

"And when Elliott met Adam that December night, he saw his brother trapped inside a monster. I think that helped him with his own demons; it made these monsters he chases human...troubled, but human. I think his started to go away."

"Carol Mason is the perfect vessel for Elliot. We brought her along the right way and introduced her at the right time. The rest just happened."

"Are you certain Carol knows nothing? She has been talking about *Gilgamesh* and Elliott has started to ask me about it."

Rudy smiled. "By the time they get anywhere on *Gilgamesh*, Elliott's future patriarch will be a toddler." Rudy lost the smile. "Unfortunately, when Adam killed his other brother we lost our insurance policy. Jack had a role, the reduction of risk; we live in a complex and dangerous world now and must always have a contingency plan."

"It's always been about protecting the assets, hasn't it?"

"That sounds a little cold, Albert. I think it's about family."

That's the way you justify all of it. Everything is really about assets.

"Did you purchase *BelMed?*" asked Albert.

"Yes, buried deep in the books—another family asset hidden beneath a half dozen shell corporations. Jack set up both companies in December 2004, locking Medino out. I suspect he didn't completely trust Enrique at that time. Our people took care of all the paper."

"I am sure Jack trusted Dr. Medino later. Everything he said he could do, Jack validated. Mr. Chambliss tried to get access to the Medino files in November."

"That covert government agency tried to get Medino to join them for years. He'd have nothing to do with them," said Rudy.

"His recovery from pancreatic cancer in 2004 was telling. No doubt the man figured out something," Albert baited.

"That photo-shopped government video was a lame effort to gain access to some of the boxes down in those Brent catacombs."

"So your people got a look at the video, too?" Albert asked softly, encouraging truth.

"Medino was dying of pancreatic cancer; that was a fact. The government took tape from the 2004 Bellow meetings in Vegas and six months later in Memphis. They used a little *Star Wars* magic and created a lie to mislead...and their actor never existed. But you already knew that, Albert. You and Elliott and Carol Mason didn't buy any of it the day of your meeting with Chambliss. Still, you had it analyzed by the best. So may I ask you, why the question?"

Albert smiled with a confidence that had always irritated Rudy, a look of greater knowledge and the complete absence of fear that Albert enjoyed wielding. "And why do you despise Dr. Medino?"

Flustered, Rudy snapped, "Because he stole from the Bell family. But I am not going there with you today. Before Elliott shows up, what can you tell me about *Life2?*"

Albert looked into his coffee cup in silence, as if he had reached a decision. Then he spoke. "Our people inside the S.E.C. have everything handled. The family will have controlling interest when the dust settles."

Rudy shifted in his seat. "What about the Medino files."

"What Medino files?" asked Albert, although he knew where it was going.

"We have gone to considerable lengths to locate Medino's private files. We believe he got there—biogenic immortality."

"What have you done?"

"We searched every square foot of his Nashville farm last month; found nothing. To eliminate risk we flooded that location. We have been all over the Exchange Building downtown too. Again, nothing. We may need to demolish that building if we can't get comfortable."

"You are really afraid of Medino's research getting out, aren't you?" Again, Albert knew the answer, but he had his reasons.

"That bastard stole Bell patriarch DNA and focused a lifetime on duplicating what belongs to this family."

He saw William at the glass door, about to come on the patio. He timed his most frustrating question for last. "And how is that different from *Gilgamesh?*"

"We have been over this ground. The difference is..."

William appeared behind Rudy and cleared his throat. "Excuse me, Sir. Your first appointment has arrived."

Albert smiled at Rudy. "Sorry." He turned to William. "Give us a minute and bring him out."

He pointed to Rudy's eating area; in seconds servants removed all signs that anyone had been there; they laid out new place settings and restocked the table with blueberry muffins, iced butter, juices and a sterling silver urn of fresh coffee.

"They're getting good at that," said Rudy getting up and out of the way. "Guess we will continue our discussion later. Don't let me forget where we were. I'll be in the greenhouse playing with the orchids. You can send someone for me when Elliott arrives." Rudy left the terrace to the south. A minute later William brought Officer Starnes out.

■ ■ ■

Albert stood to embrace Willie. "Hello, my friend." He stepped back and held his arms at his shoulders, still hard as chiseled granite, the strongest person Albert had ever known. Until Adam.

"Good morning."

"You look wonderful, Willie. You look as young and strong as the day Rudy introduced us twenty-five years ago. Are you coloring that gray?"

Willie got a good laugh. "No, that's a gift from Mama. She never had a gray hair on her head. Lived to be ninety-two."

They sat down and William brought Willie his special coffee.

"I understand you have something for me," said Albert.

Willie pulled the thin leather box from his inside breast pocket and set it on the table. After they looked at it a few seconds, Willie smiled and slid it across the linen tablecloth to Albert. Then he took a long sip of his special coffee: one part hot cream, two parts coffee and two pinches of sugar. Mr. Albert's William always got it perfect.

"Help yourself to a warm blueberry muffin, and that's real butter."

"Thank you. Blueberry muffins and real butter; I sure know what this means." Willie helped himself.

"I know you do." Albert turned the box so the embossed word in the center was right side up. He smiled, placed his napkin over it and took another sip of coffee. "Willie, are you about ready to retire?"

"Well, Sir, ya know how I miss Mr. Bellow. I've been looking out for him for a long time. I'm not use to him not being around."

"I know, Willie."

"I remember, the basement of the Exchange Building, October 15, 2009, when he gave me that little leather box. Jack hugged me hard and then went down the sewer pipe. I felt like he knew that would be the last time."

"I know the feeling, Willie. I wish we had both known Jack was my son when he was alive," said Albert as he looked into his coffee cup at his reflection.

"Mr. Albert, you know Mr. Kohl never told me either or I would have talked to you. I just knew I had my job—to watch over him. I guess I should have asked why. But, I thought Mr. Bellow was a special man that attracted the interest of the Bell family. He was so very smart and a good man, Mr. Albert."

"Willie, when we look back over our life and get to see most of our story, I guess it is normal to wonder why we failed to get around to a lot of things."

"Yes, Sir, seems like life happens and sometimes we just don't keep up."

"Willie, at the end Jack was desperate. He didn't know who was after him. Someone had killed his partner—Dr. Medino—greedy investors stole his company, the Memphis police accused him of being the Bluff City Butcher and he had unsavory and covert groups trying to steal his secrets. I don't know how he managed as long as he did."

"I guess that is a lot for a man to carry."

"You took care of him much of his life and he never knew it. At the end, he was blindsided and he came to you, Willie. That says a lot. He trusted you like I do and many others in this world that know you."

"I guess he did trust me." Willie thought for a few seconds, smiled and popped a blueberry muffin into his mouth. He chewed with a big smile as he looked up to where Jack surely was this morning.

"So, are you going to retire, my friend?" asked Albert.

"Not much I can do now. Guess I better find me that porch to sit on." They both laughed. Willie got up. They shook hands and embraced.

No matter what I tried to give you over the years, you would only accept my blueberry muffins and you would only take a piece of my heart...which has always been fine with me.

"Willie, you've been a millionaire for about twenty years now. Do you remember that little retirement account? Go get you a porch wherever you want and let me know when you do so I can come do some rocking with you, my friend."

"Yes, Sir." Willie stopped before entering the mansion and turned back to Albert. "Is Mr. Alberto hiding in the greenhouse?"

Albert smiled. "What do you think, Willie?"

"I think he ain't ever gonna change." Willie disappeared into the mansion with a big smile on his face.

Breakfast with hot blueberry muffins and real butter meant Alberto Bella was around and that would make him 165 this year. That family sure does live long.

"No, Sir, Mr. Albert," he bellowed. "Ain't nothing ever gonna change." Willie's laughter faded into the depths of the Bell mansion.

■ ■ ■

Albert pulled the white linen napkin off the thin leather box, closed his eyes and ran his finger over the embossed word, *GILGAMESH*. "On the contrary, Willie, everything is about to change for everybody," he whispered with an eye on the greenhouse.

William stepped out on the patio. "Albert, may I...?"

"Yes, but Rudy is nearby playing with the flowers."

William leaned close to Albert and whispered, "Max phoned. Miss Duncan has been located. She never married. The records in Texas were bogus, Sir. She had to disappear. She wants to see you but is afraid."

"She is alive! Where is she?"

"Peru, Sir...she is somewhere south of Arequipa."

"Wait for Alberto to leave the estate grounds before we revisit this topic. I will want Elliott involved. We will be planning a trip for one of us when the time is right."

"Dr. Sumner is in the study, Sir. May I ask, does he know Rudolph Kohl is Alberto Bella?"

"No. That is what this meeting is about. However, I am sure Elliott will handle this encounter well, as he does all unexpected matters."

"I don't know, Sir. Meeting your great grandfather can be a bit alarming, if you know what I mean, Sir." William rarely offered his opinion or smiled; this was one of those special occasions. Albert returned an appreciative smile.

"I think you may be right, William."

"I will bring him from the study, Sir." William turned to leave.

"Oh…William, please take this." Albert handed him the thin leather box. He covered it with the white napkin draped on his arm, no questions asked. "You know where to put it," said Albert. William disappeared into the mansion.

Beneath the thick canopy of giant oaks Albert smelled his coffee while watching the cascading sunbeams disperse the lingering morning mist that clung to the manicured lawns. He felt at peace for the first time since the death of his father. Now, his son would make the dream possible.

Elliott would learn he had another gift, one unique to Bell patriarchs: an unexplainable, genetic anomaly passed only to the first conceived male of each generation. *Did Dr. Medino learn how to reproduce it?*

One day soon I will tell you the whole truth about Gilgamesh, Dr. Medino and our mission against unstoppable legions, he thought. Albert's smiling eyes followed Elliott brusquely passing by the tall windows of the mansion on his way to the veranda. Then his pupils contracted when Alberto Bella pulled out his chair.

"What a wondrous day," said Albert.

CPSIA information can be obtained at www.ICGtesting.com
Printed in the USA
LVOW081750140912

298871LV00007B/87/P